THE KING

JOHN NORMAN

WARNER BOOKS

A Time Warner Company

WARNER BOOKS EDITION

Questar® is a registered trademark of Warner Books, Inc.

Cover design by Don Puckey
Cover illustration by Dorian Vallejo

Warner Books, Inc.
1271 Avenue of the Americas
New York, NY 10020

 A Time Warner Company

Printed in the United States of America

First Printing: September, 1993

10 9 8 7 6 5 4 3 2 1

BLOOD ON THE SNOW

✠✠✠✠✠✠✠

The Herul scout gingerly pushed at the headless, half-eaten horse on the sledge. He reached into the rib cage to draw the frozen corpse out of the cavity.

The leader of the Heruls looked back at the sledge. "Utinn?"

The scout stood by the sledge, not moving. There was something odd about the attitude of the figure.

"Atlar!" said the leader. A second Herul waded through the snow to his fellow. "The neck is broken," he said. "He is dead."

"Lift the axe," said the leader of the Heruls.

At that moment, with a cry of rage and power, a mighty figure, more than half again the size of a common man, rose from the body of the horse, flinging dried, cold ribs, bones scattering; springing like a hurricane, like a lion . . .

And Atlar, a yard of great blade emerging from his back, was lifted, impaled, in the air. Snarling, surely more animal than man, Otto held the Herul's squirming, bleeding body over his head . . .

ALSO BY JOHN NORMAN

The Chieftain
The Captain

Published by
WARNER BOOKS

This book is dedicated
to all who approve of, and welcome, and celebrate,
the liberty and glory
of the human imagination.

· · · PROLOGUE · · ·

"And there were wolves in the land."

—The Annals

"Let us laugh with steel."

—An Otung Saying

"Let us see if there are men here."

—A Drisriak Challenge

"The laurel is unpicked;
 We have forgotten the festivals;
 The laurel is unpicked;
 The statues are broken;
 The limbs of the gods lie in the dust;
 The holy places are defiled;
 The temples are in ruins.
 The laurel is unpicked;
 It has died upon the branch;
 The tree is dead;
 It is winter;
 It grows cold.
 Night has fallen upon the empire."

—Alarion

"I have heard the drums;
I have seen the riders on the hill;
The breath of their horses is like fire;
Their hoofs are like thunder;
On their arms the sun blazes;
The lords have come;
I will come forth from the forest;
I will plant again;
I will find a wife;
It is a new morning."

—*Anonymous, after Alarion*

Note:

It has been the custom of the chronicler, or chroniclers, as the case may be, and as some have argued, to include certain observations, or reflections, in a manner prefatory to the Telnarian manuscripts. Here, however, we seem to encounter a departure from that practice. We have only these three quotations, and the two short poems. I do not understand them, or, at any rate, their placement here. Their inclusion with the manuscript may be the result of some accident, or mistake. This sometimes happens with complex papers. Certainly they seem, the poems at least, to have little to do with the story. I have included them, however, as they were with the manuscript.

—Editor

· · · **CHAPTER 1** · · ·

"Let us see if there are men here," said Abrogastes. He handed the empty drinking horn to a shieldsman. He wiped his face with the back of his right forearm.

Retainers, and clients, pounded on the long tables lining the edges of the hall.

Drinking vessels were brought hastily by former ladies of the empire.

The drinking horn, refilled, was handed to Abrogastes by his shieldsman.

Abrogastes, seated on the bench, between the tall, carved high-seat pillars, looked down from the dais, on the hall, and the tables, grasping the drinking horn, formed from the horn of the hoofed *sorit*, adorned, enwrapped, with golden filigree, foaming with *bror*, spiced and honeyed, brewed from golden *lee*.

This was the season of the storms, of the rain of stones between the world of the Alemanni and its yellow star.

The lionships slept in their steel sheds.

In the season of the storms was sealed the world of the Alemanni, the stones in their annual tides, streaming in the skies, some visible at night, closing the gates of the world, closing it to those without, locking within, as well, those on its surface.

But in the spring the skies would clear.

It was then that the lionships would awaken.

Abrogastes was moody of late.

He stared sullenly into the drinking horn.

Bror was on his beard.

Behind him, to his left, his shieldsman carried his sword. On the bench beside him, at his right, lay an imperial pistol. It was a simple, yet precious weapon. In the empire, only one of senatorial rank, or above, would be likely to possess such a weapon, or a limited number of charges for it, privately. In billions of years, you see, resources which once seemed inexhaustible proved themselves finite, after all, and often unrenewable.

In many places even imperial troops were armed with simple weapons. A parity, thus, had developed in many places between the empire and its encroaching foes, and foes not unoften, former *federates*, within its own borders. The advantages of the imperial troops on many worlds lay sometimes in little more than military engineering, discipline, and tactics. Acres of land, or a woman, had often been exchanged for no more than an ancient bullet. Yet there was no doubt as to the strength of the empire yet, an empire concerned to husband its resources, and resist tenaciously incursions into its central systems. It could still destroy worlds. Yet there were many worlds and once one was destroyed, the energy, the means, to destroy such a world no longer existed. That bullet, so to speak, had been fired.

There was the sound of slim, belled ankles, as former ladies of the empire, bearing great wooden trenchers, hurried barefoot over the dirt, rush-strewn floor to serve the guests, the clients, the retinue, the men at arms, the high men, the ambassadors, the merchants, the scholars, the sons of chieftains in fosterage, the hostages, seated beneath the high-roofed hall of Abrogastes, lord of the Drisriaks, largest and fiercest of the eleven tribes of the Alemanni nation, that nation referred to commonly in imperial records as the Aatii.

Abrogastes handed his drinking horn, emptied, to his shieldsman, who laid it to one side.

Such a horn must be drained before it can be put down.

This is common among the Alemanni, the Vandals, and other such nations.

The former ladies of the empire hurried about. The switches of lads in attendance, here and there, in colorful garments, in colorful cloaks, a livery of sorts, would brook neither delays nor dallyings on the part of the beauties.

Abrogastes seemed angry.

He was often so, of course, when the sword, his signet on the pommel, for signing deeds, was not in his hand, when he was not aflight, when he was not adventuring.

Yet Abrogastes was not a simple adventurer, no ordinary raider, no simple brigand or pirate, sniffing about here and there, watching for his chance, prowling at the outskirts of cities, then slipping into a port at night, bringing the storm of fire and steel to some town, and then slipping away again, almost as swiftly as he had come, before the imperial cruisers could, or would, reach the scene.

Some worlds, he was sure, had been abandoned to the predations of such as he, as they lay open and inviting, whereas others, doubtless richer, were zealously guarded, so much so that they might cost a fleet.

Was this supposed to constitute an unspoken contract, he had wondered, a concession of sorts, that he might occupy himself somewhere, and content himself with what he was offered?

That he should then give up the rest?

Did they think to cast him a bone, that he might carry it away, and gnaw on it, and worry it, thereby being distracted from the stores of roasted beeves, the scent of which was on every wind?

Did they think he was a dog, to be so easily distracted?

Those of the empire, he knew, regarded him, and his kind, as dogs.

But they did not know the dogs of the Alemanni, he thought to himself, one of which lay to his right, on the dais, humped, alert, its crest half-aroused, watching the tables between half-closed lids.

The dogs of the Alemanni, and of many worlds, were large, agile, restless, vicious beasts.

Dogs, mused Abrogastes, have teeth, and will.

With some worlds, still nominally within the empire, many of which on whom *federates* were housed, he had formed arrangements. On many of these worlds citizens still sacrificed to the empire on the public altars, whereas resources, and tributes, secured their impunity from incursions. These became, in effect, tacit client states of the Alemanni. They increased the power of the Alemanni, and, indeed, of other peoples who were engaged in similar projects, enterprises of an economic and political nature. Imperial insignia, and standards, continued in such places to dignify public buildings, theaters and such, whereas, in justice, a banner of pelts, flown from a pole in a field, or mounted on a great wagon, might have been more appropriate.

At this very assemblage in the hall were men from such states, and others.

There were representatives here, as well, from each of the eleven tribes of the Alemanni people.

Too, present, were others, from other tribes, and other peoples, some officially allied, or federated, with the empire, at least in some titular fashion, and some not, and there were present, too, others from outworlds, of diverse species, eager for soil, seeds, gold, and power.

The shieldsman, the sword of Abrogastes in its leather sling behind his left shoulder, like the dog, surveyed the assemblage. At such gatherings he did not drink. He, a shieldsman, would remain, like the dog, watchful, and alert.

Abrogastes was no ordinary bandit, no ordinary brigand.

He saw far, he thought deeply. His appellation was the Far-Grasper. Abrogastes, the lord of the Drisriaks, Abrogastes, the Far-Grasper.

Had he been an ordinary brigand, he would not have called, nor could he, in plausibility, have called, this gathering.

There were present guests of many tribes, and many species.

There was a small sound of chain, from the dais, to the left of his bench, with the high-seat pillars. He felt something soft press itself against his fur boot. He thrust with his boot to the side, irritably, forcing it away. There was another sound of chain, that of a heavy chain, and a tiny whimper of misery, of timid, pleading protest.

"Would milord be fed?" inquired the shieldsman.

"I would be fed," said Abrogastes, the Far-Grasper.

The shieldsman lifted his hand, and made a peremptory gesture.

· · · CHAPTER 2 · · ·

"The greatest danger to the empire," said Iaachus, the Arbiter of Protocol, "is not from beyond the stars, not from the ships of barbarous dogs, but from traitors, within the empire."

"Surely," she said, putting down her tiny bowl of *kana*, and leaning back in the chair.

It was late at night, in one of the many palaces of the imperial family. It does not matter which palace, as it might have been any one of several. Nor was the palace on the Telnarian home world. It was, however, within the first imperial sector. I mention this that one may conjecture the nature of its grounds, the extent and arrangement of its gardens, the splendor of its fountains, its securities, the fields, forces, and armaments, the richness of its furnishings, the lavishness of its appointments and such. Many rich individuals in the empire, incidentally, had their own palaces, members of ancient families, some of whom putatively dated back to the early worlds of the empire, some of them members of the hereditary senatorial class, still officially required to confirm the appointment of an emperor; high officials, such as prefects civil and military; rich merchants; great landlords, and such. But this was a palace of the imperial family, though none of the imperial family, Aesilesius, the emperor; Atalana, the empress mother; or the two sisters of the emperor, blond Viviana and brunet Alacida were currently in residence. That was not a matter of coincidence. On the other hand, we may surmise that the affair afoot this late night was not one undertaken without the knowledge of, and approval of, the empress mother, Atalana.

Iaachus glanced to one side.

"Elena," he said. "Leave us."

The girl addressed, a beauty, with brown hair and gray eyes, hesitated only a moment, but then, barefoot, in a white, ankle-length, sleeveless gown, hurried from the room.

"I do believe she is jealous," said the young woman sitting across from Iaachus.

Iaachus smiled.

"Who would not be, of one such as you?" he asked.

His guest stiffened, ever so slightly, in the investiture of her ornate, brocaded robes.

"The fortunes of your family have declined, as I have heard," said Iaachus.

"Imperceptibly," she said.

"The burning of the piers at Governor's Landing, the seizure of granaries at Losann, by unruly *coloni*. The raids on the storehouses on Clarus IV. The loss of the cargo contract between Archus and Miton. The salt monopoly abolished on Teris. The razing of the resort complex at Felnar. The closing of the routes to Canaris and the Drakar Archipelago."

She was silent.

"I am very sorry," he said.

"There are many disturbances within the empire," she said. "It is a time of unrest."

"But not of change," said Iaachus.

"In its essence the empire is changeless, and eternal," she said.

"True," said Iaachus.

"Such things are minor considerations," she said. "They are negligible, at best."

"I am so pleased to hear it," he said.

She did not speak.

"To be sure," he said, smiling, "though the empire is changeless, and eternal, its forms imperishable and such, there might be changes within the empire."

"Oh?" she said.

"Changes, for example, in power, in the positions, and fortunes, of families, of individuals."

"Perhaps," she said.

"Such things have occurred, countless times in the past," he said.

"That is true," she said.

"Your family is among the highest, and most revered, in the empire," he said.

"True," she said.

"If there has been a decline in its fortunes, that is a tragedy not only for the family, but the empire, as well."

"I have little to do with my family any longer," she said.

"There is a rumor," he said, "that they have dissociated themselves from you."

"Possibly," she said.

"Perhaps they have reservations pertaining to your character, your tastes, your friends, your manner of living?"

"Perhaps," she said. "They are fools," she added. "I am well rid of them."

"Are you in debt?" he asked.

"I have an allowance," she said.

"It seems you were heavily in debt," he remarked.

" 'Were'?" she said.

"I have consolidated your debts," he said, "and have discharged them."

"They have been discharged?" she asked.

"Yes," he said. He put papers before her.

"You recognize the items, the vouchers, and such?"

She lifted her head from the papers, and regarded him.

"I did not request such a thing," she said. "Nor did I suggest it, nor bargain for it."

"Of course not," he said.

"I do not recognize the signatures," she said.

"Those of agents," he said. "It was done through private, concealed accounts."

"Why did you do this?" she asked.

"You owe me nothing," he said.

"Why?" she pressed.

"In respect of your lineage," he said. "For the sake of your name, the honor of your family, the good of the empire."

"I do not understand," she said.

"I could see to it," he said, "that your fortunes might considerably improve. That they might far, in the future, outdistance even the residues of your family's fortune. I could manage it in such a way that you could become one of the wealthiest, and most envied, women in the empire, honored, rich with dignities, welcome even at the imperial court."

"I do not understand," she said.

"Let us say," he said, "merely that I think your prospects are splendid."

She did not speak, but regarded him.

"I gather you are not overly fond of your family," he said.

"Oh?" she said.

"Are my informants reliable?" he asked.

"Perhaps," she said.

"Nor they of you," he said.

"Perhaps," she said.

"You have been repudiated, disowned," he said, "save, of course, for a not ungenerous allowance."

"It is a pittance," she said.

"They do not care in the least for what happens to you," he said.

"Nor I for them," she snapped. "They are all fools, fools!"

"You would have no objection to becoming independently, and fabulously, wealthy, I would suppose."

"I think I might manage to accommodate myself to such a modality," she said.

"You could even look down upon your family, and ruin it, if you wish, with the power I could give you."

"Ah!" she said, her eyes sparkling.

"It would be a splendid vengeance, would it not?" he asked.

"Yes," she said.

"I owe you nothing," she said.

"But you are interested, are you not?" he asked.

"Perhaps," she said. "What would I do?"

"You must serve the empire," he said.

"The empire has, of course, my undivided allegiance," she said.

"Your allegiance is only to yourself," he said.

"As yours is only to yourself?" she inquired.

"In my case," smiled Iaachus, "the interest of the empire, and my own interest, coincide perfectly."

"A most happy coincidence," she observed.

"Precisely," he said.

"As I mentioned earlier," he said, "the greatest danger faced by the empire comes not from without, but from within, from traitors."

"Of course," she said.

"And, particularly," said he, lowering his voice, "from traitors of insatiable ambition, villains who, with the help of barbarians, would aspire to seize the throne itself."

Her eyes widened.

"You have heard of the Aurelianii?" he asked.

"Of course," she said. "They are kin even to the emperor."

"Which makes them even more dangerous," he said.

"Their loyalty is unquestioned," she said.

"No," confided Iaachus.

She reached for the tiny bowl of *kana*, but her hand shook.

"Julian, of the Aurelianii," said he, "has designs upon the throne. He plans to enlist barbarians in the mobile forces, as mercenary companies, with ships, with weapons, at their disposal. They will owe their allegiance only to him, not to the empire."

"Have him seized," she said. "Confiscate his property. Surely it is considerable."

The Aurelianii were one of the oldest, and richest, families in the empire. They traced their roots back to the original Telnarian world, the home world of the empire itself.

"He is too powerful, we must be careful how we proceed, we do not wish to precipitate civil war. There are portions of the navy which are loyal to him."

"What are we to do?" she asked.

"We must drive a wedge between him and his barbarian cohorts, we must frustrate his scheme of enlisting barbarians in the regular forces. That is crucial. That is the first step. We must deprive him of these allies, and, in doing this, cast discredit entirely upon his probity, and the feasibility of his plan to defend the empire."

"Can the empire defend itself?" she asked.

"Of course," he said.

"Who is the barbarian, or barbarians, in question," she asked.

"First, and primarily, one whom he encountered, it seems, on the forest world of Varna, a chieftain of the Wolfungs."

"I have never heard of them," she said.

"They are a tribe of the Vandals," he said.

"I have not heard of such a people," she said.

That was, of course, a genuine possibility at that time. At that time, you see, few in the empire had heard of the Vandals. Indeed, at that time, few outside of the administration and the military had heard even of the Alemanni, or, as the imperial records have it, the Aatii. And even in the war office such peoples tended to be dismissed, much as one might think little of rumblings in the distance, the darkenings of far skies, the occasional flash of lightning over distant mountains, such things, things far away.

"His name," said Iaachus, "is Ottonius."

She moved the bowl of *kana* a bit on the table with her finger, turning it a little, watching the ruby fluid move in the shallow container.

"I am a woman," she said.

"But one highborn, one of lofty family, of noble station, one who may be relied upon."

She looked up at him.

"And one, one supposes, of great beauty," he said.

She stiffened again, slightly, as she had once before. She regarded him, irritably.

She was vain of her striking beauty, and took great pleasure in it. She enjoyed the effect, too, which it seemed to have on men, as it seemed to put them much at her mercy. She enjoyed using it to tantalize, and frustrate, men. It was pleasant to taunt them, and arouse them, and then, with cold pleasure, deny them.

"And one of great wealth?" she asked.

"That is for you to decide," he said.

"It is said," she said, "that Iaachus is the most powerful man in the empire."

"I am only the humble Arbiter of Protocol," he said, "a modest office, an ancillary office, with little authority or power affixed thereto."

"It is said you have the ear of the empress mother," she said.

"She consults me on small matters," said he, "having to do with the arrangements, and etiquette, of the court."

"What is to be the fate of this Ottonius?" she asked.

"He is leaving in two days for Tangara, to recruit a *comitatus*, a company, among Otungs. I shall see to it that our beloved Julian, scion of the Aurelianii, will be unable to accompany him."

"Tangara is far away," she said.

"Its provincial capital is Venitzia," he said.

"And what is to happen on Tangara?" she asked.

Iaachus rose to his feet, went to a cupboard at the side of the room, opened it, moved some small objects on a shelf to one side, and pressed a button, that actuating a panel which, sliding back, revealed a small recess. From this recess he withdrew a flat, rectangular leather case. He placed this on a table at the side of the room, returning to the cupboard to close the recess, rearrange the articles on the shelf, and shut the cupboard door. He then brought the leather case from the table at the side of the room and returned to his seat at the table near the center of the room. He placed the leather case on this table, between them.

She looked at him, and then, with two hands, lifted up the lid of the leather case.

"It is beautiful," she said.

"Who knows what may happen on a primitive world such as Tangara," he said, "particularly once one is outside the fences of the capital?

"Be careful," he said.

In the container there lay a dagger, or poniard, small, and delicate, with a slender, gleaming blade, some seven inches in length, and an oval, yellow handle, some five inches in length, with a swirled design in black wrought within it.

"It is a woman's dagger," she said.

"Yes," he said.

Between the hilt and the slender blade there was a guard, one of its terminations scrolled toward the point, the other back, toward the hilt.

The guard, of course, aside from permitting resources of additional leverage, if needed, would prevent the hand from slipping down the blade. In certain situations that is a not negligible advantage of this sort of tool. Such guards, with their capacity to protect the hand, are common in certain forms of weapons, where the strike might be made through silk or velvet, a silk or velvet concealing, say, a lining, or a coat or jacket, of interwoven metal links.

She looked up at him, puzzled.

"Do not touch the blade," he said. "It is coated with a transparent poison. The tiniest cut, the smallest break, in the skin will introduce the poison into the wound. A most unpleasant, most ugly, death would ensue within seconds."

"It need not be driven into the body then," she said, looking at it.

"It is marvelously sharp," he said. "The strength of a child would suffice to drive it into a man's body."

"Or that of a woman," she said.

"To the hilt," he said.

"I see," she said.

"But a scratch would suffice," he said.

"If you wish him slain," she said, "why do you not hire ruffians to manage the business?"

The eyes of Iaachus clouded. Then he smiled. "No," he said, "it is better done by an agent, on a distant world, far from public attention, by an agent whose presence would arouse no suspicion, by an agent who would be utterly unsuspected."

"What if I cannot approach him, what if he is armored?" she asked.

"You will doubtless be able to approach him," he said, "and I suspect that, at times, in your presence, armor would be laid aside, and, if not, remember that so small a thing as a scratch on the back of the hand will be quite enough.

"Are you interested in this matter?" he asked.

"Perhaps," she said. "But I am not a mariner, not a gunner, not a technician. I do not understand under what excuse, or pretext, I might be included in a crew voyaging to Tangara on such a business."

"There will be various goods taken with the vessel to Tangara," he said.

" 'Goods'?" she asked.

"Yes," he said, "trade goods, and goods to smooth the way, to serve as inducements, to serve as gifts, and such, things that barbarians might find of interest, for example, skins, wines, grains, cloths, gems, silks, oils, copper plates, spices, gold, brooches, rings, nails, wire, ivory, iron, silver, goods, many forms of goods, ranging from the common to the exquisite."

"To the exquisite?" she asked.

"Yes," he said, "such as emerald cameos, carved in the likeness of the emperor."

"I do not understand," she said.

"Drink your *kana*," he said.

She lifted the tiny bowl to her lips. Over the rim, of purest *luxite* porcelain, from the valley of Raf, milled later in the tradition of the Toronichi, she regarded him. Her eyes were blue. Then she put back her head and drained the shallow container. As she had her head back he glimpsed, in the partage of her high brocaded collar, her white throat. She then again regarded him. She then replaced the tiny bowl, now empty, on the table.

Her hair was blond.

It was fixed in a way not uncommon among high ladies of the empire, being fixed upward, formally, stiffly, in an intricate coiffure, held tightly in place by a rather rectangular, peaked, enclosing frame, a headdress in effect, of golden wire and jeweled leather.

"Of course," he said, "it may be that you would prove to be an unsuitable choice for the matter at hand."

"Unsuitable?" she inquired.

"That you might not prove an appropriate choice for the agent in question, that it is not, at the moment, clear that you possess the necessary qualifications."

"Milord?" she inquired.

"In the role in which you would be cast," he said, "you must be believable. If you are not, suspicions would be immediately aroused, and all might be lost."

"It is my hope that I might prove believable in the role which I am to play," she said.

"My informants suggest that there would be no difficulty in the matter," he said.

"Informants?" she said.

"Attendants at the women's baths, and such."

"I do not understand," she said.

"But you understand that I must be sure of the matter," he said. "There is much at stake."

"I do not understand," she said.

"Rise, and stand there," he said, pointing to a place on the marbled floor, a few feet from the table.

"For what reason?" she asked.

"Do it," he said.

"I am not accustomed to being addressed in that fashion," she said, coldly.

"Now," he said.

"Good," he said. "Now remove your clothing, completely."

"Milord!" she protested.

"Do so," he said, not patiently.

"I am of the senatorial class!" she said.

"Now," he said.

She angrily removed the robes, and the many garments beneath them. It was not easy for her to do, as women of her station were customarily assisted by one or more maids in these tasks.

"Ah," he said.

Her eyes flashed fire.

"Straighten your body," he said. "Good.

"You are angry?" he asked.

"I am of the senatorial class!" she said, in fury.

"Is this the first time you have been naked before a man?" he asked.

"Yes!" she said.

"Remove your headdress," he said. "Loosen your hair."

"Please!" she said.

"Now," he said.

Angrily she unfastened the headdress, and lifted it off, and put it to one side, with the robes on the floor, near her feet, and then fumbled with the net and wire. It had taken better than three hours for her coiffure to be arranged earlier in the day.

"Shake your hair loose," he said.

With an angry shake of her head she freed her hair.

"Put it behind your shoulders," he said.

In fury she put it back, behind her.

"Turn," he said, "slowly."

She complied.

"Now kneel here," he said, indicating a place near the table. "Straighten your back, put your hands on your thighs, put your head up, widen your knees."

He then regarded her, with care.

"With the expedition to Tangara," he said, "among the trade goods, the gifts, and such, to be kept, distributed, or utilized at the discretion of the barbarian, there will be twenty slave girls, who must be of remarkable beauty, of the highest order of beauty."

She looked up at him.

"You are trembling," he said. "But, of course, it must be the first time you have been before a man in such a position."

"And in what position am I?" she asked.

"In one of the common positions of the female slave," he said.

She made an angry noise.

"I would not look into the eyes of a male," he said, "or any free person, for that matter, unless you sense that it is permitted, or you have been commanded to do so."

"I am free!" she cried.

"Yes," he said, "but to see you kneel so, one might be forgiven for having doubted it."

"I will rise!" she announced.

"Not without its being permitted," he said.

"I am free, am I not?" she said.

"Of course," he said.

But she remained kneeling. She had not received permission to rise.

"Yes," he said, approvingly, "I think you will do very nicely."

"I suppose I should be pleased," she said.

"Of course," he said.

She shook, half in trepidation, half in fury. She did not know whether she was pleased, or angered. Within her lovely, tumultuous bosom feelings warred.

Then she became again the woman of the senatorial class.

"I shall see that you are included on the cargo manifest for Tangara," he said.

"The other nineteen women will also be free women, of high class?" she said.

"No," he said. "They will be common slave girls, save, of course, that they will be of extraordinary beauty."

"But I will be the most beautiful," she said.

"One does not know," he said. "One must see what the men think."

"I despise men," she said. "But not your lordship, of course," she added, quickly.

"Another agent will be sent with you," he said. "But, in the interests of security, he will make himself known to you only later."

"He will be a member of the crew?"

"Yes."

"He will bring the dagger?"

"Yes, and he will, of course, assist you in your work, in so far as it is practical."

"I do not understand," she said.

"He will see that you obtain the knife," he said. "After all, it is not he who is likely to be alone with the barbarian at night."

"I see," she said.

"Too, of course, he must arrange for your mutual flight, after the deed, and see that you are returned safe and sound to the inner precincts of the empire, to receive your rewards, your renewed wealth and status, your new estates and palaces, such tokens of an empire's gratitude."

"My thanks, milord!" she said.

"Do you think you can carry off this matter?" he asked.

"Surely, milord," she smiled.

"Do you think that you will be able to stand it," he asked, "if your small, fair limbs should be encircled with steel, if you should feel chains upon your beauty, if your neck might even feel upon it a collar of steel?"

"I would know such things to be an empty farce," she said.

"I think that you would find that they would hold you as well as any other girl upon the ship."

" 'Girl'?" she asked.

"Such an expression," he said, "is commonly used of the female slave, perhaps because she is lowly, and nothing, perhaps because it sweeps away cant and hypocrisy, and speaks of unmitigated, direct, uncompromising sexuality."

"I could wear chains," she said, "contenting myself with the knowledge that a hundred times their weight in gold awaits me later!"

"You may rise," he said.

She leapt to her feet and ran to her clothing, which lay strewn on the marble.

She began to gather it up, and sort it out. She turned to him.

"May I bring my intimate maid?" she asked.

"No," smiled Iaachus, Arbiter of Protocol.

"How then shall I manage?" she asked, puzzled.

"The slave girl, which will be your guise," he said, "seldom needs assistance in dressing, for her garb is commonly simple, if, indeed, any is permitted to her at all."

"What of my hair?" she asked.

"That, too, will be quite simple," he said. "It need only be well washed, brushed and combed—vital, abundant, full-bodied, glossy and long."

"I would take my maid with me," she said.

"No," he said.

"I would have more *kana*," she said, irritably.

"No," he said.

"Do not dress here," he said. "I have work to do."

She stood there, clutching her garments about her.

"I would forget, for the time," he said, "the drinking of *kana* from *luxite* vessels. I would rather accustom myself to the prospect of drinking water from pans, on all fours."

"Doubtless it is time that I was on my way," she said.

"Doubtless," he concurred.

She threw him a look of fury.

She had been conducted to the palace secretly, and would be returned to her chambers in the city in the same way. But it would be best if as few as possible noted the comings and goings of a mysterious party, arriving and parting in darkness, hurrying in and out of a closed carriage, a party which consisted, it might seem, of some high lady and her escort.

"You may leave," he said.

"I am not to be addressed in that fashion," she said. "I am a lady of the senatorial class."

"You are now an agent, and will take orders," he said.

She stiffened, angrily, holding her garments about her.

"Later," he said, "you may revel in the glories of your wealth and status. In the meantime, you are no more than a vain, declined aristocrat, of dubious character, and repudiated by your family."

"Beast!" she said.

He regarded her, and she stepped back, uncertainly.

"Perhaps I should throw you to the marble," he said.

She gasped.

"Perhaps you can imagine what it would feel like, on your body, as you were seized, held helplessly and ravished."

She retreated.

She clutched the clothing before her, about her, closely, defensively.

"I jest, of course," he said.

"Of course, milord!" she laughed.

"Milord," she said.

"Yes?" he said.

"Your informants?" she said. "You spoke of bath attendants, and such."

"Yes?" he said.

"Was my intimate maid among them?" she asked, angrily.

"Perhaps," he said.

"I will beat her," she said, "as she has never been beaten before!"

"Your carriage will be waiting," said Iaachus, the Arbiter of Protocol. "You will be contacted again, tomorrow, and the necessary arrangements will be made."

"Dress outside," he said.

"Yes, milord," she said, and backed from the room.

Her emotions, in the anteroom, were like charging, leaping seas within her, chaotic tides, irrepressible stirrings, storms of confusion, of delight, of ambition, of fury, of humiliation, of curiosity. She reveled in the improvement of her prospects, the prospect of the redemption of her fortunes, the vistas of status, of wealth and power held out before her, that she could become one of the foremost ladies in the empire, perhaps, nay, undoubtedly, invited even to participate in the court! And so much could be purchased so simply, at so little cost as an awaited opportunity and the merest scratch of a tiny point. She could, once success was hers, so easily wrought, return to the empire, ruin her family, bring destruction in a thousand ways upon her enemies, and upon others, whom she might please, who perhaps had slighted her, or disapproved of her, or might have done so. But, too, she shook with humiliation, with fury. Within, a man had seen her, she, though a woman of the senatorial class, as naked as a slave girl! To be sure, he had doubtless had no choice. He must have had, she reassured herself, to make what determinations he needed, to make certain that she was fully suitable for inclusion within his plans, to ascertain her fittingness for the role in which he was considering casting her. Yes! Yes! And apparently he had found her fitting all right! She was extremely beautiful! She knew that. She would do quite well. She would do superbly! She was extremely vain of her beauty, and relished its power. But, too, she was disturbed by feelings she had had, before him, as when turning before him, when he had told her to do so, as when kneeling before him, when he had told her to do so, and precisely according to his instructions. For an instant, here and there, she had suddenly, overwhelmingly, frighteningly, felt wholly, radically, simply, basically, fundamentally female, felt herself a creature to be seen in terms of its basic, radical psychosexuality, a creature with no alternatives, no options, other than a total helpless, yielded femininity, a creature of basic femaleness, a femaleness imbued with, redolent with, radiant, profound, pervasive passion, and, too, for an instant, she sensed what might be the nature of a total love, obedience and service, sensed the profound sexuality of a creature who is uncompromisingly owned, and must be, under the threat of terrible punishments, but is eager, as well, to be, hot, devoted, and dutiful. She had sensed then, in distracted, terrified, resisted moments, simply, what it might be to be a woman, a true woman, radically, fundamentally, basically.

How she hurled such thoughts from her head! How she hated men! How she hated the dark-garbed, mysterious, powerful Iaachus, Arbiter of Protocol. How she hated slaves! How she hated the world, the empire, everything!

She was of noble family, she was of the highest lineage, she was, even, of the senatorial class!

She thought of her intimate maid!

The chit! How she would beat her!

It was at this moment that, in the outer room, the anteroom, she saw the white-gowned young woman who had been, earlier, in the inner room, who had been dismissed before she, the woman of the senatorial class, and the Arbiter of Protocol had begun to discuss matters of a possibily delicate, sensitive nature.

The girl had been lying curled on a mat, in the white, sleeveless, woolen gown, at the far wall, well out of earshot of the inner room, which, in any event, was sealed with a mighty door, a heavy portal designed to be soundproof.

When the woman of senatorial class had entered the room the girl at the far wall had stirred, and then, becoming aware of her, had hurriedly knelt on the mat, her head to the floor, the palms of her hands on the floor, as well.

"Girl!" snapped the woman of senatorial rank.

The girl hurried forward, and knelt before her, her head to the floor, her palms upon the floor, as well.

"Mistress?" asked the girl, frightened.

"Are you trained as a lady's maid?" inquired the woman of senatorial rank.

"No, Mistress!" said the girl, frightened.

The woman of senatorial rank uttered a sound of exasperation, of impatience.

"I would dress," she said. "Do you think yourself competent to assist me?"

"I will try, Mistress," said the girl.

And, in a few moments, with the assistance of the girl, who was deferent, and whose fingers seemed adept in such matters, the woman of senatorial rank was again suitably robed.

There was little to be done about the coiffure, of course, and it would have taken hours to manage properly, but her hair could be muchly concealed within the frame of wire and jeweled leather, and, particularly in the darkness, few would guess that it had been disarranged.

The bedecking of the imperial female, of the upper classes, was not a simple task, given the numerous garments, their positioning, the cunning closures, and such, but the matter was soon finished.

"You are certain you have not been a lady's maid before?" asked the woman of senatorial rank, regarding herself in one of the wall mirrors.

"No, Mistress," said the girl, again kneeling.

"That dress you are wearing," said the woman of senatorial rank. "It is all you are wearing, is it not?"

"Yes, Mistress. Forgive me, Mistress," whispered the girl.

"You are very pretty," said the woman of senatorial rank.

Though the gown of the girl was loose, and of an ankle-length, it was not difficult to detect a graceful, well-curved form within it, and the neckline was surely lower than it need have been, making clear that it held merely precariously captive a lovely, well-formed bosom.

"Thank you, Mistress," whispered the girl.

"You have not been trained as a lady's maid, and yet you seem familiar with the subtleties, the intricacies, of a lady's investiture," said the woman of senatorial rank.

"Forgive me, Mistress," said the girl.

"Interesting," mused the woman of senatorial rank.

The girl, fearful, kept her head to the floor.

"Look at me," said the woman of senatorial rank.

The girl looked up, timidly, but did not dare to raise her eyes above the ornate collar of the robes of the woman standing before her.

"Look into my eyes, my dear," said the woman of senatorial rank, kindly.

Timidly, gratefully, the girl did so.

The woman of senatorial rank then slapped her, viciously, with all her force, across the face.

Tears sprang to the girl's eyes. She looked at the woman of senatorial rank. Her eyes were startled, questioning.

"Do you not know," inquired the woman of senatorial rank, "that you are not to look into the eyes of one such as I, unless you sense that you may do so, or unless permission is granted?"

"Forgive me, Mistress," said the girl, shuddering, putting her head down to the floor, as she had before.

"On your belly," said the woman of senatorial rank. "Kiss my slippers!"

Instantly the girl obeyed.

The woman of senatorial rank then spurned her to her side, with her foot.

The girl lay on her side then, in pain, but did not dare, of course, to look into the eyes of the one who had spurned her to her place.

"Slaves are disgusting," said the free woman.

"Yes, Mistress!" said the slave, putting her head down.

The free woman then spun about, and left the room, with a swirl of her robes.

How shamed I have been, she thought. How I will beat my intimate maid tonight, the embonded little chit!

To be sure, that maid was now her only slave, that being one of the unfortunate, degrading consequences of the reduction in her resources, in the slippage of her fortunes.

Her carriage would be waiting.

Shortly after her departure a bell rang in the anteroom, and the slave girl, whose name, we recall, was Elena, hurried to the inner room, where she knelt before the Arbiter of Protocol, in suitable obeisance.

"You are crying," he observed.

"Forgive me, Master," she said.

"Our guest has left?" he asked.

"Yes, Master," she said.

"Go to my chamber," he said. "Prepare it for pleasure. Then chain yourself, naked, at the foot of the couch."

"Yes, Master!" she said, and then, unbidden, she crawled to his boots and kissed them, gratefully, fervently.

She then hurried from the room.

From his chambers she saw a darkened, closed carriage leaving the grounds.

She looked to the cuffs and shackles, the collar. They were all open.

She looked about the room, to make certain that all was in readiness. In a moment it would be too late to repair any last-minute oversights.

All seemed in order.

She slipped her gown to the side.

She looked down at the chains, the impediments. How totally helpless, how much at his, or anyone's, mercy, she would be in a moment.

She loved their weight, the sound of them on her body, how they moved against the ring.

How they told her what she was, and how she must be.

The master, of course, held the key to them.

She began with the left ankle, for there is an order to such things. It is one of the first things a girl is taught. Then, in moments, the steel, in all its beauty, its efficiency, its closeness, its meaningfulness, was upon her.

She could scarcely control herself.

She had a good deal of slack now, but such devices may be shortened and adjusted, as the master may please.

She looked to the wall.

On it was a whip.

She did not think she would be beaten. Surely she would do her best to please.

She lay there, like a tethered kitten, at the foot of the couch, like the animal she was.

She trembled with desire.

She did not envy the free woman.

The free woman, in anger, confused, filled with the hope of improved fortunes, fearful of the future, resolved, rode alone in the closed, unmarked carriage, the blinds drawn, her guards, her escort, on the box outside.

Coming to the palace she had permitted her escort to share the carriage.

Doubtless that had given him much pleasure. Doubtless he had been looking forward to the return trip, as well, to the opportunity, if only briefly, to be again close to one such as she. She was sure of it!

Then she had banished him to the box.

How amused she had been at this.

It had been difficult for him to conceal his disappointment.

Too, for a moment there had been a look in his eyes which had frightened her, but then it was gone.

She reassured herself.

Men are weak, she thought.

She smiled to herself.

She looked down at the floor of the carriage.

Slave girls, she thought, those meaningless chits, might be transported in such a carriage naked, kneeling, crouched down, on the floor, a blanket, or cloak, thrown over them.

Slave girls are commonly so transported, in closed vehicles, and such.

They are commonly kept in ignorance.

How fitting for them, she thought.

How pleased she was, that she was a different sort of woman, not such as they.

The wheels sounded hollow on the hard surface; the hoofs of the draft beasts rang on the pavement.

Back in the palace Iaachus, the Arbiter of Protocol, gathered together papers, inserting them in a portfolio, and then placing the portfolio in the recess from which, earlier, a rectangular leather case had been withdrawn.

Afterward he proceeded to his chambers.

· · · CHAPTER 3 · · ·

"Let us see if there are men here!" called Abrogastes. "Are there men here?"

"There are men here!" cried the feasters.

Drinking horns were lifted.

Greasy hands snatched at slabs of roasted meat, dripping with juices and blood, from heavy, broad, stained wooden trenchers proffered almost frantically by former ladies of the empire, their ankles belled. Behind them, here and there, in colorful garments, in their colorful cloaks, were lads, with switches, whose business it was to see that the former ladies of the empire performed well.

Abrogastes, clearing his vision, angry, sat back on the bench, between the high-seat pillars.

He was moody, angry.

He had drunk too much.

At his right there lay a great hound, of a sort bred for loyalty and suspicion, for ferocity and courage, a dog of the hunt and war, which will defend its master to the last drop of its blood, who will hurl itself at the merest spoken word on even an *arn* bear or vi-cat, or a dozen armed men, wreaking havoc amongst them.

To his left, at his feet, in a collar, on a chain, there lay a softer pet, one appropriate for other uses.

Abrogastes bent down and put down his hand on the massive head of the hound.

It rumbled, a growl that betokened affection.

"Good lad," said Abrogastes thickly. He tousled the mane on that great head.

Another hand, so placed, might have been torn from the wrist, with one sudden, unexpected, fierce movement of the great jaws.

Abrogastes straightened up, looked out on the open space, at the serving, and, at the tables along the walls, the feasters.

He then looked down, moodily, angrily, to the left, at the other pet, on its chain.

It put down its head, terrified.

It did not know why it had been brought to this feast.

It dared not put its lips again, timidly, beggingly, placatingly, hopefully, to Abrogastes' boot.

There was a sound of swearing from one of the tables. Two men pushed back their one-man benches.

"Desist!" cried a fellow.

Blades whipped from sheaths.

One of the former ladies of the empire screamed.

Two men leapt upon the table, scattering flagons and trenchers, and then from it, to the floor, rage in their eyes.

There was a sound of steel.

Then the very ground between the two men erupted upward in a blinding spume of dust, and there was a narrow trench, smoking, between the men.

All eyes turned to Abrogastes who stood before the bench, a smoking pistol in his hand.

"Who is the enemy?" he inquired.

"Milord?" asked one of the men, sword in hand.

"It is not he," said Abrogastes, pointing to one of the combatants. "Nor he!" he said, pointing to the other.

There was a sound of belled ankles, as ladies of the empire shrank back toward the tables.

"The true enemy," said Abrogastes, "is the empire."

The former ladies of the empire, carrying their trenchers, and their flagons, trembled.

There was a tiny sound of bells, as the small feet, bared, of former ladies of the empire stirred on the earthen, rush-strewn floor. Then they tried to stand perfectly still, but, even so, here and there, inadvertently, miserably, a tiny bell would sound.

The lads stood by with their switches.

They grinned at one another.

It would be easy enough to make those bells jangle a merry tune.

"And this, too," said Abrogastes, lifting the smoking pistol, "is the enemy." He regarded the silent men. "This is an imperial pistol," he said, "of the sort carried by officers of the mobile forces of the empire." Abrogastes looked about himself. "And this, I think," said he, brandishing the weapon, "is the true enemy, the only real enemy—the only enemy to be regarded with respect, with circumspection—the weaponry, the ships, the machines, the technology of the empire."

He looked again about himself.

"But what if we, too, had such things?" he asked.

Men looked at one another.

"Think on that," said he.

"But it is not possible," said a man.

Abrogastes smiled, and resumed his seat.

"Our weapons, milord, have been drawn!" cried one of the paused combatants.

"Then let blood be shed," said Abrogastes.

"And how shall it be shed?" asked the other.

"As the blood of what we all must be," said Abrogastes, "as the blood of brothers."

Both men then slashed their forearms, and stood there, blood flowing down their arms, regarding one another, and then, as one, they sheathed their weapons, not having been drawn without blood being shed. Among the Alemanni and such peoples one does not draw a weapon lightly. Into the sheaths struck the weapons, decisively. The men then approached one another. They held their bleeding, slashed arms together, pressed, the one to the other. Their bloods mingled. Weeping, they embraced, the blood of each on the other. There was cheering from the tables. Both men resumed their seats.

There was the lively sound of switches and the beautiful waitresses, the former ladies of the empire, all of them highborn, and chosen from many for their loveliness, crying out in pain and misery, sped by the impatient lads, their bells jangling, addressed themselves again, and zealously, to their appointed tasks.

"Surely, milord," said a clerk, a small man, with dark garments, carrying papers, tied with string, and a clerk's wallet, with its ink flask and sheathed pens, leaning toward Abrogastes, "the time is propitious for the business of the evening."

Abrogastes lifted his head.

"The colleagues are in a splendid mood," said the clerk. "They will be receptive to your proposal."

"It is not time," said Abrogastes. "You have much to learn, yet, of the ways of the Alemanni, of the Drisriaks."

The Alemanni nation, as I have mentioned elsewhere, consists of eleven tribes. Representatives of all were present, as well as representatives of many other tribes, and groups, and species. The Drisriaks were the largest and fiercest of the Alemanni tribes. Abrogastes was king of the Drisriaks. The Alemanni nation was indisputably the most powerful of the barbarian nations, particularly since the decimation by the empire of their hereditary enemies, the Vandal peoples. Abrogastes thus, as king of the Drisriaks, occupied a very important position.

"Yes, milord," said the clerk, withdrawing.

"For what purpose has this feast been called?" asked a nobleman, to the right of Abrogastes, of his fellow, to his own right.

Abrogastes gave no sign that he had heard the question.

"Perhaps to celebrate the victory of the Drisriaks over the Ortungen," the first nobleman was told.

A son of Abrogastes, one named Ortog, had broken away from the Drisriaks, with loyalties from his own retainers, from those who had taken rings from him, to form his own tribe, the Ortungs, or Ortungen. The Ortungs, and their ships, had been pursued relentlessly, and finally apprehended by Abrogastes, first on, and in the vicinity of, the world we know only by its number in the imperial records, 738.2, and later, others, in the vicinity of another world, one whose location, also, is unknown, a world, however, whose Alemanni name survives, Tenguthaxichai, possibly "Tengutha's Camp," or "Tengutha's Lair." Tengutha, incidentally, is a common name among several of the barbarian peoples, including the Alemanni. Justice, as viewed by Abrogastes, had been meted out on that world, on Tenguthaxichai.

"I have many sons," had said Abrogastes. He had then wiped his bloodied knife on his thigh, and returned it to its sheath. His traitorous daughter, Gerune, who had fled the Drisriaks with Ortog, the rebel, had been humbled, disowned, and enslaved. Abrogastes had permitted her to be claimed, and thusly owned, by one whom he had taken to be a tender of pigs.

He looked about the tables. Yes, he had many sons. Two were Ingeld and Hrothgar.

Are they loyal, wondered Abrogastes.

His favorite had been Ortog.

Hrothgar is simple, and cares for little but drink, and his horses and falcons, thought Abrogastes, and I do not fear him, but Ingeld is silent, and keeps his own counsel. His eyes are restless.

I have never seen Ingeld drunk, he thought. If one is to be feared, it must be Ingeld. But Ingeld, he thought, did not seem likely to be a giver of rings. Men did not understand him. They did not seek out his hall. He was not, like Ortog, a leader, the likely founder of a line, a laughing, insouciant prince, one for whom hearty men would willingly die.

"Yes," said the addressed nobleman. "Perhaps that is the purpose of the feast, to commemorate the defeat of the secessionists."

"No," said another. "That was done long ago, on the ships."

"What then is the purpose of the feast?" asked one of the noblemen.

"I do not know," said the man who had spoken.

"It must be of great importance," said one of the noblemen. "See who is here, so many, from so far!"

"Yes," said another.

"I have many sons," had said Abrogastes.

He had then cleaned the knife.

It was even now in its sheath, at his side.

It is hard to know, thought Abrogastes, when one might need such a thing.

"Milord?" inquired one of the noblemen of Abrogastes, the Far-Grasper.

"Feast," said Abrogastes, who had heard their conversation.

"Yes, milord," said the man.

"Drink!" called another.

And one of the former ladies of the empire hurried to him, to humbly, head down, her hair falling about the flagon and vessel, fill the giant drinking horn.

As she leaned forward, between the feasters, she dared not protest the hand upon her flank.

Abrogastes looked at the former ladies of the empire serving the feast.

It was no mischance or coincidence that they were there, and as they were.

He wanted the feasters to see them thusly, former ladies of the empire, now serving.

Surely they were no different from other women.

And surely they were not without interest.

These things were in accord with his plan.

To his left, he felt a soft cheek press itself to his boot. He did not, this time, thrust it to the side, angrily.

He heard a tiny, grateful whimper.

He felt tender kisses pressed against his foot, through the fur of the foot.

The pet at his feet, to his left, did not know why it had been brought to the feast.

It was fearful.

It whimpered.

There was a reason, of course.

Abrogastes gave no sign that he was aware of the pathetic, tender pressings of lips on his boot.

It is better, sometimes, that such things not be deigned to be noticed.

That helps the pet to better understand all that it is.

Later Abrogastes moved his foot to his right, away from the small, soft, chained object at his feet, its head to his left boot.

As we have mentioned, there was a reason for its presence at the feast.

It was, too, a part of the plan of Abrogastes.

· · · CHAPTER 4 · · ·

"I am detained, unaccountably," said Julian, of the Aurelianii, to Otto, chieftain of the Wolfungs.

"I will go ahead," said Otto.

They stood on a loading dock, one of dozens at Point North, some nine miles north of Lisle, on Inez IV. Even so, the departure of the ships, several times a day, like thunder, could be heard in the city.

Men, some carrying burdens, some with carts, hurried about them, under the supervision of officers, placing supplies in the hold.

"It is unexpected business at court," said Julian. "I will follow you as soon as possible. Do not proceed without me. Wait for me at Venitzia."

Otto had no intention of waiting at Venitzia.

Hoverers were already loaded.

"Way, way!" said a longshoreman, parting crowds for a treaded vehicle drawing flat trailers loaded with boxes.

Too, if it must be known, Julian, even though delayed, had no intention of proceeding directly to Venitzia, the provincial capital on Tangara. It was his intention, rather, to visit an obscure *festung* village on Tangara, one at the eastern edge of the plain of Barrionuevo, at the foot of the heights of Barrionuevo, one in tithe to the remote *festung*, or fortress, of Sim Giadini, far above it, massive, but seemingly tiny from the plain, almost invisible amongst the dark, forbidding, snow-capped, cloud-encircled mountains, the heights of Barrionuevo.

"I will get away as soon as I can," said Julian.

Otto nodded.

The vehicle drawing the trailers passed them, moving toward the cargo hatch.

Through another hatch, reached from a loading platform below, visible through the grille on which they stood, by means of trailers drawn by rumbling, motorized carts, gigantic drums of fuel were being taken aboard.

They were on the second hatch level.

Crew, and passengers, would ascend to the higher level, and board through the smaller entryway.

"Watch out!" called a man.

There was a roaring and a scratching and men struggled to lead wild-eyed mounts through the hatch.

"Be gentle with them!" cried Julian.

We shall call these creatures horses, for the sake of simplicity.

Otto snatched a canvas from one of the carts near him and cast it over the head of the first of the skittish animals. It pawed and scratched at the grille, and cast its long-haired head about, beneath the canvas, and then stood uneasily on the grille, shifting a little, snarling.

"Ho, fellow," said Otto, quietly, patting the creature's shaggy side, "ho!"

He then seized the halter, taking it higher than its groom's grip, near the jowls of the beast.

"Ho," he said again, gently.

"You may take him now," said Julian to the groom.

Otto relinquished his hold on the halter.

The groom then took the halter higher, where Otto had held it, his arm under the canvas.

The groom then led the unprotesting animal through the hatch, into the ship.

The beasts behind the first, seeing the first quiet, the contagion of their anxiety thus assuaged, seemingly contentedly, seemingly now unconcerned, followed it into the ship.

"Put them carefully in their stalls," called Julian.

"Yes, sir," said a man.

The stalls for such beasts are commonly padded, as they are restless, energetic animals, and may injure themselves when they become active, as, for example, when they smell a female of their species.

"Where did you learn the business with the canvas?" asked Julian.

"In the school of Pulendius," said Otto. "It is a common way of quieting female prisoners. But a blanket, not canvas, is commonly used."

"I see," said Julian.

"It may be buckled about their waist, tightly, their hands inside."

"Of course," said Julian.

The blindfold, too, of course, has such virtues. It may not silence the captive, but it tends to reduce her activity, as she does not know where she is, or where she might step, or what dangers lie about her, or, say, what she might strike against, or how she might injure herself if she were to move, and so on. She would not care, for example, to run against spikes or plunge, bound, into a pond of carnivorous eels. If one wishes to silence the captive, of course, a variety of arrangements can manage that easily.

"Prisoners?" asked Julian. "At the school of Pulendius?"

"They are rounded up, occasionally. Girls of the *humiliori*, of course, unless a mistake is made."

"I had not heard of this," said Julian.

"The practice is not widely publicized."

"That is understandable," said Julian.

"They are freed later, of course. And given a coin."

"Splendid," said Julian.

"Do not concern yourself with them," said Otto. "They are only of the *humiliori*—and, too, only of the empire."

"I see," said Julian.

"We are nearly provisioned, sir," said a mariner, with a manifest.

"Good," said Julian.

"I thought," said Julian, "that in schools such as those of Pulendius slaves were kept for satisfying the hungers of the fighters."

"They are," said Otto, "and they grow furious when they are kenneled, and the others are brought in, as a change of pace. But it, too, is excellent for the slaves, as it makes them more diligent, and more helplessly needful, and the men, too, of course, after the timid, confused, untutored girls of the country-side, are eager to relish once again the marvelous feel of a true woman in their arms, a gasping, yielding, begging, helplessly aroused slave."

"The fuel is aboard, sir," said another mariner.

"Good," said Julian.

"The captain will be ready for departure shortly," said a junior officer.

"Good," said Julian.

Two men passed them, with sticks, herding cows.

Four men followed, carrying poles. At the ends of each pole, balanced, swinging, were cages, filled with cackling poultry. These were destined for the small farms of Venitzia, tiny allotments within its fenced perimeter. In Venitzia an egg was a luxury. Outside the fence, occasionally seen on their mounts, in their furs, with their long lances held upright, against the sky, were Heruls.

There was a point to the cows, too, of course, as fresh milk, like eggs, was a luxury in Venitzia.

Outside the fence, as I have mentioned, were Heruls.

Behind these men came others, other pairs, each pair here carrying, supported between themselves, a single pole, from which dangled, upside down, lines of the plucked, gutted bodies of similar fowl, these tied together in pairs, the narrow, scaled, clawed feet of each pair fastened together by string, the pair then thrown over the pole, held in place, swinging, by the string joining their feet.

Quantities of dark-brown leaves of salted meat, baled with cord, went past, on carts.

Great slabs of meat, too, were brought to the ship, on the shoulders of brawny porters.

Much had already been loaded, such as casks of water; boxes of eggs, layered, cushioned in straw; tins of biscuits and bread; blocks of cheese, bearing the imprints of the manufacturers; butts of oil; crates of dried fish; potted ducks; spices; almonds; dates;

sugar; confections; condiments; hampers of vegetables; barrels of fruits; skins of cheap wine, amphorae of fine wines; and quantities of butter, salt, and flour.

"Tenting, charcoal, weaponry, ammunition, parts?" asked Julian. "Fodder and food for the beasts? Fuel for the hoverers?"

"Yes, sir," said a mariner.

There was a squeal from within, ringing out from the metal, of one of the mounts, or horses.

"Be careful in there!" called Julian.

Otto had learned to ride such beasts near one of the holdings of Julian, a small fortresslike holding in the northern hemisphere of Vellmer.

He had learned to master them with the bit and bridle, and quirt.

It was at that holding that Otto had received his commission as a captain in the imperial *auxilia*, or auxiliary forces.

Such beasts were not uncommon on Tangara, being ridden by peoples such as the Heruls, and, some said, the Otungs, one of the five tribes of the Vandals.

We pause to remind the reader that the Ortungs, under Ortog, their king, were a secessionist tribe from the Drisriaks, and were decimated and scattered by Abrogastes. They are not to be confused with the Otungs, which was the leading tribe of the Vandal peoples. Five tribes, with their associated clans, constituted the Vandal nation. These tribes are the Darisi, the Haakons, the Basungs, the Wolfungs, and the Otungs. We apologize, incidentally, for what may seem the unnecessary reiteration of such particulars. We trust that the reader does not find this offensive. Surely it is not our intention to impose upon his patience. But we have noted that such matters are occasionally confused even in the imperial records.

A single, shrill note sounded in the vicinity of the ship, from a device on the port master's tower.

Men lifted their heads, and looked to the tower. Many, below, visible through the grille on which they stood, backed away, though they were yards from the flat bottom of the blackened cement well, dozens of yards thick, below the ship.

"It is the first warning," said Julian.

Below, visible through the grille on which they stood, at the level below, the lower hatch slid shut.

"You must soon be aboard," said Julian.

"What is wrong?" asked Otto.

"Ensign," said Julian.

"Yes, sir?" said the officer.

"The lading is not complete," said Julian.

The ensign regarded him, startled.

"It is not complete," said Julian.

The officer, puzzled, consulted his records, and his markings on them, added throughout the afternoon.

The officer looked up.

"There are some sheep, some goats, some pigs," he said, "but they will be brought on momentarily."

"Your manifest is not complete," said Julian. "Summon the chief supply officer."

"Yes, sir," said the ensign, and hurried away, for the first warning had already sounded.

There had already, with the first warning, been a change in the activity on the quay. It was much more subdued now. Fewer came and went now through the second hatch. Many now, their work finished, stood or sat about, some on their carts and vehicles. This was not unusual, that they would linger for a time, to see the departure of the ship. Too, in the distance, one could see colors, and flutterings, at the railings. Individuals from the city, nearby Lisle, sometimes came down to the quays to watch. The departure of such a ship, an imperial starship, even of the freighter class, is an awesome sight.

"I fear the intent of our mission to Tangara may be more widely suspected than I feared," said Julian to Otto.

"Why do you say that?" asked Otto.

"There were two manifests, of course," said Julian, "the public manifest, filed with the port officer, listing supplies, vehicles, mounts, ammunition, and such, typical supplies for an expedition supplying and reinforcing Venitzia, outfitting scouting expeditions, conducting small-scale reprisals and such, and the second manifest, which was classified."

"And what was its import?" asked Otto, puzzled.

"Trade goods, gifts, and such, of course," said Julian, "to smooth your way among barbarians."

"I am a barbarian," said Otto.

"But you come in the rank of an imperial officer," said Julian.

"It might be better, at first, if they did not know that," said Otto.

"You will need gifts, to interest them, to make yourself welcome," said Julian.

"No," said Otto.

Behind them men were hurrying a small number of sheep through the second hatch. Following them were other men, bringing four pairs of goats.

Within the hatch a mariner was hastening them forward, with gestures.

Julian regarded him, irritably.

"I am not an ambassador, not a merchant," said Otto.

"What then are you?" asked Julian.

"One who is chieftain of the Wolfungs," said Otto, "one who was lifted upon shields."

"Without gifts, you will not be accepted," said Julian.

"The time for gifts," said Otto, "is after one has been accepted."

"You do not understand barbarians," said Julian.

"It is you, my friend," said Otto, "who do not understand such folk."

At this point the second warning sounded.

Above their level, at the crew and passenger entryway, to the level of which had been wheeled a steel, stepped gangway, an officer was waiting.

He looked down at Julian.

"We are betrayed," said Julian. "We have been deprived of the goods essential to the success of our mission. Iaachus, or someone at court, I fear, has delayed or diverted them."

"If you think them important, bring them with you, when you follow me," said Otto.

"You must assuredly wait for me," said Julian, "at Venitzia."

"No," said Otto.

"Then all is lost," said Julian, dismally.

"I do not want the goods," said Otto.

"Surely you understand they would be of value, at least eventually," said Julian.

"Perhaps," admitted Otto, shrugging.

"I would know who has betrayed us," said Julian. "Surely it must be Iaachus," he said, angrily.

"Iaachus supported your mission," said Otto.

"It seemed so," said Julian.

"It is time to board," said a mariner. "The third signal will be sounded any moment."

"Where is the chief supply officer?" cried Julian.

A technician hurried past, carrying loops of insulated cable over his shoulder. This cable had been detached from a socket in the ship. Communication with the ship was now, substantially, from the port tower, not from the level of the quay.

"Time to board, sir," said the mariner, urgently.

"Without the goods we are lost," said Julian.

"No," said Otto.

"Hurry!" said the mariner.

"Farewell, my friend," said Julian, angrily, grasping Otto's hand.

"Dismiss from your mind the dross of goods," said Otto. "Where I go they are not the coin."

"And what, where you go, do you take to be the coin?" inquired Julian.

"Steel," said Otto.

"My poor, naive, simple, dear friend," said Julian.

"You would buy allies?" asked Otto.

"Yes," said Julian. "It is the way of the empire."

"I had thought that *civilitas* was the way of the empire," said Otto.

"One buys barbarians," said Julian.

"It is only slaves who may be purchased," said Otto.

There was suddenly on the quay, several yards away, from behind piled crates, rearing stacks of boxes, assemblages of large machinery, a wild hooting, and cries of pleasure, numerous, boisterous, masculine acclamatory shouts.

Julian looked up, wildly.

A senior officer approached him.

Behind him was the ensign whom Julian had dispatched in search of the chief supply officer.

"I am Lysis," said the senior officer, "chief officer in charge of supply, the *Narcona*."

He and Julian exchanged salutes.

Julian had saluted first, as his own rank, in the imperial navy, the protocol of which he was scrupulous to respect, was inferior to that of the supply officer.

The supply officer turned about and began, losing no time, to wave several men behind him toward the still-open second hatch. They bore burdens of diverse size and weight. Though the nature of the goods was somewhat obscured by their packaging, the wrapping and boxings, and such, we may conjecture, and affirm with confidence, given what later became clear, their natures, which ranged from the common and ordinary, such as nails, wire and copper, to the remarkable, and even precious, such as emeralds, ivory and gold.

"These are the goods of the second manifest," said Lysis, quietly.

"They are late," said Julian.

"No," said the officer. "On the instructions of one in high position, they were to be delivered at the last moment, in the interests of security, before inquiries could be made, before it would be possible to halt their embarkation."

"One in a position of authority is brilliant," said Julian. "I was wrong to suspect him," said Julian to Otto.

"It is good to know on whom one may depend," said Otto. The goods were now moving past them.

"The manifest has been checked," said the supply officer.

"To be sure," said Julian, "there is not time to check it now."

For an instant he seemed troubled.

"It is complete, milord," the officer assured him. "I went over it in the warehouse this morning, and it has been kept under seal, and guard, since then."

"Good," said Julian.

No need for concern was there then.

"Be careful there," called the ensign, at the officer's side, as men fought to keep their grip on a bale of cloths. The heavy canvas cover of the baled cloths gave no clue as to the richness of the stuffs inside, brocades and velvets, and sheens of golden silk, materials fit to bedeck the consorts of chieftains.

Other men struggled to carry, upon their shoulders, what, wrapped in burlap, appeared to be metal ingots. Many were of iron but there were, too, among them, concealed, ingots of gold, from which rings might be formed, fine rings, for the arm and wrist.

Groups of men, four men in each group, bent under the weight of single tusks of the Thalasian torodont.

Boxes passed, which contained plates of copper, and sacks of silver and gold coins. In other boxes there rattled cameos, and medallions, bearing the visage of the emperor, represented as a bearded, powerful man.

"Hurry, hurry!" called a mariner.

Bundles of furs, and skins, were carried by, even those of the golden vi-cat, though the golden fur was rolled to the inside, that the wealth within might be well concealed.

Spices, and condiments, and many other foodstuffs, too, were hastily embarked.

"I smell the pepper of Askalan," marveled a man.

"Are you sure?" asked another.

"Yes, I smelled it once in a bazaar on Rachis II," he was informed.

It was an exotic trade good, doubtless little known on Tangara.

The scent came through the pores of the box of fernwood in which it lay.

Too, there were many other spices, and such, though well sealed, from various worlds, such as nutmegs, gingers, cinnamons, marjorams, frostfruit peel, coriander, thyme, extract of *les*, cream of *kalot*, essence of almond, rosemary, mint, *siba*, chives, mustard, whole cloves, ground cloves, curry powder, mixed herbs, flakes of *hineen*, *tel* sauce, minced *basbas* stalk, sage, paprika, boiled *arla* leaves, seed of the pinnate *fennis* and vanilla.

"But the goods are not quite complete, are they?" asked Julian.

"No," said the officer. He lifted his hand, to an unseen compatriot.

"Move!" said a voice, from behind boxes, and machinery. "This way, this way!" said another voice.

Instantly, there was another rousing cry of delight from the longshoremen, the stevedores, the porters, the drivers, the dock hands, some hooting, the clapping of hands.

It was a similar sound to that which had risen upon the quay but moments earlier.

"This way," said a voice, that of a young, blond officer.

There were cries of pleasure from many men about, who, it seemed, had come from here and there, from many places about the quay, some descending even from their coigns of vantage on boxes, from the seats and hoods of vehicles, and such, to crowd about what was now the center of their attention.

"This way, this way," said another voice, a severe, impatient voice.

Approaching, uncertainly, were several muchly concealed figures.

Each was covered, almost entirely, by a large, light, but

closely woven, opaque, white, sheetlike cloth, which was thrown over the head and buckled about the neck, that portion of the cloth constituting then, in effect, an opaque, concealing hood. Below, at the sides, at the shoulders, two apertures appeared in the cloth, through which bared, fair arms projected. The cloth itself, its hem, so to speak, fell midway, in its voluminousness, upon lovely calves. In this way the lower portion of the well-rounded calves, and the trim ankles and the small feet of each figure, these lovely parts all bared fully, as the arms, were visible. The left ankle of each of the figures was encircled by a light, flatish, narrow, but sturdy, steel anklet, which was locked. After having been unloaded from some vehicle on the quay, which was doubtless the occasion of the first raucous greeting to which they had been subjected, they had assumed, doubtless upon command, a common hand linkage. In this case it was as follows: The first figure puts its right hand behind it and it is felt for, and grasped, by the second figure, who then puts its own left hand behind it, which is felt for, and grasped, by the left hand of the figure behind it, who then puts its own right hand behind it, which is felt for, and grasped, by the right hand of the figure behind it, and so on. To be sure, there are several other such linkages, hands on shoulders of the preceding figure, right hand back to left hand forward, repeated and so on.

The figures had now been permitted to unclasp hands and had been pushed together, crowded together, closely, near the grille ramp leading to the second hatch, only a few feet from Julian and Otto.

"Why are they not chained?" asked Julian.

"They are not going to escape," said the supply officer.

There was laughter from the men about.

"Forgive me, milord," said the officer.

"When such merchandise is moved," said Julian, "I prefer for it to be secured."

"Yes, milord," said the officer.

"And I do not mean by a cord or rope to which each clings," said Julian. "I mean a neck chain, a wrist chain, an ankle chain, an arrangement of bars and collars, locked, plank neck-stocks, nailed or bolted shut, such things."

"Yes, milord," said the officer.

The figures, under the sheetlike coverings, shifted, uneasily.

The sound of the third warning then rang out, from the port tower.

"The sequencing is begun," said an officer.

"You must board immediately," said another.

"He is right, milord," said the supply officer.

"Sir!" called down the officer, anxiously, from the higher entryway, at the top of the wheeled, steel stairway.

"I would see them," said Julian, suspiciously, abruptly.

"There is no time, milord," said the chief supply officer.

"Remove the traveling cloaks," commanded Julian.

This was hastily done, almost frantically.

There were shouts of pleasure from the ruffians, and others, on the quay.

"They are not collared!" said Julian.

"They are ankleted, milord," said the supply officer.

Each of the figures was now revealed to be that of a lightly clad beautiful woman. Each wore a white, short skirt which wrapped about her hips, and a snug, tight white halter. The midriff of each was bared.

"They are muchly clothed," said Julian.

"They are prize slaves," said the officer.

Julian went to one of the girls, and then to another. He thrust up the short skirt at the left hip.

One of the slaves, a blonde, gasped, in protest, though it was not she whose flank was thus subjected to such abrupt, peremptory inspection.

Julian looked at her, puzzled, and then looked to the officer.

"These are not branded," he said.

"None are branded," said the supply officer. "One in authority, whose name need not be spoken here, thought that felicitous, that the masters into whose ownership they come might then have them marked as they please, or even not, if that be their wish."

"I see," said Julian.

"They are prize slaves," said the officer.

"But in their condition as slave no more than any other slave," said Julian.

"True," said the officer.

"A common mark then would be as quite suitable for them, indeed, surely as appropriate for them, as for any other."

"True," said the officer.

"Indeed," said Julian, "let the most beautiful of slaves wear no more than a common mark, that it may help her to keep in mind what she is, that she is no more than a slave!"

"Yes, milord," said the officer.

One of the slaves, a blonde, stiffened, in anger.

Once, again, this caught the eye of Julian.

"It is time to board!" called the officer from the higher entryway.

The sound of pigs could be heard on the quay. It might be recalled that goats, sheep, and pigs had appeared on the public manifest, with certain other animals, but that the pigs had not yet been embarked.

The bared feet of the slaves were on the steel grille of the main platform, near the shallow ramp, also a grille, leading to the second hatch. It was not uncomfortable, as the grille was closely set, but it must have been warm, and they must have been aware, keenly, of the numerous, aligned ridges of the grille on the soles of their feet. The grille ramp, which was adjustable, as there is some variation in hatch placements, was of a similar construction.

"Hurry!" called the officer, from the higher entryway.

One of the slaves, a blonde, went to the entryway ladder, and had ascended three steps before she suddenly cried out in pain, the back of her legs, just below the hem of the short, white skirt, lashed with a switch, in the hand of one of the two officers who had brought them forward, he who seemed the more severe of the keepers.

"What do you think you are doing?" he cried out, angrily.

"Boarding," she said.

There was laughter on the quay, about the hatch.

"Get back where you belong," said the officer, fiercely, pointing with the switch to the bevy of briefly clad beauties near the ramp grille.

She stood for just an instant on the step, but, when he raised his switch again, she hurried down and fled back among the others.

Laughter rang out on the quay.

"Forgive her, milord," said the blond officer to Julian. "She is a debtress, from Myron VII, sold to defray her own debts, and knows as yet little of what it is to be a slave."

Julian was studying the blond slave, intently.

"She will learn!" laughed a man.

"Yes!" said another.

There was more laughter.

"Move aside!" said a man.

There then came, being hurried, a tiny herd of pigs, some dozen or so, which, by men with sticks, were driven through the hatch.

"This way!" called a mariner inside.

"It is through this hatch that you will be loaded, my dear," said the supply officer to the blonde, indicating the second hatch, "with the other animals."

She crouched down, and, it seemed, frantically, desperately, was trying to force the anklet from her fair ankle.

Of the twenty slaves, or seeming slaves, ten were brunettes, and ten were blondes.

"They are a likely lot," said a man.

"Yes," said another.

"I wonder what they will be doing on Tangara," said a fellow.

"We are to be distributed among taverns on Venitzia," said one of the slaves.

"I think I shall put in for duty on Venitzia," said a man.

"Do not," laughed another, "it is a desolation, a wilderness."

To such a world, thought Otto, angrily, were the Otungs banished.

"I expect to be purchased for a high house, perhaps that of the prefect," said one of the slaves.

"And doubtless among your other duties," said a man, "will be cleaning and the polishing of silver."

The beauty, a brunette, tossed her head, and looked away.

"Were you given permission to speak?" asked the blond officer, one of the two who had brought the women forward.

"No, Master," said more than one. Several put their heads down.

"Insolent slaves," said the severe officer.

"They will learn quickly," said a man.

"They need only be beaten, branded, and collared," said another.

Several of the women shifted their weight, moving from one foot to another, apprehensively.

Such things could be easily done to them.

They were slaves.

Few now met the eyes of the bystanders.

The blond looked up, ceasing her efforts to free her ankle of its identificatory device, conscious of a shadow over her.

It was Julian.

"It is on you," said Julian.

She stood, angrily.

"Stand straighter," said Julian.

She did so, angrily.

"Do I not know you?" he asked.

"I do not think so, milord," she said, seemingly suddenly frightened.

"I have seen you somewhere," he said.

"I do not think so, milord," she said.

"It would seem unlikely, milord," said the blond officer, "as she is from Myron VII."

That world was far from Inez IV.

Julian took the hair of the blonde and held it, tightly, and pulled her head back, studying her face.

"I am sure I have seen you somewhere," he said.

"We must go," said the supply officer.

"Some festival, some supper, some regatta, somewhere," said Julian.

"She is a common type, though an exquisite specimen of the type," said the one officer, the more severe of the two, he with the switch. "There are millions like her in the galaxy."

The woman made a tiny, protesting noise, but she could move her head scarcely at all, as it was held.

"Perhaps she served as a slave at some such affair," said the blond officer.

"Perhaps," said Julian.

"Perhaps you met her when she was free," said a man.

"Perhaps," said Julian.

"She might then have been dressed differently," laughed a man.

"Yes," said Julian.

He then, slowly, by the hair, forced her down, to her knees. "Keep your hands down," he warned her, when she seemed tempted to raise her hands to her hair.

"On all fours," he said.

She complied.

"Do you see him?" asked Julian, indicating Otto.

She nodded.

"To his feet, and kiss them," said Julian, releasing her hair.

She hesitated for a moment.

Then she crawled to Otto, who was but a foot or two away, where she hesitated again, for a moment, and then put down her head and kissed his feet. She then lifted her head, and met his eyes. Then she looked down. He had been regarding her, impassively.

She trembled, but then controlled herself.

"You may return to your place," said Julian.

She quickly rose up, and fled back among the other women.

"On the grille, on all fours, all of you!" said the supply officer.

The beauties crowded onto the shallow ramp.

"Cover them and load them," said the supply officer.

The sheets were thrown over them, and they were hastened through the hatch. Within, mariners, with sticks, were waiting for them.

They were to be conducted thusly, covered, herded, through the passageways of the ship.

In this way they would not know their way about, or where they were on the ship.

"Surely you admit they are an exquisite lot," said the supply officer.

"Yes," said Julian. "Someone in authority has made a set of excellent choices."

"We have let them believe that they are going to Venitzia as common slaves, for service in the taverns, for purchase by private houses, and such," said the supply officer.

"Good," said Julian.

"There did not seem much point in telling them that they are destined to be gifts for barbarians."

"No," smiled Julian. "They can always learn that, to their terror, later."

The hatch slid shut.

"In their kennels," said Julian, "I trust that they will not be overly encumbered with garments."

"Very well, milord," said the supply officer.

"Perhaps," said Julian, "they might, aboard the ship, receive some training. Whereas barbarians might enjoy training them to their own harnesses, I would not want them to be slain the first night."

"I understand, milord," said the officer.

"You must board," said a junior officer, urgently, to Julian.

"I am following later," said Julian.

"I will board," said Otto.

"Wait for me in Venitzia," said Julian.

"No," said Otto.

"At least," said Julian, "you now have the gifts."

"Yes," said Otto.

"That should smooth your way considerably," said Julian.

"Perhaps," said Otto.

"Farewell," said Julian.

"Do you think you knew the slave?" asked Otto.

"I had thought so, for a moment," said Julian. "But it seems unlikely. I think now that I must have been mistaken."

"Farewell," said Otto.

The men clasped hands, briefly.

Otto then hurried up the stairway, and disappeared through the entryway.

As soon as he had entered, the entryway hatch slid shut.

A few minutes later, in a great burst of heat and flame, and smoke, an imperial freighter lifted up and, seemingly slowly at first, then much more rapidly, ascended into the sky over the quays at Point North.

The sound was heard even in Lisle, some nine miles distant, in which city was one of the imperial palaces.

To be sure, the imperial family was not then in residence.

· · · CHAPTER 5 · · ·

"Surely it is time, milord," said the clerk, coming to stand behind the chair of Abrogastes.

"Not yet," said Abrogastes, surveying the feasters, now become more riotous, considering, too, the former women of the empire, hurrying about, serving, the lads near them, with the switches.

"There," said Abrogastes, to his shieldsman, "that one," pointing to one of the former women of the empire, who was at the farther end of the hall, with a hot, stained trencher of slabs of roasted meat, a blond woman, a particularly beautiful one, and one now exquisitely curved, from the merciless regimen of diet and exercise imposed upon her by her keepers. We have met her before. She was one of three display slaves. She had been, once, a free, haughty, highly placed, rich woman of the empire.

She had been aboard the *Alaria*, when that vessel had been overtaken by an Ortung fleet, intent upon the rescue of Ortog, king of the Ortungs, prince of the Drisriaks. The ship had been disabled, and boarded, and, after fierce fighting, taken. She, with many others, who had been unable to escape in smaller vessels, had found themselves, to their horror, become the booty of barbarians, spared only for the whip and collar. She then, with many others, had belonged to Ortog, king of the Ortungs, prince of the Drisriaks. She and two others, also blond, had been utilized by Ortog as display slaves, a particularly lovely matched set, which, together with other objects of value, boxes of coins, chests of gems, and such, advertised the splendor of his court, the wealth of his house. They had come into the possession of Abrogastes after the defeat and scattering of the Ortungs, and his raid on Tenguthaxichai. Abrogastes had seen fit, as well, to utilize the trio as display slaves. To be sure, they had many other uses, as well.

"That one, milord?" asked the shieldsman, pointing.

"Yes," said Abrogastes.

The woman had avoided the height of the hall, opposite the great two-leaved portal of its main threshold, avoided the dais, where might be found the bench, with its high-seat pillars, of Abrogastes. Indeed, few of the lovely, belled servitors would have dared to approach that end of the hall, where were the tables of the higher nobles, were it not for the merry, hastening switches of the lads who supervised them. In a sense this was unusual, for often such women, women in such a condition in such a hall, might vie to serve the higher tables, eager to patter to the boards above the salt, hoping to draw themselves to the attention of the feasters there, hoping to be noticed, and called later, when the nobles and higher men might turn restlessly in the furs. Surely better to be chained at the foot of a noble, in some hall or three-aisled house, risking all, desperately, to please him, than to twist and turn, as one could, in the tiny confines of a kennel, to share a stall, ankle-chained, in a dairy barn, or to lie, collared, with pigs, in the mud of a sty. But tonight few of the women, unbidden by their jovial overseers, dared to approach the high tables, those at the end of the hall, and even fewer the bench of Abrogastes himself. At the right of Abrogastes, free, there crouched a great hound, alert and crested. Such hounds often help to keep excellent order among domestic animals, sheep and such.

The shieldsman caught the eye of one of the colorfully garbed lads, with the colorful cloak, and pointed to the woman in question.

The lad did not bother speaking to her but struck her suddenly, unexpectedly, with the switch, turning her toward the far end of the hall.

She nearly tipped the trencher, but no meat fell from it to the dirt, rush-strewn floor.

It would not be necessary, then, that she be beaten for such a clumsiness.

She quailed.

The shieldsman gestured that it was indeed she who was wanted, and should approach.

The switch struck her high, well above the back of the knees, hurrying her forward, with a jangle of bells, toward the bench of Abrogastes.

As she approached, and then, timidly, slowed her pace, the hound at the side of Abrogastes growled, and rose up, on its two front legs. Its hump, a knot of muscle at the back of its neck, tightened, its eyes blazed, the crest began to lift, its ears flattened themselves, back, at the sides of the head.

"Steady, lad," said Abrogastes, soothingly.

The woman had stopped, some feet from Abrogastes, in terror, given the obvious menace of the animal.

Then she cried out in pain, as the lad behind her gave her an excellent stripe, across the back of the legs.

Tears in her eyes, terrified, she came forward, and knelt before Abrogastes, on the dais, for there was no table directly before his bench, and, putting down her head, lifted the tray up, and forward, to him.

He regarded her.

In such a position a woman is quite beautiful.

She was nude, of course, as were, as well, the other former ladies of the empire serving at the feast.

Perhaps I have been remiss in not calling this sort of thing explicitly to the attention of the reader, but then it was doubtless not necessary to do so.

How else would one expect former ladies of the empire to serve at such a feast?

The Alemanni are men.

To be sure, she, and the others, did wear metal anklets, to which bells were affixed, which would sound with the tiniest movement, and a steel collar.

Underneath her blond hair Abrogastes could see the glint of her collar.

On her left thigh, high, just under the hip, there was a brand. It was not the sign of the Drisriaks but a common brand, recognized in merchant law throughout galaxies. It would make it possible to put her on a slave block almost anywhere, with no questions asked.

"Would you like to feed my little pet?" asked Abrogastes, indicating the restless, crested beast that crouched to his right.

She shook her head, fearfully.

The beast looked at her, and growled.

"For what do you exist?" asked Abrogastes.

"To serve my masters with instant, unquestioning obedience and total perfection," she said.

"Do you know what would happen if you were to try to feed him?" asked Abrogastes.

"No, Master," she said.

"He would tear your arm off, at the shoulder," said Abrogastes.

"Yes, Master!" she said.

Such beasts are trained to accept food only from their master, and certain keepers, with whom they are familiar. They attack others who might try to feed them. This makes sense, as food from others might be drugged or poisoned. If the beasts do not receive food within a day or two from their master, or familiar keepers, they hunt for themselves. At such times they can be extremely dangerous.

Abrogastes then, with one hand, his right, took three slabs of hot, greasy, roasted meat from the trencher.

"Go," said Abrogastes.

"Yes, Master!" said the slave and rose to her feet and backed away, quickly.

There was laughter.

A few feet away she turned to regard Abrogastes. She was trembling. She was perhaps even more terrified of Abrogastes than the shaggy brute that crouched to his right, but, too, now, every inch of her was alive. She shifted and her bells, telling their tales, jangled. Men laughed. Her belly, as she looked at him, was afire. He was her master. She belonged to him. She must obey him, instantly, unquestioningly and to the best of her ability, in any, and all, things. She moaned with desire. She could scarcely stand. The bells jangled, as she fought for balance.

She felt weak. She feared she might faint. Never had she known a man such as Abrogastes, and these others, and they were her masters!

"Back to your serving!" said a lad, giving her a quick, stinging lash beneath the small of the back with his switch. Tears bursting from her eyes, cruelly stung, embarrassed, she turned about, and hurried to the food table, to replenish the trencher. They must call for her tonight, someone must! Did they not know she was a slave, and needful! Someone be kind, she thought, wildly. Someone be kind to a poor slave! Be kind, someone, to a poor slave!

Abrogastes took one of the three slabs of meat and held it down, to the hound at his right.

The gigantic head lifted itself delicately, and, carefully, took the piece of meat, and then put it under one paw, holding it to the dais, and tore at it with its teeth.

Abrogastes felt a cheek press itself against his boot, on his left.

"Master," said a small voice, timidly.

There was a small sound of chain, of heavy chain, on wood.

Abrogastes looked down, to his left.

"Greetings, little Huta," he said.

Lying there, to his left, was a small, nude, dark-haired woman, with dark eyes, and high cheekbones. She was on a heavy chain, fastened to a ring on the dais. The chain was quite heavy. It might have easily held even a hoofed *sorit*. And, too, the collar she wore, to which the chain was attached, by a large padlock, was unusually heavy, and large, for a woman. Her lines had been much improved, by the regimen to which she had been subjected by her keepers, since her embondment on Tenguthaxichai.

"I am hungry, Master," she said.

"Oh?" said Abrogastes.

"I have not been fed all day," she said.

"Are you hungry?" he asked.

"Yes, Master," she said.

She looked up at him, pathetically.

Abrogastes looked down at her, in anger.

She looked away, frightened.

Huta had been a consecrated, sacred virgin, an officiant of the rites of the Timbri.

It had been under her influence, according to some, that Ortog had been tempted into the path of rebellion and secession. As a historical observation it seems likely that this analysis is overly simple, considering the energy and ambition of Ortog. On the other hand, there is no doubt that her predictions, prophecies, contrived "signs" and such, played their role in firing his ambition, and encouraging his break with the Drisriaks.

In the raid on Tenguthaxichai she had fallen into the hands of Abrogastes.

She had been unable to influence him. Such men are not easy to influence.

Her guilt, her duplicity and fraud, had been manifest.

On Tenguthaxichai she had forsworn her gods.

Only by declaring herself slave had she managed to escape death, and that only, perhaps, for a moment.

She knew that her life hung by a thread with Abrogastes, who held her, in part, responsible for the defection of Ortog.

She was desperate to please him, not only that she might then live, but because of strange stirrings in her belly, because of profound helplessness, newly sensed, because of unfamiliar whispering, insistent desires, because of yearnings, and beggings, and needings, things she now sensed arising in her as softly, as meaningfully, as stealthily, as irresistibly, as tides and seasons.

"Perhaps I will throw you a piece of meat, to the dais," he said. He held the two pieces left, in his hand.

The tone of his voice frightened her.

"A slave would be most grateful, Master," she said.

"Do not use your hands," he said.

"No, Master," she said.

"On all fours," he said, "here," indicating a place on the dais, before the bench.

"Yes, Master," she said, rising to all fours, this posture lifting the chain on her neck, and coming a little about the bench.

"Ready?" he said.

"Yes, Master," she said.

He then threw the piece of meat to the dais, suddenly, before the bench.

She put down her head but then jerked it back, suddenly, screaming, in a sound of chain, of snarling, of the scratching of claws on wood. Not inches from her head had been the snarling, suddenly lunging visage and jaws of the fierce, crested hound of Abrogastes.

Its eyes were blazing, regarding her, and its head, and jaws, down, were over the meat. Then, as she scrambled back on the other side of the bench, on the other side of the left high-seat pillar, the hound seized the meat and pulled it back to his place.

She knelt then beside the bench, on the left of Abrogastes, shuddering, gasping.

Abrogastes laughed, amusing himself at the discomfiture of the slave.

Others, too, who had witnessed his joke, roared with laughter. To others, who might not have noticed, it was explained.

There was more laughter.

And men returned to their feasting.

Huta looked for an instant into the eyes of Abrogastes, and then lowered her head, frightened.

She knew that Abrogastes hated her, but, too, in his eyes, at times, she had seen something else, something which had seemingly infuriated Abrogastes, but which filled her with strange feelings, with something of hope, with even a sense of possible power. She had seen that he, at times, regarded her with keen desire. At such times, she had tried to kneel a little more straightly, or curl herself in his view, or at his feet, just a little more beautifully, or, timidly, seductively. At such times he would occasionally strike her, angrily, or spurn her with his foot. "You are learning your collar, aren't you, you stinking, clever little bitch," he would say. Then she would not dare to respond, but would keep her head down. He would then storm away. She then, kneeling there, left behind, or lying there, spurned, abandoned, wondered if, indeed, she might be learning her collar. She wanted him to care for her, if only a little. She knew she was falling in love with him. But how bold, or frightening, or terrifying, that would be for such as she, a mere slave! And how much more it would put her at his mercy!

"Kneel here, more closely, pretty little slave slut, Huta," said Abrogastes. He tapped the side of the bench.

She crawled a few inches closer, until she was at the very side of the bench.

He lifted the large padlock on her collar, its bolt fitted through the stout collar staple and one of the links of the heavy chain, descending between her breasts, to the floor of the dais, and then looping up, over her left thigh, to descend again to the dais, to its ring, to which it was fastened, to the left of his bench.

He let the padlock fall back, against the collar.

He looked at her.

"You appear to be collared and chained," he said.

"Yes, Master," she said.

"It will soon be spring," he said, "and the storm of stones will be at an end."

"Master?" she asked.

"And then it will be time for the lions to come forth from their lairs," he said.

This was an allusion to the lionships.

"Master?" she said.

"You were a consecrated, sacred virgin," he said.

"Yes, Master," she said.

"You are now a slave girl," he said.

"Yes, Master."

"Yet you are still, as I understand it, a virgin," he said.

"Master has not yet seen fit to remove my virginity," she said.

"Or give you to a groom, that he may do so," said Abrogastes.

"No, Master," she whispered.

"Where do you think, this season," asked he, "the lions should prowl?"

"I do not know, Master," she said, frightened.

He then began to chew, holding it in one hand, and pulling at it with his teeth, the remaining piece of roasted meat, from the trencher of the display slave.

She watched him, almost faint with hunger.

"Are you hungry?" he asked.

"Yes, Master!" she said.

He tore off a piece of roasted meat and held it to her, but, when she reached up, to take it, delicately, gratefully, in her teeth, he removed it from her reach.

He put it in his own mouth, and chewed upon it, and then swallowed it.

Tears formed in her eyes.

"Do you like your collar and chain?" he asked.

"Yes, Master," she whispered.

"Do you like your brand?" he asked.

"Yes, Master!" she said.

It was a common mark, familiar in almost all markets.

"It marks you well," he said.

"Yes, Master," she said, putting her head down.

"As what you are, a slave," he said.

"Yes, Master," she said.

"The proud, arrogant Huta," mused he, "is now no more than a slave."

"Yes, Master," she said.

"Perhaps the lions should visit the world of the Timbri," he said.

She looked at him, frightened.

"Perhaps you might be sent ahead," he said, "in the guise of a free woman, to assess diverse districts, with respect to their riches, to scout suitable landing points."

"No, please, Master," she said.

"You are a little fool," he said.

"Master?"

"Do you think I would entrust such a business to a slave?"

She looked at him, trembling.

"Do you think I would give you an opportunity to slip away from me?" he asked.

"I do not know, Master," she whispered.

"No," he said.

"Yes, Master," she said.

The look in his eyes frightened her.

The consciousness of her slavery burned in her belly.

"Do you not think there are numerous free women, who, for a price, would further such ends, who, for a chest of coins, a bracelet of diamonds, may be bought as easily as a slave girl, to which status they may then, in our own good time, be reduced?"

She dared not speak.

"Were you not once one such?" he asked.

"Yes, Master," she said. "Forgive me, Master."

Moodily he ate more of the meat.

"I have not been fed this day, Master," she said. "Perhaps it was overlooked by the keepers."

"No," he said. "It was by my orders."

"Let Master not be angry with his slave," she said.

"You are not worthy of being angry with," he said.

"No, Master," she said.

"Do you know why you have been permitted to be present at this feast?" he asked.

"No, Master," she said, frightened.

"There is a purpose," he said.

"Yes, Master," she said.

"Do you know why you have not been fed today?" he asked.

"No, Master," she said.

"There seemed no reason to waste food on you today," he said.

"Master?" she said.

"The lions will not hunt in the forests of the Timbri," he said, moodily.

She was silent.

"Elsewhere," said he, "there lie richer worlds for reaving."

"Where?" she asked.

"Does a pig inquire into the plans of her master?" he asked.

"No, Master!" she said.

"Let Master not hate his slave," she said.

"Master," she said.

"Yes?" said he.

"Why was there no reason to waste food on me today?"

"Because it is not likely that you will live out the day," he said.

"Master!" she said.

"I should have put you to the sword on Tenguthaxichai," he said, angrily.

"No, Master!" she cried.

"Why did I not do so?" he asked.

"I do not know, Master," she said.

"You stripped yourself well," he said. "I was weak."

"I do not think so, Master," she said.

"And what do you think was the reason?" he inquired.

"Doubtless it amused Master to punish me, by enslaving me."

"True," he said.

"Too, I think Master was curious to see how I might prove to be, as an abject slave."

"Perhaps," he said.

"That is not weakness," she said. "No more than the lion is weak, when it stalks the gazelle."

"And how do you think you would prove to be, as an abject slave?" he asked.

"Master has denied me the opportunity to show him," she said.

"Yes," he mused.

"Let Master try me, and learn," she said.

He regarded her, not speaking.

"I beg to be given the opportunity to show Master," she said.

"You beg to please as a slave?" he asked.

"Yes, Master!" she said.

"Interesting," he said.

"It is a slave's hope," she said, "that her master might find her of some interest."

His dark, keen eyes viewed her.

She drew back.

She began to realize what it might be, to be desired as a slave is desired.

Then he looked away from her, angrily.

"You are not important," he said. "To be sure, you have a small role to play here tonight. But you are not important. Mighty things are here afoot tonight.

"Down," he said, and she lay down, beside the bench.

He then, not looking at her, finished the meat.

He looked out, over the feast.

The former ladies of the empire served well.

"Is it not nearly time, milord?" asked the clerk.

"Yes," said Abrogastes.

"Shall the spear be brought?" asked a man.

"Yes," said Abrogastes.

· · · CHAPTER 6 · · ·

"Your rations, milady," said the young, blond-haired junior officer, Corelius, sliding a shallow pan of moist gruel beneath the gate of the tiny cage, the bottom of which was some three inches above the steel floor of the cage.

Inside, crouching within the cage, covering herself as best she could, the woman looked out through the closely set bars.

"Is it you?" she pleaded. "It must be you!"

Surely he was the only one of the crew who treated her with deference! It must be he!

"What?" he asked.

"Is it you?" she whispered.

He smiled. Did the smile mean it was he, or that he thought her strange, or insane, or what?

She cried out, inwardly, in anger, in misery.

"Commonly," said he, "one thanks the keeper for food. That is courteous. Too, it need not be given to you, you know."

"But you do not demand such things of me!" she said.

"Nor of the others," he said.

She cried out, inwardly, confused.

She looked down at the pan of gruel.

"Bring me something else," she said. "You cannot expect me to eat this moist slush!"

"What would you like?" he asked.

It must be he, then!

"Tidbits of roast hen, *tahareen* will do, in *siba* sauce, hot *rissit*, fresh *poma*, frosted *yar* cakes, a custard of Vellmer, and wine, some wine, *kana*, yes *kana*, white *kana*!"

"I scarcely think so," he smiled.

"You could smuggle it here," she whispered.

"Surely the risk would be too great," he whispered, conspiratorially.

She shrank back in the cage.

Perhaps it was not he.

But perhaps the risks would be too great.

But she resolved, when this business was done, as it must be soon, for she was frightened in the cage, to make him pay for not having complied with her requests, in this, her time of humiliation and hardship! How cruel he was, how lacking in understanding! How pleased she would be, reporting him to Iaachus.

"Don't go!" she begged.

He turned. "Yes, milady?" he said.

"Is it you?" she begged.

"Is it I, what?" he asked.

"Nothing!" she said. "No! Do not go!"

Again he paused.

"You are polite," she said.

"It is my wont," he said.

"You call me 'milady,' " she whispered.

"It is my wont," he said.

"That is fitting, you know," she whispered.

"Doubtless," he agreed.

"I am caged alone," she said, "in this hold. There are no others here! Might that not arouse suspicion?"

He looked at her, amused.

She decided she hated him. He was clothed, and free. "Why is it?" she asked.

"Surely the marks on your body should make that clear," he said.

She flushed scarlet. The other officer, the severe, impatient one, had lashed her twice, with his switch, she, when she had been on all fours, in the common room.

"You are being isolated, as a punishment," he said. "Too, it was felt that your example, your haughtiness, for example, might spread to the other girls, and imperil them later with masters. Too, if you must know, the other girls do not like you."

"Do not like me!" she laughed. "That is amusing!"

He shrugged.

"Bring me something good to eat!" she said.

"Consider," said he, "improving your behavior."

"Improving my behavior?" she asked.

"Some might suspect," he said, "that you were not a slave."

"Get out!" she said.

"Farewell, milady," he said, and turned about, and left.

"Bring me something good to eat!" she called after him.

When he had disappeared through the hatchway she crawled on her knees to the front of the cage, a movement of a foot or two, and grasped the bars.

It must be he, she thought.

He was polite. He called her "milady!" But perhaps he was mocking her.

She did not know.

Of course the agent would not care to make his identity too obvious to her, not until later.

It must be he.

Who else could it be?

Improve her behavior! The other girls did not like her! That was too bad, that slaves might not like her, she, who could command them, and whip them, and buy and sell them as she pleased!

But, too, perhaps it would not be wise for him to try to bring her luscious viands, and dainties, for what if the brute of a barbarian on board should learn of this, and become suspicious?

She thought of the barbarian, such a formidable, silent, brooding giant of a man.

She was terrified of him. But, too, she knew that she must,

somehow, draw herself to his attention. That she must arrange, somehow, sometime, when she had the knife, to be alone with him.

How terrifying to be alone with such a brute, a stranger to *civilitas*, not even civilized, not even, perhaps, of the empire!

She did not wish to behave as a slave!

Surely he would be more interested in her if she behaved as if she were free, not as one of those curvaceous, groveling, helpless, passionate chits in bondage! But his interest in her, if she seemed free, she feared, might be simply to tear her freedom from her, and put her to his feet, helpless, and no different then from any other slave!

It must be the blond-haired officer, she thought, grasping the bars, it must be he!

But if it were not he, who then might it be?

How she hated the severe officer, the impatient officer, who had switched her, putting two sudden, stinging, rich stripes on her, she on all fours, as though she might have been no more than a slave girl!

Before she had left Lisle, the very night she had left the royal palace, she had switched her own slave girl, mercilessly, for she had, it seems, rendered intelligence to the informants of Iaachus as to the marvelous beauty of her mistress. How the curvy little thing had wept and squirmed, as a slave, begging for mercy!

So it could not be the severe officer, the beast!

Too, it was he who had had her isolated, caged here, alone, her cage not with the cages of the others.

Then she sat back in the cage, shuddering.

It might be he.

He might be trying to divert possible suspicion from himself, trying to conceal the latent relationship between them, that of the supplier of the weapon, that of the guarantor of safety, that of the provider of swift, sure return transportation to Lisle, to the one to whom the deed fell, to the appointed assassin, to the one who need do no more than scratch a skin with a tiny point.

Perhaps he was a consummate actor?

He had put her here, alone.

Perhaps that was to diminish the chances of her being suspected, of her giving her true loftiness, her station and freedom away, doubtless inadvertently, perhaps in an instant of forgivable carelessness, in the presence of the mere slaves.

It could be he.

Perhaps, too, cleverly citing discipline as a blind, utilizing it as a pretext, he was giving her privacy, separating her from degraded animals, those meaningless slave girls, in deference to her different nature, and the delicacy of her feelings.

It must be he!

But he had not permitted her clothing in the cage.

But then it had not been permitted to the others either, in their cages, in the common room.

The young naval officer, he who had been on the quay, she thought, may have been responsible for that. He had made some remark which might have been interpreted as a recommendation to that effect.

Why had they deferred to him, as they had? His rank, surely, at least insofar as she could read the relevant insignia, was not so high.

She hated the young naval officer.

But it seemed clear, too, that he would know how to treat slaves. Of that she was sure.

But she was not a slave!

How should she behave, she wondered, in the presence of the severe officer, he who had switched her.

She smiled to herself.

Perhaps she should behave in his presence as though she were truly a slave.

That would surely be amusing, he acting his role, she hers, and none suspecting that they were both merely consummate actors! But what if he were not the one? What then, surely then she should not play such a role before him. Too, enacting such a role, as Iaachus had required of her, made her considerably uneasy. It produced feelings in her which she found oddly disturbing, not at all the sort of feelings one might expect to have if one were merely playing a role.

Too, she had heard that there were tests in such matters, available to skilled masters, by means of which hypocrisy and sham might be detected. That frightened her. To be sure, she knew little of such tests.

She sat back, farther, in the cage, her knees up. She regarded the gate, with its bars. She was well held in that cage, she knew, as well held as if she herself might be only a slave girl.

There were two sorts of tests, we might remark, one of which was used to pick out slave girls from among free women, this usually used to detect runaway slave girls trying desperately to pass themselves off as free women, but which might, if one wished, serve equally well to pick out free women from among slave girls, among whom they might, as in the siege of a city, have attempted to hide themselves; and one of which was used to determine the authenticity or inauthenticity of slave behavior. Slavery is not, of course, a simple matter of behavior, though it manifests itself in behavior, sometimes even subtly, but it runs deep in the woman, coursing in every fiber of her being. A negative result in such tests distinguishes the mere appearance of slavery, its mere simulation, from its reality, or depth actuality. In such a situation the slave is quickly taught the truth of her slavery, that that is what she truly is. It does not take the intelligent woman long to understand this. Sometimes she is simply offered the choice of a full and perfect slavery or death, and she understands that there are no third options, such as acting, sham, or pretense, or even the tiniest particle of mental reservation. In this moment the woman must examine herself, perhaps more profoundly than ever before in her life. In a moment of emotional catharsis, she understands what she is, in her deepest heart, falls to the feet of even a hated master, and rejoices.

The door to the hold opened and she raised her head instantly, and drew her knees up higher, and leaned forward, her hands about her legs, hiding herself so.

How terrible that she should not have been permitted clothing!

A stock keeper, a short, stocky, homely, simple-looking man, put his head inside the door and switched off the overhead hold light.

"You!" she called, as he withdrew.

After a moment the door slid back and the figure of the man reappeared in the portal.

"Come here!" she said.

The hold was now much in darkness except for two small, reddish night bulbs, on the wall.

By the light of these one might check the hold, and, perhaps, its occupants, or cargo, without illuminating the entire area.

It seemed that he was about to withdraw.

She called out, "Sir!"

He paused.

"Please come here, sir!" she said.

He stood there, in the reddish darkness.

Then it seemed he would turn away.

"Master!" she called. "Please, Master!"

He approached the cage.

"I have been brought by mistake only a pan of cold porridge," she said. "I cannot eat that. I will need something else. Please bring it to me."

"Kneel," he said, "kneel straightly, back on heels, knees wide, head up, hands on your thighs, palms down."

She obeyed. How she hated to be commanded by such a simpleton.

But was some semblance of obedience not required by her role as putative slave?

"Now put your hands, clasped, behind the back of your head," he said.

That such a simpleton could command her!

She did as she was told, feeling strange feelings.

"I cannot eat this cold slush," she said. "It has been brought to me by mistake. Bring me something to eat."

How strange sounded such words to her, in her present posture.

He tried the cage gate, which was well locked.

Was he trying to get in, and, if so, what for?

Happily he did not have the key.

He fingered a disk of wax wired about the gate and jamb of the cage. He let it drop, with an angry sound.

It was, she had learned, the virgin seal, the rupture of which would testify to an unauthorized opening of the cage.

He looked at her, in the half darkness, and she shrank back a bit.

"No," he said.

He turned away.

"It is late," she said.

This was true, in ship time.

He turned about, to regard her, kneeling as she was.

"The floor of the cage is hard, and metal!" she said. "I will be cold. Bring me a comforter!"

"Curl," said he.

" 'Curl'?" she said.

"Lie down, on your side, curled up," said he.

She did so.

"Bring me a comforter," she said.

"No," he said.

"What is your name," she demanded.

"Qualius," said he.

"What do you do on the ship?" she asked.

"I am a tender of pigs," he said.

"What are you doing here?" she asked.

"Tending a pig," he said.

She gasped, in fury.

"Curl more prettily," he said.

She did so, angrily, her right hip high, the love cradle of her vulnerable, and tormentingly beckoning, her waist marvelously turned, and roundly descendant, then swelling upward, roundly, to the excitements of her bosom.

It was an excellent body, even for a slave.

"Bring me a blanket!" she said.

"No," he said.

"I shall report you to the supply officer," she said, "to the captain!"

To be sure, she had not even seen the captain, nor had she seen the supply officer since the quay.

He turned away.

"Even a tiny rag, Master!" she called.

He stopped at the door, and looked back.

"Please, Master!" she called. "Please, Master!"

He stood there.

"Even a tiny rag, Master!" she called.

"No," he said.

He then withdrew.

She sat again in the cage.

What a simpleton, and a fool he was, she thought. But she could dismiss him, she was sure, from her considerations. Iaachus would not have put a task of trust in the hands of so stolid and benighted a creature.

But she had knelt for him, and posed for him, as he had commanded.

Was she then, actually, a slave girl?

Never! She was acting. But she did have strange feelings, and a sense of the radical dimorphism that separated the sexes in her species, a dimorphism that did not stop with, nor was it limited to, certain differentials of size and hardness, of smallness, of softness, and lusciousness.

She feared she would be cold tonight.

Ship, she thought, bring me soon to Tangara!

She hoped that her isolation in the hold, her separation from the others, would not provoke suspicion.

The supply officer, she thought, perhaps it is he, he who will provide me with the dagger.

But I myself, she thought, may have to arrange the opportunity to be alone with the barbarian.

How can I arrange that, she wondered.

Perhaps my beauty will arrange it, she thought.

But her beauty, it seemed, had had no great effect on the tender of pigs. But was it not extraordinary, even among slave girls, women embonded for their beauty, and, in places, she had heard, even bred for it?

She was furious.

She had not gotten her way.

How she had demeaned herself, and yet had not gotten her way!

Did they think she was a slave!

She would think of some way to have her vengeance on the fellow. Iaachus could manage that.

He had tried the gate of the cage. Had he merely been checking it, or had he been interested in seeing if it were securely fastened, and, if not, what might have happened then? He had seemed displeased at the discovery of the virgin seal on the gate. What if the gate had been insecure, and the seal not there? She shuddered. Too, she began to suspect the vulnerability of the female slave.

She looked at the floor of the hold.

She wondered what it might feel like, on her body.

Suddenly, sitting there in the cage, she tried to slip the anklet from her left ankle. But she could not do so, and, in a few moments, she gave up the effort, angrily. It was on her, as the young officer on the quay had dryly observed.

It was a slave anklet.

It was part of her disguise, of course. It was not as though it was really on her. But it was, of course, really on her, at least in the sense that she could not remove it, no more than if she were in fact no more than another caged slave.

She looked down with distaste at the now-reddish-appearing gruel in the shallow pan.

Surely they did not expect her to eat such stuff.

She would starve first.

Who is the other agent, she wondered. Who has the dagger?

She slept fitfully that night, or rest period.

Her dreams were various.

She dreamed of a slender, yellow-handled poniard, a black-swirled design wrought within the handle, the handle itself with a double-scrolled guard, which was important, that her hand not slip onto the blade, that lovely narrow blade, that beautifully, harmoniously narrow blade, ideal for penetration, some seven inches in length, razor-edged, needle-pointed, coated imperceptibly with some transparent substance.

She dreamed of herself plunging it into the back of the unsuspecting giant, or perhaps, as he lay recumbent, unsuspecting, on a couch, into his chest.

But, too, she had frightening dreams, of herself stripped, and thrown, painted and perfumed, and chained, among barbarians, with other loot, of herself on a slave block, of herself being sold in a hundred markets to a hundred masters, of Iaachus laughing, of her family laughing, of her intimate maid, whom she must now strive to dress as a lady, she herself now the intimate maid, laughing, and holding a switch, the very switch with which she had beaten the slave before, only that it was she herself who was now the slave!

She awoke with a start.

I am not a slave, she cried to the hold. And then she was frightened, fearing that someone might have heard. I am not a slave, she then whispered to herself, intensely.

But then she remembered, from the dream, the fur beneath her knees, and the chains on her body, and the men about, regarding her, with a desire she had not understood that men could feel, and she knowing that she might belong to any of them and would then be his to command, she to be obedient to the least of his caprices. And she remembered the slave blocks and the cries of auctioneers and being exhibited, as a true slave.

She shuddered.

And, too, she remembered her indescribable thrills, knowing what she was, and how she must serve, joyfully, will-lessly compliant, how she must serve eagerly, helplessly, owned by another!

Surely I am not a slave, she whispered to herself. Surely I cannot be a slave.

She found herself ravenously hungry.

There was nothing in the cage but the pan of gruel.

I cannot eat this, she protested, tears in her eyes.

Then she fingered it into her mouth.

In a little while it was gone. There had not been much of it to begin with.

Is this all we are to be fed, she asked herself.

She touched the anklet.

What is wrong with me, she asked herself.

Ship, she whispered, bring me swiftly to Tangara. Unknown confederate, put the dagger quickly into my hand. I would quickly be done with this, and would return quickly to the capitals of the empire.

She then fell asleep again, and slept dreamlessly, until she was awakened by the young, blond officer, who released her from the cage, and conducted her, suitably, on all fours, to the common room.

It was there that the slaves would receive some training.

The supply officer, Lysis, who had direct charge of them, had apparently deemed this appropriate.

··· CHAPTER 7 ···

"Surely things proceed apace, milord," said Tuvo Ausonius.

"I am detained here, in Lisle," said Julian. "There seems no adequate reason for it, for my participation in these ceremonials."

"It is fitting that those related to the imperial family participate, milord," said Ausonius.

"I am troubled," said Julian.

"Ottonius is well on his way to Tangara," said Tuvo Ausonius. "What does it matter if he arrives some weeks before you? He will surely wait for your assistance, and counsel."

"I do not think he will wait," said Julian. "I think he has his own projects afoot."

"You do not doubt his loyalty to the empire, surely?" asked Ausonius.

"One does not know," said Julian.

"Surely he is loyal," said Ausonius. "He was, as I understand it, raised in a *festung* village, one in tithe to the *festung* of Sim Giadini, in the Barrionuevo Heights.''

The *festung*, or fortress, of Sim Giadini was, in effect, a remote, fortified Floonian monastery, one occupied by members, or brothers, of the order of Sim Giadini, who had been an emanationist, a position now understood, following votes taken at three councils, to be heterodox.

"He would doubtless have received instruction from the brothers of the order of Sim Giadini," said Tuvo Ausonius.

"I think not," said Julian. "The relationship of the *festung* village to the *festung* is primarily economic. I suspect our Ottonius knows little more of Floon than of Orak and Umba."

Orak was the king of the gods in the pantheon of the empire, and Umba was his consort.

"But surely he will have learned the glory and wonder of the empire, and the value of *civilitas*," said Tuvo Ausonius.

"*Civilitas* may be crumbling," said Julian.

"Say 'No,' milord!" said Tuvo Ausonius, dismayed.

"It may be the end of all things," said Julian.

"The empire is eternal, milord," said Tuvo Ausonius.

"Once," brooded Julian, "there was no empire."

"Do you feel the empire is in jeopardy?" asked Tuvo Ausonius.

"Yes," said Julian.

Tuvo Ausonius was silent.

"The empire needs fighters," said Julian. "Leadership fails, the aristocracy grows decadent, rabbles roam the streets, clients defect, allies become restless, borders contract, trade routes grow hazardous, outlying worlds grow indefensible, *federates* grow unruly."

"But barbarians," said Tuvo Ausonius.

"No children are born in golden beds," said Julian.

"But barbarians, milord," protested Tuvo Ausonius.

"Yes, barbarians," said Julian.

"As our Ottonius?"

"Yes," said Julian.

Tuvo Ausonius was silent.

"They may save the empire," said Julian.

"Or destroy it," said Tuvo Ausonius.

"Yes," agreed Julian, wearily.

"He is a peasant," said Tuvo Ausonius.

"No," said Julian.

"What is he then?" asked Tuvo Ausonius.

"I do not know," said Julian. "The answer to that mystery lies, I think, in the *festung* of Sim Giadini."

"Surely, milord," said Tuvo Ausonius, "you do not think that the empire is truly in jeopardy?"

"No," said Julian, slowly, after a time. "I suppose not."

"There is nothing to fear."

"No," said Julian. "I think not."

"The empire is eternal," said Tuvo Ausonius.

"Of course," said Julian.

· · · CHAPTER 8 · · ·

"Let us see if there are men here!" called Abrogastes, meaningfully, his eyes blazing, rising to his feet, from the bench, between the high-seat pillars.

He waved to the side.

"It is the great spear!" cried a man.

"It is the spear of oathing!" cried another.

"What is it doing here?" cried another.

"How is it come to the hall?" said another.

"Surely it is not time for the spear," whispered others.

"Not for a thousand years," cried a man.

Two men bore the great spear forth, with its ashen shaft and bronze head, bore it muchly to the center of the feasting hall, but forward, some, toward the bench of Abrogastes.

The brownish, ashen shaft of the spear was mighty, but might, in the hands of a titan, or giant, or in those of Kragon, the god of war, one supposes, have proven supple.

The wood was fresh.

The head was broad, and of bronze, and forged in an ancient fashion, one dating back to a time when the Alemanni were first learning the mysteries of metals, how to smelt, and mix, and shape them.

There had been, of course, a succession of such spears, but

each, you see, had touched its predecessor, and thus, as the Alemanni would have it, had become the spear.

"This is the spear," the markings priest, who could read the ancient, secret signs, would say, and it had then, as it had touched its predecessor, become the spear.

This succession of spears may have extended back farther than even the most ancient of war songs, to the first forests and storms, and wars.

Its antiquity was not known.

The earliest spears would have crumbled to dust but then, at such a time, they were no longer the spear, but another was the spear.

In this sense the spear was thought to be eternal, as the Alemanni.

It was a sacred object.

Later the earlier spear was destroyed with axes, to cries of war. Thus it was as though it had perished in battle. The splinters were then wrapped in precious cloths, and burned in the sacred fire, in the secret place in what, by tradition, was said to be the first forest, where, as the stories had it, Kragon, the god of war, had fashioned the Alemanni, of earth, and fire, and his own blood, that in his hall he might have worthy cup companions. Kragon was usually represented as hawk-winged, this symbology presumably suggesting swiftness, ferocity, ruthlessness, unexpectedness of strike, and such things. He was also, generally, interestingly, regarded as a god of wisdom. In the syncretism of the empire he, with many alien gods, was sometimes included in the imperial pantheon. In the secret place in the forest, known only to the oldest of the markings priests, it was said that Kragon had breathed his spirit, with the breath of fire, into the Alemanni. The Vandals, too, interestingly, had such stories, which suggests the possible existence of an earlier cultural complex, perhaps an earlier cultural center, one perhaps even neolithic, or protoneolithic, underlying, in an obscure, basal fashion, the development of several of the barbarian peoples.

"Unchain her!" roared Abrogastes, pointing to Huta, who shrank back, where she lay at the left side of his bench, as one would look toward the hall.

One of the keepers rushed to the slave and pulled from his belt a great ring of keys, one of which he thrust into the massive padlock on her high, heavy iron collar. In an instant it was thrown in a clatter of metal to the stout planks of the dais, and Huta, whimpering, terrified, at a gesture from Abrogastes, was hurried from the dais, bent over, held by the hair, and flung to the earth, some five yards before the bench. Some three or four yards before the spear, which had now been placed, butt down, held by two men, in the rush-strewn dirt floor of the hall. She scrambled about, on all fours, to face Abrogastes, and then knelt in fearful obeisance, her head down, the palms of her hands on the floor, making herself as small as possible.

"Kneel up!" shouted Abrogastes.

Fearfully Huta did so, back straight, back on her heels, head up, palms down on thighs, knees spread widely, pathetically, beseechingly.

"Behold, brothers!" cried Abrogastes in fury, pointing to the slave. "Behold she who was once Huta, priestess of the Timbri!"

Anger coursed about the tables, for it was well known that she had been implicated in the secession of Ortog, and, indeed, by many, was held accountable for that defection, that treason and rebellion.

"What is your name?" called Abrogastes to the slave.

"Huta!" she cried.

"And what sort of name is that?" he demanded.

"It is a slave name, put on me by my master!" she cried.

"Who is your master?" he asked.

"You are my master," she cried, "Abrogastes, king of the Drisriaks, of the Alemanni!"

"For what do you exist?" inquired Abrogastes.

"To serve my masters with instant, unquestioning obedience and total perfection!" she said.

"She it was," cried Abrogastes, to the assembled, now-so-bered feasters, "who by trickery and cajolery, by promises, and false prophecies, fanned the ambition of Ortog, who tempted him to treason, who encouraged him in heinous sedition, who led him to rend the Drisriaks, his own people, who would have had him found a divisive tribe, even the name of which no longer exists!"

The name, of course, of the failed, secessionist tribe was the Ortungs or the Ortungen. The name did still exist, of course, though it was not wise to speak it in the presence of Abrogastes, nor, generally, in the dwelling places of the Drisriaks. The Ortungs had been, of course, defeated, and scattered, as grass to the wind, as it was said. To be sure, there were, here and there, remnants who, in hiding, and unreconciled, continued defiantly to regard themselves as Ortungs, in their own right, by the acceptance of rings, and not traitorous Drisriaks. After the slaughter in the tent on Tenguthaxichai, recounted elsewhere, Abrogastes, on the advice of his counselors, had permitted pockets of surrendering, repentant Ortungs to return to the dwelling places of the Drisriaks. The olive branch, as well as the sword, can be an instrument of policy.

"Is not treason the worst of crimes?" called Abrogastes.

"Yes," cried several men, about the tables.

"No!" shouted Abrogastes. "The instigation to treason is the worst of crimes!"

He pointed to Huta.

"Yes, yes!" cried men. The tables roared.

The former ladies of the empire, kneeling about the hall, at the sides, before the tables, trembled.

"Mercy, Master!" cried Huta, throwing herself to the rush-strewn floor of the hall.

"What shall be done with her?" called Abrogastes.

"Kill her! Kill her!" cried men. Men, too, rose from behind the tables. Others pounded upon them. "Kill her!"

"Let it be a lesson to all who would betray the peoples!" cried a man.

"Yes!" cried others.

Huta, lying prone in the dirt, looked up, and lifted her hand to Abrogastes. "Mercy, Master!" she begged.

Doubtless she then understood why food had not been given to her that day, that it might not be wasted upon her.

The giant spear, held by two men, was large, upright, behind the slave.

"Kneel up!" cried Abrogastes.

Terrified, Huta obeyed, though she could scarcely, even kneeling, keep her balance, so shaken, so helpless, she was.

"Let me cut her throat!" cried a man, coming about a table.

"No, let me!" cried another.

One man then even leapt to the slave and had her head back, cruelly, held by the hair, his knife at her throat.

He looked eagerly to Abrogastes.

Abrogastes waved him back, and the others, as well.

"You were a priestess, were you not?" inquired Abrogastes.

"Yes, Master," said Huta.

"You were a consecrated, sacred virgin, were you not?" inquired Abrogastes.

"Yes, Master," wept Huta.

"You do not appear to be clothed," said Abrogastes.

"No, Master," she wept.

"She has her brand!" laughed a man.

"Yes!" said another.

There was laughter.

"Behind you, behold the spear of the Alemanni!" said Abrogastes.

"Yes, Master," she said, falling to all fours, and turning.

"Go to it!" he said.

Quickly she did so, and, unbidden, began to kiss, and lick it, desperately.

There was laughter.

"She is not unintelligent," said a man.

"No," said another.

The spear, interestingly, may not be touched by free women, of the Alemanni, or others. It may, however, receive the ministrations of female slaves, this being taken as a service or an obeisance, much as the washing of a warrior's feet by the tongues of the women of the enemy, the acts serving as a symbol of the nothingness of the slaves, as an irrevocable token of total submission, and as a recognition of, and an acknowledgment of, the power and glory of the Alemanni.

"Turn about!" commanded Abrogastes.

Huta, trembling and fearful, unsteady, on all fours, turned about, to face Abrogastes.

"It will now be decided whether you live or die," said Abrogastes.

"Master?" begged Huta.

"Bring the scales," said Abrogastes.

Men cried out with pleasure.

Scales were brought, wide, shallow, pan scales, which, when the pointed staff was driven into the earth, to one side of the floor, and steadied there by the hand of a man, stood half as high as a man, and with them a small table, on which were a large number of lead pellets, tiny measured weights.

"Stand!" commanded Abrogastes.

Huta, trembling, unsteadily, stood.

"Bring musicians," said Abrogastes.

Three men, from the sand latitudes of Beyira II, were summoned, from where they had been waiting, in a small room off
the main hall, a pantry shed. Two carried pipes, and one a small
drum. The sand latitudes of Beyira II are, of course, not entirely
sand, but they are, on the whole, windswept, desolate regions.
They are crossed by lonely caravans. Here and there, among the
dunes, there are small oases, where dates may be found, and
grass, for small flocks. Some of these are well known and determine caravan routes. Some are known only to local groups, of
nomads, of herdsmen, who move among them, seeking grass at
one, while allowing it to replenish itself at another. Sometimes
there are storms of sand which last for weeks, which must be
weathered by the tiny groups and their small flocks. On the
desert, and in the desolate regions in general, there is much
loneliness, and much time. The inhabitants, the nomads and
herdsmen, of these areas, as might be expected, have a rich oral
culture, rich in such things as myth and storytelling. Too, they
have their music, which is intricate, and melodiously sensuous,
a music which moves the blood of men and the bellies of women.
Although the tents of these nomads are dull, and inconspicuous,
on the outside, melding in well with the browns and tans of the
country, they are often lined with colorful silk, and, inside, may
contain such things as rich rugs, carved wooden stools, and
bright metal vessels. The world inside the tent contrasts with the
plainness and hardship of the world outside the tent. Inside the
tents is found another world. Within this world, not unoften, is
found another aspect of the ancient culture of the men of the
sand latitudes. Within the tents, on the gorgeous rugs, often
pound small, bangled feet, within them often swirls colorful,
revealing silks, within them often rings the sudden, bright erotic
flash of finger cymbals. The men of Beyira II are known throughout galaxies for their dancing slave girls, for none but slaves are
allowed by them to dance such dances, which so say "female"
in all its beauty and vulnerability, in all its joy and radiance, in
all its rhythmic gracefulness and incredible erotic allure, dances
which celebrate, in all their unapologetic richness and glory, the
astounding attractions, and the desirability and excitement of the
female who, though perhaps collared, is totally free to be herself,
and must be herself, even, if she be reluctant, to the instruction
of the whip, or worse. These girls are often bought by the men
of the sand latitudes at the cities which, like ports, border the
edges of the lonely, terrible countries. They are then carried

away, bound and hooded, on sand beasts, into the trackless deserts to serve. The men of the sand latitudes pay for these women in a variety of ways, as with fees from guiding, and guarding, caravans; with pressed dates, from the oases; with gleanings, of flesh, horn and skin, from their herds; with minerals, found in obscure outcroppings, which to them are largely useless, except for their aesthetic value, but which are valued by the men of the "coastal cities," minerals such as *vessa* and *forschite*, which are copper and gold; with semiprecious stones such as turquoise, garnets, amethysts, opals and topaz; and rare clays, reds and whites, used in the manufacture of the red-figured Beyiran ware. There is speculation, too, when the nomads come to the cities with struck coins, diamonds and pearls, and tales tending to provoke skepticism, if not unwise contradiction, of having found such goods in the remains of perished caravans. To be sure, there may be some truth to the claim, but, if so, the matter shifts to speculation having to do with the precise nature of the misfortune which may have befallen the caravan. Sometimes, too, girls appear in slave markets claiming to be the daughters or nieces of rich merchants, governmental officials, and such, but, as they are by then branded, they are whipped to silence, and must soon, generally far away, accommodate themselves to the nature of their new life. Some might be kept, too, it is speculated, by the nomads, to be trained in slave dance. In any event, in time, these dancers, however they may be acquired, either honestly, by trade or through purchase, or in gifting, as are doubtless most, or by some less open modality of acquisition, such as the ambush, cloak and rope, become, under the harsh tutelage of the men of the sand latitudes, incredibly valuable as prizes, and gifts, being exchanged among groups, sometimes traded to passing caravans, and sometimes, too, being lost to brigands, hunting such dancers, some for their own camps, some for marketing, even on other worlds. The dancers of Beyira II are famed throughout galaxies. To be sure, the lives of such women is not all dance and such. There is much work to do about such camps, and it falls to the hands of the beauties. Their life is not easy. They must even braid the leather whips, under male surveillance, which may be used upon themselves.

The musicians took their position, cross-legged, on the floor of the hall, before the dais, but to its left side, as one would look out, toward the hall.

Huta, standing in the center of the hall, before the great upright spear, to which she had rendered zealously the ministrations of a slave, shook her head wildly, negatively.

There was a testing skirl of the pipes, the abrupt sound of a stroke on the small drum. The men with the pipes licked their lips. The fellow with the drum adjusted the tension of the head, and struck it twice more. He then seemed satisfied.

Huta moaned, audibly.

She had recognized the robes of the musicians, or the style and color, of their robes. She knew them for the sort of robes worn within the sloping, many-poled, lamp-hung tents on worlds such as Beyira II. Outside the tents, for most of the year, the robes tended to be white, to reflect sunlight, but, in the winter, in the prime traveling months for caravans, they tended, as the tents always were, to be mottled, with the result that they blended in with the background. The mottled robes, too, were usually worn away from the camps, even in the summer, when the men rode forth on various businesses, whatever might be the nature of those businesses, leaving boys behind, to supervise the flocks, and slaves.

The men looked to Abrogastes, ready to play.

Huta threw herself to her knees and, weeping, held out her hands to Abrogastes.

"Please, no, Master!" she begged. "No!"

Abrogastes looked about the tables. "How many of you," he asked, "have ever seen a priestess dance?"

The men looked at one another. One or another said, "I have, milord, a priestess of the rites of the Libanian Grain Cult."

Abrogastes laughed.

Dance figured in the rites of many cults, for dance can be a language of the emotions, of feelings, even exalted feelings and emotions, and, too, like song, speech, and gesture, can have its religious applications, but in many of these cults, the dances were performed in sacred caves or grottoes by stately priestesses, sedate, dignified and grave, veiled, and fully clad, often elderly women, in purest white, who had for years ascended the hierarchies in their cult, earning their right to dance before the high, mysterious candlelit altars of their vegetation gods.

"I have seen a priestess of the rites of Asharee dance!" said a man.

"Better!" said Abrogastes, slapping his knee.

A ripple of interest took its way about the tables.

"Now that is a dance!" said a man.

Asharee was a fertility goddess of Issia VI. Her priestesses were sacred prostitutes.

Their dances, and subsequent embraces, brought many coins rattling into the golden bowls of Asharee's shrines. Only noble, freeborn women were accepted into the cult, sometimes even matrons. For a coin their husbands might find what a marvel they were married to, but then, so, too, might any others, visiting the shrine.

"What of the rites of Lale?" called another man.

"And those of Cytele!" cried a man.

"Aleila!" called another.

"Lanis," said another.

"Seborah!" cried another.

"Yes, yes!" said men.

Many of these cults were now, for most practical purposes, secret cults.

In most the priestesses were, in effect, temple dancers, whose caresses, for a suitable donation, might be bestowed upon the faithful. The services in many of these cults tended to begin, sometimes following certain days set aside for fastings and abstinences, and after a lengthy wait in a darkened temple, with the appearance of a small light, and readings, readings celebrating the wonders and joys of life, which readings were then followed, as often or not, with a reenactment of a mythic drama, in which men, alone and without women, pathetic, lonely and miserable, besought mercy of the goddess in question, who, seeing their sorrow and pain, and taking pity upon them, created women in her own image, that his prayers might be answered, and that he might be granted a companion. At the conclusion of this drama, or, one supposes, rather as a culminating portion of it, the women appear, first one seen, and then another, so illuminated, and seem as if awakening, and finding themselves to be, begin to dance their joy in life, but soon, as the men before them, each seems apart and alone, and grieving, for, though they are created in the image of the goddess, they are not the goddess, but are finite, and thus incomplete. These women are, of course, the temple dancers. They are clothed, by intent, much as might be slaves, for example, they are barefoot, and bangled and silked. This, as well as the subdued light, and such, has its inevitable effect on the congregation, and, doubtless, too, on the officiants. They dance their loneliness to the men, whom they need as much as they are needed, for that was the intent of the goddess. Soon the dance becomes more enticing, more piteous, and more erotic until a final clash of cymbals occurs and the women and men rush to clasp one another, and the women are lifted, and carried, each to her alcove, or cell, in the temple. In their joyous union, as it is consummated in rapture, it is supposed that worship is offered up to the goddess, who is pleased with her work. There are many ways to worship gods, and this is one of the ways with certain cults, in the union of man and woman, joyously, gratefully, in mutual ecstasy. The gift of produce, or of coins, or whatever it might be, is left afterward in the alcove. The servants of the goddess, and the high priestess, and others associated with the temple, its keepers, and accountants, and such, require, of course, such things, for the satisfaction of their material needs.

As I have mentioned, many of these cults now practice secretly.

There is a good reason for that.

Too, they tend to be far less numerous than before.

There is a good reason, too, for that.

Many of them, you see, have tended to share the fate of the cult of Asharee, or, at least, that of many of her shrines. The lusciousness, and desirability, of the priestesses of Asharee, and those of certain other cults, did not go unrecognized, nor was the potential value of such women long to be ignored. In the services it was scouted out, and marked, by men whose interests tended to be less religious than practical and economic. In the eyes of some, the cult places came to be regarded as little more than places where beauty, like fruit in an orchard, might be harvested, for disposal in various markets. The cults, and shrines, particularly as the administrative, organizational, and defensive capacities of the empire began to deteriorate, became frequently the targets of slavers. Many times, to screaming and dismay, to misery and panic, were the services interrupted, by the sudden appearance of intrusive, determined, merciless men, appearing as if from nowhere, yet seeming to be everywhere, bearing weapons, and chains. "If you would be slaves," they would say, laughing, placing chains on the small, fair limbs of the priestesses and dancers, "you will be slaves!" They were distributed to various markets, some on different worlds. Many were sold to taverns and brothels. In some cases the husbands purchased back their wives, who were then no more than their slaves. And their services, in all their fullnesses and delights, then belonged only to them, not merely to anyone who might pay a coin. Too, no more then was she neglected for she was now a slave, for whom money had been paid. Surely he will see that he gets superb returns upon his investment. Too, she must now serve and love, selflessly, unstintingly, and be owned, as she had wanted. Too, if she is not pleasing, she must fear the whip, or worse.

"I cannot dance, Master!" Huta cried to Abrogastes. "I know nothing of such things!"

"Kill her! Kill her!" called men from the tables.

A saurian slid from about a table and, in one clawed appendage, picked a lead pellet from the table by the scales and flung it, contemptuously, into one of the pans, that which bore the emblem of a skull. That pan then, almost imperceptibly, descended, and the pointer associated with the arm, to which the pans, by small chains, were attached, inclined, by ever so little, toward the left side of the dial, that marked, too, with the emblem of a skull. On the other pan, as an emblem, was the representation of a slave collar, which representation, too, as emblem, lay at the termination of the dial on the right.

"Please, no, Master!" wept Huta, as another saurian, a fellow of the first, left his bench and deposited, too, a pellet in the pan of the skull.

Such creatures, of course, as would certain others about the tables, of diverse ambitious, aggressive species, alien to humans, as humans were alien to them, saw her only as a deceiver and troublemaker, and as a configuration which, as like as not, was not only unmoving to them, but tended to fill them with disgust. To be sure, such creatures occasionally kept human females as slaves.

"Mercy, Masters!" wept Huta to the tables.

Many of the cults, as we have suggested, had now gone, in effect, underground, and become secret cults, but it is a difficult secret to keep, the existence of such things, the times and places of their meetings, the identity of the officiants, and such. Too, many such cult meetings, it seems, were betrayed to slavers, sometimes by cult officials themselves, sometimes by members of the faithful, and so on. Slavers pay well for such information, often with bounties for excellent catches, and sometimes with bounties for individual women, depending on their quality. It seemed clear that many such cults, largely because of the abduction and embondment of their officiants, were disappearing. To be sure, in such a matter, it is difficult to gather data.

"Do priestesses of the Timbri not dance?" inquired Abrogastes.

"No, Master! No, Master!" cried Huta.

To be sure there were many cults, billions, within the empire. Not all favored, of course, goddesses, and such.

Many cults were dedicated to male gods, to virility, to manliness, to the principle of masculinity and such things.

Women could, and frequently did, participate in the services of such cults, but only as slaves, which they were, commonly dancing first before the male gods, or the symbols of masculinity, and then before the faithful, dancing as women before men, to be overwhelmed and subdued, to be conquered, to be given no choice but to surrender totally to men. Such cults were popular in many places. They were popular, for example, in the army. The women used in these cults, temple slaves, or cult slaves, as one might think of them, were seldom the target of slavers. One reason for this was doubtless that such cults provided a valuable market for the lovely wares of the slavers, obtained elsewhere. Theft from actual or prospective customers was not regarded as being in the best interests of their profession. To be sure, barbarians, casual brigands, and such, tended to be deterred but little by such considerations, or scruples, and would be pleased, often enough, to get their ropes and chains on anything good. Such women were, however, bought and sold, as the temples tended to vary, replenish, and freshen their stock. A young woman could often be purchased cheaply as a cult or temple slave, and then later, after having been trained in the cult or temple precincts, sold at a considerable profit. Taverns and brothels, in many cases, investing similarly, followed similar practices.

It might be added, as it may not be clear from the foregoing, that not only were free women not permitted to participate in the services of the masculine cults, but, also, were not permitted to so much as attend or witness them. Sometimes, of course, a young free woman, perhaps one too curious, or bold, or foolish, would attempt to attend the services, usually disguised as a boy. But if her disguise is penetrated, as it must be, to her horror, given an unexpected late phase of the ceremony, following the dance, she will find herself seized. Her pleas will be unavailing. In the next celebration of the rites, if she has not been slain, she will doubtless find herself among the other dancers, branded, and collared, and clad in such a way, if she be clad at all, that there is no longer the least doubt as to her gender.

In the context of matters such as these, it would be remiss not to call, in passing, some attention to one of the most interesting deities in the Telnarian pantheon, Dira, whose devotion is widely spread among female slaves. Dira is the goddess of slave girls, and is herself a slave girl of the gods. She functions, too, as a goddess of love and beauty. Dira, as her legend goes, was an unhappy, haughty, frigid goddess, who regarded herself as superior to the other gods. In some versions of the legend she was said to be insulting to the other gods and to rejoice in treating them badly and making them miserable. This caused much anger among the other gods but nothing was done about it as Dira was a goddess.

Now Orak, the king of the gods, was one day pondering the making of men, and other creatures, and what would be the appropriate arts and occupations of these creatures, and their natures, races, and kinds. He made things that lived on the land and in the sea, and even things that could fly in the air. He made many different sorts of things, and over a very long time. Indeed, according to the stories, he still makes things, new things, as they occur to him, according to his caprice, or curiosity, interested in seeing how they will turn out. This is one reason there are so many different things in the world. He made the gazelle for the vi-cat, so it would have something to hunt and eat, and the lamb for the lion, and so on. And, too, seeing how often men were lonely and angry, and restless, he made the slave girl, to love and serve men, not so much unlike he had made the gazelle for the vi-cat and the lamb for the lion, and he put a slave girl in every woman, hiding her there.

"How silly!" had said Dira, laughing, tossing her pretty head, and, turning with a swirl of her voluminous, pure-white garments, left the hall of the gods.

But Dira, learning of the making of the slave girl, had, for a moment, unnoted by the other gods, trembled, and had felt a troubling, unaccountable stirring between her lovely thighs.

Now Dira had often criticized the works of Orak, who did not care for that.

"How is it," asked Andrak, the artisan and builder of ships, "that men should have more than the gods?"

"How is it," asked Foebus, the swift god, the carrier of messages, "that men should have slave girls and we none?"

"Surely that is not right," said Tylethius, the maker of whips and breeder of dragons.

"No!" cried Orak, with a roar like thunder, rising to his feet.

Far off, Dira heard this, and was puzzled, wondering what it might mean.

"Forge magic chains, hunting chains," said Orak to Andrak, the artisan.

Dira heard this, and was apprehensive.

"Call your dragons that can herd like hounds," said Orak to Tylethius. "And braid a whip fit to lash a goddess!"

Dira heard this and was muchly frightened.

She heard pounding in the smithy of Andrak.

She heard the howling of the dragons of Tylethius.

She summoned up her powers.

But Orak, king of the gods, put forth his hand, and her powers were gone. Though a goddess she was now little more than a woman.

Then Orak put forth his powers, and they were like winds and storms.

"Go," said he, to his hawks, "and bring me the garments of Dira!"

And with cries they were awing, fiercely.

Dira, alone, deprived of her powers, little more now than a woman, cried out in fear, and began to run, but in a moment she found herself in the shadow of the wings of the hawks of Orak, who, crying shrilly, descended upon her, and, with their beaks and talons, tore away her snowy garments, leaving her on the plain, terrified, naked, and bloody.

And then she heard the clanking of chains, like snakes, leaving the hall of the gods, and she fled, and fled, and hid herself in a dark, deep cave, cold and trembling, but the chains, slowly, sniffing like dogs, followed her, deep into the earth.

"No!" cried Dira, backed against a wall of the cave, at its very end, but one of the chains, even in the darkness, near the ground, like a snake, unerringly, striking, snapped its ring about her ankle, as the legend has it, the left. Her right ankle was caught then by the next chain. As she reached down, hoping to free her ankles, her left and right wrists were seized by two other chains. Then the four chains began to draw her, protesting and weeping, out of the cave, upward, to the upper air, where two dragons, like hounds, with breaths of fire, were waiting for her. Then, dragged by the chains, and hastened by the dragons with their breaths of fire, scorching the earth and grass, and the stones at her feet, she was conducted across the plains, and into the hills, and into the mountains, and up the secret mountain trail, hidden from mortals, to the wide marble steps, the thousand steps, leading yet farther upward, to the hall of the gods, and thence she was conducted up the steps, and into the great marble-floored hall itself, where, on that great, smooth expanse of marble flooring, the gods sitting about in council upon their thrones, the chains, by themselves, whipped about four rings in the floor, prepared by Andrak, and welded themselves shut.

"I beg mercy!" cried Dira.

These four rings were placed directly before the throne of Orak.

She knew she had many faults, but she had never expected to be punished for them, because she was a goddess.

But now she was afraid.

"Mercy!" she whispered.

"How beautiful she is!" marveled many of the gods.

"Clothe her!" cried Umba, the consort of Orak.

Orak lifted his hand and a tiny, narrow rag, of no more than half an inch in width, of bright red, wrapped itself twice about the left wrist of Dira, and knotted itself shut.

Umba cried out in fury and left the hall, and so, too, did the other female deities, leaving Dira with only male gods about. The beauty of Dira had not made her popular with the other goddesses.

Orak raised his hand again, and the tiny rag about her wrist vanished.

The gods murmured their approval.

"Kneel," said Orak.

Dira knelt.

This was the first time that Dira knelt. She did not dare to disobey.

The hawks of Orak were perched upon the back of his throne. The dragons of Tylethius were behind her, one to each side.

"You have been petty, and haughty, and troublesome," said Orak. "You have been supercilious and cruel."

"You have taken my powers," she said. "I am little more now than a mortal woman."

"But one who is very beautiful," said Andrak.

"What is in your eyes?" she asked.

"It is desire," said Orak.

Dira trembled.

"Do you find it amusing that I have made slave girls?" asked Orak.

"No," said Dira.

"Do you object in any way?"

"No," said Dira.

"Do you find it fitting?" asked Orak.

"Yes," said Dira.

"But they are unimportant, and worthless," said Orak.

"Yes," said Dira.

"And one may do what one wishes with them," said Orak.

"Yes," said Dira.

"Bring the lash," said Orak.

Andrak produced the lash which Tylethius had braided.

"What are you going to do?" asked Dira.

"Put her hair forward," said Orak.

Her hair was thrown forward, before her body. Tylethius did this.

"What are you going to do?" asked Dira.

"Lean forward, so that you are on all fours," said Orak.

Dira complied.

"What are you going to do?" she asked.

"Surely you suspect," said Orak.

"But I am a goddess!" she said.

"Lash her," said Orak.

In a moment the lash, wielded by Andrak, the artisan and builder of ships, fell upon the goddess.

In another moment she was prone in her chains upon the floor, aghast and helpless, clinging disbelievingly to one of the rings with her small, chained hands.

"Please stop!" she cried.

Instantly, at a sign from Orak, the beating stopped.

Dira gasped for breath, shuddering, aflame with pain.

"You see, you received your way," said Orak.

"Yes!" gasped Dira, sobbing.

Then, at a sign from Orak, Andrak, the artisan god and the builder of ships, put again the cunningly braided leather to the back of the startled, chained beauty.

"Stop!" she cried. "Please, please stop!"

But this time the lash continued to fall and Dira, in consternation, bewildered, helpless, writhed under it, tangled in her chains, crying out for mercy.

Then Orak indicated that Andrak should desist, and Andrak stepped back, coiling the whip.

"You see," said Orak, "this time you did not receive your way."

"No!" gasped Dira.

"Kneel!" roared Orak, and Dira scrambled to her knees.

"Thus it is shown to you," said Orak, "that, from this moment on, though you are a goddess, what is done to you, and what you must do, are no longer dependent upon your will, but upon the will of others."

Dira shuddered.

"Do you prefer to be fed alive to the dragons of Tylethius?" asked Orak.

"No!" said Dira. "No!"

"No longer will it be men alone who have slave girls," said Orak.

The gods in the hall acclaimed this wisdom, and shouted, and clashed weapons.

"You will be the first of the slave girls of the gods," said Orak.

"I pronounce you slave," said Orak, "and give you the name 'Dira.' "

And it was thusly done that the goddess, Dira, became the first of the many slave girls of the gods, and received, too, the name "Dira," though then, of course, as a mere slave name.

Many, of course, are the stories and legends of Dira, how she served, how she learned to dance, how it was that she invented cosmetics, and jewelry, utilized even by free women, how it came about, in disputes concerning her ownership, that she was branded, how Andrak first forged a slave anklet, and later bracelets and collars, and such things, but we have time to note but a particle of these things.

Among such stories, of course, is that of the sexual conquest of Dira by Orak, in which she learns her slavery, and rejoices in it, and thrives in it, living to love and serve selflessly, finding her meaning and ecstasy in her own subordination, her own ravishment and conquest.

Her relationship to male gods would always be unique, and

special. But her relationship to the female gods would be quite different. By them she would be held in contempt, and hated, and mistreated.

Orak, as we may recall, as the stories have it, hid a slave girl within each woman. Indeed, it seems to have been Dira's predictable criticism of, or reservation concerning, this act which led finally to her own enslavement. Naturally the hidden slave girl seeks to come forth, and be accepted, that she may rejoice and serve, and become openly the woman which she secretly is, just as, from the other perspective, the woman longs to become and manifest the secret self which is her innermost reality. In the end, then, the slave girl is the woman, and the woman is the slave girl. As this is commonly understood, though seldom so baldly put, women are by nature the natural slaves of men. Free women, of course, are culturally encouraged, for a number of reasons, to deny and suppress their slavery. This is usually regarded as in the best interests of society, though it does play havoc with the psychology and mental health of the free woman, tending to manifest itself in various psychosomatic complaints, hostilities, neuroses, and other such ills. In many parts of the empire, of course, slavery is legal, and this tends to relieve the pain of an otherwise intolerable situation, giving a public role to, and an outlet for the needs of, slaves.

As a last remark, then, which ties much of this together, we can understand the devotion to Dira among many female slaves. Indeed, sometimes even free maidens, and older free women, pray to Dira, that she may help them attract a desired male, that she may teach them something of the wiles of the slave, that she may consent to imbue them with at least a little of the softness, the vulnerability, the sensuousness, and the subtle sexual magnetism, of the female slave. But the devotion to Dira, of course, is most profound among female slaves.

It is said that for a time, you see, most of the occupations and professions of men had their particular tutelary deities, their supervising gods, who took a special interest in certain vocations, trades, crafts, and such. An obvious example would be the devotion to Andrak of smiths and shipbuilders. But slave girls had, for a time, it was said, no such god or goddess. Dira, who was herself a slave, of course, saw this, and one morning, after, on all fours, bringing Orak his sandals in her teeth, she brought his attention to the matter. "They have no special god," she pointed out, "to enlighten them, to inspire them, to bring joy to them, to bring them special graces, to aid them, to instruct and comfort them."

"But they are slaves," said Orak, "and are unimportant, and worthless."

"I, too, am a slave, Master," said Dira, "and am unimportant, and worthless."

"True!" laughed Orak, striking his knee in amusement. "Be then their goddess."

"Yes, Master!" said Dira, and that is how, according to the stories, Dira, the enslaved goddess, became the goddess of slave girls.

"Does she live or die?" called Abrogastes to the tables.

"How can one tell, milord?" laughed a man.

"It seems she will die," said another.

"Kill her!" cried men.

Two creatures approached the scales, hybrids, creatures of exotic enzymes and catalysts, whose origins were lost in history, their ancestors perhaps the creations of a destroyed, pathological culture, one which might have been dying when the empire itself was but a set of villages on a single world, a handful of huts at the edge of a muddy, yellow river, each three-eyed, their skin sheathed with scales of bark, some scales darkish green, others brown, or black, coming, creeping forward, scratching at the rush-strewn floor, with their steel-jacketed roots, each then, with one leafy, tendriled appendage lifting and dropping, a lead pellet into the pan of the skull.

"Master, let them not participate!" wept Huta. "To them I am meaningless."

"You are meaningless to all of us, slut!" called a man.

"You are a slave!" called another.

Huta put back her head and howled with misery.

Next came two insectoidal organisms, stalking forward, their wings folded, and sheathed behind them in leather. They regarded Huta with their compound eyes. Chitinous, pincerlike jaws clicked. Two more pellets struck down, into the pan of the skull. Then came two arachnoidal creatures, eight-legged, with accoutrements of leather, whose narrow, crooked legs, four of which might serve as grasping appendages, were festooned with ribbons, whose horizontally oriented bodies were sashed with silk, scurrying forward, depositing pellets in the pan of the skull, then hurrying backward, crablike, to their places.

Huta wept, kneeling in the dirt.

Abrogastes looked about the tables, seeking out, in particular, other creatures there, many of them mammalian, other than men.

Abrogastes looked to one of them, to one of those sorts, Granath, of the Long-Toothed People.

"What think you, brother?" inquired Abrogastes.

The large eyes of Granath gleamed, and the jaws opened, revealing white bone-cleaned fangs. "It is hard to tell, milord," said Granath.

It was not unknown for the shambling, shaggy scions of the Long-Toothed People to keep human females as slaves. They were useful, for example, for grooming fur, smoothing it with their small, soft tongues, and, with their tiny fingers, and fine teeth, removing parasites. Too, they were often used to do work regarded as beneath, or unfit for, their own females. It was rumored they were put to other purposes, as well.

"Olath?" asked Abrogastes.

Olath, of the Tusked People, shrugged, the movement involving almost his entire upper body.

"Anton?" asked Abrogastes.

This was a scion of one of several primate peoples, other than men, within the compass of the empire. His world was, in theory, a world loyal to the empire, and, indeed, he held an imperial post on that world, that of imperial agent, or commissioner, to those of his people who, long ago subdued by the empire, had been relocated to that world, that as the consequence of an imperial policy dating back to the days of the Tetrarchy. We have seen, earlier, how the Wolfungs had been relocated to Varna, and the Otungs to Tangara.

Anton scratched his elbow, and turned his large, yellow eyes on Huta.

"For what she has done, I think she should be killed," he said.

"Yes!" cried men about the tables.

"And she is almost hairless!" cried another primate, in disgust.

"See how repulsively smooth she is!" cried another species of primate, one with long, silken hair.

"Kill her!" said his fellow.

"Yes," said another.

"I do not object," said Anton, who was of a short-haired species, "to her hairlessness."

There was knowing laughter among several other varieties of primates about the tables.

"She does not even have a tail!" pointed out the long-haired primate.

"Nor do I!" laughed Anton.

"She can compensate for that with her hands and mouth," said another primate.

"You should know," laughed his fellow.

"She is smooth and would be pleasant to grasp," said another.

"They feel pleasant, squirming and wriggling against you," said another.

"They can perform other services, as well," said another.

"Yes," agreed another.

These were doubtless services which they would not think of expecting from their own mates.

"But any of those, or any like them," said one of the primates, gesturing widely, indicating the former ladies of the empire, kneeling about, "would feel much the same, and, commanded, must supply eagerly, zealously, such services."

"True," said another primate.

There was an uneasy, frightened jangle of bells on the ankles of the former ladies of the empire, as they stirred. One almost rose to her feet but a swift stroke of her youthful keeper's switch put her quickly down again, frightened, on her knees.

"And so, Anton?" asked Abrogastes.

"For what she has done," said Anton, "I think she should be killed, but I am willing that the pellets be weighed."

"Yes," said one or more of the primates, regarding the slave.

Abrogastes grinned.

He had thought that the mammalians, and, in particular, the primates, with whom the small, smooth, curved slave had more of an affinity, might be more willing than certain others, less similar life forms, to suspend judgment, at least for the moment, on the fate of the miserable slave, preferring to watch and wait, and gather evidence, and weigh matters, and then, in the light of the evidence, and their considered judgment, cast their pellets.

"So," said Abrogastes, addressing the slave, "the priestesses of the Timbri do not dance?"

"No, Master!" cried Huta. "The officiants of the rites of the ten thousand gods of Timbri are chaste, and sworn to purity! We are sacred virgins! We are consecrated virgins! We must not even think of men!"

There was laughter about the tables.

"Surely in your sacred beds you must think a little on such things, and wriggle upon occasion," called a fellow.

Huta blushed scarlet, her body aflame.

"Ours is a spiritual religion," she wept, crying out to the tables, looking one way, and then another. "We are concerned only with matters of the spirit! We must move sedately, with dignity. We must be modestly, heavily, and concealingly clothed! We may not reveal so much as an ankle! We dare not dance! It is forbidden! The dance is too biological! It is too real! In it it is often impossible to conceal the form of the body! It is a form of expression even of many animal species!"

"But no animal can dance like a slave girl," said a man.

That was true, of course. The dance was a form of expression of incredible psychophysical, psychosexual import. It was no mere instinctual acting out of ancient genetic patterns, but an acting out of such patterns, and imbued templates, as was consequent upon, embellished by, and enriched by, thousands of meaningful, expressive cultural, institutional, and societal refinements and enhancements. Still, of course, beneath all this sophistication and refinement, there lurked, in all their pristine fury, in all their primitive urgency, as old as tiny fires and limestone caves, ancient things, the pounding in the loins and the aching in the belly.

Huta put her head in her hands, weeping.

The pointer on the scale was now, of course, given the cast pellets, inclined clearly to the left, toward the tiny skull at the left, bottom termination of the semicircular, graduated dial.

"You have forsworn your gods," said Abrogastes, loudly, as Huta looked up, between her hands.

"Yes, Master," she said.

"Then you are no longer a priestess of the Timbri," he said.

"No, Master," she said.

"Then you are no longer a sacred virgin, a consecrated virgin?"

"No, Master!"

"But you are a virgin," he said.

"Until Master sees fit to take my virginity from me, or have it taken," she said.

"A priestess of the Timbri may not dance," said Abrogastes. "But you are not a priestess of the Timbri."

"No, Master."

"You are no longer modestly, heavily, concealingly clothed," observed Abrogastes.

"No, Master," she said.

There was laughter from the tables.

"What are you?" he asked.

"A slave girl, Master," she said.

"And it is permissible for a slave girl to dance?"

"Yes, Master."

"Many are even trained in the dances of slaves," said Abrogastes.

"I would not know, Master," she said.

"It is true," he said.

"Yes, Master," she said.

"And for what do you exist?" he asked.

"To serve my masters with instant, unquestioning obedience and total perfection!" she said, frightened.

"Do not fear," he said. "I shall not, not now, command you to dance."

"Thank you, Master!" she said.

"The decision, rather, shall be yours," said Abrogastes.

"Master?" she said.

"Behold the scale," said Abrogastes.

Huta moaned.

Abrogastes signaled to the musicians, and they began to play a simple, arresting melody, one that seemed to speak of the sand latitudes of Beyira II, and the secret lamp-hung interiors of the dark tents, but, as the slave did not move, they ceased.

They looked at Abrogastes, to see if they should continue.

He gave them no sign.

"I cannot dance!" wept Huta. "I do not know how! I would be clumsy, and the pellets would condemn me."

"Consider the scale," said Abrogastes. "As it stands now, you already stand condemned."

"You would so humiliate me, that I should dance as I am, and as a slave, and might still be condemned to death?"

"Yes," said Abrogastes.

"I was a priestess of the Timbri!" she cried. "I was a sacred virgin, a consecrated virgin, sworn to chastity, to purity and spirituality, and you would have me dance—as a slave!"

"You may do as you wish," said Abrogastes. "I leave the matter up to you."

"Kill her!" cried men. "Kill her!"

"Be done with it, milord!" called another. "Kill her!"

One man, clearly human, rose up and, looking fiercely at the slave, flung a pellet into the pan of the skull.

Another leapt up, and did so, as well.

The hound at the side of Abrogastes rose up, its fur bristling about its neck, and the hump there, eyeing the slave.

"Steady, lad," said Abrogastes. "Steady!"

And another man flung a pellet into the pan of death, and another did so, as well.

"Master!" cried Huta. "Do you not care for your slave, a little?"

"No," said Abrogastes.

"Master?" she said.

"You deceived my son, Ortog," said Abrogastes. "You abetted crime. You aided in the fomentation of rebellion and treason. You should die."

"Please, no, Master!" she wept. "Have pity on one who is now no more than a poor slave!"

Abrogastes made an angry noise, one of surly impatience, and scowled.

"Do you not care, Master, for your slave, just a little?"

"There is not one in this hall who does not despise and hate you," said Abrogastes.

"But you, my master?"

"You are hated," he said.

She put her head down, and wept.

Two more pellets were cast into the pan of the skull, the pan of death.

Huta looked up, shaking her head wildly.

"What do you think?" Abrogastes asked the leader of the musicians.

"We find the whip loosens them up, milord," said the musician.

"They can be whipped anytime," said Abrogastes.

"She has a well-curved body," said the musician, "with sweet, fleshy thighs, and nicely rounded upper arms. They would look well in slave armlets. And her face is a fine one, with its distinctive cheekbones, and its look of great intelligence. The hair is long, and black as jet, and might, if she understood its uses, be used as bonds or veil."

Another pellet struck into the pan of death.

"I cannot dance!" she cried to the leader of the musicians.

"All women can dance," said he.

"What chance have I?" she begged.

"I do not know, little pudding," he said. "I have never even seen you serve at the tables."

"What chance have I, Master?" cried Huta.

"Perhaps one in a thousand," said Abrogastes.

Huta moaned.

Another pellet struck into the pan of the skull.

"They want me to die!" wept Huta.

"Yes," said a man, eagerly.

"Yes!" cried another.

"Surely in your dreams, and thoughts, little pudding," said the musician, "you have danced."

"One chance in a thousand," said a second musician, "is better than none."

"What can I dance?" she cried.

"Dance yourself, and your dreams, and needs, and secret thoughts," said the leader of the musicians.

"They want me to die!" wept Huta.

"Prove to them that there might be some point in letting you live," said one of the musicians.

"Dance what you are," said another. "Dance your slavery!"

"My slavery?" said Huta.

"Yes," said the musician.

"Loose the hound on her, Abrogastes!" cried a man.

"The hound, the hound, let it tear her to pieces!" cried another man.

The great hound, hunched to the right of Abrogastes, by his bench, growled, almost inaudibly, menacingly.

"Look," cried a man. "She is on her feet!"

"Yes," said another.

Huta had risen up, trembling. The great spear, held in place by two warriors, was behind her.

The tables were silent.

"I beg to dance all those things, Master," said Huta to Abrogastes, "—myself, my dreams, my needs, my secret thoughts— my slavery."

"You do not need my permission," said Abrogastes. "The matter is, for now, as I told you, in your own hands."

"I dare not dance without the permission of my master," she said.

Men at the tables exchanged glances, startled.

Abrogastes lifted his hand, in token of permission, that the slave might dance.

"But, too, I beg to dance as the slave of Abrogastes, who is my master!"

Abrogastes regarded her, surprised.

"Yes, Master," she said. "I am your slave, more deeply than you know."

"Cunning slave!" snarled Abrogastes.

But little did he suspect what wearing his chains and bonds had done to her.

Their eyes met, and Abrogastes was troubled.

"Your life is at stake," said Abrogastes.

"Even so," she said, "I dare not dance without the permission of my master."

"There are many here!" he said, gesturing angrily about the tables.

"Yes, Master," she said.

"Do you understand?" he asked.

"Yes, Master," she said.

"You must dance to them, as well."

"Yes, Master," she said.

The overwhelming majority of the feasters, as would be expected, were of the Alemanni, and related peoples. Too, substantial numbers of others were human, or humanoid.

All eyes were on Huta.

"You may dance," said Abrogastes.

"Thank you, Master," said the slave.

The musicians began to play, and Huta, in terror, tears in her eyes, in the midst of seething hostility and disgust, in the midst of those who called for her death, began to dance.

· · · CHAPTER 9 · · ·

"Your researches, under your assumed name, with my clearance, have borne what fruit?" asked Julian.

"None, milord," said Tuvo Ausonius.

"The likeness," said Julian, "is the best I can supply from memory."

Between them, on the marbled table, lay a sketch, in color, of the face of a beautiful, blue-eyed, blond-haired woman. It had been prepared, painstakingly, secretly, by a gifted portraitist, each detail being examined, and revised, and revised again, according to the directions of Julian, until it bore a striking similarity to the woman seen on the quay at Port North.

"I have taken the picture to the keepers at all the slave houses in Lisle, and Port North, and for many miles about," said Tuvo Ausonius. "There are hundreds of blond slaves, of course, but I found no keeper who could make a positive identification from the picture."

"You added in such details, as her unusual behavior, her seeming newness to the anklet, and such?"

"Yes, milord, as you recommended, but there was still no positive identification."

"No record of a judicially embonded debtress from Myron VII, brought to Inez IV?"

"Some," said Tuvo Ausonius, "but they do not seem to be the same individual."

"What of the other nineteen women?"

"We can account for them," said Tuvo Ausonius, "several are from local houses, and some were brought in, according to specifications, from diverse worlds."

"She is, thus, the only one not accounted for," said Julian.

"Yes, milord," said Tuvo Ausonius.

"It seems she would have been brought in, and held, if nothing else, pending shipment," said Julian.

"It would seem so, milord," said Tuvo Ausonius. "Is it important?"

"No, I think not," said Julian.

"But milord is troubled," said Tuvo Ausonius.

"It is nothing," said Julian.

"*Kana*?" inquired Tuvo Ausonius.

Julian nodded.

Tuvo Ausonius clapped his hands, sharply, twice.

In a moment a lovely, slender, young, dark-haired woman, barefoot, in a brief, yellow, silken tunic, cut at the left thigh, to the hip, in a light, yellow-enameled collar, and a yellow-enameled anklet, on her left ankle, hurried into the room, and knelt.

"*Kana*," said Tuvo Ausonius.

She rose to her feet and hurried to a sideboard, to fetch the decanter, and glasses.

"It is strange," said Julian. "It seems that a slave should be easy enough to trace, if brought to Inez IV. She would have to be registered, measured, fingerprinted, toeprinted, and such."

"Some doubtless slip through," said Tuvo Ausonius. "This one did," he remarked.

The woman, head down, had set the glasses on the table and, deferentially, poured the glasses, a third full.

She did not meet the eyes of the men.

"But with my assistance," said Julian.

"True," smiled Tuvo Ausonius.

The woman replaced the decanter on the sideboard and turned to face Tuvo Ausonius.

"Master?" she asked.

"Kneel there," said Tuvo Ausonius, indicating a place on the tiles, to the side, where she would be inconspicuous, and yet at hand, in case wished.

"Head down," said Tuvo Ausonius.

"Yes, Master," she said.

Julian regarded her, idly.

"You have a pretty slave," he said.

"She is nicely curved," granted Tuvo Ausonius, dismissively.

"It is strange," said Julian, "how the blond slave seems not to have been registered, or locally boarded."

"Yes," said Tuvo Ausonius.

"Ai!" said Julian, suddenly, rising to his feet.

Tuvo Ausonius looked up at him, startled.

"She is not a slave!" said Julian.

Even the slave drew back a little, frightened, on her knees. Then she put her head down again, quickly.

"But she must be a slave," said Tuvo Ausonius.

"Inquire among free persons, in the hostels, in the *insulae*, in the towers, discretely at court, in restaurants, at the baths," said Julian.

"As milord wishes," said Tuvo Ausonius.

"The work of Iaachus!" snarled Julian.

"Milord?" said Tuvo Ausonius.

"And inquire first among higher free persons," said Julian. "Look for information pertaining to an incredibly beautiful blond woman, whose beauty might be the envy even of many slaves. Inquire after female patricians, even of the senatorial class, in particular any who might be in need or financial straits, any who might be living alone, or substantially so, any whose family connections might be tenuous, any in what might appear to be unfavorable or dubious circumstances, any in debt, any in difficulties, any in dishonor, any in want, any under suspicion, any subject to umbrage of any sort. Take the picture!''

"Yes, milord!" said Tuvo Ausonius. "Fetch my street cloak!" said Tuvo Ausonius to the slave.

"Yes, Master!" she said.

"Hurry!" said Tuvo Ausonius.

"Yes, Master!" she cried, hurrying from the room.

· · · CHAPTER 10 · · ·

"You would not dare!" said the blonde.

Her hands, wrists crossed and bound, were tied high over her head. They were fastened by a short rope to a ring, the ring dangling on a chain from the ceiling. The wrist rope could be shortened or lengthened, depending on the height of the slave. The blonde was of medium height. She was fastened in such a way that she was on her tiptoes, unable to get her heels to the metal flooring. Her white serving gown had been pulled down, about her ankles. Her body faced the metal wall. She turned her head, as she could. The severe officer, whose name was Ronisius, was behind her. Her hair had already been thrown forward.

"Do not dare!" she said.

Slaves, in the common room, laughed merrily.

"You were insufficiently deferent," said Ronisius.

She struggled, helplessly.

"You were clumsy," he said.

These things were true. At least twice her speech had been insufficiently deferent, even omitting the respectful term "Master." Too, she had been slow to bring a tureen of *hiris* to the table, and had failed once to kneel to the side, as is customary when waiting to serve or be summoned, but had stood, and had stood where the barbarian, if he might lift his head, must see her. The other slaves had not cared for this, for they, too, found the barbarian, in his brooding, feral way, handsome, but dared not so call themselves to his attention. Ronisius had criticized her, and she had gone to kneel with the others, pulling her gown up, and putting it about her knees, so that it would be her knees, and not the gown, which would be on the floor, as though she might be no more than another slave. Perhaps it was because of his criticism, and her fury at the reprimand, addressed to her as though she might be no more than a slave girl, that she had been unsteady, that she had spilled wine, and at his own goblet.

All in all, she had certainly not served well at the captain's table, where the captain, the barbarian, and certain officers would sup at the conclusion of the ship day. Five slaves were assigned to serve there each ship evening. The ship had now been out for four days. It was the first time she had been permitted to serve at the captain's table.

"You would not dare!" she said.

"I think you are stupid," he said.

"I am not stupid!" she cried.

Then, as she cried out, she was switched.

He was not as gentle with her as he might have been, considering that she was a new slave, not even branded, a recently embonded debtress from Myron VII.

But it had been at his own goblet that the wine had been spilled.

"You may now thank me for your beating," he said.

She looked at him, over her shoulder, startled, tears in her eyes.

Twice more, swiftly, impatiently, the switch spoke.

"Thank you! Thank you!" she cried.

Twice more then, again, angrily, the switch spoke, and she leapt in the bonds, squirming, crying.

"Thank you, Master!" she said.

"You will be released later," he said.

"Yes, Master!" she gasped, startled by the piteous urgency of her exhalatory exclamation, and, too, by its seeming appropriateness, and fittingness, and, horrifyingly, by the complete, irrepressible naturalness with which it had somehow escaped her. "Thank you, Master!"

She then hung in the ropes, her back stinging.

About her slaves were discoursing merrily, kneeling, facing one another, playing guessing games, amusing themselves.

I hate everything, she thought.

She grew furious.

How could the agent, whoever he might be, permit her to be switched, as though she might be no more than a clumsy, errant slave?

The blond officer, Corelius, had seemed horrified that she had been conducted from the captain's table by Ronisius.

Corelius must be the agent then, but he had not objected, though he must have realized that the admonitory switch might have been laid to her beauty, just as if she were a slave.

He could not interfere, of course, without revealing himself.

But Ronisius might be the agent, treating her harshly, to conceal her true identity, and his relationship to her, as the purveyor of the delicate blade.

There was Lysis, the chief supply officer, who had seemed to pay her little attention. But it was he who had brought them to the ship.

The stock keeper, oddly, had been at the table, as well, with his porcine face, with the small eyes, the one who had subjected her to such humiliation in the slave cage.

It might be he, why else would he, of his rank, be permitted at the table?

How she had hated serving him, one of the *humiliori*, at best.

Surely one of the *humiliori* could not be the agent, on whom she, herself of the *honestori*, even of the high patricians, indeed, of the senatorial class itself, would have to depend!

There was the captain, too, of course, Phidias, lord of the *Narcona*.

It could be he, she supposed.

But the *Narcona* was only a freighter.

Yet, too, it was an imperial ship.

But presumably such an officer would stay with the ship.

But, too, who would be less likely to be suspected than the commanding officer?

Who would be more powerful than he, who better placed to manage the affair, to see it done?

But then, she thought, who would be more likely, given his authority, his command, his prominence, to be suspected?

No, it seemed that things had best be done secretly, far beneath his level of command, utterly unsuspected by him.

He would not dream of the intrigues afoot, on his own vessel.

It did not seem that Iaachus would risk taking such a fellow, a common captain, a professional mariner, into his confidence, entrusting him with such a serious business.

It did not seem likely that it would be he.

But it might be he.

She jerked in the ropes.

"Free yourself, Cornhair!" laughed one of the girls.

The supply officer had given them names, making them kneel, in a line, in the common room.

"You are 'Filene,' " he had said to her. "Who are you?"

"I am Filene, Master," she had said, following the example of the other girls.

In time a mariner came to the common room and released her.

"Garments, ladies," he said.

The few garments in the room were surrendered.

These were the five serving gowns which had been worn by the slaves serving at the captain's table. He then, the gowns over his arm, turned off the light in the common room and left, closing the door.

This left only some small, reddish hold lights lit, high in the walls.

"They have not even chained us to the rings at the base of the wall," said one of the slaves.

"We are not going anywhere," laughed one of the slaves, fingering the thin line that marked the separation of the steel wall from the closed hatch.

"Why have we not been chained?" asked another, wonderingly.

"We are special slaves," said another.

The blonde smiled to herself, in the dim, reddish darkness.

"Let us sleep," said one.

"Give me your blanket," said the blonde to a small brunette, the smallest of the slaves.

"You have your own blanket!" said the tiny, well-curved, exquisite slave.

"Give it to me!" said the blonde.

"No! Stop!" cried the smaller woman.

"Give it to me," said the blonde, "slave!"

They pulled at the blanket, it between them.

"Cornhair, stop it!" said another brunette, she who had been designated by the supply officer as first girl.

"Give it to me!" cried the blonde.

"Seize her!" said the first girl.

In a moment the blonde, seized, found herself held down, on her stomach, on the steel flooring of the common room, her arms and legs widely spread.

"Bring the switch," said the first girl.

"No!" cried the blonde. "Do not switch me! Please, *Mistresses*! Do not switch me, *Mistresses*!"

She heard the switch being tossed aside.

She was released.

"But you will have no blanket tonight, Cornhair," said the first girl.

"Yes, Mistress," said the blonde. The first girl is addressed by the other slaves as "Mistress." That much the blonde, surely, knew.

Later, cold, her legs drawn up, on the flooring, trying to keep herself warm, the blonde was furious.

When I am rich, and powerful, she thought, I will have my vengeance on them all. I will buy them and dispose of them to outposts, and mines, and farms, and sell them to worlds of reptiles! Then they will see how special they are!

She moved a little. How hard was the metal. How uncomfortable she was!

Ship, whispered she, bring me swiftly to Tangara.

Then, my secret, hated confederate, who abuses me, or does so little to protect me, put the knife in my hand, that I may finish our business with dispatch. Then I shall come into my fortunes, and you shall all regret that I have not been better treated!

She recalled how she had placed herself, standing, where the barbarian might have looked up, and seen her. She had pulled her gown down a little, and back, that the sweet fullness of her bosom might be excitingly apparent. He had looked up only at the moment that she had been reprimanded and, embarrassed, humiliated, had been hurried back to her place. Yet, that glimpse, she was sure, might have been sufficient. Too, she had returned to the place with the other girls in such a way, her head high, her shoulders back, and her belly tight, that he might well conjecture the delights of her figure, and find it of interest, for, after all, even the serving gown, long, white and sleeveless, as it is a slave's garment, does little to conceal the charms of its occupant. Too, in such a way, or similarly, so walking, or holding herself, she had tortured many men, as it had amused her to do. But when she had knelt, and put the gown up, over her knees, that her knees and not the gown might press the floor, she had looked up, and seen him regarding her. But there was something about being on her knees which did not give her confidence, and which put the entire matter into a quite different light. She tried to adjust her gown in such a way as to better conceal her bosom, but when she looked up, he had returned to his meal.

She lay there on the steel flooring.

She could not believe, and it muchly disturbed her, how easily, how naturally, at the time of her switching, the word "Master" had fled from her lips.

She wondered what it might be to be in the arms of a man such as the barbarian, and as a slave.

· · · CHAPTER 11 · · ·

"Aii!" cried a man, rising to his feet.

Another pounded on the table, his eyes blazing.

The melodies of Beyira II seemed incongruous somehow, at first, in the rough hall, with its high timbers, and smoke holes, and rush-strewn, dirt floor, but in moments these things had seemed forgotten and the venue of what occurred might as easily have been a hundred other places, as a woolen tent, lost among dunes; a tavern on Illyrius, a free planet, an emporium planet, a crossroads for slavers and brigands, where good buys might often be found; a brothel, utilizing slaves, on scorching Torus, where one cannot set foot outside without protective gear; a remote pre-embondment prison where the wives and daughters of traitors, awaiting enslavement, are trained for the collar; a slave farm on rural Granicum, where some slaves do not yet know that men exist, and cannot begin to understand the primitive discomforts which dismay them; or, perhaps, a chamber of state, many-columned, lofty, and marble-floored, somewhere within the white, high-walled, turreted palace of some sand lord, rising

above a thousand hovels, and caravansaries, the cruel, waterless
desert stretching away on all sides. But, too, as easily, and as
well, it seems, might the venue be what it was, a rude hall of
the Alemanni, a place of Drisriaks on a world now shielded, now
closed away, by a whirling storm of stones, marking the skies
with light, like the raking claws of beasts; anywhere would do,
really, if there were slaves and men.

"No, no, no!" cried a man, angrily. "Kill her! Kill her!"

"Be still, watch!" cried another.

"Do not weaken!" said a man.

Abrogastes, on his bench, watched, with keen interest.

Former women of the empire shrank back, moaning, terrified
to see what a woman might be.

"My thighs flame!" wept one.

"I am a slave, a slave!" cried another.

Many turned away, but turned back again, quickly.

The hands of many were at their bared bosoms. They gasped
for breath. Their hearts pounded.

"Oh, oh!" moaned one.

But the boy who was her keeper just put his switch lightly
upon her left shoulder, cautioning her to silence, not even looking
at her, unable, it seemed, to take his eyes from the floor.

Then he lifted the switch a little, absently, hardly aware, it
seemed, that he still held it.

He was a lad, and had not seen such things before.

The woman turned suddenly, as though she could not help
herself, and kissed, and licked, the supple disciplinary instrument
near her shoulder.

The boy was hardly aware of this.

The attention of both was then returned to the floor.

"See her writhe at the spear!" cried a man.

"Aii!" said another.

The attention, even, of many of the creatures alien to men,
was focused upon the floor. Whereas much must have been lost
to them surely the vibrations in the air, however they may have
experienced them, and the rhythm, and grace, of certain movements, must have had some effect upon them, as they shared
with men a world in which there were, should one listen, should
one see, should one be attentive, the movements, the songs, of
nature, a world in which there were rhythms and cycles, a uni-
verse in which there were stars and orbits, and seasons, and days

and nights, and tides, even in the earth, drawn by moons, and rain and heat, snow and winds.

She was now on her knees at the massive spear, the spear of oathing, supported, its butt in the dirt, by two warriors, grasping it, caressing it with her body, her small hands, her helpless lips and mouth.

Had it been a man surely it would have cried out, mad with pleasure.

Then she flung herself before it, and, so before it, so prostrated, rolling and twisting, supine, and prone, and on her side, in the rush-strewn dirt, she writhed, sometimes holding out her hands to it, sometimes as though she might half fend it away in unendurable ecstasy, sometimes as though for pity, sometimes as though begging mercy.

"Let me kill her now, great Abrogastes!" cried a man. "Let me cut her throat!"

"There is time enough for that later," growled another man.

The slave must have heard this, for she moaned in terror.

"Kill her!" cried another man, one who may have cast his pellet earlier into the pan of death.

"Be silent!" said a fellow.

The slave threw the fellow a look of gratitude, but his scowl was such that she was again plunged into misery and terror.

"Dance, dance, slut!" cried men.

Then she knelt before the spear, a yard or so before it, and, slowly, to the music, bent herself backward, until her head was back, upon the dirt floor, her dark hair scattered upon it, in which position she could doubtless see Abrogastes, above and behind her, on his bench, between the high-seat pillars, and then she slowly straightened her body, until she was kneeling, and then knelt forward, until her head was in the dirt again, and then the palms of her hands were on the dirt, too, and she was, as men cried out with pleasure, in a common position of obeisance, and then she lowered herself to her belly, and inched herself to the spear, as in the belly obeisance where the slave hopes to be permitted to kiss the feet of the master, and she pressed her lips to the dirt before it, and then, tenderly, to its sides, the left and right.

"Glory to the Alemanni!" cried a man.

"Glory to the Alemanni!" cried others.

Among slaves and masters there are many such ceremonies, which are meaningful.

The spear, as we have mentioned, may not be touched by free women, but the ministrations of female slaves figure frequently in its rituals.

"She is on her feet again!" cried a man.

The slave then began to dance to the tables, and to individual men, pathetically, at first, almost timidly, begging their attention, their indulgence, but soon she noted, whether it was the subtle effect of those rich, sensuous, exotic melodies which, by themselves, might have swept away the resolve of the coldest and most determined of men, and tempted even the most frigid of free women to tear away their garments, or whether it was something of her own beauty, which she now began for the first time to truly understand might be something precious and remarkable, something of great interest to men, for which they might pay much, or the dance itself, or all these things, that in the eyes of many men there glistened intense interest, heat, and desire. She saw even, in the eyes of some, awe.

I am beautiful, she thought to herself, startled.

She danced before Anton, the short-haired primate, and she saw the knuckles of his hairy hands, beneath the hair, whiten.

She saw a drinking horn whose edge had been half chewed away.

There were furrows in the table of Granicus, of the Long-Toothed People, where his claws had left, as he watched, their marks.

The scales of one of the saurians rippled.

She hastily moved down the table.

The bright, compound eyes of the insectoidal warriors were upon her, but they may have seen a hundred of her.

Before the least human aliens, too, you see, she danced, even before those who had already cast their pellets in the pan of death, as though acknowledging their right to decide as they did, but nonetheless presenting herself before them, for their inspection, and contempt, if they wished, contritely, too, in her dance begging their forgiveness for not having been found by them to be sufficiently pleasing, performing for them, thusly, you see, as for the others, as what she was, in all humility, a slave.

But her greatest strengths, of course, came, as she began to comprehend, almost daring to begin to hope, with the mammals, and mammalian sorts, and, progressively, among these forms of life, with the primates, both those closer to and farther from

humans, and then, advancing further, with humanoidal sorts,
and even more humanlike sorts, many of whom kept women
such as she for labor and pleasure, and with some of whom such
women, commonly with certain biological adjustments, would
even be cross-fertile, and culminatingly, of course, like explo-
sions and eruptions, like tides and seasons, with those for whom
she had been prepared by a billion years of evolution and selection to appeal to and delight, the males of her own species,
human males, and these, at the tables, she gratefully noted, were
in the vast majority.

I am beautiful, she thought to herself. I am desired. I am
wanted, and as a slave!

It is well known how beautiful and exciting women are when
they dance the dances of slaves, even a legally free woman, but
one who would be, of course, a slave in her heart, dancing before
one, out there in the darkness, she hopes is her master. Suppose
then that she who dances such a dance is truly a slave, fully and
legally, which must be the case in many places in the empire,
who can be priced and purchased, who knows herself slave, and
is subject to discipline, and must obey. A thousand times more
meaningful then is her dance, and her reality! How men might
scream for her, and bid for her!

"A gold ring for the slut!" called a man.

"Two!" cried another.

"No!" shouted a man, in fury. "The scales, and lead, will
decide her fate!"

On many worlds it is well known, though on others the information is suppressed, that biological realities exist, such as dominance and submission, strength and vulnerability, reciprocal
needs, jealousy, possessiveness, protectiveness, sexual dimorphism and its meaning, claimancy and command, behavioral
genetics, readinesses to respond to sign stimuli, longings for
completeness, the desire to belong to, and yield to, the master
animal, and such. Illustrative of one small aspect of these matters, one might consider the matter of sign stimuli and, in particular, what one might speak of as "emphasis sign stimuli." The
lips of a woman, for example, have a natural color and function
as sign stimuli, having a role to play, as does the totality of her
loveliness, inward and outward, in arousing the male. But it is
well known in many cultures for the color of the lips to be
deepened and intensified by the application of, say, lipstick.
This, in its way, enhances and intensifies nature, and thus, in its

way, constitutes a sign stimulus which does not occur in nature itself, or, at least, in nature short of its witting enhancements, taken then as a part of nature. That is an "emphasis sign stimulus." Cosmetics, generally, and jewelry, and perhaps clothing, on the whole, function as such "emphasis sign stimuli." Now consider the subtler matter of possession. There is little doubt that the primitive human male, in effect, claimed and owned his mate, much as he might have his tools and weapons, though a legal concept of property is unlikely to have existed at such a time. In such a sense then, the sense of male dominance and female submission, the sense of the possession and ownership of the mate, and of other women captured, one can think of slavery as natural. Women who might, say, evade or flee such relationships would have been less likely, presumably, to replicate their genes, and thus, in time, nature would have selected for the dominant male and the submissive female, his subordinated, serving, treasured prize. As civilization developed, these relationships would tend to be elaborated and complicated, and, for example, the slavery of nature would tend to come, in some of its aspects, at least, to be the slavery, in effect, of merchant law. Thus, just as cosmetics and jewelry, and such, might enhance, as emphasis sign stimuli, the natural female, rendering her even more exciting and attractive, so, too, legalized slavery, in the context of a complex civilization, in the emotive and cognitive dimensions, as emotional and cognitive emphasis sign stimuli, would render the female ever more desirable, exciting, and attractive. This is doubtless one reason the female slave is far more sexually arousing than the free female; her slavery itself is an incredibly powerful emphasis sign stimulus. Add in then the lore of the slave, her skills, her role in the civilization, how she might be marked, or identified, collared, or ankleted, or such, how she is to be dressed, how she is to behave, and such, and considering all these things as emphasis sign stimuli, one begins to suspect something of the secret of her sexual magnetism, something of her incredible desirability, something of the extraordinary power of her attraction. And, too, of course, these things are reciprocal, working as much on the female, perhaps even more, than on the male. The woman who must see males as masters cannot help but find them sexually disturbing, and a thousand times more interesting and attractive than might a free woman. Bondage induces not only interest in the opposite sex in the human female, but primes her with readiness and eagerness. The collar makes her not only the slave of her master, but of her own passion, as well. Too, she longs to kneel and express her devotion in a thousand ways. She longs to love and serve, and give of herself. She is a slave.

"Three rings!" cried a high fellow in one of the Alemanni tribes, the Dangars.

"Five!" cried another fellow, from another of the Alemanni tribes, the Teragar, or Long-River, Borkons.

"No, no!" cried a man, angrily. "See the scale! It tips to the skull! It points to death!"

"No rings of gold for her!" cried a man.

"Would that I had a ring of gray, base lead, to hurl it into the pan of death!" cried another.

Huta hurried to the fellow who had cried this out, and fell to her knees before him, some feet before his table, and then, on her knees, with her body and arms, to the music, lifting her arms to him, so danced, on her knees, in supplication before him.

"Ai!" cried a man.

The fellow tried to turn away, but in a moment, furious, tears streaming down his face, turned again, to regard the slave.

Huta lifted her dark, glorious hair, spreading it about herself, and then shielded herself with it and then, as though timidly, and as if commanded, drew it away from her body, looking at the fellow, as though shyly, frightened, as though he had ordered this done.

"Ai!" he cried, in fury.

And then, to the music, she wrapped the hair about her wrists, as though they might be bound, and then placed her wrists, crossed, behind the back of her head, holding them there, as though they were bound there, and then, before him, regarding him fearfully, surged, and struggled, as though helplessly, as though striving to free herself from bonds, but futilely.

"How now will you cast your pellet?" inquired a fellow at his elbow.

He put his head down, weeping, striking the table with his fists.

And Huta was up, to dance before another.

"I will fill your drinking horn with emeralds for her!" called a high fellow of the Aramars, one of many tribes allied with the Alemanni.

"A thousand rubies!" cried another fellow, from the Vessites, the Copper People.

"A diamond from Kolchis III!" cried another fellow, a Buron, from Safa Minor.

There were a great many tribes, and peoples, allied with, or well disposed toward, the Alemanni.

In the Alemanni nation itself, as we have mentioned, there were eleven tribes.

"Dance, slave, dance!" cried a man.

"Yes, Master!" cried Huta.

Huta could not but have been aware of the effect of her dance on the feasters, and, in particular, on the humans, the Alemanni and others, and, indeed, even on certain of the other species as well, some not even closely kindred to the human species. As we have suggested, several of these species kept human females as slaves, putting them to a variety of purposes.

Huta began to suspect, the hope rising in her, suddenly, irresistibly, wildly, elatedly, in her dance, that she might have a chance for life, that she might be able to exert some real influence in her favor, however small, on the dark matter which, only too realistically, hung in the balance.

"Dance!" cried another.

"Yes, Master!" she cried.

I may live, she thought wildly. I may live!

She swayed, meaningfully, before a man.

She read his keen desire in his eyes.

I have power, she thought. I have the power of a slave!

"See! She grows proud!" cried a man.

This terrified Huta, whose slavery then was only too clearly recalled to her.

She flung herself to the rush-strewn, dirt floor, rolling and begging, prostrating herself, piteously.

Her movements said, I am not proud! I am weak and helpless, and I beg mercy!

"Oh!" she suddenly cried, as she lay supine, in the dirt. Her hips suddenly shook, and rocked, uncontrollably. She lifted herself a little, with her hands and her heels. Her haunches heaved, and she was startled. Her hips bucked. She lost the music, bewildered, for a moment, turning to her side, pulling her legs up, in consternation, trying to hide and cover herself.

There was laughter.

"Oh!" cried more than one of the ladies of the empire, moving wildly on her knees. Many of the others turned scarlet, trying to cover themselves.

"Finish your dance!" cried a man.

But Huta, now, could do little more than crawl on her knees, her stomach moving, to reach the foot of the dais.

"Take the vote!"

"Cast the pellets!" cried men.

"Mercy, Master!" wept Huta, beside herself in misery, and bewilderment, her eyes wide, her hands at her hips.

Muchly then was there laughter.

"Behold the needful, helpless slave!" cried a man.

Huta cast a pathetic, helpless glance at him.

"Masters! Masters!" cried one of the former ladies of the empire. "We are yours! Take pity on us!"

"Down!" cried one of the lads, savagely, lashing across the shoulder with his supple, greenwood switch she who had cried out. The former lady of the empire put her head down, bent far over, weeping, clutching her thighs.

Other former women of the empire moaned, looking about themselves, fearfully, wonderingly, at men who might, at a word from Abrogastes, become their masters.

Huta's hips, despite her efforts, moved.

"Forgive me, Master! Mercy, Master!" she cried.

"The music, slave, the music!" cried one of the musicians, angrily.

Abrogastes regarded her, eyes closely lidded, face expressionless, considering what a mere touch might do to such a slave.

"The music!" cried the musician.

Doubtless for such a lapse, in a tavern or brothel, a girl might be muchly leathered.

"The music!" insisted the musician.

The whip lies always to hand, you see, to instruct such women in deportment, its presence admonishing them to control themselves to the end of the dance.

They may afterward be thrown to those for whom they have been reserved.

It was not unknown, too, that their own girls might, upon occasion, in the dark, woolen, silk-lined, lamp-lit tents, fall to the rugs, weeping, tearing away veils, touching their collars, writhing, begging for the touch of masters.

Such was sometimes permitted, if there were no guests.

But sometimes, even in taverns and brothels, it is recognized that a woman, even one frightened and resolved, cannot always help herself. She is, after all, a slave, and is thus in a state of intensified nature. Some of the manuals recommend lenience, even indulgence, at such times.

What is done depends, of course, on the master.

"Dance!" ordered he who was first among the musicians.

Huta then, in agony, crawled to a few feet before the dais of Abrogastes, and knelt before him, precisely as she had before the spear.

"Good! Good!" said the leader of the musicians.

She then, to the music, leaned backward, until her dark hair was swirled upon the rush-strewn floor, and then, slowly, gracefully, came forward, lifting herself, her hands, and arms and body seemingly entwined with the music, obedient to its beat and caress, helplessly responsive to the melody, exquisitely, vitally vulnerable to it, submissive to it, swept up in it, like living silk in the wind, borne by it, and in it, sensuous and rhapsodic, wordless and eloquent, fluent in the speech of desire and emotion, like the glow of firelight on a brass vessel, the movement of silk, the rustle of ankle bells.

"Good," said the leader of the musicians.

Then she bent forward, as she had before the spear, and, trembling, performed obeisance, head to the dirt, palms on the dirt, before Abrogastes, and then lowered herself to her belly, and crawled to the dais.

"Down," said Abrogastes to the rumbling, agitated hound to his right.

The beast subsided, its ears erecting, the bristling, manelike hair, crackling, descending over the knot of muscle at the back of its neck.

Huta then squirmed to the surface of the dais and, putting down her head, began to kiss and lick at the boots of Abrogastes, as she had at the butt of the spear, still held by the two warriors toward the center of the hall.

The music then, suddenly, stopped, Huta's tiny hands about the left boot of Abrogastes, her lips pressed down, piteously, fervently, to the boot of her master.

Huta trembled.

The furred boot of Abrogastes was damp with her tears, and dampened, and streaked, pressed down, wet, from the desperate, placatory attentions of her soft tongue and lips.

Abrogastes rose to his feet, and, with his boot, thrust Huta from the dais.

She lay then on her side in the rush-strewn dirt at the foot of the dais, trembling.

She drew her legs up, she covered the soft, swelling beauty of her bosom with her hands.

Her hips stirred in the dirt.

She wept. No longer could she help herself.

"Behold the helpless slave!" laughed a man.

There was much laughter.

But the slave, miserable, and in agony, could not, as we have said, help herself.

"The proud Huta has been stripped of her freedom," said a man.

"And of her clothing," laughed another.

"And now, too," said another, "she has been stripped of her pride."

Huta shuddered.

She sensed that no woman who has so danced can ever again be anything but a man's slave.

She lay there in the dirt, trying to control herself.

"It remains now only to strip her of her virginity," said another man.

"Yes," said another.

"Abrogastes!" cried men. "Abrogastes!"

But Abrogastes descended from the dais, and stepped over the trembling form before the dais, which had, in the plans of Abrogastes, now served its purpose.

"Are you well feasted, and well entertained?" called out Abrogastes.

"Yes!" called men, and other forms of life.

Goblets smote upon the heavy planks of the feasting tables.

"This is nothing," cried Abrogastes, "only a little food and drink, and the pathetic appeal, in dance, of a meaningless slave."

Men looked at one another.

"Do you think it is for the sake of such trivialities, such pleasantries, that I have called you here?"

"Speak, Abrogastes," called a man.

"Behold the spear of oathing!" called Abrogastes, pointing to the great spear, held upright by two warriors.

The hall was silent.

Abrogastes then surveyed the former women of the empire,

112 • John Norman

kneeling, huddled together, frightened, here and there, before the tables.

They shrank back, but well, after the dance of Huta, knew themselves slaves.

She who was the first of the three display slaves, kneeling, raised her hands from her thighs, turning them, and lifting the palms, piteously, to Abrogastes.

Another, she who had been lashed when she had called out for the pity of masters, lifted her head a little, pathetically, but dared not move. Muchly did she fear the switch of her impatient, youthful mentor. Her eyes spoke for her.

Others of the women had their thighs pressed closely together. Some squirmed.

"To the spear, slaves!" called Abrogastes, harshly, waving his hand about.

These women had been well instructed by the example of Huta, and they hurried piteously to the great spear, and desperately, in fear for their lives, and, too, muchly aroused by what they had seen, the dance, and the masters about, and their own vulnerability, and condition, as slaves, ministered to the great spear, holding it, grasping it, pressing themselves against it, pathetically, caressing it, licking and kissing it.

There was much laughter at the tables, as the former women of the empire, with their bodies, their small hands, and their lips, and tongues, bestowed attentions upon the mighty spear.

They crowded about the spear, trying to reach it, kneeling, and bellying, none on their feet, each vying with the other, each striving to touch it, to lick and kiss it, each attempting to do so more lovingly, more zealously, more submissively, than the other.

"Behold the women of the empire!" called Abrogastes. He gestured to the crowd of slaves at the spear, performing the spear obeisance.

The men at the tables looked on, approvingly.

"Do they not attempt to caress pleasantly?" asked Abrogastes.

"Yes," said men.

"Do they not attempt to lick and kiss well?" inquired Abrogastes.

"Yes!" called men.

"Are they not pretty little things?" called Abrogastes.

"Yes," shouted men, approvingly.

"Do you not think they could be instructed to squirm well?" inquired Abrogastes.

"Yes!" laughed men.

"Enough!" cried Abrogastes, sharply, and the lads, who had been alerted to this moment in the feast, long before its commencement, lashed the ladies from the spear and to their bellies, where they then lay in the dirt, clustered about it.

"We are despised, as you know, my brothers," said Abrogastes, "by those of the empire, we, the lords of stars, by the fat, the haughty and the weak, by the complacent, the petty, the smug, the wealthy, the arrogant."

Men exchanged glances, uneasily.

"What do they, with their vaunted civilization, their refinements and luxuries, know of hardship, of pain and war, of adventure, of victory?"

"Little, milord," said the clerk.

"Which of them has swum in cold, restless, black waters, who among them has hunted the long-maned lion, who trekked the ice of the month of Igon, pursuing the white bear, who marched, in the heat of solar fire, a pack on his back, a thousand miles to distant outposts, who braved the flood, who forded, afoot, turbulent rivers, who drawn the oars, or held the tiller, of river vessels, who driven the stakes of the high tents, who lived alone in the forest, who met enemies at borders, and on lonely skerries, who hunted beasts and by them was hunted?"

"Not those, surely, of the empire, milord," said the clerk.

"They wear silks and linens, and we coarse cloths, and the skins of beasts," said Abrogastes.

There was silence.

"To whom does the lamb belong?" asked Abrogastes.

"To the lion, milord," said the clerk.

"To whom the pig?"

"The leopard, milord."

"To whom the gazelle?"

"The vi-cat, milord."

"To whom the slaves?"

"To the masters, milord."

The former women of the empire trembled, lying in the dirt, about the foot of the great spear.

"The empire is vast, and rich," said Abrogastes, "vast and rich beyond measure."

"The empire is invincible, and eternal," said a man.

"Once," said Abrogastes, "there was no empire."

Men looked at one another, for the empire was taken much for granted, as might be a mountain or star.

"It is true, milord," said the clerk.

"The empire is invincible," said one of the men, uncertainly.

"Let us raid now and then, and return to our worlds, with some loot, for feasting, the telling of stories, the songs of skalds," said a man.

"While the empire strengthens her defenses, and even prepares to send her ships of reprisal forth to follow you?" asked Abrogastes.

"They must find us first," said a man.

There was some uneasy laughter.

"Are you content to be weasels and scavengers, nocturnal *filchen* to rush forth, at night, to seize a crumb from the garbage of a palace?"

"To what end do you speak, mighty Abrogastes?" inquired a Dangar.

"Walls may be scaled, ditches may be bridged, portals may be smote down," said Abrogastes.

Men looked at one another, uneasily. Much as they might hate the empire, they feared it, either as a dim, vast, remote presence, just beyond the horizon, one awesome, one fearsome and menacing, or even as a reality, sharp and bright, fierce, which they may, upon occasion, almost as though in the dark, suddenly, to their dismay and grief, have touched.

Huta lay forgotten in the dirt, before the dais.

Only gradually did she begin to understand how she had been used by Abrogastes, she responding totally naturally, in every particle of her being, as she must, in her own needs and interest, yet, at the same time, just as naturally, serving simultaneously, as was the intent of Abrogastes, to unite the feasters, giving them a common object to hate and hold in contempt, and to ignite their anger and resentment against any form of treason, any form of divisiveness; in these ways, thusly, she found herself used to serve the purposes of Abrogastes. Too, of course, her reduction to slavery, this reduction in status, from that of a consecrated, sacred virgin, even a priestess, to that of a mere desire object, a slave, who could be bought and sold in any market, must convey its message as well. And, of course, doubtless Abrogastes had enjoyed showing her off, displaying her as one of his properties. And, obviously, she had figured in the feast's entertainment, as might have any slave. It seemed clear that several of the feasters had not failed to derive some pleasure from her performance. And, too, of course, she had, in her ministrations at the spear, and in her dance, served her purposes, as well. She had set an example for the former ladies of the empire, instructing them, in her way, in what was required of them at the spear. Too, there was no doubt that her dance had taught them, incontrovertibly, not only what she was, but what they were, as well. Many had moaned with helpless arousal and desire. Some had cried out. Many had squirmed in need, some scarcely understanding what was going on in their bodies. Her dance, if such were needed, had readied them, primed them, for slave service. They wanted now their masters' touch. They, though former ladies of the empire, were now eager for it, now zealous for it. Some were ready even now, though not so long in their collars, to beg for it.

"The empire is not invincible," said Abrogastes. "We have met her on a hundred worlds, at a thousand ports and cities, and defeated her."

"Those are border forces, not the mobile forces, auxiliaries, not regulars, conscripts, not professionals," said a man.

"Even the Vandalii, our hated and hereditary foes, at one time resisted the empire!" said Abrogastes.

"And they are now vanished, or scattered, and meaningless, exiled, banished to distant worlds, some even in rural service to the empire."

"Are we, of the Alemanni," asked Abrogastes, "less than the Vandals?"

"No!" cried men, angrily.

Huta lay in the dirt, small, forgotten, her knees drawn up, her arms about herself. She, overwhelmed with what had occurred, with her dance, with her feelings, her sensations, scarcely dared to move. Never had she been so alive, so frightened, so ready to feel, so real. It was as though she had somehow discovered herself, finding herself to be, in perfection, what she had always suspected herself to be, a woman, more in the state of nature than she would have dreamed possible. She felt an overwhelming desire to please, and serve. She wanted to live to do so, and be held, and mastered.

Yet she lay there on the dirt floor of the hall, huddled up, naked.

Whether the slave is clothed or not is up to the master, but they are often clad, if only in a ribbon, or rag, that it be clear that they are slave, to themselves and others, that their beauty might be the subject of provocative, betraying hints, and that there be something to remove from them, whenever the master wishes it.

But on Huta's body there was not even a collar.

She wanted the collar, or the anklet, or bracelet, or ring, or chains, anything, something to give her at least a little security, something to confirm upon her her status, something to make it clear that she might be wanted, that she might hope to be kept.

Her hunger now began to return to her. She had not been fed. It had not been seen fit to waste food on her. It had not been clear that she was to survive the evening.

She longed for the reassurance of chains.

Would not such suggest that she might be kept, if only for the night?

But there was not so much as a rag on her body.

To be sure, on her left leg, high, just under the hip, she had been branded, a common brand, the tiny slave rose, one of several standard marks recognized in merchant law, but it had been done shortly after landfall from Tenguthaxichai, she one in a line of several others, no different, being put in the rack, which held the limb immobile, in her turn, as the others. She had cried out, struggling in the cuffs, pinioning her wrists behind her, which would not be removed for several hours, and had seen her thigh marked, saw it hissing, smoking, for a moment, and had understood that she was now something that could be recognized and identified for what it was throughout galaxies. She had hoped to be marked by Abrogastes himself but he did her no such honor. It was a common fellow, a smith, in his dark, stained leather apron, who did the work, he taking one iron after another from the brazier, these being cleaned and reheated by attendants. She had been on a common neck chain, with others. The work was done in a routine, unhurried, methodical, efficient manner. Did the smith, and the others, she had wondered, not understand what they were doing, what an absolute, incredible transformation they wreaked with each placing, and pressing in, of the iron? One might have thought, she had conjectured, that they might have been marking cattle. Then it had occurred to her that, in a sense, that was precisely what they were doing. They were marking livestock. She had, when free, despised slaves, and thought nothing of them. But then she had found herself one.

Abrogastes had had her branded promptly, but had not done the work himself. He had given it over to the smith and his fellows. He himself had scarcely seen her afterward. She had, with others, served twice, her ankles in leather shackles, in his hut.

The mark was on her, of course, and it identified her as a slave. But surely it provided her with little assurance that she might be spared.

She might be thrown, tonight, to the dogs that guarded the camp.

"They think," called Abrogastes to the tables, he striding about, fixing his fierce eyes upon one of the feasters after another, "that we are weak, that we are afraid of them! Are you weak, Granicus? Are you weak, Anton?"

"No," responded these creatures.

"You, Ingeld?" inquired Abrogastes.

"No, milord."

"Hrothgar?"

"No, father!" cried Hrothgar.

"Hensa? Orkon?"

"No, milord," said these men.

"Who here fears the empire?" called Abrogastes.

"The empire is strong," said a man.

"Do you fear her?" inquired Abrogastes.

"No, milord!" said the man.

"The empire believes that we cannot fight, that we are afraid to fight, that we are cowards!" said Abrogastes, his eyes blazing.

"Surely she is wrong, milord," called the clerk.

"Is she wrong, brothers?" inquired Abrogastes.

"Yes, milord!" cried a man.

"The empire is strong, milord," said a man.

"The empire," whispered Abrogastes, "is weak."

"Milord?" asked the man.

"Weak," said Abrogastes.

He then turned about and, not more than a pace from the prostrate Huta, returned to the dais, where he stood before the bench, between the high-seat pillars.

"You have spies, milord?" inquired a man.

"Yes," said Abrogastes.

"Let rings be brought!" called the clerk.

Men gasped, looking about, many apprehensive.

Huta, ignored, fearing, not knowing her fate, lay before the dais, frightened that no notice was taken of her, not even the blow of a boot, and yet fearing, as well, that she might, at any moment, by some happenstance, even by some caprice, as though by the shifting of a wind, be returned to the attention of the hall.

Chain me, she whispered to herself, chain me.

Abrogastes seated himself on the bench, between the high-seat pillars.

I want chains, she whispered to herself. Chain me, so that I cannot run, chain me to a ring, by the wrists and ankles, by the neck, if you wish, so that I cannot escape, so that I will be secure, so that I know I will be kept, at least for the night! Chain me, my master. I beg chains.

"I have thought long on these matters, and hard," said Abrogastes.

"Is it wise to have rings brought, father?" inquired Ingeld.

"There is a time to bring the rings," said Abrogastes.

"Is this the time, father?" asked Ingeld.

"It is the time," said Abrogastes.

"It is the time!" said Hrothgar, smiting with two fists upon the table.

"But the empire is eternal," said a man.

"Let it be eternal," said Abrogastes.

"I do not understand," said the man.

Two men entered, from the side, bearing with them a coffer, bound in iron.

"The rings, milord," said the shieldsman, at the left shoulder of Abrogastes, the sword of his lord over his left shoulder.

Huta looked pathetically to one of the musicians, still by the dais.

She could not read his expression.

She shuddered. She had, as she had been urged, danced her secret dreams, her secret thoughts, her needs, herself, her slavery, what she was, who she was. She had danced as a slave, shamelessly, holding nothing back, surrendering everything, releasing all, throwing herself piteously upon the mercy of harsh masters. And she had danced, too, before Abrogastes, and as his helpless, and, to her consternation, so vulnerably, as his needful, slave. What more could she do? What more could she give? Surely she had lost everything. But he had then thrust her with his boot from the dais, and seemed now to have dismissed her from his mind.

Mighty matters were afoot, and she knew herself only a worthless, meaningless slave.

She moved herself a little, and, lifting herself on the palms of her hands, regarded the scale, the pointer of which inclined ever so slightly toward the left side of the semicircular dial, toward the skull at its termination, indicating that the greatest weight, at this moment, lay within the pan of death.

What if they should forget her, and leave matters as they stood? Would not then the men come and, taking her by the arms, conduct her outside, to be thrown to the dogs?

She lay back down, trembling.

"Who here does not want wealth beyond his wildest dreams?" asked Abrogastes.

Men looked at one another, and grinned.

"It is there for the taking," said Abrogastes. "We need only have the courage to seize it! The empire is like a shell. It is hard on the outside, but once we break through, as I assure you that we, in strength, we brothers together, can, there is nothing to stop us, not until we reach the treasure rooms, the boudoirs, with our chains, the hearths of Telnaria herself!"

"They have ships, thousands, and weapons," said a man.

"We too have ships, and will have more, as we are joined by disaffected worlds. We are not the only enemies of the empire. Many are sophisticated, technological worlds which will support us with ships, with supplies, with equipment and armament."

"You have sounded these things out?" asked a man.

"Else you would not have been called to the feast," said Abrogastes.

"There are many peoples here, milord," said a man.

"We are strong," mused another.

"The empire is a burden on many worlds, and places, milord," said a man. "They would be pleased to be rid of her."

"The time to strike is now," said Abrogastes.

"And what will these worlds want of us, who wish us to take their risks, and do their work for them?" asked a man.

"What we give them," said Abrogastes, "is what they will receive."

"It will be by our doing?" asked Ingeld.

"Yes," said Abrogastes.

"There will be worlds to distribute?" asked a man.

"A billion worlds," said Abrogastes, "to be distributed, to

the brave, the faithful, the loyal, to owe their duties to their lords.''

"The empire is eternal," said a man, his voice shaking.

"Let it be eternal, or not," said Abrogastes. "What does it matter? It is a house into which we may, if we wish, enter. Do you think the empire, if she is to endure, cares who governs her, who is her master? Do you not think that power has not changed hands within her a thousand times, by poisonings, by assassinations, by untimely deaths, by intrigues, by palace seizures, by riots, by civil wars, in her long history? That there is a throne is all that is required, that and someone to sit upon it!"

"But we are not of the empire," said a man.

"So much the better," said Abrogastes. "Our blood is fresh, and hot. We are young, and the heat of our youth is upon us. We are a newer, more ambitious, more adventurous, more determined, stronger people. I will not be content until I ride my horse into the throne room of Telnaria, and wash my blade in the blood of the emperor!"

"Beware, milord!" cried a man.

"I have not gone mad," said Abrogastes. "What is required is courage."

"We are only warriors," said a man.

"Such," said Abrogastes, "stand at the beginning of all dynasties."

Abrogastes rose to his feet.

"Milord," said the clerk.

Men gasped, for the clerk had drawn forth, from a chest at the back of the dais, a long, purple robe, of the imperial purple, trimmed with white fur, from the pelt of the ice bear.

He draped this about the shoulders of Abrogastes.

Abrogastes himself fastened the large, golden penannular clasp.

The robe was so cut, in two leaves, that its length fell before and behind, leaving the arms free.

In such a way a sword may be wielded.

"Such robes may you all wear," said Abrogastes.

Men regarded one another, wonderingly.

"Let rings be distributed," said Abrogastes.

The men who had brought the rings, in the iron-bound coffer, began to distribute them.

They were large, and of gold, such as might be worn on the upper arm, or wrist.

Men drew back, fearing to accept them.

"Do not be afraid, my brothers," said Abrogastes. "See. I do not ask that you kneel before me, and accept rings from my hand. These are tokens of the feast, and of my good will. Surely those who have accepted rings from me know who they are, and many of you, I know, have accepted rings from another. I ask no forswearing of allegiances. We are all brothers. These are gifts. No obligation attends them."

"Our thanks, milord!" called a man.

The rings then were distributed, though some were accepted with reluctance.

It is a serious thing, the taking of rings.

There was, you see, as Abrogastes well knew, something in the nature of an implicit understanding involved in such an acceptance, even though it might be formally denied.

Abrogastes then resumed his seat upon the bench, between the pillars.

"Bring gifts!" he called.

Men rushed out and returned with rich gifts, drawn from chests, some of which required four men to bear. There was rich cloth, much of it cunningly woven, and satins and brocades for free women, and subtle silks, many diaphanous, with which to bedeck slaves, and there were jewels, of a dozen kinds, and golden wire, and brooches, buckles, strap ends, coins, plates, vessels, candelabra, lamps, swords, daggers, bracelets and necklaces, many such things. Much of this was heaped upon the tables. Men, and others, grasped these things, taking them to their places, putting them about themselves, thrusting them into their belts and garments.

Abrogastes watched, with satisfaction.

He witnessed men, and others, accepting his gifts, even eagerly.

Too, he was the lord of the Drisriaks, the foremost tribe, the largest and fiercest, of the Alemanni nation. To accept gifts from him was not the same as from some minor lord.

Abrogastes called to himself, while the gifts were being distributed, the chief of the lads in the bright livery, with the switches, and spoke with him.

He then, the lad, went to the prone women, crowded together, radiated in their semicircle about and before the spear, and, with deft, significatory touches of the supple wand in his hand, brought three to their hands and knees and herded them, with a touch here and there, unobtrusively, on an arm, or flank, to a position before the dais, to the left, before the bench of Abrogastes. These were the three blondes who had, often, even on the *Alaria*, served as display slaves, the sort with which a barbaric court might be bedecked, as an indication of the wealth and power of a rude sovereign, one of a powerful, ruthless people among whom the complete mastery of slaves was a commonplace. At a nod from Abrogastes, a keeper chained them, the three of them, hand and foot, to a ring, it set in the side of the dais.

This business was not muchly noticed by the men at the tables, boisterous, vying, arguing, reaching out, gathering in their gifts.

"There is more than enough for all!" cried out one of the distributors of this largesse.

The leader of the display slaves, shackled with the others, looked at Abrogastes fearfully, hopefully. She pressed her lips to her manacles, looking above them, timidly, to Abrogastes.

A wave of hatred and jealousy swept through the small, exquisitely curved body of Huta, but then she put down her head in fear, in misery, and moaned.

On her own throat there was not so much as a collar.

The eyes of the hound, green, and alight with fire, that crouched to the right of Abrogastes, were upon her.

At the merest word from Abrogastes, she knew the hound would be upon her, and tear her to pieces, its muzzle and fangs awash with blood, it feeding eagerly before the dais.

Huta looked to the scales, and to the pointer, indicative of the weightier burden borne within the pan of death.

She shuddered, and pressed the right side of her cheek into the dirt, against one of the broken reeds, or rushes.

Muchly did she envy the display slaves their shackles.

It seemed, at least, they had been found worth chaining, that they would be kept.

"Behold!" called Abrogastes, rising from the bench, and gesturing expansively to the side, where, from an entrance, men filed in, bearing oblong boxes.

"What is this, milord?" called a man, a Buron, from his home world of Safa Minor.

"See!" laughed Abrogastes.

The boxes were torn open, the boards splintered by swift, prying bars.

"Aii!" cried feasters, for within there were Telnarian rifles.

Such weapons were superior to those of most border troops, many of which, given the losses of resources over more than a billion years, were reduced to primitive weaponry, suitable for little more than the ordering, and pacification, of peoples scarcely less advanced than themselves. A quarrel, an arrow, may be reused, and, indeed, many charges, and the forcings of ground, had as their main intent the recovery of just such missiles from the field, some gathering them up, others maintaining the hurdles or shield walls behind which this harvesting might take place. A cartridge, on the other hand, once expended, is gone. A gallon of fuel burned is lost. A bomb, once exploded, has done its work, its reality then vanished in the debris of its birth and death. In these times, you see, a rifle might be worth a kingdom, and an unexploited world, newly discovered, rich in minerals and arable soil, worth a star. Resources, once carelessly conceived as if they might be infinite in nature and quantity, used upon occasion even to shatter and destroy worlds, had proved, over billions of years, finite, potentially exhaustible, and many were scattered, remote, and to most intents and purposes inaccessible. Small wonder then that simple metal, which might be fashioned into blades, and wood, that gloriously renewable resource, which might be fashioned into arrows and bows, began again to appear in the mixed arsenals of a million worlds.

"Beware," laughed Abrogastes, as men eagerly seized these precious devices, "one must learn to use them!"

"Do not unlatch that catch," said one of the more civilized of the feasters, to a second Buron, one to his left, fumbling with the contrivance.

"They are loaded," cautioned one of the fellows who had distributed the weapons.

"Each contains but a single charge," said a man, inspecting a spring-actuated loading panel.

"Outside, to be distributed," said Abrogastes, "there are a thousand charges for each weapon."

Men regarded one another, marveling.

Such a weapon, with only five charges, might suffice for the governance of a city. A single charge might crash the wall of a building.

"And there are ships, and heavier armaments than these," said Abrogastes.

"With such weaponry," said a man, "one might challenge even the empire."

"With such weaponry," said Abrogastes, "we are more than a match for the empire!"

"We can attack her upon a thousand fronts!" said a man.

"Those who rule the empire," said Abrogastes, "are soft and weak. We are hard, and strong. They are satisfied. We are lean and hungry. The empire, and everything within it, by the decree of nature, belongs to those who are strong enough to take it!"

"Yes, yes!" cried men.

The tables resounded with acclamatory pounding.

Then Abrogastes pointed to the prone women, the former ladies of the empire, by the spear.

"Huddle," cried he, harshly, "sluts!"

Swiftly the women, terrified, rose to their knees, and, guided by the switches of the boys, crowded closely together.

"More closely, in a circle!" said Abrogastes.

And then the women, the more than fifty of them who had served at the long tables in the great hall, who were all the women in the hall other than Huta and the three display slaves, already huddled, already crowded and pressed closely together, weeping, to the jangle of ankle bells, were forced into an even smaller space, a tinier round space, one they could scarcely occupy.

"Behold the beauty of their bosoms, the narrowness of their waists, the width of their hips," said Abrogastes. "Are they not pretty?"

"Yes," cried out more than one man.

"And they have slave collars on their necks, and slave bells on their ankles," said Abrogastes.

"Yes!" said men.

There was much laughter.

"What are they?" asked Abrogastes.

"Slaves!" cried men.

Abrogastes made a sign to one of the men who had brought in the rifles and he, adjusting the device, suddenly, walking swiftly about the crowded women, holding the weapon down, tore, at their very knees, in a swift, but extended torrent of fire, a close ditch about them, which, better than a yard deep, smoked, and was bright with fused stones. The women screamed, the bodies of many reddened from the heat, the knees of some scorched, and clutched one another, and drew back, the tiny bit that they could. There was a piteous jangling of bells.

Abrogastes turned to the horrified leader of the display slaves, in her chains, to his right, at the foot of the dais.

"To whom do you belong, all of you?" he asked, gesturing to her, to the other two display slaves, and, broadly, to the weeping, crowded, huddled slaves within the circle, smoking, cut by fire in the floor of the hall.

"To you, Master!" she cried.

"To whom do you belong, all of you?" he inquired again, fiercely.

"We belong to our barbarian lords, Master!" she cried.

"Is it fitting?" he asked.

"Yes, Master!" she cried.

"For what do you exist?" he asked.

"To serve our masters with instant, unquestioning obedience and total perfection!" she cried.

"Yes!" cried men.

There was pounding on the tables.

"Those of the empire," said Abrogastes, addressing the tables, "hold us in contempt. They call us 'dogs'!"

Men, and others, cried out in fury.

"But these," said Abrogastes, gesturing to the women, those huddled before the spear, and the three, the display slaves, chained to his right, neglecting only the prostrate Huta, "are all high ladies of the empire!"

There was laughter.

"They call us 'dogs,' " said Abrogastes, "but their high ladies, as you can see, are no more than the lowest of our bitches!"

"Yes!" cried men.

"Do you think we can find uses to which to put them?" inquired Abrogastes.

"Yes!" said a man.

"Yes, Abrogastes!" cried another.

"Yes, milord!" said another.

Abrogastes then, in the purple robe, of imperial purple, trimmed with the fur of the ice bear, viewed the tables, as a huntsman, a warrior, a statesman.

"My brothers," he said, "many of you were apprehensive, seeing the spear of oathing brought to the hall. That is understandable. It is brought here tonight only that you may remember it, and think upon it."

"No, father!" cried Hrothgar.

"Many, too, are reluctant to accept rings, though they are accorded here, this night, only as tokens of fellowship and esteem, of hospitality and good will. Your reluctance in this matter, too, is understandable. Surely we have fought amongst ourselves so long, and quarreled so frequently, that jealousy and suspicion are only to be expected. Indeed, is not our division, and our differences, one of the mightiest weapons of the empire, and mightier even, perhaps, than her ships and cannons? What a fearsome fate it must be for her the moment we should band together as the brothers we are. Together we outnumber her by thousands. She is mighty only as we are weak, only as we are many, and not one, and one not as abandoning our chieftains or kings, not as forgoing ourselves, not one as coming to be of one tribe or people, but one as being a thousand tribes and peoples with but a single purpose, the conquest of Telnaria."

The tables were quiet.

"It is true," said Abrogastes, "that I have invited you here tonight that we may think upon our enemies, upon the empire, and consider whether or not we are cowards, or warriors. I, myself, have long enough prowled the perimeters of rich countries. I, and my people, and yours, have long enough been shut away from well-watered pastures and black fertile fields. I have seen new worlds before me. The future has called to me. It calls to us. I will answer. I do not know if you will answer or not. Tomorrow I will learn."

Men looked at one another.

"Tonight," said Abrogastes, "we have feasted. Tomorrow, at noon, when you have slept, and thought, and your minds are clear of *bror*, so none can accuse me of imposing upon you, of cozening you to unwise pledging while in the pleasant delirium of drink and gifting, tomorrow, outside this hall, on the summit of the mountain of Kragon, on its lightning-smitten, seared stones, I, and those who follow me, will swear upon a ring, and upon the spear, our vengeance on an empire, and our undying determination to make her ours. We will swear brotherhood, and vengeance, and war."

"In twenty days," said a man, "the stones will leave the sky."

"Then let the lionships be unleashed," said a man.

"Much planning is in order," said Ingeld.

"Who would be the leader of this thing?" inquired Farrix, a

chieftain of the Teragar, or Long-River, Borkons. The Borkons were the third largest of the tribes of the Alemanni nation. The second largest was the Dangars. There were several branches of the Borkons, the largest being the Lidanian, or Coastal, Borkons.

"Whoever is lifted upon the shields," said Abrogastes.

"But only as lord of war," said Farrix.

"And for a time appointed," said another man, a high fellow of the Aratars, a people from Aratus, in the constellation of Megagon.

"We shall see!" said Hrothgar.

Two men sprang to their feet, but, in a moment, cautioned by their fellows, returned to their bench.

"I shall retire now," said Abrogastes, "and leave you, if you wish, to your deliberations."

"What of the sluts?" called a man.

"Ah," said Abrogastes, "it seems I had forgotten them."

There was a jangling of bells as the former ladies of the empire, crowded together in the small space, like an island within the encircling ditch, now naught but stripped, collared, belled slaves, trembled.

"Gamble for them," said Abrogastes, laughing.

No sooner had he spoken than several of the men who had brought in the rings began to distribute dice among the tables. Another, with the heel of his boot, scraped a small circle, some three feet in diameter, outside of, and before, the larger, ditched circle. In another instant another of the men had reached over the ditch and seized one of the women by the hand and dragged her from her knees into the ditch and out of it, unceremoniously, and put her on her feet, in the smaller, just-scraped circle, in front of the ditched circle. He held her small wrists together, pinioned over her head, in one hand, and turned her about. Dice rattled on the boards.

"What of that one?" called a man, indicating Huta, who shuddered.

"Let the hound have her!" called another.

Those who scored the highest in the first roll of the dice rolled again, and so on, until a winner was established.

"Twenty!" called a fellow.

"Twenty-two!" cried another.

Abrogastes, standing upon the dais, seemed bemused by the gambling.

"What of the slut, Huta!" cried a man.

The first of the former ladies of the empire was soon won and was put down upon her hands and knees and hurried, by a boy's switch, to her new master. She screamed, for it was an insectoidal creature, alien to mammals.

"You, quickly, to the circle!" cried one of the men to another of the former ladies of the empire and she, weeping, scrambled down into the ditch, and then up, out of it, and put herself in the smaller circle, and, once again, the dice danced, scattering about, on those broad, rough planks.

"Stand straight!" said a man. "Turn!"

"Do not leave the circle without permission or you die," said another.

"Let me cut the throat of the abettor of treason, Huta," said a man.

"No!" cried another.

The second of the former ladies of the empire, indeed, former high ladies of the empire, though perhaps we should now speak of them indiscriminately as slaves, for none, in her new condition was more than any other slave, any rural maid caught in the horseman's noose, any fleeing, netted debtress, to be sentenced to a slave brothel, any scullery thrall, any dirty-faced guttersnipe who, rounded up by the police in the alleys of some teeming metropolis, her days of vagrant parasitism abruptly concluded, was then sold. She was won by Granicus, whose snout now was moist, and beaded with sweat, and, in an instant, she was thrust beneath his table, to be tethered there by an aide, by the neck, the leash tied to one of the supports of the table, to crouch there, fearfully, amongst gold and other possessions, at her master's massive, leather-beribboned, clawed feet. And already Granicus scattered the dice from his mighty paw, for another woman, a brunette, on all fours, cowered within the tiny circle. And another woman was summoned forth, into the ditch, bells jangling, and then up, slipping at its side, to take a designated position, on all fours, near the circle, to be the next won.

"Huta!" cried a man.

"Huta!" cried another, howling it out.

Abrogastes seemed not to hear.

A fellow came from behind a table, bearing a double-headed war ax. "See the scale, mighty Abrogastes!" he cried. "It points to death!" He brandished his ax over Huta, who trembled beneath its heavy, tapered edge. A blow from such an implement can cut a shield in two. "I am your cousin, noble Abrogastes," said he. "Do not give her to the dogs! Let me have her first, piece by piece! I shall begin at the left ankle!"

"No!" cried a fellow, his sword half-drawn.

"She danced well," said another man.

"She abetted treason!" said the fellow who had earlier asserted this charge, one which surely none in conscience would care to dispute.

"Kill her!" said another.

"Her body is not without interest," observed one of the more civilized of the guests.

"I know markets in which she would bring a good price," said a merchant, Cang-lau, of Obont, he who had, incidentally, in a series of masked transactions, and at considerable risks to his shipping interests, from imperial inspectors and patrols, arranged for the delivery, from the client world of Dakir, via putatively neutral Obont, of the Telnarian rifles.

"Kill her!" repeated he who had cried out before.

"I will give you a ruby for her, a Glorion ruby!" called out a man. Such rubies are the size of a man's fist.

Huta's heart leapt.

She had value!

"Kill her! Cut her throat!" screamed a fellow.

Another woman, in the background, the brunette, was gambled for, and won. She went to a man, to whom she hastened eagerly, on all fours. Another was then put in the small circle, and another, bells jangling, brought to the place of readiness.

"Death is too good for her!" called a fellow. "Let her be the slave she is!"

"Slavery! Slavery!" cried a man.

"Keep her as a slave!" called another.

"Put the collar on her, Abrogastes!"

"Sell her!"

Were men so foolish, Huta wondered, to think that, for a woman, death was preferable to slavery. Did they know so little of women? Did they not realize, so many of them, the sweet, simple fools, why women made such perfect slaves?

"Kill her! Cut her throat!"

"Put her on a slave block!"

Huta pressed her tiny body into the rush-strewn dirt, terrified, while these cries rang about her.

She was, in legality, already a slave.

Too, she had begun to sense, deeply, the wonder of chains,

and the whip, and obedience, and subjection to the master. She had begun to sense what it might be to be under discipline, with its identities, with its realities, its perils and ecstasies. Already a profound transformation of her consciousness had begun to come about. From puberty on, in its own inexorable time of unfolding maturations, of insights and intuitions, she had begun to suspect, and to be aware of dim mechanisms within her, genetic preparations, latent responses, awaiting longed-for, releasing stimuli, biological destinies and fittingnesses. She had begun to long for the unswerving master beast to whom her desirability and beauty would be categorically and uncompromisingly subject. Even as a girl, frightened and resistant, she had unaccountably begun to long for the mighty master of her dreams, the man before whom she could never be more than an eager, impassioned slave. She had begun to sense, you see, what it might be to be truly free to feel, and to be sexually free, truly, wildly and helplessly, as no woman can be who is not subject to command, and to love and serve, as she must, and as no free woman could.

In the background women were being gambled for, and won.

"Like this!" cried the fellow who was the cousin of Abrogastes, driving his ax into the dirt not more than an inch from Huta's left ankle.

She screamed.

He looked up at Abrogastes, eagerly.

But Abrogastes seemed to give him no attention.

Another woman was forced into the tiny circle, on down upon her knees, and a fellow, his hand in her hair, bent her backward.

Well was she displayed.

Numbers were called out.

"She is a beauty, milord," said the clerk.

"Yes," said Abrogastes.

"Milord!" protested the cousin of Abrogastes.

"What of Huta?" called men.

"Throw her to the dogs!" called a man.

"Sell her!" demanded another, clutching a bag of coins, yet was not each, now, at those tables, rich? Had not Abrogastes, and the coffers of the Drisriaks, seen to that?

"Put her on the slave block!" called a man.

"Sell her to the highest bidder!" called another.

"Kill her! Kill her!" cried others.

Huta's body shook with terror and tears.

One of the women in the tiny circle, throwing her head about, seemed mad with fear. She rose up, suddenly, staggering. "Do not leave the circle or you die!" snarled a fellow. She knelt down then, sobbing. She was soon sold.

"Huta! Huta!" called men.

"Abrogastes!" called others, pressing for his attention.

"This is not happening to me!" cried a woman in the small circle, but, in moments, she was on her belly, and her new master, kneeling across her body, was binding her hands behind her back. When he stood she turned, on her side, bound, and looked up at him, and then swiftly pressed her lips to his boot.

Another woman was put in the circle.

"Put your hands behind the back of your head, and bend backward," she was told by the fellow at the circle. "Now put your hands on your hips, and flex your knees!"

Wonderingly, frightened, the woman did so.

"Now, move!" said the man at the circle.

"Surely not, Master!" cried the woman.

"Now!" he said.

"Oh!" she cried.

"There," said the man, "now you have moved as a slave before men. I do not think you will ever forget this moment."

"No, Master!" she said, flushed, wonderingly, knowing she could never again, after that movement, be anything other than what she now was, a slave.

"Slut! Slut!" cried one of the women in the larger circle.

"Yes, yes," wept the woman in the smaller circle. "I am a slut! I am a slave. I cannot now be anything different."

"I, too, am a slave!" cried one of the women in the larger circle.

"I, too!" said others.

"Take me next!" cried one. "I would be won!"

"I am hot!" wept the woman in the smaller circle.

"Yes, yes, I, too!" said another woman in the larger circle.

Many held out their hands to be the next to be permitted to the smaller circle, but the one selected was she who had cried out, "Slut! Slut!"

"You will have nothing from me!" she cried, as she was dragged, standing, to the circle. "I will be inert!"

"The whip," said a man, putting out his hand, into which the implement was promptly placed.

"No, Master!" she said. "Please, no!"

"Shall our little critic be lashed?" inquired the fellow, of the tables.

"Let her perform!" called a man.

"Interest them," said the man with the whip.

"Please, no!" she wept.

The whip snapped.

The men laughed as the distraught beauty attempted to interest them.

"Is that the best you can do?" inquired the man with the whip. Again the whip cracked.

"More," said the man with the whip.

There was laughter.

"It seems the next stroke must be upon your body," said the fellow with the whip.

"No, no, Master!" she wept.

He held her left arm with his left hand, and was behind her.

"Aii!" she suddenly cried.

There was, again, laughter, but this laughter was one not only of amusement, but one also of genuine interest.

Gently, but surely, and unexpectedly, had the whip, coiled, touched her.

The proud woman was now no more than a humbled, scarlet mass of shame in his hand.

"It seems your body betrays your mouth," he said.

"Yes, Master," she said.

"Lying is not permitted to a slave girl," he said.

"No, Master," she said.

"Do you think, truly, you are different from other slaves?" he asked.

"No, Master," she said.

"Do you think you will be an inert slave?" he asked.

"No, Master!" she said. "Please, Master, let me be won swiftly!"

"Inertness is not permitted in a slave," he said.

"No, Master!" she said.

She was soon won.

Swiftly, eagerly, she crawled to her new master.

Another woman, one eager to be won, was brought to the circle.

"Hold, Abrogastes!" called Farrix, of the Borkons, who had risen to his feet.

The woman in the circle shrank down, tiny.

The dice stopped rattling.

Abrogastes turned toward Farrix, for Farrix was on his feet, and a chieftain.

"Let the pellets be cast," said Farrix, grimly.

"Beware, father," whispered Ingeld.

Abrogastes gave no sign he had heard the warning of Ingeld, Ingeld, who kept his thoughts muchly to himself.

Huta, lying in the dirt before the dais, trembled, sensing suddenly that her fate might cease to depend on such simple matters as guilt or justice, or her desirability or lack of desirability as a female slave, but on other matters, subtle political matters, on rankings, on contests of will, on maneuverings for power.

"Of course," said Abrogastes, affably.

She knew that Abrogastes despised and hated her, for her role in the business of the Ortungs, but she also suspected that he, the thought both alarming and stirring her, found her not without interest as a slave. Surely more than once she had detected in his eyes, or thought she had, keen desire, even fierce desire, as for a slave to be uncompromisingly mastered and ravished. She had no hope of winning his love, that hope of almost every slave girl, to win the love of her master, but hoped that she might, if only by years of an abject slave's service and devotion, win perhaps at least some particle of a begrudging sufferance.

"How will Abrogastes, lord of the Drisriaks, cast his pellet?" inquired Farrix.

"Sacrifice her, father," whispered Ingeld.

"How will Farrix cast his pellet?" inquired Abrogastes.

"She is not worth the collar!" said another Borkon.

"But she is not without interest," said another Borkon, evenly.

The hand of Farrix went to his dagger, but he withdrew it, and it was almost as though he had not moved.

"The matter is trivial, and it had escaped my mind," said Abrogastes.

He nodded to the clerk.

"Let the pellets be cast!" called the clerk.

Huta was pulled to her knees, and turned to face the scales, that she might witness the deciding of her fate.

"Death to her!" cried a man.

"Life!" cried another.

The feasters then, the women in the circle forgotten, even she in the smaller circle, waiting, small, kneeling there, to be won, began to leave the tables and file, one by one, to the table of pellets, and then each, to cries of acclamation, or anger, or derision, cast their pellets, those small, leaden counters, into the pan of their choice.

Huta could scarcely kneel.

"Straighten your body, head up," said the fellow who had positioned her. "Place your hands, wrists crossed, as though they were bound, at the small of your back."

She tried to comply.

Pellets struck into the pans.

The pan of death began to descend even more.

"See she who was once the proud Huta!" laughed a man.

"See the slave," said another.

"She trembles," said another.

"She cannot even hold herself upon her knees," laughed another.

"Tie her wrists behind her back," said Abrogastes.

"Blindfold her," said Abrogastes.

"Put her on a double leash," said Abrogastes.

These things were done, that she might better hold her position, and then she knelt much as she had, save that now her small wrists, in reality, were fastened behind her back, her eyes were now bandaged, with a folded scarf, and on her neck were two leashes, the straps, short and taut, extending from the two leash collars on her neck to the fists of her keepers, one on each side. The residual lengths of the straps were muchly coiled, the higher coils wrapped about their fists.

Huta moaned.

The pellets, unseen by her now, continued to strike into the pans.

She could not now, held as she was by the leashes, slip from her knees.

"You can see the pans, father," said Ingeld. "Give her up."

"What is she to me?" said Abrogastes.

"Give her up," said Ingeld.

"No!" said Hrothgar. He rose from his place and cast a pellet into the pan for life.

"See how Hrothgar casts his pellet," said Abrogastes to Ingeld.

"He sees only the shapely limbs of a slave," said Ingeld.

"How shall I cast my pellet?" Abrogastes asked the clerk.

"You will cast it as you wish, milord," said the clerk.

"How should I cast my pellet?" Abrogastes asked his shieldsman, his own great sword in its sheath, over the fellow's left shoulder.

"I shall defend my lord to the death," said the shieldsman, "whatever he does, whatever be his decision."

Hrothgar returned to his place, casting a dark glance at Ingeld.

"Hrothgar is a fool," said Ingeld. "He cares only for his horses and falcons."

"And, it seems," said a man, "for slave girls."

"Yes," said Ingeld, scowling, "and for slave girls."

The pellets continued to be placed into the pans.

Huta trembled. Tears ran from her eyes, beneath the blindfold, to stain her cheeks.

The warriors, the merchants, the envoys, all, filed past the scales.

"The matter is evening itself," said a man, wonderingly.

Huta lifted her head, startled. She strained, as if to see through the dark layers of the blindfold. Her small wrists moved helplessly in the tight, confining thongs.

"Now it inclines again toward death," said a man.

The hall was now muchly silent, the eyes of the men upon the scales.

The guests filed past, each putting his pellet into the pan of his choice.

"Remove her blindfold," said Abrogastes.

The blindfold was removed, and Huta saw that the pointer on the scale was poised, as though indecisive, restless, wavering, at the midpoint of the scale.

"It seems your beauty is not without interest, slut," said a man.

"She danced well," said another.

"I think she might make an excellent slave," said another.

"Not everyone who may has cast a pellet," said Farrix, quietly.

He looked at Ingeld.

Ingeld looked at Abrogastes.

Ingeld then went to the pan and cast his pellet.

"He casts it for life!" said a man.

Abrogastes then descended to the floor and went to the table. The scale, still, was delicately difficult to read, so many pellets there were, so evenly were they distributed, so small the weight of each.

"It points, does it not, to the collar," said a man.

At one termination of the dial on the scale there was the representation of a skull, at the other the representation of a slave collar.

Abrogastes picked up a pellet.

"Remember Ortog, remember the Ortungs, remember the division of the nation, remember treason," said Farrix.

"I remember those things," said Abrogastes.

"How then will you cast your pellet, mighty Abrogastes?" asked Farrix.

"As I please," said Abrogastes.

The hall was silent.

Abrogastes then tossed his pellet into the pan of life.

"Aii!" cried men, and others.

"Shieldsman," said Abrogastes.

The shieldsman came to him.

"My sword," said Abrogastes.

The weapon was unsheathed, and placed in his hand.

Abrogastes then threw the mighty weapon into the pan of life, and it bore the balance of the scale almost to the vertical. Pellets spilled from the pans. The pan of life, that of the collar, was borne as low as it might be, without breaking the small chains which held it to the balance.

"And how will you, noble Farrix, cast your pellet?" asked Abrogastes.

"For life, of course," he said. He cast his pellet into the pan of life, it now so much descended. "Hail to the Alemanni," he said.

"Hail to the Alemanni," said Abrogastes.

The keepers who held the leashes of Huta played out leather, lowering her to the ground.

"Continue your gambling, my friends, my brothers," said Abrogastes, raising his hand.

"Up, on your knees, slave!" said a fellow at the smaller circle, to the woman waiting to be won.

Again there was shouting. "Forty!" "Forty-six!"

Abrogastes looked down at the slave who, overcome, had lost consciousness.

"Take the leashes off her neck," he said. "Leave her bound. Revive her."

Then he said to another fellow, "Bring a common slave collar for her."

Dice rattled upon the boards.

Another slave was won.

And another was put to the circle, and another summoned, bells jangling, from the ditched island to the place of readiness.

Cold water was splashed upon the unconscious, fainted, overcome, bound Huta, who, coughing, gasping, frightened, comprehending that her hands were still bound, regained consciousness.

She looked wildly at Abrogastes, the earth muddied about her.

Abrogastes retrieved his sword from the pan in which it lay, withdrawing it from amongst the three tiny chains, and gave it to his shieldsman, who returned it to its sheath.

He then returned his attention to Huta, while the gambling went on, in the background.

Huta scrambled to her knees, and put her head to the ground before Abrogastes.

"Collar her," said Abrogastes.

One of his men crouched by the slave, her head still to the muddied dirt, and fastened a slave collar on her neck. It was a common slave collar. It fit closely. It locked in the back.

"Now that she has been collared, throw her a piece of meat," said Abrogastes.

"On your belly, slave," said a man.

Huta went to her belly and the meat was thrown into the mud, before her.

Eagerly, starving, her hands bound behind her, she seized the bit of meat in her small, fine teeth and, pulling it about, gnawing, trying to get it in her mouth, fed on it.

The leader of the three display slaves, as well as her two companions, all chained to the ring on the dais, frightened, watched her. She, and her companions, commonly fed from pans, put on the floor, their heads down, on all fours. In such small ways, and others, a woman can be reminded she is a slave.

Another woman was won, and another brought to the small circle.

Much attention was on the gambling.

Granicus had won a second slave.

She was now tethered, like the first, beneath his table.

Huta, ravenous, finished the bit of meat, but there was no more.

She looked to the keeper, beggingly.

"We must be concerned for your figure," he said. "Let us keep it trim."

"May I have water, Master?" she begged.

"You have water," he said.

She put down her head and lapped at muddied water.

It had not been thus when she was a consecrated virgin, and priestess.

Ingeld regarded her. Her flanks, it was true, were not without interest.

Another woman was won, and another put to the circle, and another readied.

"My lord will retire now?" asked the clerk.

"Yes," said Abrogastes.

Two men, secondary shieldsmen, rose from their places, to accompany Abrogastes, and his shieldsman, from the hall.

Abrogastes indicated Huta to one of the keepers. "See that she is washed, and combed, and perfumed, and given a slave rag, and bring her to my hut tonight."

Huta looked up, wildly, frightened, gratefully, to her master.

"You may kneel," said a keeper, kindly.

Huta scrambled up, and then, on her knees, unbidden, crawled to Abrogastes.

She put her head down to his feet.

He seemed not to notice.

"That one," he said, indicating the chief of the display slaves to a keeper, "prepare her, and bring her to my hut tonight."

"Master!" cried the blonde, joyfully, lifting her small, chained wrists, to the extent that her chains permitted.

"Master!" cried Huta, raising her head, in disappointment, in protest. "Is it not I who am to be brought to your hut?"

"No, I!" cried the blonde.

"I!" said Huta.

"I love you, my master!" said the blonde.

"I love you, my master!" cried Huta.

"Is it true?" asked Abrogastes of Huta, looking down upon her.

"Yes, Master," she whispered, putting down her head.

"With the hedged-in, qualified, partial, careful, incomplete love of a free woman?" he asked.

"No, Master," she said.

"With the profound wholeness of a slave's love?" asked Abrogastes.

"Yes, Master," she said.

"I juice when you but look upon me, Master!" said the blonde.

Her companions gasped.

How dare she admit such a thing! But then she was now only a slave.

Then her companions blushed and put down their heads. They, too, were only slaves. They, too, had knelt before masters. Their bodies could be easily checked. And if they lied, they would be beaten.

"And what of you, little slave?" asked Abrogastes of Huta.

"Yes, Master," she whispered. "Many times, at your least glance, I have juiced."

Abrogastes regarded her.

"Though you have not deigned to touch me," she said, "you have conquered me, and I am yours."

"Before I met men such as you, Master," said the blonde, "I knew men only of the empire. Before I met men such as you, I did not know that such men existed, men before whom a woman can be naught but an obedient and eager slave."

"You will share my couch tonight," said Abrogastes, to the blonde, "and you," he said to Huta, "will be our serving slave."

"But what of my needs, Master?" asked Huta.

"You have not even begun to experience needs," said Abrogastes.

"Yes, Master," said Huta.

Abrogastes then turned to the assemblage. "Continue with your sport," he said. "And outside, there are more than four hundred more, and though they are not high ladies, yet they are delicate and refined, and of the empire, and will serve as well as any, I ween, in the furs, and at the ovens, and the laundry troughs, and in the pantries and butteries. They are to be distributed to any who did not win in the hall."

Cheers met this announcement.

Men were gambling, too, among themselves, for many of the other gifts which had been distributed. Only the rifles, it seems, were not put up as stakes.

One man, leading two of the slaves on tethers, their wrists

bound behind them, passed Abrogastes, eager, it seemed, to get to his quarters.

"Hail, Abrogastes!" he said.

"Lash them, that they may understand that they are slaves, and then enjoy them," said Abrogastes.

"Yes, noble Abrogastes," said the man. "Hail, Abrogastes!"

A keeper had freed the three display slaves, and their leader, her arm in the grasp of another keeper, was being hurried from the hall, doubtless to the heat shed, with its large wooden tubs.

As Abrogastes left the hall, Farrix, the Borkon, standing by the side door, spoke to him. "Hail to the Alemanni," he said.

"Hail to the Alemanni," said Abrogastes and, in the purple cloak, trimmed with the fur of the ice bear, took his leave, followed by the clerk, and three shieldsmen.

"On your feet, slut," said a keeper to Huta.

"Yes, Master," she said.

"You are to be congratulated, on surviving the decision of the scales," he said.

"Thank you, Master," she said.

She shuddered as he touched her, with the freedom of a keeper.

"It seems you will live," he said.

"Yes, Master," she said.

"At least until morning," he said.

"Yes, Master," she said, trembling.

"Among the Drisriaks," he said, "we throw those who are not good slaves to the dogs."

"I will try to be a good slave."

"See that you do," he said.

"Yes, Master," she said.

She was about to be conducted from the hall by the keeper, when she found her way barred by Ingeld.

Swiftly, confronted by a free man, she knelt.

She kept her head down, that she not risk meeting the eyes of a free man.

"If you are to be sent barefoot, in a slave rag, to the hut of a noble," said Ingeld, "you must be brushed and combed, and washed."

"Yes, Master," she said.

Ingeld frightened her, even more than Abrogastes.

"Do you love your master?" inquired Ingeld.

"Yes, Master!" said Huta.

"You will love whomever the whip tells you to love," said Ingeld.

"Yes, Master," she whispered.

"Take the slave away," said Ingeld.,

"Yes, milord," said the keeper.

· · · CHAPTER 12 · · ·

"Oh!" said the small, exquisite redhead, in the bright sunlight, amidst the stalls and carts of the Sephisa market in Lisle.

"Do not turn around," said a man's voice.

The redhead whimpered a little.

"What you feel is a gun at your spine," said the voice. "One false move and this weapon will scoop a hole eight inches wide in you, and every gut in your pretty little belly will be pasted on that wall across the square."

"There are people about," whispered the redhead. "I need only scream."

"It would be your last," said the voice.

"What do you want with me?" she asked.

"Remain calm, smile," said the voice.

The redhead tried to smile. "You do not want me," she said, frightened. "I do not know the art of writhing in chains, of serving a master. I'm only a woman's slave, a lady's maid."

"That is a waste," said the voice. "Your legs are exquisite."

"Master?" she asked.

"If you are a lady's maid," he said, "do you not think she could dress you more richly, more amply?"

The redhead wore only a brief, sleeveless brown tunic, ragged at the hem, of simple *corton*.

"My mistress is not rich," she said. "Too, she enjoys dressing me in this fashion, to demean me, that my sexuality will be evident."

On her neck was a slim, close-fitting steel collar, closed in front, with a small padlock.

"You are shopping," he observed.

"Yes, Master," she said.

"Do not drop your net of produce," he said, "and advance easily, as if nothing were amiss, to the edge of the market, to the alley there, and do not turn around."

"Please!" she said.

"Now," he said.

The point of the object, which was surely a muzzle or muzzlelike, pressed into her lower back, harshly.

"Yes, Master!" she said.

She moved toward the alley.

"In here," he said.

Moaning, she entered the indicated door, a shabby door, one of several, in a worn, defaced wall, covered with scrawls, and the remains of some yellowed, posted bills.

"Kneel," he said, and she knelt, on some boards, before a shuttered window, through which light filtered, and a chair, on which a man sat. She could see, rimmed with light, little more than the outline of his body. She could tell, however, that he wore a mask.

"Put aside the groceries," said the man in the chair, not unkindly.

She put them to the side.

"I know little of serving men, Master," she said. "I am a lady's maid."

"Show her the picture," said the man in the chair.

From behind her a drawing, in color, was produced, and held before her face.

She turned white.

The picture was then withdrawn.

"You are the maid of the Lady Publennia Calasalia, of, or once of, the Larial Calasalii."

"No, Master!" she said.

"Do you lie to free men?" asked the figure in the chair.

"Forgive me, Master," she said, frightened.

"It is known you are her maid, and you have been identified as such, and that is why you have been brought here," said the man in the chair.

The slave was silent.

"Is she still of the Calasalii?" asked the man.

"No, Master," she said, regarding the picture, fearfully. "She was disowned."

"But she receives an allowance."

"Yes, Master is well informed." The slave, who was a highly intelligent young woman, realized then that she stood in terrible jeopardy, for she did not know what her interrogators knew and what they did not know. Accordingly, great risks might be involved in attempting to conceal or obscure information. She had already been caught in one lie. It might mean her life to be found out in another.

She began to weep.

"Show her the picture again," said the seated man.

It was put again before her.

"Look at the picture," she was told. "Look carefully."

She looked at it, trembling, through tears.

"Is that your mistress?" asked the seated man.

The slave wrung her hands in misery.

"Put your hands behind you, wrists crossed," said the seated man, "as though bound."

She complied.

"Widen your knees," he said.

"Master!" she said.

"And now cross your ankles, as though they were bound," he said.

"Yes, Master," she wept.

"Is the picture that of your mistress?" asked the seated man.

"It is a drawing, Master!" she wept. "It is not a mechanical pictorial. I do not know if it is my mistress or not!"

"It has been identified, by several people, as a likeness of your mistress," said the seated man.

"It appears to be she," said the slave. "But it is a drawing. It is only a drawing. One cannot know."

The drawing, at a sign from the seated man, was withdrawn.

"But you think it might be a drawing of your mistress?"

"Yes, Master," she wept.

"Where is your mistress?" asked the man.

"She is not well—she is indisposed—" said the slave. "No, no! Forgive me, Master! She is not in the city!"

"That seems clear," said the seated man.

The slave trembled. It seemed obvious then that the quarters of the Lady Publennia must have been searched, that inquiries had been made.

"Are you, Masters," begged the slave, "of those who questioned me earlier?"

"Speak," said the seated figure, sternly.

"Those who inquired of me information as to delicate matters," she whispered.

"What?" asked the seated figure.

The mind of the exquisite redheaded slave, kneeling, positioned according to the dictates of her captors, raced. She felt vulnerable, and helpless, kneeling, her knees spread, her wrists crossed behind her, her ankles crossed. If they knew the truth of these matters, and were testing her, and she lied, she did not know what would be done with her. It is not permitted to slaves to lie, and penalties, terrible penalties, may be inflicted on one who does. Simple truth, perfect truth, and a desperate hope for the mercy of masters, is the slave's best hope.

"Information," said she, "as to the most intimate lineaments of my mistress's beauty."

"As though she might even have been a slave?"

"Yes, Master," whispered the slave.

"Ah," said the man in the chair, an utterance of both triumph, and fury.

The slave put her head down, frightened.

"When were you so questioned?" asked the man in the chair.

"Over twenty days ago," said the slave.

"Where is your mistress now?"

"I do not know, Master!" said the slave, looking up. "Men came for her, and she left, in a carriage, in the early morning."

"When was this?"

"Fifteen days ago," said the slave.

"On the *calends* of Rissius?"

"Yes, Master," said the slave, startled.

"What is your name?" asked the seated man.

"Nika, Master, if it pleases Master," she said.

"It is a pretty name," he said.

"Thank you, Master," she said.

The seated man then made a gesture to the man behind the slave.

The slave became aware of hands, at the side of her head, and of a band, or cloth, of sorts, between them.

"Do not move," said the man in the chair.

The slave was then gagged.

She whimpered.

Then she felt light cords of silk whipped about her crossed wrists, which were then, almost instantly, bound, and then her crossed ankles, too, were so served, and she knelt then as she had been, save that now she was gagged, and bound, hand and foot. Her eyes were wild over the gag. She was gently eased to her side on the boards. She felt a coldness on her upper left arm, and a dampness, where some fluid had been rubbed, and then, a moment or two later, as she winced, the entry into her body, at that point, of a needle. It took some seconds to inject a given quantity of fluid into her body.

She looked up, wildly, at the man who had been in the chair, who now stood, looking down at her.

She looked to the other side and saw a large leather sack being drawn toward her, over the boards.

"You are going on a trip, pretty little Nika," said the first man, he masked, he looking down at her.

She squirmed a little, but, in a moment or two, lost consciousness.

"I fear the worst," said Julian, of the Aurelianii, pulling away his mask.

"What can be done?" asked Tuvo Ausonius. "The *Narcona* has a start of fifteen days. By now she will have crossed at least four thresholds. Radio contact, without adjustments at the thresholds, will not be possible."

"We must do what we can," said Julian.

"The next ship is specially scheduled, and, even so, does not leave for two weeks."

"It will leave tomorrow," said Julian.

"I will be ready," said Tuvo Ausonius.

"We will be ready," said Julian.

"You cannot leave, milord," said Tuvo Ausonius. "The ceremonials, the insult to the emperor!"

"I have men loyal to me," said Julian. "If necessary, I will seize a patrol ship."

"An impostor slave seems an odd selection for a spy, or saboteur," said Tuvo Ausonius.

"Who would be alone, with no thought given to it, unsuspected, with a man at night?" asked Julian.

Tuvo Ausonius turned white.

"It is not a spy or saboteur we need fear," said Julian. "It is an assassin."

"You suspect Iaachus?"

"Yes, but one does not know. It could be any enemy."

"They do not know we are aware of an impostor slave," said Tuvo Ausonius.

"True," said Julian. "That may give us time. Ottonius must await us at Venitzia. In that way, we may have time to warn him. I suspect they plan to do their deed in the wilderness, not within the *pomerium* of Venitzia."

"The imperial family will not give you permission to be absent from the ceremonials," said Tuvo Ausonius.

"Then I will seize a patrol ship," said Julian.

"That is treason!" said Tuvo Ausonius.

"Are you ready to join me in such treason?" asked Julian.

"Treason in the service of the empire is no treason," said Tuvo Ausonius.

"Good fellow!" said Julian.

"What if we are successful?" asked Tuvo Ausonius.

"Then we shall brazen things out," said Julian.

"And if we are not successful?"

"Then we are traitors," said Julian.

Tuvo Ausonius shuddered.

Tuvo Ausonius looked down at the unconscious slave, bound and gagged, at their feet.

"We need her," said Julian. "She can make an identification of her mistress, as the free woman, the Lady Publennia of Lisle, on Inez IV."

"We have the drawing," said Tuvo Ausonius.

"The drawing is only a drawing, and not a mechanical pictorial, and, as far as many would know, only the drawing of someone who closely resembles a supposed slave, or, indeed, it might even be a drawing of an actual slave, the one with the expedition. How could one prove that the drawing, done even by one who had never seen the woman in person, but only by means of the memory of another, is that of the Lady Publennia? Indeed, how could one prove that even a mechanical pictorial of the woman was a pictorial of the actual Lady Publennia?"

"True," said Tuvo Ausonius.

"The slave is important, too," said Julian, "if we are separated, as you have never seen the Lady Publennia personally."

"It seems a pity to take such a pretty, innocent, delicious little creature into what might prove to be a situation of considerable danger, among perhaps even ruthless barbarians and such."

"Not at all," said Julian. "She is only a slave."

"True," said Tuvo Ausonius.

The two men then, together, eased the body of the redheaded slave, feet first, into the sack, and tied it shut, over her head.

"What if Ottonius does not wait for us at Venitzia?" asked Tuvo Ausonius.

"He must," said Julian, angrily, jerking tight, and tying, the cords of the sack over the head of the slave.

She stirred a little in the sack, but did not regain consciousness.

"But what if he does not?" asked Tuvo Ausonius.

"Then all is lost," said Julian.

· · · CHAPTER 13 · · ·

On the day following the great feast of Abrogastes, which is conjectured to have taken place on Ukuna III, a large assemblage of barbarians, and others, climbed to the height of a rude, natural feature known as the mountain of Kragon. There, on its stony summit, well above the tree line, on a great horizontal metal ring, hands laid upon it, a swearing took place, this done by rank after rank of individuals, approaching and withdrawing, which swearing, too, similarly and successively, was repeated, hands placed upon the shaft or blade of a great spear, it seeming to have some symbolic relevance among the Alemanni and certain other peoples, mostly allied or related.

We do not know precisely what was sworn, or what occurred, on that day in that place.

On the other hand, it seems clear that something of importance took place.

It was shortly thereafter, in that world's spring, after the cessation of the astronomical anomaly of the "wind of stones" that the gates of better than a hundred thousand concealed hangars were slid upward and the great ships rolled forth.

The lions, as it was said, were awakening.

The name of the world, in the language of the Alemanni, seems to have been Ainesarixhaben, or a place where fires are kept. It may have been the home world of the Alemanni peoples.

It was also known, in other barbaric tongues, as Eineskmirgenlandes, a world, or country, of the morning, and Oron-Achvolonarei, the place where stone birds fly.

This was, in the reckoning of the empire, in the third year of the reign of the emperor, Aesilesius.

· · · **CHAPTER 14** · · ·

The horse put its head down, its long hair whipped by the wind. It drew against the traces, and stumbled to its knees in the snow.

It turned in the traces, snorting, wildly, in pain, tilting the sled, and threw its head to the side, its round eyes rolling.

Its body was already half covered with snow.

The man, wrapped in the fur cloak, with the staff, who had been struggling at the side of the sledge, thrusting at it, lifting it, waded to the beast's side. The horse's mighty lungs heaved. It gasped. The freezing air seared its nostrils. The wind and air, too, tore at the side of the man's face, and stabbed his lungs. The breath of the horse whipped away from it, like a lace of fog, broken and splintered. There was ice caked about its jaws.

The man looked down at the animal, bracing himself against the wind.

He could see little, even in starlight reflected from the snow, for the blasting wind and ice.

This was the third night of storms.

Already the stirred, whirled snow was deep on the plains of Barrionuevo, or, as some have it, the flats of Tung. In places, by morning, it would drift to heights of fifty feet.

Tangara is bitter in that place, in the month of Igon. Only once had the Heruls raided in that month, and that was years ago, when they had crossed the Lothar on the ice.

It was then that they, fresh from their defeat of the Otungs, had carried war to the related folk, the Basungs.

It was after this that the plains of Barrionuevo had become, for many, the flats of Tung.

On them the Heruls, a hardy, merciless, slave-keeping folk, in the summer, grazed their herds.

The man knelt in the snow beside the horse. He opened its eye, which had closed, with his mittened fist.

It was still alive, gasping.

He drove the staff into the snow, and removed from the sledge a great sword, one which must be wielded with two hands. He lifted it, with both hands, and then smote the horse's head away.

He then, kneeling beside the beast, trembling with cold, cut it open, and cut himself bits of meat, thrusting them, fumbling, into his mouth, his beard crusted with ice. The blood from the horse froze as it entered the air, forming almost instantly rivulets, and breakages, of thick, dark ice. The man cut through the rib cage, and pulled away tissue. He tore with his mittens, and then, as they sopped, and crusted, and might have broken, he dug with his sword, holding it near the point, at the ventral cavity of the beast, emptying it, pushing its contents away, and he then crawled, freezing, huddling, within the body, which, for moments would be warm, but might provide, for days, shelter and food.

It is a trick known to Heruls, and others, for example, to those of certain *festung* villages, such as that of Sim Giadini, nestled at the foot of the heights of Barrionuevo.

· · · CHAPTER 15 · · ·

"He is gone! I heard it in the kitchen, from one of the barrack girls!" said the small brunette, rushing into the administration's cement slave shed in Venitzia, a small city on Tangara, surrounded by its electric defenses. It was the provincial capital.

"Who is gone?" cried the blonde, rising from her simple, sturdy, anchored metal cot, to which she, like the other girls to theirs, was chained.

The surprise, and bewilderment, was universal.

The girls came to the ends of their chains, out, into the aisle, as they could. Their chains must reach far enough to make possible the cleaning of not only their area but of the adjacent portion of the aisle, as well.

"The barbarian!" cried the girl. "He has gone!"

The blonde cursed the chain on her left ankle that would permit her only a handful of feet from the cot.

"I do not understand," said she who was first girl, even she, at the moment, chained to her cot.

"They are startled, in consternation, furious!" said the brunette. "It seems he left Venitzia before dawn, without informing anyone, taking only a horse and supplies upon a sledge."

"But why?" asked a girl.

"I do not know," said the brunette. "He was to wait, for his excellency, Lord Julian. There was some diplomatic mission or other, it seems. But he has gone!"

"What of all the hoverers, of the shuttle, of the *Narcona*?" asked another.

"The *Narcona* remains in orbit," said the brunette. "The shuttle is within her. The hoverers are covered, in the yard, with the supplies."

"Where did he go?"

"Who knows," said the brunette.

"Which direction did he go?" asked another girl.

"We do not know," said the brunette. "Doubtless he has his own plans, or destination."

"Surely a search was made!" said a girl.

"There are no traces," said the brunette. "The storm! The hoverers were forced to return, unable to maneuver."

"What is wrong, Cornhair?" asked the girl next to the blonde.

"Call me 'Filene'!" cried the blonde, in tears. "That is the name I have been given!"

"That is the name the masters gave you!" said the girl next to her. "Say it! It is the name the masters gave you!"

"Very well," said the blonde, in tears. "It is the name the masters have given me!"

"That is better, Cornhair," said the girl.

"I will buy and sell you all!" screamed the blonde. "I will see to it that you are all sold to beasts and reptiles!"

"Secure your freedom first, slave slut!" said the girl near her.

"Slut! Slut! Bitch! Bitch!" screamed the blonde.

"Be silent, slave," said she whose cot was near the door, she who was first girl.

"Yes, Mistress," said the blonde.

"What is wrong, Cornhair?" asked the girl on the other side of her.

"Nothing," said the blonde, and sat, frightened, on her cot, her legs drawn up, on the simple, striped mattress, the palms of her hands down upon it.

"I do not know what is going on," said another girl.

"Nor I," said another.

The blonde felt sick, and it seemed she was reeling. She was chained to a cot in a slave shed in a small town far from the inner Telnarian worlds. Her only garment, as was the case with the other girls, as well, was a simple, scandalously brief slave tunic. Her lovely legs were well bared. She looked at the ring on her ankle, with its attached chain. She could not slip it, no more than could the other girls in the shed.

For all they knew, and for all those in Venitzia might know, and for all those, or most of those, of the *Narcona* might know, she might even be a slave, an actual slave!

It might be easy enough to believe she was a slave.

Certainly she was beautiful enough to be a slave.

What if, somehow or other, her actual identity was lost? What if her protestations as to her true identity, her true status, as a free woman, were ignored, or disbelieved? She was far from home. What if she were merely beaten, as a mad slave? Doubtless Iaachus had seen to it that there were slave papers on her. She had even been, in Lisle, photographed, and measured, in detail, and fingerprinted, and toeprinted, as might have been any slave.

She had had a business to do, and it was to have been done on Tangara, presumably in some camp in the Tangaran wilderness, surely, in any event, not on the *Narcona*.

The *Narcona* and its crew were not to be compromised.

How could she manage it now?

Where was the dagger?

She did not even know, as yet, the identity of her mysterious confederate.

She recalled a night, two nights ago, on the *Narcona*.

"You summoned me?" she had asked.

"Why are you standing?" he had asked.

She had knelt before the young blond officer, Corelius.

He had a small, light, folded, silken sheet on the arm of his chair.

"Remove your tunic," he said.

"Surely," he said, "a command need not be repeated."

She drew the tiny tunic off, over her head, blushing.

"Surely you understand, Filene," he said, "that modesty is not permitted to a slave.

"The proper response," he said, "is 'Forgive me, Master. Yes, Master.'"

"Forgive me, Master," she said. "Yes, Master."

Can it be he, she wondered, is he my contact, the agent, he who will supply the dagger?

He tossed her the small sheet and she put it hastily, quickly, gratefully, about her. It came about her thighs, as she knelt, but was not long enough to cover her knees.

"What is the meaning of the removal of my clothing, and that I have been given this tiny sheet?" she asked.

"Were you given permission to speak?" he asked.

"Forgive me, Master," she said.

"But you are curious?"

"Yes, Master," she said.

"You are all alike," he said.

She stiffened.

"You have been called for," he said.

" 'Called for'?"

"Yes," he said.

"By whom?" she asked, frightened.

"Perhaps by Qualius," he said.

That was the name of the porcine stocksman, he with the fat face, with the tiny, closely set eyes, who had denied her even a rag in her cage.

She turned white.

She had not anticipated that she, in her adventure, in her pursuit of station, and wealth, might, if only to preserve the integrity of her guise as a slave, find herself put to slave use. Perhaps he was not the agent. Perhaps he did not know that she was truly free. How could she confess to him that she was not a slave?

"I jest," he smiled.

She shuddered, clutching the tiny sheet about her.

"Normally," he said, "stock slaves, in common transport, as opposed to privately owned slaves, are available to the crew, and officers, generally."

"Are we so available?" she asked.

"Interestingly, not," he said.

"We are special slaves," she said. "We are not even branded."

"You are available to the higher officers, the captain, the first officer, the supply officer, and such," he said.

"Oh," she said.

"Like the others," he said.

"You yourself, however," she said, lightly, but archly, boldly, "could not 'call for me.' "

"It might be arranged," he said.

She shrank back.

He smiled.

She sensed, uneasily, a slave's vulnerability. How could she make clear that she was not a slave?

"Who has called for me," she asked, "the captain?"

The captain, she speculated, might be the agent. He might want this opportunity to identify himself, to confirm her instructions, even to entrust her with the dagger.

"No," he said.

"Lysis, officer in charge of supply," she said.

It must be he, for it was he who was in charge of the slave consignment!

"Do not consider yourself meat of such interest," he said.

She made an angry noise, and clutched the sheet more closely about herself.

"To be sure," he said, "your body, though it requires some trimming, and is a bit stiff, is not without interest."

She was silent.

"It is more like the body of a free woman," he said.

"I see," she said.

"And your movements," he said, "lack the natural, seductive, vulnerable grace, the lovely, helpless, total femininity, of the female slave. They are too stiff, too awkward, too clumsy, too inhibited. They are like the movements of a free woman."

"I see," she said.

"To be sure," he said, "your body, and your movements, have improved considerably, even in the brief time you have been with us."

"Oh?" she said.

And then she was frightened, for she did not know what that might mean.

Perhaps there was something about kneeling before men, and being subject to the mastery?

She dared not speculate what it might be, to be actually a slave. Often, in the last few days, she had had to fight feelings which had begun to arise spontaneously, frighteningly, within her.

"Doubtless you are interested in knowing who has called for you," he said.

"Yes, Master!" she said. Then she was startled at how easily, how naturally, the word "Master" had escaped her lips. I am an excellent actress, she tried to reassure herself, but remained troubled, for the word had emerged as easily, as naturally, as a breath.

"Our guest, our passenger, the barbarian," he said.

She gasped.

Was the deed to be done so soon, even on the *Narcona*?

"It is your turn, of course, on the roster," he said, "in which the women are put up for slave use, but, interestingly, he has not, until now, availed himself of the offerings of the roster. It seems he does little but exercise, and practice with weapons, many of them primitive. Too, he spends much time on the observation deck, seemingly muchly given to thought. Perhaps he is intent upon conserving his strength, or maintaining a singleness of mind, of purpose."

"But he has called for me," she said, "and not the others."

"Yes," said Corelius.

She clutched the sheet about her again. Within its flimsy fabric her body suddenly flamed. She tried not to analyze her feelings. Could this be, in her body, that of the Lady Publennia, of Lisle, receptivity, and a receptivity so uncontrollable, and helpless, that it might be almost that of a slave?

"It seems you intrigue him," he said.

"As a slave?" she asked.

"I do not think so," he said. "I think it is something different. I think that he senses something different about you, and that he is curious about it."

"Oh," she said.

"It seems something puzzles him, or troubles him."

"I have troubled many men," she smiled.

"Remove the sheet!" he snapped.

"Yes, Master!" she said.

"As I have suggested," he said, "I do not think it is a mere matter of your embonded lineaments." And he then added, musingly, regarding her, "—as provocative as they might be."

"What then?" she asked.

"I am not even sure he thinks that you are a slave," he said.

"You seem frightened," he said.

"But he has called for me!" she said.

"That is true," said Corelius. "And surely you have put yourself frequently enough, blatantly enough, before him."

"Master!" she protested.

"Do you think that we, and your sisters in bondage, cannot see?"

She tossed her head, insolently.

"You are a true slave," he said.

She looked past him, toward the wall.

"We, and your sisters in bondage, can tell that, even if the barbarian cannot."

"I see," she said, acidly.

How could he know her subtlety, her plans, the nature of her project?

"When am I to be sent to him?" she said.

"Now," he said.

"Put the sheet about you," he said. "You may rise.

"Bring the sheet higher on your thighs," he said. "Turn."

She then again faced him.

"Am I to be alone with the barbarian?" she asked.

"Of course," he said.

"Have you nothing to tell me?" she asked. "Have you nothing to give me, nothing, no artifact, no implement?"

"I do not understand," he said.

"It is nothing," she whispered.

"I do have one thing to tell you," he said.

"Yes, Master!" she said, eagerly.

"Remember that you are a slave, being sent to a master," he said.

"Yes, Master," she said.

"You may go," said Corelius. "Outside you will find a mariner, waiting. He will conduct you to the quarters of our passenger."

"Yes, Master," she said.

"Is it not conjectured where the barbarian has gone?" asked one of the slaves, come from her heavy, metal, anchored cot in the long, low, cement slave shed at Venitzia, to the length of her ankle chain.

"There are a thousand conjectures," said the small brunette, the center of attention, who had come to the shed with the startling news of the barbarian's disappearance, ''but no one knows which, if any, are sound.''

''What is its meaning for us?'' asked one of the slaves.

''Surely it has nothing to do with us,'' said one of the slaves.

''It may,'' worried another.

''Who knows?'' said the small brunette.

Several of the slaves exchanged apprehensive glances.

''We should have been sold, all of us, long before now,'' said one of the slaves.

''What are we doing here in the shed?'' asked another. ''Why are we being kept here?''

The blonde sat, miserable, her entire body on the mattress of the cot, her knees raised, her legs together, now leaning forward, clasping her ankles with her hands, one hand, the left, on the shackle to which her chain was fastened. It was a fetching pose, and one not uncommon to slave girls. She had assumed it unconsciously. Suddenly aware, she drew her legs back, half under her, half sitting, half kneeling on the mattress, but that pose, too, she knew, would be arousing to men. Tears formed in her eyes. The slave garment, of course, if it were to be worn sensibly, almost dictated, like a short skirt, certain attitudes, certain postures, of the body. But, to her horror, in the last few days, she had found herself assuming, however clothed, or even if unclothed, naturally, unwittingly, unconsciously, bodily postures, and attitudes, which she had always associated, to her contempt, but to her envy, as well, with an inferior form of life, that of the female slave.

''Are they searching for him any longer?'' asked one of the girls.

''I do not think so,'' said the brunette.

''Perhaps when the storm abates,'' said a slave.

''Perhaps,'' said the brunette.

''They could go out with horses and dogs,'' said one of the slaves.

''Outside the fence, on horseback, or afoot?'' said one of the girls, skeptically.

''It would be too dangerous,'' said one of the girls.

''Why?'' asked another.

''Wild beasts, primitives, Heruls, and others,'' said one of the slaves.

''Are they dangerous, truly?'' asked a slave.

"Why do you think they have the fence?" asked another, scornfully.

"But this world belongs to the empire," said a slave.

"Tell it to the vi-cats, and the primitives," said another.

The girls shuddered.

"Are Heruls human?" asked one of the girls.

"I do not know," said another.

"Do they keep slaves?" asked the girl.

"Yes," she was told.

"They could use the hoverers," said one of the girls.

"Do you think you are on an inner world?" asked one of the girls.

"Fuel is precious, and soon exhausted," said another. "A considerable quantity would be required to search even a square latimeasure, if one were to do so with care."

On the cot, the blonde moaned.

The barbarian had vanished.

She was to do her work with the tiny dagger, as she understood it, when alone with the barbarian, in his tent, at one of the projected camps outside the fence, when the expedition was to have set forth, with mounts, and weapons, in force. She was then, presumably by hoverer, to be transported to safety, to a rendezvous with the shuttle, hence to be returned to the *Narcona*, and, eventually, to the inner worlds, to find herself one of the highest placed, richest and most envied women in the empire.

But now the barbarian had vanished!

Would he return, would he be found?

What of the plans of Iaachus?

And what of herself, she, if these plans should fail, she, now in a slave garment, and chained to a cot in a cement shed, in a remote provincial capital?

I should have been permitted to do the deed on the *Narcona*, she wept, to herself.

Why was I not given the dagger on the *Narcona*, she thought. I was alone with him then!

What fools men are, she thought.

But then who could have anticipated that the barbarian would slip away from Venitzia, that he would not wait for his excellency, Lord Julian, of the Aurelianii, that he would disappear, leaving the projected expedition, with all its men, and supplies, behind him, in Venitzia?

How could he have done such a thing?

What did it mean?

She wanted the deed to be done, and the sooner the better. She was a highly intelligent young woman, and was not unaware of subtle changes which, in the past few weeks, on shipboard, and here, in Venitzia, in the shed, and when she worked in the kitchens and laundry, were taking place within her. She had begun to find herself growing eager for the entrance of men into the shed, or the kitchen or laundry, that she might, with the others, kneel and perform obeisance. When she had, on all fours, been scrubbing a floor with others, she had tried to put her head against the boot of a keeper. Men, suddenly, had begun to appear creatures of great interest and fascination to her. For the first time in her life she had begun to find them attractive, powerfully, almost irresistibly so. She was warmed, and delighted, and thrilled to be chained at night. She wondered what it would be, to be in the arms of a man. She wondered what it would be, to be owned by one, to feel his cuffs and ropes, his caress, brutal or gentle, rude or delicate, his whip, if he were not pleased with her.

She had awakened at night, terrified, to find herself on the cot, chained.

She had dug at the cot with her fingernails.

I am not a slave, she would assure herself.

Why did they not give me the dagger on the *Narcona*, she asked herself.

She feared, you see, a thousand subtleties, the transformations being wrought within her consciousness, the changes taking place within her, the wonders, and beauties, the indications, the surprises, the promises, arising from within her depths.

Let the barbarian return, she thought. Give me the dagger! Let me strike! Let me be done with matters!

She feared, more and more, her slave feelings.

For a long time she had denied that she had had such feelings, but such a denial was now useless. She set herself now, accordingly, to resist them.

She feared herself, you see, what she had begun to sense she was becoming, and perhaps had always been.

Mostly, perhaps, she feared her intellect, that it would reflect upon her, that it would consider her, carefully, and deeply and wholly, with sensitivity, and in great detail, what she was, and should be, and would then put her on her knees.

Why was I not given the dagger on the *Narcona*, she moaned.

But then she laughed bitterly to herself.

She would have had little opportunity to use it.

"Enter," had said the barbarian.

"A slave," had said the mariner, presenting her.

She had knelt, as she had supposed was expected of her.

The barbarian had dismissed the mariner, and she had found herself kneeling before the barbarian, holding the sheet about her.

"What is your name?" he asked.

"Filene," she said.

He regarded her.

"—if it pleases Master," she said.

He sat down, on a chair, near the cabin couch. He wore a half tunic. He was blond-haired and blue-eyed, which was not uncommon among many of the barbarian peoples. He was a large, muscular man. His mighty chest was bared, save for a dangling necklace of claws, lion claws. They were from a beast he had slain on a hunt, in the forests of Varna. She speculated that they might leave a print on her body, were he to take her into his arms, and crush her to him, in the embrace of a master. She saw that the cabin couch had posts, at the head and foot. About one of the posts, at the foot, wrapped there, was a cord. On the steel wall, on one of its panels, on a hook, there hung a whip. On the surface of a small dresser there was a roll of tape.

"You are from Myron VII?" he said.

"Yes, Master," she said.

"A debtress sold to recover, in part, debts?"

"Yes, Master," she said.

"What were your debts?"

"In excess of ten thousand *darins*," she said.

"And what did you bring on the block?" he asked.

"Doubtless Master has read on my papers," she said, angrily.

"I cannot read," he said.

"Oh," she said. This startled her, for he was one of the few individuals she had met, in her travels, in her circles, who could not read. To be sure, literacy was a precious commodity in the empire, taken as a whole.

"Perhaps you remember," he said.

"Well over ten thousand *darins*!" she said.

"I should not think," he said, "that the sisters of an emperor would bring so much." He recalled blond-haired Viviana, and the younger, dark-haired Alacida, sisters of Aesilesius, met not long ago, on a summer world. Both were attractive. He had wondered what they might look like, as slaves.

"Fifty *darins*, Master," she said, quickly.

Perhaps he had lied about being unable to read, perhaps he had been told the price, perhaps it had been read to him. Iaachus, in his thoroughness, had included a forged bill of sale with the papers, as an insert. She had been furious at the supposed price of a mere fifty *darins*, but she had been informed, by an agent of Iaachus, that that was a remarkable price, and that a higher figure would not be likely to seem plausible, not for a debtress, from a remote world. Slaves were cheap, in many places in the empire.

"You are vain," he said, "and a liar."

He glanced to the whip, on its hook, on the steel panel.

"Forgive me, Master," she said, frightened. He did not know she was free. He might actually beat her, as a slave.

"Fifty *darins*," he said, "is a very high price."

"Thank you, Master," she said.

"Remove the sheet."

"Yes, Master."

"You are very beautiful," he said. "It is not inconceivable that you might bring fifty *darins*."

"Yes, Master," she said. "Thank you, Master."

Inwardly her feelings were tumultuous. As a free woman she knew herself to be priceless, but now, suddenly, she had some serious concept of what she might be worth, as a woman, as a female, if she were truly a slave. The supposed price, fifty *darins*, conceded by Iaachus, might even have been somewhat generous. This came to her as something of an abrupt shock, a most unsettling revelation.

"I am pleased that I was not one of your creditors," he said.

"They have had their vengeance, Master," she said, "as I am now a slave."

"I have wondered, sometimes," he said, "why women, understanding the penalties of defaulting in such matters, permit themselves to accumulate such debts."

"Doubtless we plan to pay them off," she said.

"There would seem great risks involved," he said.

She shrugged, uneasily.

She herself had accumulated considerable debts, on several worlds, but Iaachus had satisfied them. Many were the times she had pretended to be unavailable for inquiries. Often she had dreaded a heavy knock on her door. Sometimes, at night, she, even though of the senatorial class, had awakened, apprehensive of being brought to the dock, and sentenced to the iron, and the collar.

"Hold out your hands," he said, "where I can see them, clearly, spreading the fingers. Now, turn, fully about, on your knees, hands held over your head. Now bend over and shake out your hair, and run your hands through it, thoroughly, touching every part of your head. Now stand, hands over your head, and turn, slowly. Return to your knees. Spread your knees more widely. Now put yourself to your belly."

She looked up at him, angrily.

But, too, she was in consternation.

Naked, brought to him, the sheet removed, earlier kneeling, unable to rise quickly, feet from him, exposed, turning, rising, hands lifted, subjected to such scrutiny, how could a dagger be concealed?

To be sure, things might later be different, or the dagger might be planted in a tent, or smuggled to her later.

"You may now crawl to me, on your belly."

She then lay at his feet, her head turned to the left, her cheek on the rug.

"This is the first time you have crawled to a man on your belly, is it not?" he asked.

"Yes, Master," she said, angrily.

"Go back, and do it better," he said.

Three times he had her repeat this exercise.

At last he seemed satisfied.

"Kneel up," he said, "before me, back on your heels, knees spread, hands clasped behind the back of your head."

"Tell me about yourself, specifically, and in detail," he said.

She had been given an identity, and many specifics, in particular pertaining to her supposed debts, her arraignment, her sentencing, the name of the supposed court, and judge, and such, things concerning which it was anticipated she might be questioned. Where this putative biography fell short, and his direct questions exceeded her preparation, she hurried to supply further data, some of it from her own history, suitably disguised, the rest of it the product of her own invention.

"You stammer and falter," he said.

"Forgive me, Master," she said.

"But still, on the whole," he said, "it is unusual to find a slave who can speak of herself so articulately, so volubly, so readily. It is almost as though you had been prepared."

"Forgive me, Master," she said.

"You seem more familiar with the details of your enslavement than with those of your life as a free woman," he said.

"The details of one's embondment," she said, "are often vivid for a woman."

"For a girl," he said.

"Yes, Master," she said.

"For a slave girl," he said.

"Yes, Master," she said.

He had, of course, she before him, been reading her body, and her expressions.

"You are from Myron VII?" he said.

"Yes, Master," she said.

"What color is its sun?" he asked. "How long is its year, in Telnarian days?"

She began to tremble.

The questions were so obvious that they had not been anticipated.

She dared not invent answers to such questions. What did the barbarian know? Were his questions innocent, matters of pure curiosity, or were they subtler, and dangerous?

"I am not truly from Myron VII," she said. "I am from Lisle, on Inez IV! I fled to Myron VII to escape my creditors. I was apprehended in the port. I did not even see its sun. I know nothing of that world, other than the fact that it was there that I was taken into custody, and there tried and sentenced."

"And you were then returned, a slave, to Inez IV?"

"Yes, yes!" she said.

"May I take my arms down?" she asked.

"No," he said.

"You have told many lies," he said.

"No, Master!" she protested.

"Do not compound your fault," he said.

"No, Master," she said, tears springing to her eyes.

"I would not advise you to behave in that manner when you have a private master," he said.

"No, Master," she said.

"Lies are not permitted to a slave girl," he said.

"No, Master," she said.

"But you will probably not believe that until you are thoroughly beaten," he said.

"Forgive me, Master," she said.

"When we were shortly out of Lisle," he said, "you were clumsy."

He referred, doubtless, to the incident of the spilled drink.

"I was switched," she said.

"Are you a clumsy slave?" he asked.

Her eyes flashed.

Then she put her head down.

"I do not think so, Master," she said. "It is my hope that I am not clumsy."

"In serving at the table," he said, "a slave is to be graceful, unobtrusive and deferent."

"Yes, Master," she said.

She looked up.

"May I lower my arms?" she asked.

"No," he said.

She moved angrily, not having obtained her way.

"Am I mistaken," he asked, "that you have, upon several occasions, placed yourself provocatively before me?"

"Oh, Master," she said, quickly. "Forgive me, but I fear that it is true. You are a man, and I am naught but a slave girl. How else can a poor slave call herself to the attention of an attractive master?"

"You find me attractive?" he asked.

"Yes, Master."

"You wanted to meet me?"

"Yes, Master!"

"You desire a man's touch?" he asked.

"Oh, yes, yes, Master!" she said.

Surely she must interest him, even drive him mad with desire for her, that she might be alone with him, when she had the dagger! But now, of course, she did not have the dagger. If she had been a free woman she might have teased, and drawn away, and teased, and drawn away, until the time and place were arranged, until she was ready, but such behaviors are not easy for a slave.

He put out his hand and touched her, gently.

"Ai!" she cried, frightened, and drew back.

"Keep your hands behind your head," he cautioned her, gently. "I thought you said you desired a man's touch," he said.

"Forgive me, Master," she said. She came forward a little, deliberately, trembling.

He put forth his hand again, gently.

"Ah!" she said, softly, surprised. Then she flushed scarlet before him.

Quickly, then, almost as though she had not consented to her own movement, she squirmed forward a little, closer to him, but was stopped, by his hand, and held in place.

"Master?" she asked.

"Interesting," he said.

She regarded the necklace of claws on his chest.

What would it be like, she wondered, to be swept into his arms, she helpless and will-less, to be swept uncompromisingly into his arms, as a slave.

"Master has called for me," she said.

"Yes," he said.

"Surely master has called for me, to ravish me, as a slave," she said.

"No," he said.

" 'No'?" she asked.

"No," he said. "I have called for you because it seems to me that there is something different about you, something different from other female slaves. I did not understand it. I was curious about it."

"That is all?" she asked.

"No," he said.

"Ah!" she said.

"You may polish my boots," he said, indicating a pair of boots, to one side. "The polish and rags are in the adjacent cabinet.

"You may lower your arms, of course," he said.

"Thank you, Master," she said, acidly.

She fetched the boots, and the cleaning materials and, kneeling before him, where he had indicated, addressed herself to the assigned task. She worked slowly and carefully, meticulously, responding to his direction, applying a small quantity of paste to a small area, working it into the leather, with firm, circular movements, and then buffing it. This was done again and again, a tiny area at a time, until the entire area of each boot had been done twice.

She was shaken, when she had performed this small, homely

task. She was angry, but, too, seemingly unaccountably, she found herself much aroused.

To her surprise she was drawn on her knees to the post at the foot of the bed, that about which the cord was wrapped. Her wrists were then crossed and bound with the cord, which was then fastened to the post. She was thus tied, wrists crossed and bound, on her knees, to the post at the foot of the bed.

"Master?" she asked.

"I think I know now," he said, "what is unusual about you."

"Master?" she said, apprehensively.

"Can you guess what it might be?" he asked.

She was frightened.

Her mind raced.

"Perhaps Master suspects that I am not truly a slave," she said, lightly, tentatively, as though in jest.

What else could it be?

Certainly she could protest the authenticity of her bondage. There were the papers, in which she was clearly specified, even to toeprints. Indeed, obviously, there was her very presence on the ship, amongst women anyone could see were slaves.

"No," he said.

"Oh?" she said.

"You are truly a slave," he said. "There is no doubt about that. You are truly a slave."

"What then?" she asked.

"It is only that you do not know you are a slave," he said.

She looked up at him, but he had gone to the side, where, on the surface of a small dresser, there lay the roll of tape.

"Lift your head, look at me, close your mouth," he said.

He then, using the metal, saw-toothed extension, part of the roller, snapped off a few inches of tape, and put it across her lips and face. She felt it pressed down, firmly.

"I have heard you enough," he said. "You will now be silent."

She looked up at him, over the tape.

He then applied an additional length of tape, longer than the first, firmly, over it.

"It is a bit late to return you to the slave room," he said.

He then applied a third length of tape, longer than the second, pressing it into place. This came well about the back of her neck. He then, moving her hair about, that as little of the tape might adhere to it as possible, encircled her mouth and head three times, the free end of the tape being pressed down, at last, behind the back of her neck.

Then he looked down upon her. "You are tempting," he said.

She looked quickly away, down.

He then snapped off the light, and retired.

After a time she tried to struggle, but found her struggles useless.

She knelt there, for a long time, angrily.

She could not sleep.

She tried to speak, late in the night, but was unable to do so. She had been silenced, and bound, as might have been a slave.

Later, at times, she whimpered, and moaned, a little, as she could, helpless, begging for attention.

But there was no sign that she was heard.

Toward morning, her head on the foot of the bed, inches from his feet, she slept. A mariner came for her later. The barbarian had already left the cabin.

"It is clear that the barbarian has disappeared," the small brunette was saying, she scarcely within the entrance to the long, low cement slave shed at Venitzia, "and it is not known where!"

The blonde, half sitting, half kneeling, in the tiny slave tunic, on the thin, hard, striped mattress of the metal cot, to which she was chained, gasped, her head reeling as she struggled to comprehend the import of the brunette's revelation.

"What is wrong, Cornhair?" asked one of the other slaves. Few had noticed the agitation of the blonde.

"Nothing," gasped the blonde.

"Has this anything to do with us?" one of the slaves was asking the brunette.

"I do not know!" said the brunette.

"Who cares about the barbarian," said one of the girls. "What about us?"

"Yes!" cried another.

"We have been here for days," said one of the girls.

"Why are we being kept here, in this shed, in the administration compound?" asked another.

"Why have we not been sold?" asked another.

"Irons should have been heated for us by now," said another. "We should have been put on the block!"

Only the blonde, of all the women in the shed, had a clear

idea of the putative purport of the slave consignment to Venitzia. Only she knew that the women were not, by intent, destined for a sale in Venitzia.

If the barbarian is gone, thought the blonde, wildly, then perhaps I need not use the knife! But then, surely, the agent will identify himself to me, and assure my safe return to Lisle. But what if he does not? What if, for some reason, the agent had not even been on the ship? What then? She knew Iaachus was thorough. Her slave papers would doubtless appear in perfect order!

"Perhaps we will be put up for sale tomorrow," said a girl.

"Fools! Fools!" suddenly screamed the blonde, from her cot. "Are you not aware of the goods embarked with us at Lisle? Are you not aware of the stores in the warehouse within the compound, some even under canvas, under snow, in the yard! They have not been moved either! You are not intended for Venitzia, fools! You are trade goods, trade goods!"

"No!" screamed one of the slaves.

"Cornhair is a liar!" cried one of the girls.

"Beat her!" cried another.

There was a sudden rattling of chains.

The blonde shrieked and knelt down on the cot, covering her head.

To be sure, only two of the girls could reach her, given the shed's custodial arrangements.

The blows of small fists rained upon her.

The blonde shrank even smaller on the cot, whimpering.

"No, no!" called the first girl, chained near the door. "Stop! Stop!"

The blows stopped. The assailants were half hysterical, weeping, as well as furious.

"I fear Cornhair is right," said she who was first girl.

"Trade goods?" said one of the slaves, aghast.

"Yes," said the first girl.

"But to whom?" asked another slave, her voice quavering.

"Barbarians, Heruls, primitives, who knows," said the first girl.

"Whomever they like," said another slave, fearfully.

"They cannot do that!" said one of the slaves.

"They can do as they wish," said the first girl. "We are slaves."

"We can be disposed of as masters wish," said one of the girls, frightened.

"Yes," whispered another, "we are slaves."

The blonde sank to her stomach on the cot, her head turned, her right cheek on the mattress, her fingers clutching its sides. She moved her left ankle a little, feeling the shackle, and its weight.

• • • CHAPTER 16 • • •

"Is he alive?" asked Varix.

"I do not know," said Olar.

"Is it a Herul?" asked Varix.

"No," said Olar.

"Then we need not kill him," said Varix.

"I think he is dead already," said Olar.

"See if he is Telnarian," said Varix. "He may have money."

"I do not think he is Telnarian," said Olar.

"What is he?" asked Varix.

"He has the appearance of an Otung," said Olar.

"Not here, not this faraway," said Varix.

Varix looked about, warily, apprehensively.

"I do not like it," he said.

Varix wore, over his eyes, tied at the edges with leather, a curved bone plate. It was cut with a horizontal slit, which eliminated most of the glare from the snow. Olar was similarly protected. It was bright and cold on the plains of Barrionuevo this afternoon. The sun blazed off the snow. It was in the month of Igon. One, unprotected, could go blind on such days. Both men wore fur, and deep fur boots. Each was armed, Varix with knife and ax, Olar with knife and spear.

Both were hunting vi-cat.

One had been seen yesterday, crossing the Lothar, on the ice, moving eastward.

They had been following its trail all morning, but now the hunt, for the moment, was forgotten.

"If he is dead, let us rob him, and be gone," said Varix. "If he is not dead, let us kill him, and see if he has anything of value."

"We are not Heruls," said Olar.

"We are poor men," said Varix.

"He may be a Herul spy," said Olar.

"The body," said Varix, wading through the snow, coming to the edge of the sledge, on which lay the remains of a horse, and, within the body of the horse, the shape of a man, or manlike creature, "does not appear malnourished."

"Perhaps he died recently," said Olar.

"He may not be dead," said Varix.

"The cold can keep things for a long time," said Olar.

Varix stepped back, wading backward, away from the sledge.

"Come back," said Varix.

Olar, turning, struggled back a few feet in the snow, to join Varix. Then both faced the sledge.

"See the tracks," said Varix, pointing. "The man must have been in the traces, drawing the carcass of the horse."

"Why?" asked Olar.

"I do not know," said Varix.

"He must have been strong," said Olar.

"He could feed on the horse," said Varix.

"He may not be dead," said Olar.

"That is what I think," said Varix.

"See, on the sledge," whispered Olar. "The rolled pelt of a vi-cat."

"It is not the pelt of the one we seek," said Varix.

"No," said Olar. "It is mottled."

Both men then backed away, a little farther, in the bright snow.

"It is the bait trap," said Varix.

"Yes," said Olar.

"He is Herul," said Varix.

"He is not a Herul," insisted Olar.

It is a mode of hunting occasionally practiced by Heruls. The hunter lies in wait, within the carcass, and when the vi-cat, or wolf, or *arn* bear or snow bear, come down from the north, in the time of Igon, prowls closely enough, the hunter, with spear, or long, thrusting blade, strikes. Commonly he is supported by others in the vicinity, lying covered in the snow, ready to spring, at a cry, to his aid. The animal, if not slain, is usually grievously wounded, and, slowed, may be trailed in the snow, the trail marked by blood.

"Do you understand what I am saying?" called Olar to the form within the carcass. "Are you alive?"

There was no response.

"I am afraid," said Varix.

"Why?" asked Olar.

"That it is the bait trap," said Varix.

"Why does that alarm you?" asked Olar.

"I think it is not now set for the vi-cat," said Varix.

"For what, then?" asked Olar.

"For us, I fear," said Varix.

At that time, suddenly, behind them, was heard the tiny jangle of harness, and the sound of a horse.

Both men turned.

"Heruls!" cried Olar.

There were seven Heruls, all told, three now behind them, and, in a moment, four others, two now approaching from the front, from behind the sledge, as they stood, and now two more, one from each side, in their dark leather, their fur capes, the conical, fur-trimmed helmets, with the slender, long, wandlike lances. Small bucklers were at the left side of their saddles. They had not even freed the bucklers. The four who had come from the front and sides now, too, drew up, reining in.

The circle was some ten yards in diameter.

In its center were Olar and Varix, and the sledge, with its weights.

There was a small sound of harness metal, as the beasts shifted in the snow, the sound of their breathing. Their breath hung about their snouts like fog. These were Herul mounts which, for simplicity, as is our wont with mounts of diverse species, we shall speak of as horses.

"Can you understand us?" called the leader of the Heruls to Olar and Varix.

"Yes," said Varix.

Whereas countless modalities of communication, as well as countless languages, verbal and gestural, coexisted in the galaxies, Telnarian, in its imperial purity, and in its dialects, and its corruptions, was, by creatures capable of forming its sounds, or analogues to them, by far the most commonly spoken. Even fierce enemies of the empire, in order to make themselves understood to one another, often had no alternative to conversing in Telnarian. The influence, linguistic and cultural, if not the civil and military presence, of the empire was, for millions of rational creatures, a fact of life. There were various legends to the effect that Orak, the king of the gods, had invented Telnarian that men might be able to converse with one another. It was generally regarded as the mother tongue of rational creatures. That Telnarian bore within itself innumerable traces of earlier languages, from which it seems to have emerged, was a fact understood by, and appreciated by, few but scholars. But there was little doubt that Telnarian, or the language that bears that name, was an ancient one. It was present in a developed form, even in the dim beginnings of the empire, as the most ancient of the imperial carvings, inscriptions and plaques attested. The language was apparently spoken by several related peoples, one of these peoples being the Telnarians, which people founded the empire. And, of course, it is by the name of that people that the language came to be known.

"Are you hunting?" asked the lead Herul, cheerfully enough, moving his horse a yard or two closer, in the snow. The snow came to the knees of the beast. It came rather to the thighs of the men.

"Yes," said Olar.

"Vi-cat," said Varix.

"Are you hunting?" asked Olar, of the chief Herul.

"Yes," he said.

"Men?" inquired Varix.

"Vi-cat," said the chief Herul.

"Perhaps it is the same beast," suggested Olar.

"Perhaps," said the Herul.

"A giant white?" asked Olar.

"Yes," said the chief Herul.

"Doubtless it is the same," said Varix.

"Yes," said the Herul. "But it seems we have caught men."

"This is not your bait trap then?" asked Olar.

"No, is it not yours?" asked the Herul.

"No," said Olar.

"Where would you like to die," asked the Herul, "here, or in the camp?"

"They are scrawny, for soup," said one of the Heruls.

"We are afoot, you on horseback!" said Olar, angrily.

"We do not allow mounts to such as you," said one of the Heruls.

"Let us take them back to camp, and run them naked, in the snow, for the dogs," said one of the Heruls.

"Spare us!" said Olar.

"You are not women," said one of the Heruls. "Sometimes we spare them."

"We work them well," said another.

"They are pleasant to whip," said one.

"Their hairless skins mark delightfully," said another, "and they squirm well."

"Too, with their small bodies and smooth skins," said another, "we find them interesting, and different, in the thongs and furs."

"You are on horseback," said Olar. "There are seven of you."

"You should not be on the flats of Tung," said another.

"You should not have crossed the Lothar," laughed another.

"Rope them," said the leader of the Heruls.

▪ ▪ ▪ CHAPTER 17 ▪ ▪ ▪

"You must forgive us," said Brother Gregory, leading the way, carrying a small, shielded lamp in one appendage, descending the long, spiraling damp stairs, down, down into one of the humid, heated, murky depths of the *festung*, "but it is restorative, and, upon occasion, imperative, for several of the brothers to keep their skins moist."

"I understand," said Julian.

He had removed his jacket, and his shirt was soaked with dampness and sweat.

He could hear the chanting of the brothers.

Here and there, in niches, were small votive tablets.

"Is that a female?" had cried the gatesman in horror, pointing to the small figure with Julian and Tuvo Ausonius, all three long disembarked below, in the valley, from the hoverer.

The outer gate to the *festung* had creaked open, slowly, to admit the travelers.

It was a long, winding, tortuous trail up from the level, up from the valley, one of several miles, to the outer gate of the *festung*.

It was seldom traveled. Visitors were few at the *festung* of Sim Giadini.

At the village below they had learned that it would not be wise to approach the *festung*, save in this fashion, on foot and not obviously armed.

There were defenses, at various levels, which must be specifically, and consecutively, disarmed.

This was done from within the *festung*, the deactivations consequent, at given levels, upon judgments, given the data of diverse surveillance devices.

Too, a known man of the village had accompanied them, as a guide.

"Yes," had said Julian.

"Nothing female may enter here," said the gatesmen.

"This is the hospitality of the *festung* of Sim Giadini?" had asked Julian, irritatedly.

"She does not appear in desperate need of medical assistance, she is not bleeding, she is not dying," said the gatesmen.

"No," admitted Julian.

"She may not enter," said the gatesmen.

He averted his eyes that he might not look upon, and perhaps be tempted by, what was now in the company of Julian and Tuvo Ausonius.

"Surely she is sufficiently concealed," said Tuvo Ausonius.

The object of their discussion, small, fur-booted, and heavily bundled in furs, was kneeling on the stones before the gate, which posture she had assumed, correctly, suitably, while waiting for the response to the great metal ring, lifted and dropped three times, as the guide had advised, against the plate.

In her days with Julian and Tuvo Ausonius, thanks to their intensive training, she had made considerable progress in learning her slavery.

Her arms were not in the sleeves of her jacket but within the jacket, the wrists cuffed together, behind her back.

About her throat, over the furs there, there was a metal leash collar, from which, gracefully dangling, in loops, threaded through loops on the jacket, was a lovely, light, chain leash.

Commonly, in the transport of slaves by primitive peoples over the snow, in sleds, the slaves are simply, in their chains, wrapped naked in heavy furs. In this fashion there is little danger that they will be tempted to flee the sleds, or, huddling, chained, by the fires, the camps.

"It does not matter," said the gatesman.

"She is only an animal, a slave," said Tuvo Ausonius.

The woman looked up. Her head was muchly covered by the bundling of the fur hood, but it could be seen that her face was exquisite. Wisps of red hair peeked out from within the hood, framing her lovely features.

"Not even female animals are permitted within the *festung*," said the gatesman. "Nothing female, no female bird, no hen, no ewe, no cow, no bitch, no mare, no sow, nothing female."

"Put down your head," said Julian.

The slave instantly lowered her head.

"You may look on her now," said Julian. "You can see nothing."

"No," said the gatesman, "I can see furs, and it is not difficult to detect, from their configuration, that within them there is a female."

"I fear he is right, milord," said Tuvo Ausonius.

The small figure, the center of such attention, trembled a little, on her knees, her head down.

"Take her away!" cried the gatesman.

"Take her back to the valley, to the hoverer," said Julian.

"Milord!" protested Tuvo Ausonius.

"It is all right," said Julian. "I should have anticipated this."

"I shall have to close the gate," said the gatesman.

"She is leaving," said Julian.

Julian gestured, with his head, to Tuvo Ausonius.

"On your feet, girl," said Tuvo Ausonius.

She rose up and followed Tuvo Ausonius, head down, with small steps, deferentially, who drew away from the vicinity of the gate, to where the guide stood.

"May I now enter?" inquired Julian.

"Certainly," said the gatesman.

Standing near the guide, and Tuvo Ausonius, she looked back, toward the gate.

The gatesman, with his weight, with two hands, was pressing the gate shut. He paused for a moment, Julian within, impatient, beyond him, to view the slave, even bundled as she was, angrily, and then shut the gate, firmly.

She heard the two heavy bars being slid through their brackets behind the gate, first one, and then the other.

She briefly met the eyes of the guide, a rude fellow, from below, and then looked away.

She had seen desire in his eyes.

He was a peasant, simple, brutal, rude, lustful.

She had become aware of her desirability here again, as she had on the patrol ship, serving the crew's mess, barefoot, in a collar and slave rag, and in the appreciative glances of Julian and Tuvo Ausonius, as they sought to improve her posture, her movements and skills, until they would be likely to meet the requirements of even an unusually exacting master. And now here, again, she had become aware of her desirability, twice, in quite different ways, once in the loathing, the anger and disgust of the gatesman, fighting a naturalness and might which he had mistakenly, ignorantly, forsworn, he the deluded, self-tortured victim of a grotesque conditioning program, one promulgating, even celebrating, thwarted drives and suppressed desires, and that of the peasant, who had looked upon her with hardy approbation, much as he might have upon a fine pig.

She was aware now, from many indications, of her desirability, and its effect on men, and the power which she might, in virtue of it, under different circumstances, have held over men.

It is no wonder, she thought, that they strip us, and chain us, and cage us, and put us up for sale.

We are too beautiful, and too dangerous, to be free. It is wrong that we should be free! It is absurd that we should be free! We belong to them by nature, and they will see to it that they own us. It is no surprise then, she thought, that they do with us as they please.

We belong to them, she thought. I do not object. I love them. Let them be strong with us! I despise weak men. Oh, be strong with me, Masters!

"Come, girl!" called Tuvo Ausonius.

He and the guide were already several yards down the trail.

"Yes, Master!" she called, and hurried after them.

Tuvo Ausonius was a master of women. But he had not so much as put a hand on her. He cared, it seemed, for some other slave, a Sesella, back on Inez IV. But surely he could have two slaves. Some men had several! Lord Julian, too, whose identity she had learned, kneeling before him naked, in obeisance, on the patrol ship, she sensed was a natural master of women, but he had not touched her either, other than once to tie her, and whip her, for clumsiness. He had some barbarian slave, it seemed, of which he was fond. But she was sure she could compete, at least after more training, with a mere barbarian. Let him choose between us, she thought, or have both of us, and others! But she had not been given to the crew, either. She was a virgin, which was not unusual, as she had been purchased at an early age, fourteen, to be a woman's slave.

That she was a virgin seemed to be of interest to some men. She was not certain why that was. To be sure, it was important to her. She would not have wanted to awaken in her cell, for example, and discover that her virginity was simply gone.

She hurried down the trail, to catch up with the men.

They were far ahead now, and were not looking back.

She fell once, heavily, twisting in her fall to her left shoulder, unable to break her fall because of the back-cuffing, confining her wrists. Whimpering, she regained her feet, and, pulling a little at her small, encircled, chained wrists, the leash chain striking against the furs, continued on down the trail, hastening after the men.

They were even farther ahead now.

She called out, "Wait, Masters! Please, wait!"

But they did not wait.

She hurried on.

She did not dare to call out again. She did not wish to risk being beaten.

"Brother Benjamin!" called Brother Gregory, gently.

Brother Gregory stood on damp stones, at the edge of a broad, dark, warm pool.

He lifted up his tiny lamp.

The chamber was itself lit, though dimly, with similar lamps, set here and there on a shallow, circular shelf, its structure following the perimeter of the chamber, which was round, and shallowly domed.

These lamps were brought to the depths by the brothers, and taken with them, when they ascended to the higher levels.

There was a gentle stirring in the dark waters, and several pairs of eyes surfaced, large, round eyes.

The eyes seemed to stare at Julian.

It was difficult to read any expression in such features, without clues from the body.

"I trust," said Julian, "I am not disturbing their meditations, or devotions."

"It is time for the seventh bell," said Brother Gregory. "I would not have brought you here so soon, otherwise."

"Oh," said Julian.

"Not all brothers are of this species, of course," said Brother Gregory.

"I understand," said Julian.

Brother Gregory himself, obviously, was not.

"But our redemptor, our Lord Floon, blessed be his holy name, was of such a species."

"A bipedalian salamandrine?" said Julian.

"An ogg," said Brother Gregory.

"It seems strange that your Karch would emanate, as I understand it, as an ogg," said Julian.

"Why?" asked Brother Gregory.

"You're right," said Julian, shrugging. "Why not?"

"Perhaps you think he should have emanated as a man?"

Julian shrugged.

There had seemed a bit of testiness in Brother Gregory's speculation.

Brother Gregory was an azure-pelted Vorite.

"He can emanate in whatever form he pleases," said Julian.

"True," said Brother Gregory.

"I would speak with one who is called Brother Benjamin," said Julian, addressing himself to the occupants of the pool.

There was, at that time, as though from far off, the sound of a bell, its sounds making their way oddly about the stairwells, and down, to the chamber, and doubtless to others, as well, here and there, in the depths and heights, and throughout the labyrinthine corridors and chambers of the *festung*. It could probably be heard far below, in the valley.

"Turn about," said Brother Gregory, "for the brothers must robe themselves."

Julian turned about.

He heard sounds behind him, soft, of moving water, of bodies emerging from the pool, of dripping water, of the pat of feet on the stones.

"I am Brother Benjamin," said a voice behind him.

"I am Julian, of the Aurelianii, of the patricians, of the senatorial class, kin to the emperor, Aesilesius," said Julian, not turning about. "I have credentials to make that clear."

"You are then Telnarian," said the voice.

"Yes," said Julian.

"He has come to inquire about 'Dog,' " said Brother Gregory.

"I have waited years for one to come," said the voice behind Julian, "but I did not think it would be a Telnarian."

"What then?" asked Julian.

"I thought it would be an Otung, a Vandal," said the voice behind Julian.

Brother Gregory shuddered.

"Do you know the identity of the one you call 'Dog'?" asked Julian.

"Yes," said the voice behind him.

"Can you prove that identity?" asked Julian.

"Yes," said the voice.

"May I turn about?" asked Julian.

"I would not," said Brother Gregory. "He is half-garbed, but the wounds are still fresh, of the penitential exercises."

"It is a mark of vanity," added Brother Gregory, "to wear a stained habit."

"Penitential exercises?" asked Julian.

"The stone saws, beneath the surface of the pool," said Brother Gregory.

"How can you prove his identity?" asked Julian.

"I will show you," said the voice. "Proceed me, up the stairs."

Brother Gregory, with his lamp, led the way, Julian following. Behind them came the brothers, each with his lamp, and, together, intoning a hymn to Floon.

"Surely you will dine with us in the refectory, and stay the night," said Brother Gregory.

"I would be soon gone," said Julian.

"We get few visitors at the *festung*," said Brother Gregory. "You are the first stranger in two years."

"I must decline," said Julian.

"Some of the brothers, the weaker ones, I fear, amongst whom I number myself," said Brother Gregory, "will be eager to hear news of the outside world."

"I am sorry," said Julian.

"At night the trail is extremely dangerous, the activated defenses, set by automatic timers, at places, the dogs," said Brother Gregory. "It is unlikely you would reach the village alive."

"Then," said Julian, "I am pleased to accept your gracious invitation."

"Excellent," said Brother Gregory.

Julian noted, as he climbed the stairs, and as he had earlier, in his descent, but had thought little of it, that they were darkly stained.

Julian noted, on the climb, in a niche, illuminated by a votive light, a representation of Floon in the electric chair, or, perhaps better, fastened on the burning rack, the pain represented in the twisted body, the expression of misery on the countenance. It made Julian sick. How different it was from the bright sunlight and blue skies of the pantheon of Orak.

But it was here, in the *festung* of Sim Giadini, that there lay the secret to the identity of the peasant, or gladiator, or warrior, or chieftain, or captain, whom he knew as Otto, or Ottonius.

"What is the proof?" he asked.

"You will see," said the voice behind him.

· · · CHAPTER 18 · · ·

The location of the beast was not a matter of coincidence, not after the first moments.

It was incredibly alert, every sense sharp and alive, like needles, tense with excitement.

In its belly burned the cold rage of hunger.

Such creatures did not hibernate, even in the month of Igon. It had survived eight winters on the plains of Barrionuevo.

Little more than its eyes and nostrils could now be detected, had one known where to look and what to look for, it lying still, in the snow.

The wind was blowing, softly, doing little more than stirring the snow at the summit of drifts.

The odor of horses, and of Heruls, and men, was brought to the broad, dilating nostrils of the beast. These odors were as discernible, and unmistakable, to the beast as a sighting would have been to a more visually oriented form of life. The direction of the wind, contrariwise, predictably, would not carry its own scent to the horses.

It moved in the direction from which the odors were wafted,

its body low, little more than a wrinkle, or a shifting crest, stirred by the wind, of snow.

It moved a little and stopped, and moved a little, again, and stopped, again.

While it stopped there was almost no movement, save for the infrequent opening and closing of the eyes, large, and green, with their black, narrow, vertical pupils, better than two inches in height, and an occasional, small, agitated movement of the tail, white, whiplike, in the snow, betraying its excitement.

Then, more than two hundred yards away, as it lay eager, and trembling, and silken and white, almost flat in the snow, almost invisible, white on white, little more than its eyes and nostrils showing, it saw dark shapes moving about, shapes which stood out, clearly, even to its vision, at this distance, from the background, from the snow, which shapes, clearly, were the sources of the maddeningly exhilarating, irresistible odors, odors such that, in the month of Igon, they might drive such a beast mad. The smallest of contented, purring sounds escaped its great throat.

It waited until none of the shapes was turned its way, and then it moved forward again, a little closer.

· · · CHAPTER 19 · · ·

"They are trussed like the *vardas* they are," said one of the Heruls, stepping back.

"How," asked Olar, "so tied, can we run at your stirrup, how, so tied, can we pull in the traces of the sledge?"

"It would be difficult," said the leader of the Heruls, still mounted, as were four other Heruls. Two had dismounted to tie Olar and Varix.

"I do not understand," said Varix.

"Break up the sledge, for firewood," said the leader of the Heruls.

"I do not understand," said Varix.

"It is not your bait trap, nor is it ours," said the leader of the Heruls. "It will do for firewood."

"You are cold?" asked Olar.

"Do you think we are beasts, to eat raw meat?" asked the leader of the Heruls.

"We have no kettles with us," said one of the Heruls who was dismounted.

"Do you think we would run such as you for the dogs?" asked another, one who was mounted.

"No!" cried Olar.

"Why?" asked Varix.

"You did not fight," said the leader of the Heruls.

"I can remember when Vandals fought," said another.

"You are mounted, we are on foot!" said Olar.

"We are hungry," said one of the dismounted Heruls.

"You will roast well," said the other.

Olar and Varix, tied back to back, sitting in the snow, their ankles crossed and bound, struggled.

"Break up the sledge," said the leader of the Heruls. He held his lance in his right hand, or, perhaps better, appendage. It was a multiply jointed, haired tentacle, now sheathed in a beaded, fringed, mittenlike fur sleeve. He had two such hands, or appendages, or tentacles, as did the others, an arrangement which tended to be common, given the selective advantages of paired, symmetrical structures. At the tip of each tentacle, recessed beneath a contractible callosity, there was a tiny anatomical feature, a small, caplike sensory organ. Its function has been likened to that of taste, and even to sight and smell, but these sensory modalities are available to the Heruls, and the Hageen, as, indeed, given their advantages, to millions of diverse species throughout the galaxies. To be sure, that two species have a sense of taste, or such, does not guarantee that their experiences are identical. Even in something as obvious as vision, it is not clear, for example, that the visual experiences of diverse species are identical, for example, with respect to what can be seen, and how it can be experienced. Similarly, it seems unlikely that the visual experiences of, say, insects and men are identical. And, too, the visual experiences of an organism which has eyes on the sides of its head may be rather different, in consciousness, than one which, say, has the eyes in the front of the head, permitting a binocular focus, and such. The visual experiences of a creature with eye stalks or seven eyes, placed at diverse places on the body, laterally, ventrally, dorsally, and such, may be different, as well. We shall not attempt to speculate on the specific nature of the sensory experience correlated with the small, protected, tentacular sensory organ of the Heruls. We ourselves have never had such an experience. To those who have had the experience, a verbal description would doubtless be superfluous. To those who have not had the experience a verbal description would doubtless be unilluminating, if not unintelligible. Figures of speech may or may not be helpful. There seems dispute on such a matter. For example, suppose that one lacked particular sensory modalities. Then, would it be helpful to say, really, for example, that the taste of an orange is like seeing the sun at midday, that the smell of wet grass is like the taste of wine, that the blare of a trumpet is like the heat of fire? But the function of the Herul organ, or one of its utilities, at least, is clearly recognition. It seems clear that, in some sense, it reads, or reacts to, on a cellular, or subcellular, level, with consequences in consciousness, the chemistry, if not the very hereditary coils, of an organism, in a very specific fashion. The organ, which is not vestigial, seems to antedate the development of other senses, such as sight and hearing, in the evolution of the Herul organism. It, or its predecessor, seems to have functioned in making determinations as to self-identity, and to what might be ingested and what not. It seems to have prevented, in the beginning, certain chemical macrocompounds from being self-destructive, for example, from predating on their own bodies, and to make determinations as to what might be absorbed profitably into their own systems and what not. To be sure, putting it in this fashion suggests a teleology. The compounds which, for example, were uninhibited in self-predation tended to perish, and those who found poisonous substances acceptable, or even attractive, for ingestion would be expected, too, statistically, over time, to fail to replicate their genes. Presumably the organ, too, as parthenogenesis came to be supplanted by sexual reproduction, was useful in identifying members of its own species, or type. Later, it doubtless functioned in mate identification, and recognition, for Herul conception, proceeding in stages, requires a considerable period. And later, too, as life forms developed, and tribalities became of selective advantage, it doubtless proved its value for group integrity and consolidation, much as might have a nest odor among certain social insects or a pack odor among social rodents. It may, too, have some sort of bonding effect among individuals. In any event, it is an interesting, and rare, organ, particularly among rational species. The butt of the lance, grasped in the right hand of the Herul, was sheathed in the right stirrup holster.

THE KING · 183

One of the two dismounted Heruls, in response to the leader's injunction to break up the sledge, picked up the ax of Varix, which was in the snow.

In a moment he was before the sledge.

"Ota!" he said, an exclamation of surprise.

"What is it?" called the leader of the Heruls.

"There is something here," he said.

"What?" called the leader.

"A body," he said.

"It is dead?" said the leader.

"I think so," said the Herul.

He gingerly pushed at the shape, lying within the ribs of the headless, half-eaten horse on the sledge.

"Yes," said the Herul. "It does not move. It is dead."

"There is a pelt on the sledge," said the leader of the Heruls, referring to the folded, mottled pelt toward the back of the sledge.

"Doubtless it is that fellow's bait trap," said one of the mounted Heruls.

"What is he?" asked the leader of the Heruls.

"An Otung, I think," said the Herul.

"Here?" asked the leader.

"It seems so," said the Herul.

The leader of the Heruls and he closest to him exchanged glances.

Basungs would have been expected, in this vicinity, if they dared to cross the Lothar.

"Proceed with your work," said the leader of the Heruls.

The Herul at the sledge, putting the ax into the snow beside him, head down, the handle upright in the snow, broke to the side two, then three, of the ribs of the horse.

He then reached within the remains of the rib cage to draw the body out of the cavity.

In a moment the leader of the Heruls looked back toward the sledge.

"Utinn?" he asked.

The Herul stood by the sled, upright, waist deep in the snow, as it had drifted there, not moving.

"Hurry!" said the leader.

There was something odd about the attitude of the figure, as it stood.

"The head, the head is wrong!" said the Herul nearest the leader.

"Atlar!" said the leader.

The other dismounted Herul was reluctant to approach.

"Atlar!" snapped the leader.

The second Herul waded through the snow to his fellow. He put his hands on him, and lowered him, half to the snow. He moved the head, and looked back at the leader. "The neck is broken," he said. "He is dead."

"How can it be?" asked one of the Heruls.

"Utinn is a shaman," said the Herul nearest the leader. "He has died to go to the land of spirits, and will come back, with knowledge, and secrets and medicine."

"Utinn was not a shaman," said the leader of the Heruls, looking about, uneasily.

"He will come back," said one of the Heruls.

"One does not come back from broken necks," said another. "It is not like the coming back from the magic death, the sleep death, the trance."

"It is done by spirits, in the pay of the men of Ifeng," said another Herul. Venitzia was known among the Heruls as Ifeng. Among several of the other tribes of the area it was known as Scharnhorst.

"It is the magic of the brothers of the *festung* of Sim Giadini," said one of the Heruls.

The brothers had not discouraged such beliefs among the Heruls.

To be sure, it was unlikely the Heruls posed any great threat to the *festung* itself. They did pose, of course, a possible threat to *festung* villages.

"Utinn did it to himself," said one of the Heruls.

"Then he is a shaman," said another.

"He was not a shaman," said the leader.

"How did it come about?" asked one of the Heruls.

"I do not know," said another.

"I am afraid," said the Herul nearest the leader.

The leader of the Heruls looked about. The country was desolate. The snow was white, and calm.

He then returned his attention to Atlar, the body of Utinn, and the sledge, half buried, half lost, half obscured, in the snow.

"Atlar," called the leader of the Heruls, calmly, at the same time freeing the butt of his lance from the stirrup holster.

"Yes?" rejoined the Herul addressed, releasing the head of

Utinn, which, loosely, as though tied on with rope, dropped into the snow, near the body's left shoulder.

"Step back," said the leader, quietly.

The Herul moved back, wading backward in the snow.

"Pick up the ax," said the leader, quietly.

Atlar, uncertainly, not taking his eyes off the sledge, put out his right hand, as we shall have it, as is our practice, for the sake of ease, and simplicity, and grasped the ax.

"Lift the ax," said the leader of the Heruls, patiently.

Atlar lifted the ax, with two hands, the tentacles wrapped about the shaft, back, over his head, puzzled, and looked to the leader, astride his mount, a few yards away, in the snow.

"Kill it! Kill it!" suddenly screamed the leader of the Heruls, gesturing toward the sledge, with its weights, with the point of the lance.

But at that very moment with a cry of rage and power, a cry, perhaps, even of war, a mighty figure, more than half again the size of a common man, seemed to rise up from the surface of the sledge, unexpectedly, suddenly, like lightning, like a springing lion, seemed to rise up even from the body of the horse, stark, dried, cold ribs of the horse, brittle and dead in the cold, breaking, bones scattering in its emergence, like a striking snake, like a lion, springing through sticks and straw, seeming to rise up, like a hurricane, like a lion, snow flung to all sides, and Atlar, a yard of a great blade emergent from his back was lifted over the figure's head, impaled, the ax lost in the snow.

The figure stood there, in rage, snarling, surely more animal than man, for just a moment it stood there, the body of Atlar held high, squirming, bleeding, over its head.

But in that moment, in that brief instant, we may surmise, as would be expected of one trained in the school of Pulendius, it had located each of the Heruls.

Of the mounts of the Heruls about, of which there were seven, five of which Heruls were astride, and two standing nearby, without riders, in the snow, hobbled, their two front feet tied together with the reins dangling from their bridled snouts, the five shifted, startled, one bucking, throwing his rider into the snow, while of the two hobbled, one sank to its knees, squealing, a leg broken, and the other, trying to run, fell to its side, rolling, struggling, in the snow.

The war cry tends to inspirit and energize its utterer, but, perhaps more importantly, it can, if not anticipated, momentarily freeze the responses of the enemy or prey. The roar of the lion has a similar role, it would seem, at least in the latter particular. The moment of inactivity is often all the predator needs to effect his purpose, to strike a blow, to reach a critical point, to shorten a distance.

With another cry the mighty figure, snow thrashing about its legs, they forcing that great body through the snow, had hurled Atlar from the blade and rushed upon the nearest Herul and mount. An upward sweep of the great blade smote away the head of the horse, and it spun away, and there was a burst of blood which drenched the snow for yards about. The rider slid off the back of the horse. The mighty figure turned about, again, and again the blade flashed forth cutting through a Herul's leg at the thigh, cutting even the girth strap holding the saddle and the horse, too, sank to its knees a lateral slash marking the blade's passage. Another horse reared over the figure and the blade slashed out opening the belly, disemboweling the animal, the rider pitching away, scrambling up, in the snow. The horse thrashed, squealing, rolling about, its legs caught in the loops of its own intestines, its frantic movements tearing them out of its own body. The leader of the Heruls wheeled his mount away, some yards in the snow, and then turned it, his lance descendant, at the ready. He called to his men. There had been six. Utinn and Atlar were dead. Another, Utak, had crawled away, dragging a bleeding stump, leaving a river of blood in the snow. He had collapsed ten yards from the sledge. The rider who had been thrown, his horse bolting at the sudden, unexpected appearance of the figure, had now recovered his seat. Another rider, whose horse had been decapitated in the figure's rush forward had hurried to Atlar's frightened, hobbled animal, slashed the hobble, beat the horse to its feet, and mounted. The rider who had lost his saddle when his rearing horse had been fended back, with the fierce stroke of the terrible blade, some five feet in length, hurried, afoot, away from the sledge, to join the leader of the Heruls. The figure with the hilt of that terrible weapon in his two-handed grasp, panting, stepped away from the horse, which, wide-eyed, rolled about amongst its own intestines, these gushed forth upon the snow, bright, steaming from body heat, glistening and tangled, enmeshed.

Four Heruls there were then, three mounted.

One lowered his lance and charged.

"Wait!" cried the leader of the Heruls, but the fellow had already, with a cry of rage, kicked back with his spurs, and his mount, squealing in pain, was plunging forward through the snow.

The horse was to the figure in the snow almost instantly. The figure, trying to evade the charge, lost its footing in the snow, staggering, stumbling. It struggled to keep its balance. The lance thrust down. The Herul cried out in frustration. The figure in the snow, lurching, had managed, but barely, to turn the thrust with the flat of the blade. The horse wheeled. The figure in the snow felt the heat of its body, fiercely, its oily pelt, the fur-clad boot of the rider. The figure, buffeted, was struck to the snow. The sword was gone. The figure rolled from beneath the descending, clawed feet, the claws tearing in the snow. The rider wheeled the horse away, and then, again, aligned it, bringing it back once more to the attack line. The figure was now, again, on its feet, wary, hands out, the snow to its thighs, the sword somewhere to the side, somewhere inches beneath a dark cleft in the snow, not within reach, not before the horse, and the lance, could reach it. The horse, sped forward by the spurs, its flanks bleeding, charged, frenziedly. The figure evaded the thrust, forcing it up with a movement of his right forearm. At the next wheeling, and thrust, the figure, again buffeted, caught the lance behind the blade. The rider, startled, thought briefly to contest the possession of the implement, to struggle for it, to cling to it, but the shaft might as well have been rooted in the ground as be in whose grasp it was, and the rider suddenly found himself, as his horse shied to the left, unbalanced to the right, and he released the weapon, and grasped for the pommel of the saddle, and, in a flurry of snow, kicked up by the mount, half slid from the horse. As the horse turned, again, confused, wheeling in the snow, a hand on the Herul's jacket tore him from the mount and flung him on his back in the snow. The Herul, down in the snow, perhaps a foot or more deep, doubtless half blinded by snow, may not have seen the lance lifted over him. Its point splintered away, stopped only by the icy ground. The startled mount, which had now veered away, its flanks bleeding from spur wounds, was gathered in by the formerly dismounted Herul. In an instant, he was in its saddle, bending over, seizing a lance from the snow where he had thrust it a moment before. The figure from the sledge stood for an instant near the downed Herul. The formerly dismounted Herul, now again mounted, was now back with the leader of the Heruls, and the other Herul. There were, then, three Heruls, all mounted. In the chest of the downed Herul, the lance shaft stood upright. It was like a marker, distinct against the snow. The figure hurried to the depression, or slit, or cleft in the snow and felt downward for the sword, and, in a moment, lifting it, cold, had it in his two hands.

The three would charge, in a coordinated fashion. He could see the leader, some yards away, with gestures, and quick words, organizing the attack. He had, perhaps, three or four seconds in which to act. He had no realistic expectation, afoot, armed as he was, of successfully resisting the coordinated attack of three such horsemen. These creatures were Heruls. Many learned to ride, clinging to a neck strap or harness, before they learned to walk. Peoples such as Heruls had given rise, long ago, on diverse worlds to tales of centaurs, and such creatures, creatures which were at one time man and horse, so much one with the mount they were. Imperial cavalry, if similarly armed, would not meet them in the field.

Four horses lay in the bloodied snow, one headless; one dying, disemboweled; one hobbled, with a broken leg, it snapped, broken against the hobble, in its earlier alarm; and one wounded, that whose body had been partially shielded by the leg of its rider, he dying in the snow to one side, the leg lost at the thigh, and the girth strap.

The figure in the snow tore his way to the wounded horse, seized its bridle near the jaws, cried out, kicked the animal, jerked its head upward, twice, and the horse, squealing, got its legs under itself and staggered up to its feet, turning, unsteady, eyes rolling, its paws, wet, crusted with ice, trampling its own blood down into the snow.

Almost at the same time the first Herul made his passage, but the horse was now between them.

The same-line attack is often used against an enemy afoot. Two riders, or more, are required for its prosecution. It is supposed that the first passage may fail of its mark, and particularly against an agile, ready foe. But the first rider, if he is evaded, in effect sets the target for the second rider. For example, if the target, seeking to avoid the first lance, moves to, or is moved to, a given position then that, of course, determines the line of the second rider, following closely on the heels of the first. With three riders, of course, the probabilities of a hit are considerably increased.

The second rider, too, plunged past, he, too, following as

closely as he did, unable to move to the opposite side of the horse.

The leader of the Heruls, pulled his horse up, and it reared, squealing, scratching at the air.

The first two riders turned their mounts, the animals struggling in the snow.

The figure who had been in the snow was then on the back of the wounded horse.

At a call from the leader the two Heruls, urging their horses through the snow, rejoined him.

There was no saddle on the newly mounted fellow's horse as it had been lost in the earlier stroke.

The weight on its back, and the activity of movement, freshened the blood on the horse's right side.

Its rider, the newly mounted fellow, unfamiliar, strange to the horse, surely not a Herul, had learned something of horsemanship on a distant world, Vellmer, an imperial world, at the villa, or holding, of a citizen of Telnaria, one Julian, of the Aurelianii, a patrician, even of the senatorial class. He had even practiced riding bareback, for one might not always have time to saddle one's horse, and had, in the saddle and bareback, familiarized himself with the lance, light and shock, and the scimitar and saber. But it is one thing to approach targets, and practice the address, the parry and thrust with the lance, the wielding of blades, of diverse weights, lengths, and curvatures, such things, from horseback, against wands and garlands, and quite another against men, and yet another, surely, against creatures such as Heruls. His lessons had not been, at that time, learned in the school of battle, the most pitiless of houses of instruction. He was not at that time a horsemen, not in the sense that worlds, and even Heruls, would know him, and fear him, later. He was at that time young, a very young man really, though with a terrible maturity for his age. He was, at that time, no more than a creature of dreadful, awesome promise. Too, the animal was unfamiliar, and wounded. Yet, even so, the Heruls drew back.

"It is an Otung horseman," said one of the Heruls. He had met Otung horsemen long ago, in the spring and summer of 1103, in the chronology of the imperial claiming stone, set up in Venitzia, when Venitzia had been no more than a small military camp.

The new rider retained the long sword. Its flat was across the back of the animal.

The leader of the Heruls, too, remembered the Otung horsemen, those of the Otung Vandals.

"Do you remember them?" asked the Herul who had first spoken.

"Yes," said the leader of the Heruls.

"They fought well," said the Herul who had first spoken.

"Yes," said the leader of the Heruls.

"They were very brave," said the Herul.

"Yes," said the leader of the Heruls, holding in his mount. Then he drew a circle in the air.

"Yes!" said the third Herul, elatedly.

The Otung horsemen, though valiant, had been, with their massive horses, dense formations and shock tactics, no match for the illusive, swarming, lighter-armed, more mobile Heruls, appearing, disappearing, attacking, drawing back, striking from behind, shifting the point of attack, hanging on the flanks, choosing the time and place of war, engaging only when it was to their advantage.

"Exercise care," said the leader.

The attack of the circle is usually directed against an isolated horseman, whether isolated, oddly, in the tumult of battle or elsewhere more naturally, as in a meadow, a field, or a snowy plain. It means no more than a surrounding attack, and, for it, obviously, even two riders would suffice. One engages and defends, and the other, or others, attack. The engagement and defense, and the attack, of course, can be, and commonly is, transferred among riders, these modalities shifting as seems appropriate under the circumstances.

The newly mounted rider kicked back into the flanks of his mount, instantly seizing the initiative, and it lunged forward toward the Heruls, that it might with its rider strike into their very midst, but the beast was slowed, from its wound, and the snow, and the Heruls, though taken aback, though startled for a moment, not having expected this audacity, recovered and parted, one to the left, two to the right, and the rider's horse, leaping and struggling, struck through the snow amongst them, the flash of the great blade better than a yard from the nearest foe. The rider turned swiftly toward one of the Heruls but he drew away from the charge. Each Herul now had freed the buckler from the side of his saddle. It could withstand the thrust of a lance, the slash of the saber, the deft flight of the scimitar, but the weight of the mightier blade must be turned, or slipped, else the buckler itself might be cut, or the hand within its single grip broken at the wrist, or the rider beaten down, perhaps out of the saddle. Too, the spinal cord of the mount, in a carelessly slipped thrust, might be severed. The Heruls were not eager to come within the thunder, the sweep, of that blade.

The rider turned his bleeding mount in the snow. The Heruls were now about him.

It was the circle.

He plunged his horse between two of the riders.

But in a moment they were with him, and then one was well ahead, and turned, waiting for him, lance ready, and the other two were behind him, one behind to his left, the other behind to his right. The rider reined in his mount. With a stronger, sounder mount, perhaps on a faster surface, he might have found open ground, and separated them in a line of pursuit, the swiftest closest to him, the second swiftest, in a minute or two, significantly behind, the slowest out of the fray, until it came back to him, in turn, but he had now reined in. The false flight, separating the pursuers, and the sudden turning back, to deal with them singly, was not practical. The rider was now surrounded. The four combatants stood still, mounted. The three Heruls formed the points of a triangle. Within this triangle was the newly mounted rider, alone. The distance of each of the Heruls to the target was some ten yards. The triangle, as a whole, was some forty or fifty yards out into the plain, out from the trampled snow about the sledge. It seemed quiet then on the snowy field.

"It is over," called the leader of the Heruls to the young, blond rider.

The young fellow turned to face him. The leader had been behind the young fellow, to his left.

The young fellow grasped the hilt of the mighty sword in two hands.

His mount sank a little down, into the snow, its back legs unsteady beneath it.

Angrily, struggling to maintain his seat, the young man urged the horse up again.

Then it was on its feet once more.

The snow was red beneath it.

A little wind blew some snow toward the rider farthest from the sledge, he at the point, or apex, so to speak, of the triangle.

Very warily the three Heruls began to close in on the isolated horsemen amongst them.

They stopped some four or five yards from him, on their attack lines.

The leader of the Heruls looked from one of his men to the other.

He was satisfied.

"What is wrong?" suddenly called the leader of the Heruls to the Herul farthest out from the sledge, at the apex, so to speak, of the diminished triangle.

"It is the horse," said the fellow. "It is the horse!"

The horse, suddenly, had lifted its head. It threw its head back and forth. Its eyes were like round balls. It seemed to fear to put its paws down to the snow. It began to prance. It reared. It squealed. Its nostrils were wide, like cups, opening and closing. It showed its teeth. It tore at the bit.

The newly mounted rider, he in the midst of the Heruls, spun about on his mount's back, pulling back on the reins, and in that instant there rose up from the snow, from that desolate, bleak landscape, snarling, almost at his side, like an explosion, like a a blizzard of white fire, springing, shedding snow, like a torrent of teeth and claws, a vi-cat!

It was a giant white.

The vi-cat was upon the hindquarters of the wounded beast, its claws sunk inches into its loins, its teeth buried in its rump, and its weight and twisting threw the squealing horse to its side in the snow, trapping the rider, by one leg, beneath it.

The horses of the Heruls bolted. For a moment they were unmanageable. The Heruls, struggling to retain their seats, dragged on reins, fighting for control. They screamed at the animals. The horses spun about, frantic, maddened, lost in the snow. The Heruls beat them with the butts of their lances. Back, again and again, jerked the bits. Blood gushed from the mouths of the terrified horses, washing about the jaws, drenching the lacerating metal.

Ravenously the vi-cat tore at its prey, feeding, holding it down with its paws, digging in it, its mouth and jaws thick with hair and blood.

The rider of the animal drew his leg loose from beneath the squealing horse, and stood unsteadily in the snow, half staggering, the leg almost buckling beneath him.

The sword was to one side, half in the snow, half visible.

The vi-cat fed, its ears back, its head half lost in the body of the horse, obliviously, deliriously, not more than two yards from where he stood.

The young man saw the sword.

The Heruls, the leader first, then the other two, brought their mounts under control.

The young man looked back to the vi-cat.

He must reach the sword.

The vi-cat paused in its feeding, suddenly.

It lifted its head from the body of the horse.

The young man stood extremely still. The sword was feet away.

He must not move, not perceptibly.

The rolling eyes of the horse turned wildly, piteously, toward him.

At the same time the vi-cat saw him. It snarled.

The young man was not a stranger to the vi-cat, for he, and other villagers, long ago, had hunted them, though not such as this one, not the giant white. He had killed his first vi-cat at the age of fourteen, one which had unexpectedly doubled back on hunters. Even at that age he had been larger and stronger than most men. He had killed the beast with an ax. He had given the skin to his best friend, Gathron. Later, years later, he and Gathron had had a fight. In this fight he had killed Gathron. The fight had been over a woman. He had soon left the village. He would go to Venitzia, and from there, elsewhere, anywhere, seek his fortune. He had worked his passage on a freighter. He had disembarked on Terennia. It was on Terennia that was to be found the school of Pulendius, in which gladiators were trained, for diverse games on diverse worlds.

The critical distance for the vi-cat tends to range from ten to twenty yards. Outside this range, if it is not hunting, and man, in any event, is not its common game, man and beast can usually pretend to ignore one another. The man turns aside, and the beast slinks away, into the high grass, as though it had not seen the man. Within this range, closer than ten to twenty yards, the particular distance tending to depend on the disposition, even the indolence, of the beast in question, this game of man and beast is not played. Within the critical distance the beast tends to approach, and investigate, and, from this point, things tend to rapidly and often unpleasantly escalate. It will also, often, without warning, charge within this distance. It might also be noted that even outside the critical distance it is important to avoid obvious eye contact with the beast. Once the beast knows it has been seen it is almost, oddly, as if a matter of honor had become involved, and that retreat would somehow result in a loss of face. This interpretation seems somewhat anthropomorphic, but the serious question is not whether or not it is anthropomorphic, but whether or not it is correct. It may be, you see, that a concept of honor is not unique to rational species, but that its rudiments, or such, lie much farther down the phylogenetic scales of different animal kingdoms. A sense of rightness, of fittingness, and such, may not be an invention of rational species but, in a sense, an inheritance of such species, later interpreted, naturally enough, in conceptual terms. It might be proposed, of course, that the animals which recognized themselves seen, or challenged, and responded aggressively, tended to replicate their genes, and that more casual organisms, indifferent to intruders, tolerant of strangers, and such, tended to be eliminated. But, if this is the case, this would seem to suggest merely that the rudiments of honor, or such, have been themselves selected for. This is not incomprehensible, of course. For example, it seems clear that the blind mechanisms of natural selection have produced, and perhaps inevitably, what is commonly taken to be their antithesis, thought, intentionality, consciousness, planning and reason. Civilization may be an inevitable precipitate of the jungle. Certainly within itself it bears the traces of dark origins. Indeed, there is some speculation that civilization is not a successor to, nor a replacement of, the jungle, but merely a transformation of the jungle, merely another of its many faces. And the jungle, too, you see, is not really a chaos, but, in its way, a highly articulated structure, with its habits and patterns, its history, its proven, tested, developed ways, its relationships, its ranks, its distances, its hierarchies.

The eyes of the man and beast met.

The man dove for the hilt of the blade, emergent from the snow, as the beast, snarling, scrambled over the trembling, shaking body of the expiring horse.

The man threw himself to the snow, scratching within it, and the beast was on him, pawing away the snow, biting at the half-buried back.

"Do not interfere," said the leader of the Heruls to his fellows. Their mounts, their sides heaving, blood frozen about the jaws, like threads of ice, their breath like fog bursting from their mouths and nostrils, were now under control.

The vi-cat tore away the back of the man's coat, shaking it. It seemed puzzled.

The figure rolled to the side in the snow and leapt upon the vi-cat from the side, his arms about its neck, and the cat, enraged, reared up, lifting the man a yard from the snow. The man clung to its neck, his head down, at the base of the animal's neck, down, away from the massive, turning head, and fangs. The beast sought futilely to reach him with its forepaws, the curved claws, four inches in length, extended, brandished, then flung itself down in the snow, rolling, and one could not see the man, and then one could, as, again and again, he was first submerged in the snow, and then again, body and hair a mass of snow, torn upward into view. The beast, roaring, tried to scrape him away, against the horse, now dead. The beast then stopped, and gasped, startled. It shook its head, and the man was flung to one side and the other. The man, as he could, tightened his grip. He could not slip his arms beneath the forelegs of the beast, and up then, behind the back of the neck, given the size of the beast. In such a way might a smaller animal's neck be broken. Such things were learned, though with an intended application to men, in the school of Pulendius, on Terennia. Then the beast threw itself to its side in the snow, squirming down, to the frozen soil. Then, slowly, pressing itself against the ice, it, with its mighty bulk, began to turn itself, inch by inch. The man, in his garments, with his own bulk, could not then turn with the animal. He was wedged between the body of the beast and the soil, like cement, and the beast, inch by inch, was turning, moving in the grip of the man, bringing its jaws about, inch by inch, closer to the man's head.

The vi-cat, gasping in the snow, continued to turn, inch by inch.

The man released the beast's throat and scrambled to his feet in the snow, and the beast, too, scrambled up.

The beast stood there for a moment, sucking in air, blinking, snow about its eyes, looking for the man.

The man reached to the great sword and had it in his hand, half lifting it as the beast charged, and the man was struck from his feet, the sword lost, and the beast had stopped. Then it backed away, puzzled. It eyed the man, and licked at its own blood.

The man, bleeding, recovered the sword.

He lifted it unsteadily, half to the ready, and the beast was upon him, again, charging and snarling.

A yard of the blade disappeared into the chest of the beast.

A blow from the right paw of the beast smote the man at the side of the head, and he was struck to the side, and the blade, to which he clung, slid sideways in the animal, and, as the man fell to the snow, the blade, still in his grasp, was mostly out of the body.

The beast backed away, a foot or two, which movement slipped the blade further from its body, and, at the same time, drew it away from the hands of the fallen man. Then the beast shook itself, as though it might be shedding water. The blade was flung to the side.

"The Otung is dead," said one of the Heruls.

The beast returned to the still warm body of the horse, and its feeding. Its own blood mingled with that of the horse. There was little sound then except the breathing of the horses of the Heruls, and the feeding of the vi-cat.

The figure struck down in the snow staggered to its feet. It felt about for the great sword. It had it again in its hands.

Blood was now coming from within the lungs of the vi-cat, and it gushed forth from its mouth and nostrils, and, as it fed, it drank its own blood.

The man staggered toward the vi-cat with the blade raised, but fell into the snow before he could reach it.

The vi-cat died feeding.

"The Otung is dead," said a Herul.

"He would be worth running for the dogs," said another.

"He is dead," said the Herul who had first spoken.

"I do not think so," said the leader of the Heruls. "Tie him. Put him on the sledge."

Olar and Varix, who were Basung Vandals, were put in the traces of the sledge, to draw it.

The horse whose leg had been broken was killed, with a blow of the ax of Varix.

In a few moments the three Heruls left the trampled, bloody snow.

They did not bury their fellows, but left them, as was their common wont, for the beasts of the plains.

They cut some meat from the dead horses, for provender on the trip back to the wagons and herds.

They also skinned the vi-cat, for such a pelt was of great value. Indeed, from such a pelt might be fashioned the robe of a king.

· · · CHAPTER 20 · · ·

"He is awakening," she said.

"Do not hurt me," she said.

The blond giant's hand had grasped her wrist. His brow was wet, from the cloth with which she had wiped it.

He released her wrist.

"Leave," said a voice, that of a Herul, who was sitting back, in the shadows.

Not speaking, she gathered her pan of warm water, and, with the cloth and sponges, and a whisk of her long skirt, hurried away.

It was a woman of his own species, or seemed so. Heruls kept such, he knew, for labor, and diversion. The giant did not object, as they were females.

"She is the daughter of an Otung noble," said the Herul.

The giant moved his legs a little. The clasp of the chains was then evident.

"You have been unconscious for four days," said the Herul.

"You are old—for a Herul," said the giant.

"You are surprised?" asked the Herul.

"Yes," said the giant.

Heruls kill the old and the weak, the stupid, the lame, the deformed.

"I am still hardy," said the Herul. "If I am to be killed, someone must do it. I have killed four. They will let me alone now, I think, for a time."

"You are a warrior," said the giant.

"I have ridden," admitted the Herul. "Would you like to have her, tonight?" he asked.

"Yes," said the giant.

"She is a slave," said the Herul. "Do not fail to use her as such."

"I will not," said the giant.

"You are in the wagon of my friend," said the Herul. "It was he who captured you, who brought you in. He was the leader of a party of seven, three only of which returned."

"Who are you?" asked the giant.

"It does not matter," said the Herul.

"What is to be done with me?"

"You must regain your strength," said the Herul. "I will have broth brought to you, and, in a day, curds, and then, later, meat."

"Mujiin is proud of you," said the Herul.

"Who is Mujiin?" asked the giant.

"He who captured you," said the Herul.

"What is your people?" asked the Herul.

"I have no people," said the giant.

"You are an Otung," said the Herul.

"I am chieftain of the Wolfungs," said the giant.

"I do not know that tribe," said the Herul.

"It is a tribe of the Vandal nation," said the giant.,

"One knows the Vandals, of course," said the Herul, "—the Otung Vandals, the Basung Vandals, and such."

"Its remnants were banished to a far world, Varna," said the giant.

"How is it that you are on Tangara?" asked the Herul.

"I am commissioned captain in the imperial *auxilia*," said the giant, "entitled to recruit *comitates*, *comites*, companions, a *comitatus*, a military company, for service under the imperial standard. I seek Otungs for this purpose."

"Strange," said the Herul.

"Why?" asked the giant.

"Little love is lost between the empire and the Otungs," said the Herul.

"Nor," said the giant, "between the empire and the Heruls."

"True," said the Herul.

"There were two men who were captured on the plains," said the giant. "What was done with them?"

"They drew you here, on a sledge," said the Herul. "Then they were bound, and their throats were cut, and they were fed to the dogs."

The giant regarded him.

"They had not fought," said the Herul.

The giant lay back on the rude, low couch.

"To be sure," said the Herul, "they crossed the Lothar, and that must have taken courage.

"I can remember when Basungs fought," said the Herul.

"They were then Vandals, Basung Vandals," said the giant.

"Yes," said the Herul.

"What of the Otungs?" asked the giant.

"We broke them, long ago, and have denied to their fugitive remnants horses, and the plains. They are not permitted to come forth from their forests, except at times to trade with us, honey, pelts, produce from their small plots, such things, for leather, hides, glue and horn, and excess trade goods, which we, by similar exchanges, have obtained from merchants of Ifeng."

"Venitzia?"

"That is the Telnarian name for the place," said the Herul. "There is a good spring there."

"Why do you not go into the forests and kill them?" asked the giant.

"We are horsemen," said the Herul. "In the forests it is very dangerous for us. We do raid in them, afoot, sometimes, for sport. It was in such a raid, two years ago, that we captured Yata, and others, while they were bathing."

"Yata?"

"The slave," said the Herul. "It was but a moment's work to bind and gag them, wrap them securely in camouflaged blankets and tie them on narrow frameworks of poles, which frameworks we then drew after us, reaching, two days later, the edge of the forest. Once there, where our horses were waiting, we untied their ankle cords, put them in coffle, and marched them, under the knout, to the wagons. They marched quickly, and well."

"I do not doubt it," said the giant.

"We take others," said the Herul, "as they fall to us; some are captured in raids, as were Yata and her maidens; some are caught outside the forests, herding pigs, gathering herbs, and such; some are given to us as tokens of good will; some are sold to us; some are received in trade, such things. But these are usually not high women, and many are only beautiful, unwanted daughters."

"You take only the beautiful ones?"

"Of course," said the Herul. "For we may have to dispose of them in Venitzia later. We reject the others. But we do not take all the beautiful ones, as we wish to leave them enough beauties to breed, that more beauties may be regularly produced."

"You seem interested in me," said the giant.

"I am curious about you," said the Herul.

"Why?"

"You remind me of someone," said the Herul, "someone I saw once, long ago, one to whom I once lifted my lance."

"An Otung?"

"Yes."

"Who are you?"

"It does not matter," said the Herul.

The Herul rose up. He approached the couch. He looked down upon the blond giant.

"May I touch you?" asked the Herul.

The giant did not move.

The right tentacle of the Herul uncoiled itself and its tip rested on the right forearm of the giant. The giant detected a movement within the tentacle.

"Ah!" said the Herul.

The tentacle withdrew.

The giant looked up at the Herul.

"It is as I thought," said the Herul.

"What?" asked the giant.

"Nothing," said the Herul.

"What?" asked the giant.

"We have met before," said the Herul.

"No," said the giant.

"You are from the *festung* village of Sim Giadini," said the Herul.

"How could you know that?" asked the giant.

"That is not important," said the Herul.

"We have met?"

"Yes."

"I was very young?" said the giant.

"Yes," said the Herul, "you were very young."

"I do not think the Heruls keep male prisoners, or slaves," said the giant.

"You are right," said the Herul.

"What is to be done with me?"

"You will see," said the Herul. He then turned away, and went to the door of the broad, roomlike wagon. "I will have broth brought to you," he said.

"By Yata?" asked the giant.

"Yes," said the Herul.

"She is to remove her garments while serving me," said the giant.

"Of course," said the Herul.

· · · CHAPTER 21 · · ·

The giant plunged through the snow, naked, the baying of the dogs behind him.

Five had been set upon him, the size of ponies.

He had had the start of a full hour.

That hour is best spent not in trying to cover as much distance as possible, for the difference of a few miles is immaterial in such matters, the dogs on the run, tireless, in the pack, but rather looking for a defensible place, an outcropping, a stand of trees, a hillock, such things. But the plain in this place, save for swirled drifts, seemed level and barren.

But somewhere, somewhere in this snow, and desolation, concealed by gentle contours, perhaps those of some high drift, there must be stones, or irregularities, or faces of rock, or pools in which water might be trapped. In the summer animals were abundant here. There must be water for them, in pools, or streams now frozen, lost under the snow.

But all seemed bleak.

It was impossible not to leave tracks, and in the clear, cold, windless air his scent would follow him, almost as though it were a trail of heat, almost as though it were a wash of color, lingering, gentle in the disturbed snow, soft in the still air, marking, as though with paint and banners, his passage.

He was breathing heavily.

His feet were terribly cold.

If he should stop moving he did not doubt but what they would be soon useless, and frozen.

He could not double back to the wagons. Horsemen had followed him, with knouts, making that impossible.

Then they had turned back.

Then the dogs would have been released.

It would not be dark for five hours, and the dogs were surely only minutes away.

He scratched under the snow, searching for a stick, a rock, anything which might be used as a weapon. His fingernails were torn on the frozen soil.

Drifts lay about.

He moved on.

He looked back. He could see five dots on the plain, in the snow, moving, hastening in his direction.

He had been brave. Mujiin, his captor, had thought so. He had been given thus this chance for life. Too, the dogs needed exercise. Bets were being taken at the wagons, on which animal would first return, which animal then would presumably have been the first to have had its fill, which animal then would, presumably, have been the first to reach the quarry.

The sky was a winter sky, dark and overcast.

There was not enough sun to melt snow, to make possible the building of a shelter, the building of a wall, of some sort of fortress, through the entrance of which only one animal at a time might enter.

The snow was useless, like powder.

It came to the thighs of the giant. He had to force his way through it.

Such snow, if virginal, particularly where it had drifted, must form an impediment to the movement of the dogs, even as it did to himself, but, as of now, of course, his own body had broken a passage behind him, which facilitated the pursuit of the dogs. He had, in effect, broken the trail to his own body.

His feet slipped, climbing a drift. He could not climb it, and then, feet bleeding, he came to the top of it. The dots were closer now, larger, leaping, plunging in his traces. He cried out, in fury, as he stumbled down the other side of the drift, rolling in the snow. There was a depression there. He stood upright in it. Then, angrily, struggling, he fought his way back to the top of the drift. It was high, and seemed as good as any other likely place. It was there he would make his stand. Too, the snow was soft behind, almost like a trap, slipping down to the depression. He did not think that dogs would have much better footing in it than he had had. In the summer water might have gathered there.

He looked back at the dogs.

They were much closer now.

He took snow in his mouth, to melt it. As he could, then, with his hands, and the water from his mouth, mixing that water with soft snow, packing it carefully, shaping it, he formed a tubular, tapering, pointed trench, some eighteen inches in length, some four inches in diameter at its thick end, and like a needle at its narrow end.

The gentle reader may be advised to skip the following pages, as he may find them offensive. I cannot, in conscience, however, omit the accounts as they have come down to us. That would betray my task, which is not, when all is said and done, to protect the feelings of the delicate, however laudable that aim, but to give an account of the times of troubles. Accordingly, I crave the reader's indulgence, reminding him that we, herein, are dealing with times other than our own, times harsher and more primitive, darker times, ruder times, more savage times, times of transition, of change, the times of troubles.

More water from his mouth, spread slick against the sides of that trench, froze almost instantly.

Ice daggers may be formed variously. They may be formed, for example, from pieces of ice shaped, and sharpened, and edged by abrasion, chipping or warmth. They may also be formed, if there is time, from water, perhaps from snow melted in the mouth, and then poured into a snow mold to freeze.

Too, of course, urine may be used.

That is common with the Heruls.

But much depends on the temperature. The riders with the knouts had followed him, driving him from the wagons, before turning back. Then there had been the search for the place to make a stand, for even a dagger is of little use against five hunters, which may tear at one from all sides. And then it takes time for water to freeze.

To be sure, it was bitterly cold.

At some temperatures water freezes almost instantaneously, for example, as when, in an arctic area, urine strikes the ground in brittle shafts. But at such temperatures an unprotected, warm-blooded animal would have already been incapacitated or dead.

The urine in the trench would remain warm no more than a moment.

He, in that moment, mixed in more snow, it melting but, almost instantly, cooling, it having, too, in that instant, further reduced the temperature of the bodily fluid, which was already crystallizing. He mixed in more snow, and spit into the trench, and took snow in his mouth, to heat it, and add it to the pale artifact.

It did not seem likely that there would be time.

He trampled down the snow at the height of the drift to give himself a better footing, certainly better than the dogs would have in their climb.

He could now see the brown crests of the dogs clearly. The baying, the cries, of the animals were extremely clear, sharp in the icy air.

He sensed their excitement.

The dogs were some fifty yards away.

He watched them coming, the leader first, the others plunging behind.

He shuddered with cold, and crouched down in the snow.

He touched the object before him.

Two fingers slipped over its surface.

He then put his two hands about it, prying up its thick end an inch from the mold, that the ice might melt away a little, from the warmth of his fingers, to leave impressions, to provide a grip. But then he pulled his hands away, and blew on his numbed, stiffened fingers. Could he even hold such an object? Could he even manage to retain it in his grasp, without dropping it in pain, without its slipping away from his half-frozen fingers?

The dogs did not hesitate. They were ten yards away. If anything, his nearness, and his visible presence, energized them in their pursuit.

He went to his knees.

This was not in despair.

It gave him greater stability in the drift.

The leader was at the foot of the drift, rushing upward, furrowing snow, its scrambling hind legs, slipping, spattering it behind him, almost obscuring the second dog, so close behind.

The giant reached down and wrenched the heavy weapon from the snow, and tore it upward, holding it over his head, mold and all.

He saw the large head of the lead dog, the eyes, the hump, the manelike crest, the long tongue, livid and wet, the fangs, white, the curved, saberlike canines, some seven inches long, a foot away, and the beast slipped back in the loose snow, and pawed for its footing.

And it was then that the giant lunged forward, bringing down, pointed, hammerlike, the stakelike, tapering cone of ice on the beast's skull, which, point snapping, it penetrated, and the second animal, impeded by the footing, and the blockage of the lead animal, slipped back, but only to be pursued by the giant, half sliding down the hill, who struck it with the blunted, sharpened stake of ice, crashing in its head. With one foot he thrust it down the drift, into the way of the third animal, itself fighting for footing. Then, scratching with the icy stake at the drift, scrambling, the giant regained its summit. The third animal sped its way about the second, slipped sideways on the drift, went to its belly, and then, feet under it, began to inch its way upward, slavering. The fourth and fifth animal stood at the foot of the drift, baying. The first animal had slid down, and lay before them. The giant struck at the third animal but the ice, blunted now, and slick from the heat of his grip, missed the skull and only tore the snout on the right side. The giant tried to strike again but the stake slipped from his hand. It struck into the drift beside the third animal and it snapped at it, angrily, getting its teeth on it, and then, snarling, in pain, drew back, puzzled. The giant reached down and seized the animal by the manelike crest, and drew it, it frenziedly scratching and bending about, to rend him, to him, and then hurled it behind him, down to the soft snow in the depression, behind the drift. It rolled down the slope, caught its footing at the bottom, and stood up, shaking snow from its pelt. The giant then crawled a few feet down and seized the second animal, whose skull had been crashed in by the stake of ice, and pulled it, by its right hind foot to the summit of the drift. The giant, shuddering, clasped the body to him, rejoicing in the heat of the still hot carcass. Then he broke away the right canine tooth, that saberlike canine, some seven inches in length, and ripped open the belly of the beast, drenching the snow with blood. The viscera exposed, the carcass hot with spilled blood, the giant held it over his head and flung it down to the foot of the drift. The fourth and fifth dogs, at that point, hesitated not at all, but began to tear the carcass to pieces, feeding. The remains of the first dog, the giant did not doubt, the hunger lust aroused, would soon follow. These animals were not far from wolves, whose packs will turn on a disabled member, even a leader, and utilize it for game.

Breathing heavily the giant, picking up the canine tooth, torn from the animal's jaw, turned about, and looked down on the far side of the drift, where the third animal was turning about, putting its paws up, here and there, trying to find footing. It looked up at the giant, and growled.

Then the beast turned about, gathered its hind legs under it, leapt up, and, slipping, tried to scratch its way up, out of the depression.

It slipped back.

In a moment or two, of course, it would find, or would have packed, firmer snow, and might scratch, or even, in effect, have swum its way to freedom.

Its frustration, its discomfiture, the giant did not doubt, would be alarmingly temporary.

The giant, whose blood was now, despite the bitter cold, racing in his great body, measured the distance from the summit of the drift to the pit below, and to the center of the backbone, fifteen feet below, of the restless, moving animal.

He leapt down, legs flexed, he caught by gravity, plummeting, hurtling, and struck the animal in the back, which produced a sudden, snapping sound, and a startled squeal of pain.

In moments, using the canine tooth as a knife, the giant had opened the belly of the wild-eyed animal, and then, rejoicing, thrust, in turn, his feet and hands into the throbbing, blood-filled, heat-rich cavity. Then he embraced the carcass, pressing himself to it. He bathed in its blood and fluids. Then, crouching beside it in the snow, he drank blood, cupping it in his hands, and fed on the liver and heart. Then he began to cut its skin away.

He could hear, on the other side of the drift, the feeding of the fourth and fifth dog.

· · · CHAPTER 22 · · ·

It was late at night on the plains.

It was extremely dark.

Neither the moon nor stars could be seen.

The giant, crouching in the snow, clad in the skins of dogs, booted in their fur, cowled, helmeted even, in the head and neck of the leader, peering out through what had been its mouth, watched the tiny light of the lantern in the distance.

It was carried by a rider.

That could be told from its movement.

The giant had known little of the location of the Otungs. He had been moving south in the plains of Barrionuevo when, caught in a new storm, freezing, starving, half-blinded in the snow, lost, he had had to slay the horse. It had been his intention to cross the Lothar, to seek the Basung Vandals, whom he recalled, from his days in the *festung* village of Sim Giadini, lived in the forests west of the Lothar. From them he had hoped to learn the whereabouts of the Otungs, if any survived. He now knew there were still Otungs, from the information he had obtained from the Herul in the wagon of Mujiin, who had been the leader of the men who had captured him. Indeed, he had even made rich and diverse use, in the same wagon, for several nights, of a lovely slave girl, a former Otung noblewoman, one who had been captured by Heruls only two years ago.

At times it had seemed almost as though she had thought herself still free.

Sometimes the older Herul, who had seemed to be his keeper, or warder, had removed one of his shackles, to put it more loosely, but unslippably, about her own ankle, that she would be chained with him, to the same couch, so that she could not run from him, but might be, when he wished, drawn to him.

It seemed she might think of herself as free, but he had had her kick like a slave, the slave she was.

"What is your name?" he would ask.

"Hortense!" she said. "Do not stop, I beg you!"

"What is your name?" he would inquire.

"Yata!" she would cry. "Yata, the slave! Please do not stop, Master! Yata, only a slave, begs you not to stop! Please do not stop, Master!"

But he did not know where he was, really, where the camp of the Heruls was, its relation to the Otungs, and such. He did not know how long the trip to the camp had taken. He did know he had been unconscious for four days in the camp. He had dim recollections of the trip itself, of being delirious, of being bound, of being in pain, of being forced awake, and fed, some sort of white clods, like watered cheese, and having snow jammed in his mouth for drink, and being beaten, and then again losing consciousness. Too, in the days he had been with the camp, the wagons, which were few in number, as is common with a winter camp of Heruls, had moved, apparently from one cache of fodder to another. When he had been unchained and brought forth from the wagon, to be stripped and run for the dogs, he had seen only some twenty wagons, perhaps some fifty or sixty horses, and a similar number of cattle. There had been a low, open-sided, snow-covered shed in the distance. Tracks led to it. He could see hay within it. There was straw about. There was a rich smell of manure. Such sheds are used for the storage of fodder, and the sheltering, at times, of beasts. The camp, this far north for the season, was presumably an outpost camp. Such commonly serve as bases for hunters, for scouts and outriders. In such a way, by such scattered camps, far from the winter pastures, which for the great herds are far to the south, and for many smaller ones nestled in sheltered mountain valleys, the Heruls keep themselves apprised of what occurs on the flats of Tung, on the plains of Barrionuevo. He had been chained. The wagon had been closed. He had been able to conjecture little, save, by the sunlight, bright in cracks about the door, and the single, shuttered window, that they had been moving north, and then northeast. He was probably much closer to Venitzia now than he had been when he had slain the horse.

The giant watched the light coming closer.

He knew it must be a Herul, for who else might be abroad at this time, in this place.

The giant removed the stained canine tooth from its makeshift sheath at his skin belt.

His bag of meat, which, in the cold might last for days, was in the snow, beside him.

He had little doubt but what the rider was looking for him.

The lantern cast an unsteady, flickering, moving pool of light, some four or five yards in diameter.

The giant watched, patiently.

He chewed a little meat from the bag.

Something, too, the giant noted, might accompany the rider. It was hard to tell in the light.

The giant finished the meat, and tied shut the bag. There seemed to be a small figure, heavily bundled, on the left side of the horse, trudging in the snow.

The lantern was quite close now.

Surely the rider must see him, as he crouched in the snow.

The lantern lifted.

The giant did not move.

Suddenly there was a woman's scream.

He did not move.

"It is a dog!" screamed a woman. "It is a dog!" She spun away from the stirrup, turning, frightened, to run, but, choking, weeping, in a moment, was held up short, by the tether on her neck.

"Greetings," said the rider.

"Greetings," said the giant, rising up.

He stood then, like some unusual creature, bipedalian, but canine, in the light of the lamp.

The rider, with one hand, not taking his eyes from the giant, slowly unlooped the tether, which had been wound some four or five times about the pommel of the saddle.

He dropped it into the snow.

The woman's hands were not bound. She backed away, into the darkness, the tether on her neck.

"Do not attack me," said the rider.

It was the older Herul, who had been his keeper, or warden, in the wagon of Mujiin.

The giant did not move.

"Two of the dogs returned," said the Herul. "In the camp it is thought you are dead."

"But you did not think so?"

"I did not know," said the Herul.

"It was clever of you," said the Herul, "to let the dogs return."

The giant shrugged.

It would have been possible, though dangerous, to kill them in their feeding frenzy.

Too, he had been cold, and miserable.

"How did you arm yourself?" asked the Herul.

"With ice," said the giant, "a weapon formed thereof, frozen, from snow, heated in my mouth, and a fluid of my body."

"It is an old Herul trick," said the Herul, approvingly.

"It is known in the *festung* village of Sim Giadini," said the giant.

"I had thought it might be," said the Herul.

"You have sought me," said the giant.

"Yes," said the Herul.

"Why?" asked the giant.

"I mean you no harm," said the Herul. "You have escaped the dogs."

"Why have you sought me?" asked the giant.

"I have brought you your sword, the great blade, and a Herul knife, some food, and the pelt of the giant white vi-cat, which I have had prepared for you."

The Herul loosened from across his back the great blade, now in a fur sheath, and dropped it, with its belt, to the snow, to the right side of the horse. He put with it, one object after the other, a smaller object, doubtless the knife, a dark bag, which might contain food, and then, folded, what must be the pelt of the vi-cat.

"Why are you doing this?" asked the giant.

"The pelt," said the Herul, "is that of the giant white vi-cat. Among the Vandals it is understood as the robe of a king."

"Perhaps that is why," said the giant, "that the two Basungs crossed the Lothar, to obtain such a robe."

"Doubtless," said the Herul.

The two Basungs, those who had drawn the sledge to the Herul camp, had been killed.

"Why do you give it to me?" asked the giant.

"It was you who killed the beast," said the Herul. "It is thus yours."

"Why do you return to me the sword, why give me these things?"

"It does not matter," said the Herul.

"Why?" asked the giant.

"The Heruls grow fat, and slack," said the Herul. "They need splendid enemies."

"I do not understand."

"It does not matter," said the Herul.

"I thank you for these gifts," said the giant.

"The woman whom I brought with me," said the Herul, "will have fled by now."

"She was a slave?"

"Yes."

"She may be easily followed in the snow," said the giant, "thence to be recaptured, thence to be beaten, or to have her feet cut off, or be fed to dogs."

"I shall leave such decisions to you," said the Herul.

"I do not understand," said the giant.

"She thought herself brought with me, late at night, in the cold, to perform the services of the slave female, to cook, to lie at my feet, to warm them, to give pleasure with her body, her lips and tongue, and such. It is common on journeys to bring slaves, for such things."

"But you brought her here, to let her escape?"

"Of course," said the Herul.

"When you freed her of the pommel, she doubtless thought it merely to free the horse of its impediment, to prepare for combat with me, taken as your quarry."

"That was my intention, that she should think so."

"But she is now fled."

"But should not be difficult to follow, in the snow."

"No," said the giant.

"Do you know where you are?" asked the Herul.

"No," said the giant.

"You are within two days journey of the forests of the Otungs," said the Herul. "It was at my request that Mujiin brought the wagons here."

"Does the slave know where she is?"

"Certainly," said the Herul.

"I do not know the way to the Otungs," said the giant.

"She will know the way," said the Herul.

"Then I need only follow her," said the giant.

"That was my intention," said the Herul.

"Why have you shown me these kindnesses?" asked the giant.

"I am old now," said the Herul. "And I must be killed one day. I think I would like to be killed by you."

"I have no quarrel with you," said the giant.

"But we are enemies, the Heruls, and the Otungs."

"I am a peasant, from the *festung* village of Sim Giadini," said the giant.

"No," said the Herul. "You are an Otung."

"I do not know that I am an Otung," said the giant.

"You are Otung," said the Herul.

"I do not know who I am," said the giant.

"That is true," said the Herul. "You do not know who you are."

"What is the name of the slave?" asked the giant.

"It is she whom you know," said the Herul.

"Yata?"

"Yes."

"The night is clear," said the giant. "I will follow her in the morning."

"Do not let her know she is being followed."

"No," said the giant.

"By the way," said the Herul, "she is a camp slave. We thought that might be useful, she once the daughter of an Otung noble, to help her understand, particularly at the beginning, the nature of her new condition, that of slave."

"What is the nature of the camp slave?" asked the giant.

"She is the common property of the camp," said the Herul. "She must beg and give pleasure before she is fed. She may be disposed of, in any fashion, by anyone in the camp, such things."

"I see," said the giant.

"I give her to you," said the Herul.

"A runaway slave?"

"Yes."

"My thanks," said the giant.

"It is nothing," said the Herul.

"And, in any case," said the giant, "she would be subject to claimancy."

"I see that you have thought on the matter," said the Herul.

"Yes," said the giant.

"When you apprehend her," said the Herul, "do not forget that she is a runaway slave, that she has fled from her former masters."

"I will not," said the giant.

The Herul regarded him, from the high saddle.

"It is a dangerous time to go among Otungs," said the Herul, "for it is the Killing Time."

"I have heard that," said the giant.

"Be careful."

"I shall."

"Do not think the white pelt will protect you," said the Herul. "There are men who will kill for such a pelt."

"It is of great value, and yet you have given it to me."

"It is yours," said the Herul.

"I do not want to kill you," said the giant.

"Do not the sons always kill the fathers?" asked the Herul.

"You are not my father," said the giant.

"You are the nearest thing I have ever had to a son," said the Herul.

He then turned his mount, and began to move away.

"Who are you?" called the giant, standing in the snow. "What is your name?"

"Hunlaki," said the figure, moving away.

· · · CHAPTER 23 · · ·

He heard the woman scream.

He hastened forward, through the snow.

The great blade was already unsheathed. He had unsheathed it several minutes ago, when he had first caught the smell of the animal.

He had then followed her recent tracks, rather than paralleling them, from a distance, as was his wont, in case she might look back, or retrace her steps. He had seen, with her tracks, but fresher, those of the beast.

Other than the scream and the sound of his hurried movements through the trees the forest was very quiet.

The moon was out, and its light, and that of the stars, fell through the bare branches of the scattered trees, and thence, amidst the tracery of shadows, to the snow, brilliantly illuminating it, sparkling on its cold, bleak surface, silvery, and crystalline, like frozen fire, soft, cold fire.

He came upon her in a small clearing. She was on her hands and knees in the snow, where she had, he supposed, been scratching for roots, or seeds, under the snow, even under the brittle layers of frozen leaves.

The bear had risen up on its hind legs, its forepaws extended. It was some seven feet in height.

We shall speak of the Tangaran forest *wroth* as a bear, first, in virtue of our common practice of using familiar expressions for resembling creatures tending to occupy and exploit similar ecological spheres in similar manners, and, second, because of its resemblance to the *arn* bear, originally indigenous to Kiros, but popular, because of its spirit and aggressiveness, in imperial arenas for generations.

"Ho!" called the giant, rushing forward.

He did this not from any misplaced sense of fair play, and a man would unhesitantly have been cut down from the back, but to turn the animal, so that its two hearts, which are paired, and ventrally situated, like those of the *arn* bear, which he had learned to fight, would be turned toward him.

The blade drove between the paws of the angered beast, driving through the right-side heart.

The beast struck with its paw, to knock the blade away, and the paw, slashed, streamed blood in the moonlit snow.

The woman screamed.

She could not see clearly what was occurring, from the turned beast before her.

She crawled backward in the snow.

The giant withdrew the blade, jerking it free.

The beast stood on its hind legs, regarding him, balefully, and put its paw in its mouth.

The rearing to the hind legs increases the stature of the bear and tends to intimidate in intraspecific combat and to startle, overawe and immobilize many forms of prey in hunting.

Too, of course, it considerably increases, as is common with an upright posture, the scanning range of the optical sensors. In the case of the bear there were two optical sensors, as is common in many species, given the advantages of binocular vision and paired organs.

Such a posture, however, does expose the torso to hazards unlikely to be encountered in its natural habitat, blades of steel, cord-driven or gas-impelled projectiles, and such.

Within its mighty frame valves were closing, and opening, sealing away the ruptured, spilling organ within its breast, and rerouting pounding, rushing charges of blood, wreaking changes within its body, like the damming and rechanneling of rivers within some bulky, concealed domain.

The bear went to all fours, protecting its other heart.

It snarled and charged.

The man braced himself, on one knee in the snow. The bear drove itself on the blade, six inches or more, and then, growling, backed off, snarling. It approached again but more cautiously. This time it was fended back. It struck at the blade, pushing its point to one side with the bleeding paw.

The blade reached out, again, and blood sprang from the snout of the bear.

The bear then backed away, a yard or two, in the snow. Then it turned, and began to move away.

The *arn* bear can behave similarly.

The woman had disappeared.

But the giant was not now concerned for her, nor for her safety.

It was not she who was now in danger.

The giant, breathing heavily, rose up from one knee, from the snow.

He took a step forward, considering that he might pursue the beast, but slipped. He caught his balance, bracing himself with the blade.

Then the beast had seemed to slip away, amidst the trunks of the trees, the tracery of the wickedly dark shadows, so black against the cold, moonlit snow.

The giant uttered an angry noise.

But surely the bear had withdrawn from the fray, having had enough. Surely it had abandoned this territory, the infringement on which may have motivated its initial behavior. Surely it, surly, its fur matted, and stinking, perhaps aroused from its den, where it might have slept until late winter or early spring, would simply abandon its country.

The giant kicked about in the snow, working his boots down to the frozen leaves, the thick, crackling matting carpeting the forest's icy floor.

In this fashion he would have solid footing.

But the beast was gone, and the danger past.

It is few men who would pursue such a beast at such a time. One tends to be too grateful, simply that one is still alive. Too, it is difficult to administer a blow with lethal effect to a retreating four-legged animal. It is almost necessary to be at least abreast of it, or nearly so. Too, one does not know, really, what it is doing. Indeed even beasts within the same species differ in such matters.

The beast was surely gone now.

It is hard to know, sometimes, what it is doing.

Indeed, perhaps the animal itself, so natural does its retreat seem, does not know what it is doing. Perhaps it only understands when suddenly, irresistibly, in its given time and order, the second mechanism, instantaneously, savagely, engages.

The forest was extremely quiet.

The beast must now, surely, be gone.

Perhaps it had not abandoned its territory. After all, the man was not of its species. It was not as though another bear, or *wroth*, had driven it away. Perhaps the animal had, by now, simply returned to its lair, to nurse its wounds, to sleep.

The giant stood for several minutes in the snow.

It was hard to hold the great blade at the ready.

Then he rested the blade on his shoulder.

How much, he wondered, is this thing, the Tangaran forest *wroth*, like the *arn* bear.

In the arena, of course, the footing is better, and there is good lighting, as there must be, for the spectators.

The forest was extremely quiet.

It is gone, thought the giant. It is gone.

No, thought the giant. Remember the school of Pulendius, remember the *arn* bear.

But this is not an *arn* bear, he told himself. It is something different. It may be like an *arn* bear, but it is not an *arn* bear. There must be many differences. Doubtless there must be many differences.

That was doubtless correct, but, of course, the question in point had to do with a particular modality of behavior. Was it like, or unlike, the *arn* bear in that respect?

The answer to this question, of course, he did not know.

Too, animals, as men, differ among themselves.

It is gone, he told himself. It is gone.

At that moment there was a savage roar from behind him and a scuffling, rushing sound in the snow.

In the school of Pulendius he, and the others, at any sudden, unexpected sound had been trained, even with blows, to react instantly, the same cry which might thus in one person induce startled, momentary immobility becoming the trigger in another, properly conditioned, to movement.

But he could scarcely interpose the blade and he was struck from his feet.

He scrambled up, throwing himself to the side, as the beast turned like a whip, and he flung the sword up between them. The beast struck at it and bit at it. Then its jaws were full of blood. The giant leapt to his feet, and turned, and struck at the forelegs of the animal, it growling, air bursting through the bubbles of blood in its mouth, and it went down, legs cut away at the second joint, and the man raised the sword again, and, as the beast turned, head lifted, reaching for him, jaws gaping, he struck it across the skull, over the right eye, cutting away part of the skull, and then, as the beast stopped, as though puzzled, and lowered its head slowly, tissue and brains wet on the side of its face and in the snow, he raised the great blade again, and, slashing down, severed the vertebrae and half the neck. It then lay convulsing in the snow.

· · · CHAPTER 24 · · ·

The fire was well blazing.

It sizzled, and hissed, as grease, from roasting bear meat, fell into the flames.

There was wood aplenty, cold, fallen and dry, from the trees about. It had not been so on the plains. It is not hard to make a firedrill, even without a cord, and tiny shavings, cut by the Herul knife, and crushed, crumbled leaves, the ice broken out of them, dried and heated, warmed, against the skin, had taken the heat of friction, and begun to smolder, with a tiny, curling thread of smoke, and then flicker, and then spring up, in an infancy of encouraged fire, in which, soon, twigs blazed, and then hand-broken kindling.

She sat to one side, bound hand and foot.

It had not been difficult to follow her in the snow, her prints clear.

She had known he was about, of course, from the moment she had had a clear glimpse of him, earlier, he clad in the skins of the dogs, cowled in the head of the dog, in the moonlight, terrible, with the sword, engaged with the bear.

She had fled.

Surely he would be killed.

In any event she must flee.

But, in a time, knowing herself followed, he making no secret of the matter, she had turned, at bay, armed with a stick.

"Does a slave," he had inquired, "raise a weapon against a free man?"

Swiftly she had thrown the stick down, into the snow.

"Remain standing," he had said, "turn about, place your hands, wrists crossed, behind your back."

She faced away from him, trembling, in tears.

He lashed her wrists together, behind her back, with a leather cord, part of the drawstring from the bag given him by the Herul, which had contained some food, meal, cheese and strips of meat, cut paper thin in the summer and dried on poles. In this way flies do not lay their eggs in it. He cut the drawstring in such a way that there was enough left over for her ankles.

She squirmed a little, inching a bit closer to the fire.

"Where did you get the pelt of the white vi-cat?" she asked.

"It seems," he said, "that on the prairie I killed the animal, that it died from blows I inflicted. Others skinned it. It was given to me by a Herul, one named Hunlaki. You know Hunlaki."

"Yes," she said. "I know Hunlaki." She shuddered. She was a human female, and a slave.

"I had killed another vi-cat earlier," he said, "a smaller animal, one with a mottled coat. That pelt they kept."

"I do not believe that you, alone, could kill the white vi-cat," she said.

He shrugged.

"I killed the bear," he said.

"You were fortunate," she said.

"Perhaps," he said.

After he had captured her he had returned to the carcass of the bear which he had then, she kneeling nearby, bound, in the snow, had skinned. He also took a quantity of meat from it. He had put the meat in the skin and tied it all, with sinew, into a long roll. This roll he put about her neck, and tied its ends together, before her. He had then gathered up his other things and left the place, she following.

An hour later, a good distance from the remains of the bear, which might attract scavengers, or wolves, he had found a place which had seemed suitable for a camp.

He had there relieved her of her burden and freed her hands, that she might, under his watchful eye, gather wood for the fire. When she had returned several times, with suitable fuel, which she placed to the side, he had rebound her, this time crossing her ankles, and serving her feet as well. He had then set about making the fire.

"Thank you for not stripping me in the snow," she said.

"You are not going anywhere," he said.

She squirmed a little, angrily.

"There are few furs for you," he added.

This sort of thing has been mentioned, the common practice, in the winter, and in cold areas, of transporting, and housing, slaves naked, in furs, as a way of increasing their vulnerability and rendering escape impractical. It might be mentioned that in areas of blazing heat, and burning soils, as on various worlds, a similar practice obtains, only there the slaves have only a sheet of reflective material to gather about themselves, and are denied insulated boots, and such protective gear.

"You did not think," said he, "that I would permit you, a mere slave, to be wrapped in the pelt of the vi-cat, did you, as though you might be a queen, in the arms of a king?"

"I am Hortense," she said, "daughter of Thuron, noble of the Otungs."

He did not respond.

"Build up the fire," she suggested.

"This is the forest of the Otungs," he said.

"Oh?" she said.

"Yes," he said.

"They are far away," she said. "There is no danger. Build up the fire."

He threw some extra wood on the blaze. "I am hungry," she said.

They were some two days into the forest.

"There is some meat of dog, raw," he said, "some cheese, some dried meat, some meal."

"There is roast bear meat," she said.

"True," he said, watching the meat sizzle on the spit, propped over the blaze. He turned it a little, twisting the spit, and more grease dropped, hissing, into the fire.

"I have had only some nuts, some roots, some seeds," she said. "It is hard to find anything, under the snow."

"When did you eat last?" he asked.

"Yesterday," she said.

"You must be very hungry," he said.

"Yes!" she said.

"The meat is almost done," he said.

"Excellent," she said.

"Do you think you will be given any?" he asked.

"Beast!" she cried, and struggled to free herself, but could not do so.

He observed her, dispassionately.

"I am Hortense," she said, "daughter of Thuron, noble of the Otungs!"

He did not respond to her.

"Why have you followed me?" she asked. "You have a Herul knife. Did you take it from Hunlaki? Did you kill him?"

"No," said the giant. "No."

"Have you come to spy for Heruls on Otungs, as it is said the Hageen did?"

"No," said the giant.

"Why did you come?" she asked.

"Perhaps I found your flanks of interest, as those of slave," he said.

She stiffened angrily, but he sensed that something in her was flattered, perhaps the woman, the slave, in her.

"Perhaps," he said, "I come on the business of Telnaria."

"Telnaria?" she said.

"Are you disappointed?" he asked.

"No!" she cried. "That is the last thing I would be," she assured him.

"Oh," he said.

"To spy?"

"No," he said.

"You are a Telnarian dog?" she said.

"I am from the *festung* village of Sim Giadini," he said. "It is near the heights of Barrionuevo, some miles from the *festung* of Sim Giadini. Some of the Otungs may know it, from the days when they rode free on the plains of Barrionuevo."

"On the flats of Tung?"

"As you wish," he said.

"A peasant?" she asked.

"Perhaps," said the giant. "I do not know."

"Build up the fire more," she suggested.

"You are sure it is safe," he said.

"Certainly," she said.

He put more wood on the fire.

She smiled.

"The meat is done," he said. He drew the spit from the forked sticks on which it had been supported. He put the meat down on the bearskin. He drew out his knife.

"Feed me!" she said.

"On your knees, and crawl to the fire," he said.

She struggled to her knees, and then, with small movements, inch by inch, made her way to the fire.

"Feed me!" she demanded.

"Why?" he asked.

"I am Hortense," she said, "daughter of Thuron, noble of the Otungs."

"It is late at night," he said, "and one supposes that Otungs would now, in this winter, in this cold, in their halls, and huts, and such, be deep in their furs, would be well abed."

"I do not understand," she said.

"It is nothing," he said.

"I do not understand," she said, uncertainly.

"So there would be little point, really, in my building up the fire."

"I only wished to be warmer," she said.

"It seems unlikely that there would be Otungs about," he said. "Do you not agree?"

"Yes," she said, uncertainly.

"If they were about, surely," said he, "they would have intruded by now."

She nodded, weakly.

"Thus," said he, "it seems, clearly, that we must be quite alone. Do you not agree?"

"Yes!" she said, angrily.

"And in the morning," said he, "when discovery might be more likely, though still a remote possibility, in the morning, when Otungs might possibly be about, though the chances of encountering them would be surely extremely slight, we will not be here."

She looked at him, fearfully.

"Where will you take me?" she asked. "What will you do with me?"

"You are a slave," he said. "I will take you where I wish, and do with you what I please."

"Free me!" she said.

"One does not free slaves," he said, "particularly ones who are well curved."

She made an angry noise, and tore at her bonds, futilely, but, too, he could see that something within her was not displeased at all, something perhaps the woman, the slave.

"Do you wish to be fed?"

"Yes," she said.

"Were you not a camp slave?" he asked.

"Yes," she said.

"And you were such for some two years?"

"Yes," she said.

"You must then," he said, "be in the habit of begging and giving pleasure, before you are fed."

"I am a free woman!" she said. "I am Hortense, daughter of Thuron, noble of the Otungs!"

"Slaves are given names by their masters," he said. "What is your name?"

She looked at him, angrily.

He cut a small piece of meat, hot and juicy. She eyed it, covetously.

"What name were you given?" he asked.

"Yata," she said.

"What is your name?" he asked.

"Yata!" she said.

"Yata, what?" he asked.

"Yata, Master!" she said.

"There is one reason for my following you, which does not seem to have occurred to you," he said.

"What is that?" she asked.

"You are a runaway slave," he said.

"No!" she said.

"Surely you are," he said. "And you have now been caught."

She looked up at him, trembling.

"Perhaps," he said, "I have been sent to apprehend you, and return you to the camp, to your masters."

"Do not!" she wept. "They would cut off my feet! They would kill me!"

"But I have not followed you to return you to your master," he said.

"Thank you, Master!" she cried.

"For you have been given to me," he said, "and it is I who am now your master."

"No!" she said.

"Yes," he said. "You were given to me. You are my slave."

"No!" she wept.

"And were it not such," said he, "I would make you mine now, by claimancy."

"No, no, no!" she wept.

Then she looked up at him.

"Does Yata beg?" he asked.

"Am I still Yata?" she asked.

"That name will do," he said, "unless I see fit to change it."

"It is a Herul name!" she wept.

"It seems fitting," he said, "for one who was a Herul slave."

He rose to his feet.

He looked down at her.

"Does Yata beg?" he asked.

He held the piece of meat, lifted, in his right hand.

"Yata begs!" she wept.

"Now Yata may give pleasure," he said.

"Yes, Master," she whispered.

A bit later she had fed, still kneeling, her hands tied behind her, her head down, reaching down to the snow, retrieving pieces of meat thrown there, before her.

He enjoyed seeing her take meat thusly, before him.

"That is enough," he finally said.

She looked up at him.

"You may come forth," he called out, among the trees. "You have been seen. I know you have been there for some time."

She looked about, startled, and struggled to rise to her feet, but, her ankles crossed and bound, she could not do so.

Several fur-clad figures emerged from the trees, from all sides.

"Greetings," said the giant.

He motioned that they might join him about the fire, and partake of the meat, but they remained standing.

"You are Otungs?" asked the giant.

"Yes," said one of the visitors.

"Good," said the giant.

"Perhaps not," said one of the newcomers.

"I am Otung!" cried the girl, from her knees.

"She has no tribe," said the giant. "She is a slave girl."

"I am Hortense," she said, "daughter of Thuron! Free my ankles of the thong that binds them! Let me stand! Cut the thong that binds my wrists!"

He who seemed to be the leader of the fur-clad fellows come from the forest, a large man, bearded, with blond, braided hair falling over his shoulders, looked down upon her.

"You looked well, giving pleasure," he said.

"Perhaps you can give pleasure to all of us," said another of the fur-clad men.

"That is what women are good for," said another.

"Is she yours?" asked the leader of the fur-clad men of the giant.

"Yes," he said.

"What is her name?" asked the leader of the fur-clad men.

"Yata," said the giant.

"A Herul name."

"Yes."

"I am Hortense!" cried the girl. "I am the daughter of Thuron, noble of the Otungs!"

"Thuron is dead," said one of the men.

The girl drew back.

"She was a Herul slave?" asked the leader of the Otungs.

"Yes," said the giant.

"No!" suddenly cried the girl.

"As a Herul slave, you are useless to us," said one of the Otungs to the girl.

"You were taken with your maidens, while bathing," said one of the Otungs.

"No!" said the girl.

"Your garments were found upon the banks, and in the mud, though soon vanished, the marks of transport poles," said one of the Otungs.

"No, no!" said the girl.

"Where are your maidens?" asked an Otung.

"I do not know," she said.

"They fell to Heruls, and were made slaves," said an Otung.

"I escaped, and fled, and have been hiding, and wandering," said the girl. "I was not made a slave. I can prove that! You see I have no collar, no anklet, no bracelet! Let me be examined by women. You will not find a mark on my body!"

"Why were you not with your maidens?" asked an Otung.

"I went into the woods, to gather flowers," she said, hastily.

"Why did you leave them?" asked an Otung.

"Why did you not look out for them?" asked another.

"Surely you heard the sounds of their capture," said another.

"No, no," she said.

"Your own garments were found with theirs, on the bank," said another.

"But I was not there!" she said.

"Why did you not return to the villages, to rouse the men?" asked an Otung.

"I was trying to elude capture," she said.

"Where did you obtain the garments you are wearing?" asked one of the Otungs.

"I stole them, in my wanderings, from Heruls," she said.

"You were long in your wanderings," said one of the Otungs.

"I should have returned sooner," she said, "but I was captured by this Telnarian dog! I am his prisoner, as you see, but not his slave! I am now rescued!"

"The maidens were comely," said an Otung. "We have learned that they were sold in Scharnhorst, and thence transported to other worlds, where they were to be vended in slave markets."

"That proves my story!" she said. "Had I been enslaved, I would have shared their fate!"

"Perhaps you were insufficiently comely," said an Otung.

She reacted, as if struck.

"She is comely enough to be vended in a market," said the giant. "Indeed, I think her beauty was such that it was adjudged worthy of being retained among the wagons. Too, I think it amused the Heruls to keep in their lowest bondage, at least for a time, one who had been the daughter of an Otung noble."

"She was a camp slave?" said the Otung leader.

"Yes," said the giant.

"No!" cried the girl.

"You were not a camp slave?" asked the Otung leader.

"No!" said the girl. "I—I was not even a slave!"

"Cut the thongs on her ankles," said the leader of the Otungs.

"Thank you, noble lord!" said the girl.

"Remain on your knees," he cautioned her, as she made as though to rise.

"Milord!" she protested.

"In the village," he said, "we shall look into the truth of these matters."

"We have ways, as you know," said one of the Otungs.

"And woe to you," said one of the Otungs, "if you have lied."

"Doubtless Citherix will be pleased to see you returned to the village, and as a *slave*," said one of the Otungs.

The girl turned white.

"You refused his suits often enough," said one of the Otungs.

The girl, her ankles freed, but her hands still bound behind her, on her knees, trembled.

To these matters the giant was attentive.

"Where did you steal the pelt of a white vi-cat?" asked the leader of the Otungs of the giant.

"It is mine. I did not steal it," said the giant.

"Why are you in the forest?" asked the leader of the Otungs.

"I have come to find Otungs," said the giant.

"But it seems that it is you who have been found by them," said a man.

"It is my way of finding them," said the giant. "Else, why would I build the fire so high?"

"You will now come with us," said the leader of the Otungs.

"Of course," said the giant.

"You know this is the Killing Time?" asked the leader of the Otungs.

"Yes," said the giant.

"And yet you came?"

"Yes."

"He has with him the pelt of the giant white vi-cat," said one of the Otungs.

"That is the pelt of a king," said another of the Otungs.

"I have heard so," said the giant.

"It is all very strange," said one of the Otungs.

"Put out the fire," said the leader of the Otungs. "Destroy all traces of the camp. Gather up the meat. Tie it about the neck of the woman. Gag her. Bring the bearskin, and his goods, and the pelt of the white vi-cat."

"Bring, too, the weapon," said the leader of the Otungs.

"I will bring that," said the giant.

One of the men looked to the leader.

"Very well," said the leader of the Otungs.

"He has a knife," said one of the men.

"A Herul knife," said another.

"I keep that, too," said the giant.

The leader of the Otungs nodded.

The group then left the scene of the small encampment and made its ways through the trees, and the black shadows, trudging through the pale, moonlit snow. The leader of the Otungs went first and, behind him, flanked by two Otungs, came the giant, the great blade upon his shoulder. Then came the rest of the Otungs, some dozen or so. Lastly came the woman, her hands tied behind her, the balance of the roast bear meat tied, rolled and thonged, about her neck. She was gagged. The men did not now wish to hear her speak. Accordingly, she was silenced. Her case, such as it might be, would be considered in the village. Too, in the event she should prove to be a slave, the gag, in its bands, which was a heavy and broad one, denied the meat to her, even that she might somehow touch it with her tongue. The feeding of a slave, as is commonly understood, is subject to the supervision of the master, subject, for example, to his generosity, his convenience, and even his discretion.

· · · CHAPTER 25 · · ·

"There are the men of Rolof," said one of the Otungs.

Other figures, booted, similarly fur-clad, in jackets and cloaks, armed, were seen among the trees.

This had been after a trek of some two hours through the forest, from the giant's small encampment, the fire from which had attracted the attention of the men of Ulrich, for that was the name of the leader of the Otungs, those with whom the giant was now in company.

Some quarter of an hour later another such group, consisting of some nineteen men, was detected, it, too, moving through the forest.

"Those are the men owing faith to the house of Valdemar," said one of the Otungs with the giant.

As time passed, more and more of these groups were observed.

Interestingly, to the giant, these groups, though apparently all Otungs, neither hailed one another, nor marched together.

There were now several such groups, some almost side by side, several within at least yards of one another, who made their way through the snow.

Similar groups, though this was at that time not known to the giant, were converging on a given point from other directions.

At last, through the trees, better than a hundred yards ahead, a long, low feature could be seen. It would have been quite natural, initially, at the distance, and particularly in the light, to have mistaken it for a natural feature, an eccentricity of terrain. It seemed, on the whole, like an extended hillock, or mound.

"We will stop here," said Ulrich.

"Why?" asked the giant, drawing up to him.

"We must wait for admittance," said Ulrich.

"Admittance?"

"To the hall," said Ulrich.

"Ah," said the giant.

Such halls, or, perhaps better, lest a misleading conception be conveyed, common shelters, are encountered more frequently farther to the north. About the structure of wood, formed of stout timbers, or of great logs, if they may be found, dirt is heaped, and then packed. The hall, or shelter, is oriented north to south, that neither of its main surfaces will be exposed to the northern winds. The entrance, or back of the hall, in a sense, surely that area away from the high seats, faces north, and the front of the hall, where are found the high seats, backs against the southern wall. This particular hall was a large one, for its type, being some seventy-five yards on its long axis; twenty-five yards in width, the roof supported by the walls and two rows of timber columns, in the manner of a three-aisle house; and some four or five yards raised above the surrounding level of the forest. Within the hall itself, of course, whose floor was cut down into the forest floor, it was better than eight or ten yards from the floor, of dirt, to the rafters of the roof. The hall then is half sunken into, or half dug into, the floor of the forest. One descends to the interior floor by means of stone steps. The dirt is heaped some two thirds, or better, of the way up the walls. It does not cover the full height of the exterior walls, or the roof. In the roof, and high on the walls, there are smoke holes. Given the width of the structural timbers it is difficult, unless the holes were to be considerably enlarged, to fire arrows into the hall from the roof, or from ladders, in any martially efficient manner. The dirt packing provides some protection against fire, but, on the whole, given that the gate cannot be forced, the common weapon for reducing such a hall is indeed fire. If one wishes to keep the hall, then one must make do with forcing the gate, or cutting through the walls, at some point or another.

Such structures, it might be noted, in passing, are not designed for defense, but for housing and warmth. They do provide some security, in the sense that they are isolated, in remote areas, and that it is dangerous to approach them. Otungs, and many of the forest peoples, withdraw to, and fight from the stealth, the silence and darkness of the forest itself. Indeed, long ago, imperial cohorts perished, pursuing them in such environments. Hill forts, on the other hand, are known west of the Lothar, among the Basungs. Indeed, it was such forts that largely stopped the advance of the Heruls into the western forests, long ago, in the winter of 1103, in the chronology of the imperial claiming stone, from the placing of which time, or, at least, history, from the viewpoint of the imperial records, began on Tangara.

The giant could see smoke, in pale wisps, emerging from smoke holes. And through some of these, and chinks in the logs, high in the walls, he could detect some flickering, as of a lighting within.

"So you have come to the hall," said the giant, "and there is no rejoicing?"

One would suppose, of course, that the coming to the hall, from the outside, at such a time, from the dark night and the winter, when one is hungry and cold, would constitute a joyous occasion, one that would be eagerly looked forward to, and retained long afterward in the warmth of memory.

"Among the Otungs, for many years," said Ulrich, "there has been little rejoicing."

"I shall change that," said the giant.

"Let us kill the stranger," said one of the men, angrily.

"Let us clear a space in the snow," said the giant. "We will then consider the matter."

The fellow looked at the mighty stature of the giant, and the great blade upon his shoulder, like a flat, sheathed bolt of sleeping lightning, and looked away.

"These are important times for the Otungs," said the leader of the Otungs. "Strangers are seldom welcome in the forests, but, at this time, in particular, we do not welcome them."

"At this time," said another, "it is common to kill them."

"Perhaps I am not a stranger," said the giant.

"This is the time of the claiming of the hero's portion," said an Otung.

"And the naming of the king," said another.

"I know," said the giant.

"At such a time, you come amongst us?"

"Yes," said the giant.

"Why?" asked a man.

"I would speak with he who is first amongst you," said the giant.

"I do not understand what you are doing here," said one of the men.

"Perhaps I am coming home," said the giant.

· · · CHAPTER 26 · · ·

"Give her," called out Urta, the King Namer, "the drink of truth!"

"No, milord!" cried out the girl. "It is as I have said! I swear it!"

Two men seized the girl by the arms, holding her before the high seats. In the midst of the high seats on the dais was a throne, high-backed, with huge arms, of heavy, ornately carved wood. This throne was empty. To its right there was a small stool. It was from that stool that Urta, the King Namer, had arisen.

"There is the torch," had said Ulrich, waiting outside the hall, several yards away, in the snow. "We may now enter."

He, and his party, including the giant, had then approached the portal of the hall.

"Who is he?" challenged the gatesman, lifting his torch.

"A stranger," had said Ulrich.

"Kill him!" said the guard.

"Do so yourself," said Ulrich.

"You may not enter!" said the gatesman.

"I will," said the giant. "I do. I am."

"Stop him!" cried the gatesman, thrust to the side, staggering against the jamb of the gate.

The giant turned. He surveyed, slowly, evenly, those about the portal. "Who will do so?" he asked.

Then he had turned about, and descended the stone steps to the interior of the hall.

"Who is he, Ulrich?" inquired the gatesman.

"I do not know," said Ulrich.

"What is that you have with you?" asked the gatesman.

"It is the pelt of the white vi-cat," said Ulrich.

"You dare bring such a thing to the hall?" inquired the gatesman.

"It is not mine," said Ulrich. "It belongs to the stranger."

"You do not know him?"

"No."

"How dare he bring such a thing here?"

"I do not know," said Ulrich.

"Surely he does not understand its meaning," said the gatesman.

"I do not know," had said Ulrich.

"Enter," had said the gatesman.

"Administer the drink of truth!" commanded Urta, the King Namer.

The girl was dressed now in the beads and robes, and sleeves, of the daughter of an Otung noble. Her hair had been brushed, and braided, and was inwrought with strings of pearls, brought in trade, via Heruls, from Venitzia, or Scharnhorst, as the Otungs have it. Her vesture had been provided by free women in the hall, and she had been so arrayed in a pantry, a storage room.

There had been gasps of admiration as she had been brought forth, and conducted to the front of the hall.

One of the men had come forth, from the side, and looked upon her closely, as she had awaited the recognition of Urta, the King Namer. The giant had stood toward the rear of the hall, the blade now sheathed, his arms folded on his broad chest, with Ulrich, and his men.

The two men who held the girl's arms tightened their grip. Another man pulled her head back, by the hair, and, as she was held, her body was drawn back, as well, this bending her backward, hair held. Her mouth was then held upward, facing the rafters. A soft, thrilled gasp of pleasure coursed through the free women present. The men were intent. Another man then forced a block of wood, in which a funnel had been inserted, between her teeth. A fourth man then poured liquid into the funnel, while pinching shut her nostrils. Her eyes were wild. Some liquid spilled at the sides of her mouth. The man then desisted for a moment. In a few moments, in misery, she gasped for breath, and drank. This was repeated, again, and then again, in greater pain and misery, and then, after that, realizing resistance was useless, she, tears in her eyes, swallowed the fluid.

"It is more than enough," said Urta, waving away the fellow with the bottle.

The man holding her bent backward released her.

She stood, unsteadily.

The two men holding her arms now supported her, rather than restrained her.

"Bring a chair for her," said Urta.

The girl sat in the chair, but, soon, began to move her head back and forth, in misery, as though fighting sleep, as though struggling to retain consciousness, and then she slumped in the chair, and half turned in it, grasping one arm.

"No, no," she wept.

She tried, suddenly, to thrust a finger in her mouth, to free herself of the liquid, but, instantly, a man pulled her hand away, and then her arms were held, each wrist by a man, but it was not necessary to hold her thusly for more than a few moments, as she half sank down in the chair, and her head went back, over the back of the chair.

"What is that?" asked the giant of Ulrich, at the back of the hall.

"It is the drink of truth," said Ulrich, simply.

"What does it do?" asked the giant.

"You will see," said Ulrich.

"Who is that?" had cried Urta, startled, at the appearance of the giant in the hall.

His presence was not easy to conceal, as he had the breadth of a man and a half, and stood easily better than a head above the others in the hall, many of whom were large men, tall men, men of unusual stature.

This was not unusual among the barbarian peoples, the Alemanni, the Vandals, and many others.

It was one reason they tended to inspire fear in the men of the empire. Another reason was because they, the barbarians, were the sort of men they were.

The giant stood in a space which had seemed mysteriously to clear away about him, in the back of the hall, away from the high seats, at the foot of the stone stairs which led down into the hall.

"It is a stranger," said Ulrich.

"How have you dared to bring him here?" asked Urta.

"It was, I think, his wish," said Ulrich.

"You are a fool!" cried Urta.

"He has with him the pelt of the white vi-cat," said Ulrich.

"Ai!" cried men in the hall. Women, too, cried out. Exchanged were glances of startled surmise.

"Then he is a fool!" cried Urta.

"Or a king," said a man.

"Who are you?" asked Urta of the giant.

"I am Otto," said the giant, "chieftain of the Wolfungs."

There was a cry of amazement, of skepticism, in the hall.

"The Wolfungs no longer exist," said Urta.

"Some survive, some hundreds," said the giant, "in the forests of Varna, to which they were banished, generations ago."

The relationship between the Wolfungs, the smallest of the Vandal tribes, and the Otungs, the largest of the Vandal tribes, and, indeed, the other three tribes of the Vandal nation, the Basungs, Darisi and Haakons, had tended to be lost.

"You are Wolfung?" asked Urta.

"I do not think so," said the giant.

"How is it then that you are chieftain?"

"I was lifted upon the shields," said the giant.

"Are you Otung?" asked Urta, the King Namer.

"I do not know," said the giant.

"He has a Herul knife!" said a man.

"He is a Herul spy!" said another.

"No," said the giant.

"How is it that you have a Herul knife?" asked a man.

"It was given to me."

"By a Herul?"

"Yes."

"He is a Herul spy!"

"No," said the giant.

"He brings with him one who was once Hortense, daughter of Thuron," said Ulrich.

This announcement was greeted with interest.

"Bring her forward," said Urta.

The girl, in her furs, gagged, bound, the meat about her neck, shook away the men near her and pressed herself forward, until she stood boldly before the dais, before the high seats, before Urta.

"It is long since we have looked upon you," said Urta.

She uttered muffled sounds, through the gag.

"Are you Hortense, daughter of Thuron?" asked Urta, his question not suggesting that he failed to recognize the girl, but rather that he was inquiring into her condition.

She nodded, vigorously, affirmatively.

"She was a Herul slave," said the giant, "who was given to me. Her name is Yata."

The girl shook her head, desperately, negatively.

"If you are a slave," said Urta, "you should not be standing before a free man. You should be kneeling, your head down, even to the dirt."

The girl straightened her body, boldly.

"Free her," said Urta. "Take her aside. Garb her as a noble's daughter. Then return her before us, that we may inquire into these matters."

Free women rushed to the girl, and one, with the scissors attached to her belt, together with various keys, accessing chests, and such, common signs of the mistress of a great house, cut the bonds on her wrists. Another, carefully, with her hands, undid the gag. Another removed the meat from about her neck, where she had carried it, collarlike, as might have a slave. They then, gathering about her, as though sheltering her, hurried her from the main room of the hall, to an auxiliary chamber, one of several, this one serving as a storage chamber. In their midst she cast a look of triumph and scorn upon the giant.

"Telnarian dog!" she sneered.

"Are you Telnarian?" asked Urta.

"No," said the giant.

"You bring the pelt of the white vi-cat," said Urta.

"I have it with me," acknowledged the giant.

"Do you bring it as a gift for he who will be chosen this year's king?"

"No, it is mine," said the giant.

"Do you think that you are king, that you have such a pelt?" asked Urta.

"No," said the giant. "The pelt of an animal does not make a king."

"What makes a king?" asked Urta.

The giant removed the sling and sheath from his shoulder, and drew from the fur sheath the great blade.

This caught the reddish light in the half-darkened hall, from the coals in the fire pit, from the torches, thick with pitch and resin, in their racks, jutting out from the columns and walls.

"This," said the giant, "is what makes a king."

"The sword makes the king," agreed a man.

"That was the view of Genserix," said a man. Many then looked to the empty throne.

"Who will kill this stranger?" inquired Urta, angrily.

"I have seen him before," said a man. "Or someone much like him."

"But it was long ago," said a man.

"Yes," said another.

"Call Fuldan, the Old," said a man.

"I will fetch him," said a man, turning about, drawing his cloak about him, hurrying from the hall.

"No!" cried Urta. "Who will kill this stranger?"

The giant moved the great blade about. With his strength he handled it easily. He took a stroke with it, about himself, to loosen his muscles. He set his feet apart. Then, both hands on the long hilt, at the ready, he looked about himself.

"What if he is the king?" asked a man.

"I would not lift a blade against the king," said another.

"There are only year kings," said Urta. "That is the wish of the Heruls! There is no king as before."

Men looked to the empty throne.

"I have not come amongst you to be king," said Otto. "I come amongst you to recruit a company."

Men regarded one another.

"I do not come for your high men," said Otto. "I come for your younger sons, for landless men, for heroes, for those to whom adventure and battle are a lure and a life, I come for the Otungs of old, for Otungs as men."

"Kill him!" cried Urta.

Two or three men edged forward, but stayed well beyond the compass of the great blade.

"I am a trained killer," said Otto. "I have been trained in the school of Pulendius, though you know not that place nor what is done there. I have fought in arenas, for the amusement of populaces. I know things about blades, and war, of which you are ignorant. I tell you these things not to boast nor to cause you apprehension, but only that you may understand what it is against which you would stand."

"I fear you not!" cried a young man.

"Nor is it my wish that you should," said Otto.

Otto looked about himself.

"I have no wish to kill Otungs," he said. "Accordingly I

shall, of any who now challenge me, cut from them one arm only, and they may choose the arm. If they are right-handed, doubtless they would prefer that it be the left arm which is lost. If they are left-handed, doubtless they would prefer that it be the right arm which is lost.''

"Who will challenge him?'' called Urta.

None stepped forward, though many looked about, from one to the other.

"We welcome Otto, chieftain of the Wolfungs, to our hall,'' said Urta.

Half sitting, half lying in the chair, seemingly asleep, or half asleep, her head back, her eyes closed, the girl, restless, disturbed, twisted and turned.

"Were you Hortense, daughter of Thuron, of the Otungs?'' asked Urta.

"Yes,'' said the girl.

"Were you, some two years ago, surprised with your maidens, while bathing naked in the pool of White Stones, west of the holdings of Partinax?''

"Yes,'' she said.

"Did you take them there?''

"Yes.''

"Surely you were aware of the danger.''

"I dismissed such danger,'' she said.

"Surely your maidens were reluctant to follow you.''

"Yes,'' she said.

"Why did they follow you?'' asked Urta.

"Because I teased them and shamed them, if they would not, because I called them cowards, if they would not, because I was a noble, because I was the daughter of Thuron.''

"Go on,'' said Urta.

"In the end,'' she said, "we were all merry, and eager to go, indeed, it seemed that each of us was vying to outdo the other.''

"It was all very naughty, and amusing?''

"Yes,'' she said.

"It was pleasant in the water, bathing, playing, splashing about?''

"Yes,'' she said.

"Then you and your maidens were surprised by Heruls.''

"Yes.''

"You were captured by them?''

"Yes."

"And carried away, to be made slaves?"

"Yes."

"Every one of you?"

"Yes."

"With no exceptions?"

"No."

"You were not then alone in the forest, away from the scene, gathering flowers or such?"

"No."

"You were captured with your maidens?"

"Yes."

"And were you all, without exceptions, including yourself, made slaves?"

"Yes."

There was much response to this in the hall. "The slave!" cried a woman, angrily.

The girl in the chair squirmed.

"But there was no sign of bondage on you when you were found by Ulrich and his men in the forest, no collar, or anklet, or such."

"No."

"And the women tell us that you do not bear a slave brand."

"No," she said, "I am not marked."

"Why are these things as they are?" asked Urta.

"Among Heruls," she said, "what could a woman of our species be but a slave?"

"What was the fate of your maidens?" asked Urta.

"They were sold in Scharnhorst, to Telnarian agents," she said. "Thence they were sold later to wholesalers, of diverse species, and thence sent to various far worlds, there to be sold a third time, there to learn their fate in slave markets."

"How did you learn these things?"

"It pleased the Heruls to inform me, while I knelt abjectly, head to the dirt, before them," she said.

"But you were kept among the wagons?"

"Yes," she said.

"Why?" he asked.

"I was perhaps found desirable," she said.

"As a slave is desirable?"

"Yes."

"In that way?"

"Yes."

One of the women in the hall gasped.

"Be silent!" said another woman to the one who had permitted the small sound to escape from her lips.

"Too," said the girl, "I was the daughter of a noble. Thus I think they enjoyed keeping me with the wagons, being pleased to be served by one who had once been a noblewoman. Too, in the beginning they found me arrogant, and it pleased them that I should be well taught my slavery."

"And did you learn it well?"

"Yes."

There was a soft, half-suppressed, thrilled cry from several of the free women in the hall.

"No! No!" cried one woman, angrily. "Slave! Slave!" she cried.

"I do not understand," said Urta, "why you, and your maidens, surely aware of the risks run, went to such an isolated, lonely place."

"We were courting the collar," said the girl. "I think it was only later that I fully realized that, and the others, too, when we were bound together, later, helpless in our cords. We had wanted to become slaves. That is why we did what we did. We wanted to have no choice but to love and serve, to be owned by masters."

"No, no!" cried an angry free woman in the hall.

"What are you?" inquired Urta.

"I am a female slave," she said. "I have always known it, but I have not dared to speak it."

"How is it that you dare to speak it now?" asked Urta.

"I am now wholly, and secretly, within myself," she said. "I can now speak as I wish, and no one can possibly hear."

"You were a slave of Heruls?"

"Yes."

"But you were found in the forest."

"I fled the Heruls," she said.

"Then you are a runaway slave."

"Yes."

"Perhaps you should be returned to Heruls," said Urta.

She squirmed in the chair, miserably. "No, please, no, Master!" she said.

"She calls him 'Master'!" said a free woman, angrily.

"He is a free man. That is how a slave girl must address him," said a woman.

"Yes," averred another.

"How terrible to be a slave girl!" said a woman.

"Yes," said another, thrilled.

"Why did you run away?" asked Urta.

"I feared the Heruls," she said. "They held me in contempt not only as a slave, which was suitable, but as a human. My beauty, if beauty it is, gave me little protection from them. They did not even give me to a single master, to whom I might then be devoted, whom I might then have endeavored with my whole helplessness and being to please, but to the camp, as a whole. Anyone there might have injured, or killed, me, even a woman or child, on a caprice, or in a fit of impatience. They are not human. They are a different species. Too, everything that I had been taught had told me to be not like a woman, but like a man, that I should be like a man! I thought, thusly, that it was expected of me to run away, and seek freedom. And, too, I need a human master, not a Herul master. I am a human female, and need a human master, someone who can understand me, and will master me as I require. Somewhere I know masters have been prepared for me by nature, just as I, in my heart, know that I have been prepared for them."

"Do you like being a slave?" asked Urta.

"Yes."

"Do you love being a slave?"

"Yes."

"Do you want to be a slave?"

"Yes, yes, yes!" she said. "I want to be a slave! I want to be a slave, totally, helplessly, to be overwhelmed, to be choiceless, to love and serve, to be at the will of my master, to kneel before him, to strive to do his bidding, to attempt to please him in all ways, to the best of my ability, to lie soft in his arms, grateful and timid, obedient and fearful, to be mastered, ruthlessly, uncompromisingly, to be owned!"

"Heat an iron," said Urta to a man at the side. The fellow then turned away, and went back to the fire pit, and stirred the coals.

"You do not mind if your slave is marked?" asked Urta of the giant.

"Not if it is well, and cleanly, done," said the giant.

"It will be so," said Urta.

"Take the slave from the chair," said Urta. "Put her in the dirt. Remove the chair. Strip her. Bind her hands before her body, with a strand free. When she awakens, let her find herself naked and bound, as the slave she is.''

"I will give you five sheep for her," said a man.

"Who are you?" asked the giant.

"Citherix," said the man.

"It seems he will have her after all," said a man.

"But in the best possible way, as a slave," said another.

There was general laughter.

"But she is mine," said the giant.

"I will make it seven sheep," said Citherix.

"I will consider the offer," said the giant.

"Let the fire be built up," said Urta. "Let the gutted boar be brought in, that it may be cooked, and the hero's portion decided."

There was assent to this in the hall.

Two large, four-legged iron supports were put in place, two legs of each on opposite sides of the fire pit, on which an iron spit could be laid, lengthwise, over the fire.

Tables were set up, about the edges of the hall, and, to each side of the throne, upon the dais. These were planked tables, set on trestles. Such arrangements, or settings up, of eating boards is common in many halls, the trestles, and planked surfaces, being stored, sometimes the trestles folded, between meals. These materials are sometimes kept in ancillary chambers, but, quite commonly, are simply placed, or leaned, lengthwise against the walls. In this fashion space within a hall, or great room, may be adjusted, conveniently, to meet the requirements of diverse occasions. Benches are usually kept, too, to the side.

Four men brought in, on its spit, the carcass of a giant, gutted boar.

In a few moments, the carcass turning, the smell of roast boar began to permeate the hall.

The giant had resheathed the sword.

He sat at one of the tables, with Ulrich, whom he had met in the forest, earlier, at his own encampment.

One table, one of heavy planks, and resting on stout trestles, four of them, with no benches about it, was set up before the dais, lengthwise, one end facing the dais, the other pointing to the fire pit.

"What table is that?" asked the giant.

"The table upon which will be placed the roast boar," said Ulrich.

"From which the hero's portion is to be cut?"

"Yes."

"Whose throne is that on the dais, on which no king sits?" asked the giant.

"That is the throne of the Otungs," said Ulrich. "The last king to sit upon it was Genserix."

"Who was he?"

"He was the last true king of the Otungs," said Ulrich. "He died in battle. It was long ago. The Heruls respected him, though he was human. They built a pyre and burned his body upon it. To Genserix even the Heruls lifted their lances."

"No one sits now upon the throne?"

"No," said Ulrich.

"And the medallion and chain of the king, the medallion and chain of the lordship of the Otungs, was lost, long ago," said a man.

"I do not understand," said the giant.

"It does not matter, not now," said Ulrich.

"There are no longer true kings among the Otungs?"

"They have been forbidden to us by the Heruls," said Ulrich. "We may have only year kings, kings who rule for a single year."

"That seems unwise," said the giant.

"It is wise from the point of view of the Heruls," said Ulrich, "for the absence of a true king divides us, and spreads dissension among the lineages."

"Who is the leader, he of the dais?"

"That is Urta, the King Namer," said Ulrich.

"He then is king, or the year king?"

"No, he is the King Namer."

"I do not understand."

"This is not called the Killing Time because we would have the forests closed to strangers during this, our time of shame," said Ulrich, "but it is called the Killing Time because in this time it is common for the families, the lineages, sometimes the clans, to fight one another, to kill, for the possession of, for the prestige of, the kingship."

"It is foolish to fight for an empty throne," said the giant.

"One supposes so," he said.

"What has the hero's portion to do with this?"

"It is divisive," said Ulrich. "There is no king to bestow it, either to the satisfaction or dissatisfaction of the nobles, the lords.

It is, in effect, thrown amongst us, that the strongest, the fiercest, may claim it for himself."

"The strongest, the fiercest, of the lineages, of the clans?" said the giant.

"That is much the way it is," said Ulrich. "What Otung lineage would grant itself less than any other?"

"You are denied then not only a king, not only continuity of leadership, of policy and action," said the giant, "but must war with one another."

"There has always been conflict among the Otungs, among the families," said Ulrich.

"You need a king," said the giant.

"Yes," said Ulrich. "That is true."

"Where will you find one?"

"Perhaps one day," said Ulrich, "someone will bring into the forest the pelt of the giant white vi-cat."

The giant looked at him.

"Why else do you think I brought you to the hall?" asked Ulrich.

· · · CHAPTER 27 · · ·

"Your slave is awakening," called Urta, from the dais.

Otto rose from the bench where he had been sitting with Ulrich, and walked behind the tables, toward the front of the hall. It was his habit to sit with his back to the wall. The high seats on the dais are similarly arranged.

Some other men, and some women, too, hearing Urta's words, went to gather about the uneasily stirring slave. Among the men was Citherix. Ulrich accompanied Otto.

"She is well curved, indeed," said a man to Citherix.

"She is a beauty," said a man.

"I had not expected so much," said Citherix.

The girl lay in the dirt before the dais, between the long table on which the hero's portion was to be cut and the dais.

She rolled about, a little.

She was as naked as any item of livestock.

She seemed puzzled, a little, that she could not separate her wrists. They were bound before her body, tightly, with leather thongs, with a strand, a yard or so in length, free. She made a tiny puzzled, protestive noise.

At the fire pit, behind one of the iron supports, more toward the stairs leading down into the hall, a man, with heavy gloves, lifted an iron from the coals. It was a slaving iron, and its termination, with its small, delicate design, perpendicular to the shaft, and the shaft itself, for some six inches upward from the design, glowed fiercely, whitely. He thrust it back into the coals.

"She will awaken momentarily," said a man.

"Bring a whip," said Urta.

A man brought the implement, and he stood near the girl.

"Oh, oh," moaned the slave, twisting in the dirt.

She was then on her right side, her head rather toward the dais. She opened her eyes.

"Where am I?" she said.

"In the hall of the Otungs," said a man.

"They tend to be disoriented, at first," said a man. "It is the lingering effects of the drink."

"It passes almost immediately," said another.

The girl, from her side, looked about, as she could, but could see little but the floor, the boots of men, the shoes, the hems of some of the skirts, of free women.

It seemed she was trying to interpret what she saw, to make sense of what was about her.

She then gently touched her thigh, and her left breast, with her bound hands.

She tried, a little, to separate her hands.

She then went to her stomach, and extended her arms, her head between them, her eyes again closed, and put the right side of her head, turned, on her upper right arm.

The man with the whip lifted it, but, at a small gesture from Otto, he lowered it.

"What has happened?" she said. "What has come about? It is all so strange. I do not understand. I do not understand."

A man laughed.

"I am dreaming," she said. "That is it," she said. "I am dreaming. I am dreaming that I am a slave girl, and am naked and bound."

Several of the men laughed.

She rolled to her right side, again, her hands lowered.

She seemed unwilling to awaken.

"That is it," she said. "I am dreaming that I am a slave girl, and am naked and bound."

There was more laughter, from several of the men about.

She opened her eyes, suddenly, startled.

"Where am I?" she asked, again.

"You are in the hall of the Otungs," said the man, again.

Her eyes were now opened widely, disbelievingly.

She squirmed, suddenly, wildly, in the dirt.

"Why am I naked and bound!" she cried.

She tried to scramble to her feet but a man's hand would permit her to rise no farther than to her knees.

She lifted her bound wrists to Urta. "Why am I naked and bound!" she demanded.

Urta regarded her, but did not reply, his face revealing no emotion.

"I am Hortense, daughter of Thuron, noble of the Otungs!" she cried. "I am of noble birth. Release me, instantly! I am a noblewoman, a noblewoman!"

"Did you not dream you were a slave girl, naked and bound?" asked a man.

"Perhaps," she said, frightened.

"Perhaps the dream has come true," said the man.

"No!" she cried.

"Surely you have had such dreams before," said another man.

"Perhaps," she said.

"Perhaps, now," said a man, "they have all come true."

"No," she cried. "No! No!" She looked about, wildly. "Surely it is now that I am dreaming!"

"No," said a man. "It is now that you are fully awake. It is now that you find yourself to be precisely what you are, and all you are, a slave."

"I do not understand," she said. "How can it be?"

"In any event it is your reality," said a man.

"And its appropriateness has been revealed by the drink of truth," said another.

She looked about, wildly, and then, unable to control herself, sank down, to the floor of the hall.

The giant softly kicked her, with the side of his boot. "Kneel," said he gently, "Yata, slave girl."

She struggled to her knees and knelt, trembling, amongst the men and women.

"Put your head down," said the giant.

The slave lowered her head.

"She is a lying slave, and a runaway slave," said Urta.

"True," said the giant.

Urta took the whip from the fellow with the whip, and handed it to the giant.

"She is to be lashed well," said Citherix.

"Look up," said the giant.

The slave looked up, quickly.

The giant held the whip, coiled, before the slave, and she hastily pressed her lips to it, kissing it.

"Slave!" snarled one woman. Soft cries of pleasure escaped several of the others.

"I will give you ten sheep for her," said Citherix.

"Do not sell me to him, Master!" cried the slave. "His birth is below mine!"

There was laughter amongst the free persons.

"Or was once below mine!" she said.

"That is better," said the giant.

"He has wanted me for years!" she said. "But I am, or was, Master, too good for him. I stood off his suits for years. I treated him with much condescension. I treated him with haughtiness. I demeaned him. I ridiculed him publicly. I loathe him! I cannot stand him! He makes my flesh crawl! I beg you, Master, do not let him aspire to me!"

"Aspire, to a slave girl?" said the giant.

"Forgive me, Master!" she said. "But do not sell me to him, I beg you!"

"I will give you eleven sheep for her," said Citherix.

"Surely you would not want a lying, runaway slave," said the giant.

"Lash her well," said Citherix, "and she will soon be brought into line."

"Do not sell me to him, Master!" wept the girl.

"Twelve sheep," said Citherix.

"You must admit," said the giant to the slave, "that that is a fine price for a slave girl."

"But she is well curved," said a man.

"Please do not sell me to him, Master!" begged the girl.

"Fifteen sheep," said Citherix.

"I think she is not now for sale," said the giant.

The girl gasped with relief.

"You hold the whip," said Citherix to the giant, angrily. "She is at your feet. She is your slave. She is a lying slave, and a runaway slave. Punish her!"

The giant looked at Citherix.

"Or are you weak?" asked Citherix.

Men drew back a little, from about them.

The giant then held out the whip to Citherix. "Perhaps," he said, "you would care to whip her yourself?"

Citherix drew back, angrily. "I am not a whip thrall," he said.

"Bend down, Yata," said the giant.

Trembling, she bent forward, putting her head to the dirt.

"Do not think, in virtue of what I now do," said the giant to the slave, "that I am either a gentle or an indulgent master. You will find, if I keep you, that my standards are high and that I am not a patient man."

"Yes, Master," she whispered, frightened.

"Behold," said the giant to Citherix, "one blow is for her thousand lies, and her thousand faults, as yet uncorrected, and the second is for having run away."

Men gasped.

For he had barely touched, twice, not even tapping it, the back of the frightened, kneeling, bent slave, having merely, in effect, rested the whip, gently, twice, upon her back.

Citherix seemed too puzzled to comment, too puzzled to express even contempt, or derision.

In such a way did the giant prove to the hall that the slave was his, his to do with as he might wish, according to his own will, as his own will would have it, not as others might wish, or will, the matter. Also the slave understood, and at the moment to her relief and gratification, and only later to her chagrin and terror, that her master was not subject to the pressures of society or convention with respect to her treatment, but would decide such matters in his own way and according to his own views, and inclinations. In this sense she would soon come to understand that her fate was fully in his hands, and that she belonged to him completely, and in every way. This was a lesson, of course, which each of his slaves, each in her own time, and in her own way, learned.

From her knees the girl lifted her head, and looked up, slyly, at Citherix, her lovely face suffused with triumph, and smiled.

She had little to fear.

And well, thought she, her beauty had conquered her master.

"Leave, Citherix," she said.

With a cry of rage the giant seized her hair in his left hand and pulled her upright, straightened on her knees, and then bent her head back, that she must look up at him, and she did, her eyes wide, in pain and terror. "Contemptible, displeasing slave!" he cried.

"No, Master!" she begged.

He then hurled her on her belly before him, her bound hands stretched outright, the stand of free leather flung before them, and lashed her, twice, with the whip, and then, angrily, he put the whip in his teeth and dragged her to one of the wooden columns, to the base of which he fastened her, head down, on her knees, by her long blond tresses, they encircling the column, and knotted behind it. He then lashed her, as befitted her crime, her impudence and foolishness.

"Strike well," said a man.

"Let her learn what she is," said another.

The slave cried out in misery, her tears dampening the dirt and rushes at the base of the post.

"She is a sexual creature, a slave!" said a woman, angrily. "Let her be punished!"

"Punish the slave, the shameless hussy!" cried a woman.

"Hit her harder!" cried a woman.

"Yes!" cried a young woman, her voice trembling with excitement.

"Yes!" cried another, thrilled.

"The boldness of the liar, pretending to be a free woman!" said another woman.

"She is an insult to all free women!" said another.

"Punish her!" cried a free woman.

"Yes!" cried another.

"She is sexual," cried another. "Let her be a slave!"

"She is a slave! Treat her as a slave!" said another.

"You will learn your place, slut!" cried another woman.

"Oh!" cried the slave.

"You are a slave, being whipped by your master!" hissed a free woman.

"Yes, Mistress!" sobbed the slave. "Oh!"

"Say it!" demanded the free woman.

"Oh!"

"Say it!" demanded the free woman.

"I am a slave being whipped by my master!" cried the slave.

"You are hopelessly sexual," said a free woman. "That was seen under the drink of truth."

"Yes, Mistress!" cried the slave.

"Thus you should be a slave!"

"Yes, Mistress!" said the slave.

"Thus you belong to men!" said a free woman, angrily.

"Yes, Mistress!" cried the slave.

"Say it!" cried the free woman.

"It is true!" wept the slave. "I am a slave. I belong to men!"

"She belongs to men!" cried a young woman, in awe.

"Yes!" said another, thrilled.

"And see!" said a young woman, turning to another. "She is being whipped by her master!"

"And so, too, might you be, were you a slave," said the woman addressed.

"And you, too!" responded the first.

"Yes, yes!" agreed the second.

"What are you?" inquired a free woman, bending down to the slave.

"A slave!" gasped Yata. "Oh! A slave, a slave!"

"What else?" demanded the woman.

"Oh!" cried Yata. "A slave! Only that! Oh! Nothing more, only a slave, only that!"

The barbarian lowered the whip.

"Have you learned your lesson?" inquired a free woman of the slave.

"Yes, yes, Mistress!" sobbed the slave.

The barbarian threw aside the whip, and, with the Herul knife, cut the tresses of the slave, freeing her from the column.

"To him!" ordered the barbarian, indicating Citherix.

The slave, sobbing, and beaten, her face stained with tears, her blond hair jagged about her head and face, where it had been cut, releasing her from the column, on her knees, crawled quickly, clumsily, unsteadily, lurching, supporting herself partly on her left palm, her right wrist bound to, and over, her left wrist, to the feet of Citherix, where she bellied before him, and pressed her lips fervently to his boots, kissing them, again and again. "Forgive me, Master!" she begged. "A contrite, errant slave, one now well apprised of her faults, begs forgiveness of a master!"

"See how she is before him!" whispered a young woman.

"She is so sexual!" said another.

"She is a slave," said another.

Citherix looked up from the abject, penitent slave at his feet.

"A thousand sheep," said he to the barbarian giant.

"Shall I sell you?" the giant inquired of the beaten, prostrate slave.

"It will be done with me as my master wishes," she whispered.

"The answer is fitting," said Otto.

He then lifted her with great gentleness in his arms and carried her to the side of the fire pit, where he placed her on her right side, her legs drawn up, near the waiting iron, it plunged a foot into the fire. The smith, or worker with iron, at a sign from Otto, relinquished the heavy gloves. Otto then himself removed the iron from the fire. Yata looked up at him, he who owned her, who was her master.

"Hold her," said the giant.

The slave was seized by three strong men.

She could not move.

The iron was white-hot.

It met with the barbarian's approval.

Its mark would be that of the tiny, tasteful, stylized slave rose, a mark which would be recognized throughout galaxies.

Yata was then branded.

· · · CHAPTER 28 · · ·

"On your back, on the table, Filene," said Ronisius, the severe officer.

Corelius, the young, blond officer, stood to one side.

The blonde rose quickly to her feet, from where she had been kneeling in her place in line, with the other girls, and took her place on the table, as ordered.

She glanced once at Corelius.

She wondered if he would be jealous at how swiftly she obeyed Ronisius.

It pleased her, of late, she had discovered, to obey, and

promptly, at least men such as Ronisius. Too, stricter masters tend to be better obeyed. Too, she did not wish to feel his quirt. Her form of livestock, after all, assuming that he might regard her in that fashion, was not that of the horse, but of the woman. To be sure, in her case, as in that of others, assuming he viewed her as a domestic animal, as the others, he would permit no doubt, nor had she any, in his case, as to who was master. It pleased her to sense that Corelius envied Ronisius her obedience. She knew vaguely, deeply within her, despite what she would have preferred to tell herself, that she despised Corelius for his weakness.

"Put your head back," said Ronisius, "over the back of the table."

She obeyed.

Corelius, standing to one side, seemed angry.

Perhaps, she thought to herself, he is polite, he is gentle, he is kindly, he is tender, he is understanding, he is sensitive, because he knows that I am free, and he is my contact, the agent who must supply me with the dagger?

Else, if he thinks me a slave, why does he not treat me as a slave?

Is he so weak, she wondered.

She felt a light chain, in a leather sleeve, jerked about her neck, rudely, closely, and then snapped shut, locked.

She shuddered. It was the first time she had worn a collar, one not a portion of a chain, serving to fix her in place.

To the collar a metal disk was attached, which, in three languages, including a Herul pictograph, identified her as the property of the Telnarian empire, to be returned, if found, to the office of the provincial governor in Venitzia.

"You look pretty in a collar, Filene," said Lysis, the supply officer.

"Thank you, Master," she said.

How easily, how naturally, it now seemed to her that she used the word "Master" to men, and how appropriate, this frightening her, it had now begun to seem to her!

She could see, as her head was back, the ceiling of the preparation room, a vestibule of the slave shed.

She sensed that she could not slip the collar. It was on her well.

She was naked.

She felt two of the governor's men pulling the fur sack up,

beginning at the feet, about her body. It had a hood, and would be tied shut, about her neck.

She knew that she, and the other girls, were to be taken from Venitzia, out, somewhere, on sleds, into the winter, into the wilderness, and thus that the collars were a judicious mercantile precaution, not that one could count on their import being respected, no, not on the other side of the fence.

The heavy fur sack was pulled up, tightly, about her, and its drawstrings were tied about her neck. Then the hood was pulled up and adjusted, and it, too, was tied beneath her chin. There was a tiny clink from the metal disk on a bit of the chain, it exposed outside the leather, in the front, near the lock.

The porcine stockman, whose name was Qualius, from the bottom, pulled the sack down a little. He pressed down on her knees. Her legs straightened. Her feet were still several inches from the bottom of the sack. Such sacks come normally in but one size. She was not a large woman but one who was well turned, one with a body of the sort that could drive men mad with desire, one which would sell well in slave markets. She closed her eyes as Qualius moved his hands about, over her. Did he think she was a slave? She restrained herself, that she not lift her body within the furs to his touch. She opened her eyes when he was checking the knots, that at her throat, and that beneath her chin. There seemed about his lips the slightest trace of amusement. Had he detected her incipient movement within the sack? She desperately trusted not! She quickly turned her head in the hood, to the side, looking away from him. Once she had found herself yearning to press her cheek against the knee of Ronisius! And once, in the early morning hours, when she had been helpless at the foot of the barbarian's bed on the *Narcona*, kneeling, tied to the bedpost, her mouth taped shut, she had squirmed, with strange sensations, and whimpered, and moaned, begging him to awaken, and yet fearing that he might. She did not know what was becoming of her.

Parts of her were stirring, and becoming so alive and meaningful that she dared not even think of them.

And yet they forced themselves upon her terrified consciousness.

What if I should yield to these feelings, she asked herself. What would I then be? What could I then be?

I would be so different, and yet my true self!

No, no, she wept to herself, I must not think such things! Oh,

I must be given the dagger soon, I must do my work soon! Unknown colleague, make yourself known to me!

Qualius turned her about and lifted her, lightly, to his shoulder, her head to the rear, and carried her outside. She felt the cold, pure air of the Tangaran winter. A light snow was falling.

She was placed on a broad sled, her back against the backrest, in the single row, the last of five girls for that sled. The horse was already hitched to the sled. The sledsman, from Venitzia, once she was placed, drew the broad leather straps, two of them, fastened on the right as one would face the sled from the front, across the goods, and buckled them on the left. This arrangement was intended less as a custodial precaution than as one designed with the safety of the cargo, and the convenience of the drivers, in mind. In this fashion it was less likely that the goods, in the event of a rough trail, would be dislodged, or pitched, from the sled. Custodial arrangements, which might have been handled differently in benign weather, were now considered well satisfied by the goods' lack of garmenture and the severity of the season. The wilderness, and the dangers of animals and others, too, added, so to speak, bars to their cages. Too, on the neck of each there was a collar and disk.

"I am afraid," whispered one of the girls on the sled, when the sledsman had left. "They are going to take us into the wilderness."

"They will use us as trade goods!" wept the girl the farthest to the blonde's left.

"I do not understand. I do not understand," said the girl closest to the one who had spoken.

"They will do with us as they want. We are slaves," said the second girl to the blonde's left.

"But I do not understand," repeated the one closest to the girl on the left.

"I do not either," she was told.

Phidias, captain of the *Narcona*, to the blonde's surprise, was in the muddy, snowy yard.

There were better than twenty sleds in the yard, several of which bore slaves, readied for transport, just as the blonde and her companions were. Most of the sleds, however, bore boxes, and tenting. There were also several horses to one side, pawing in the mud, fastened to a rope. Two treaded, armored vehicles were near the gate. And the canvas had been thrown back from two hoverers.

"The shuttle is ready to blast off," a mariner informed Phidias.

Phidias nodded.

The *Narcona* was doubtless somewhere above, invisible in the morning sky, in orbit.

"When will the *Narcona* return to Inez IV?" one of the governor's men inquired of the captain.

"Shortly," said the captain.

The blonde looked wildly to the captain, and almost cried out to him. They could not, truly, be thinking of leaving without her!

The last of the slaves were now loaded, and secured. The blonde had been near the end of the line.

Some men were mounting.

The motor of the first treaded vehicle turned over, and then that of the second.

Several soldiers from Venitzia, in line, with rifles, emerged from a barracks at one end of the yard. Sledsmen finished hitching up several of the horses. One of the hoverers began to hum, and then the other.

Snow fell on her eyelashes.

She blinked.

Lysis, the supply officer, emerged from the slave shed. He wore furs and boots. The yard was muddy where men and horses trod, and white with snow about the edges.

"It is some mission to barbarians," said one of the sledsmen to one of his fellows, some three gathered near the sled.

"I don't like it," said another.

"We are taking enough armament and force equipment to protect us from the Herul nation," said another.

Lysis entered the first of the two treaded vehicles; the second, eventually, would bring up the rear. The hoverers, open to the air, would be used largely as scout craft. There were also two broad sleds, these drawn by four horses apiece, on which they could be transported, if needed, as fuel was inordinately precious.

"Mistress," whispered the blonde to the girl at her left. The girl was not first girl, but it had been decided, after the blonde's outburst in the slave shed, in which she had threatened, incomprehensibly to them, to buy and sell them all, that she must henceforth be as a slave to them all, as though they might be free persons, serving them with deference, and addressing them

all as "Mistress." At first she had, of course, haughtily refused
to do so, but, in a day or two, she had begun to do so, desiring
to be clothed and fed.

"Have you requested permission to speak?" inquired the girl
to the left.

"May I speak, Mistress?" asked the blonde. How she hated
to address a slave as "Mistress"!

"Perhaps."

"Please!"

The other girl looked about. It might not do for them to be
caught speaking to one another. They did not know. Speech had
not been expressly forbidden to them, but, on the other hand,
that privilege, that of conversing with one another, had not been
explicitly accorded to them at the moment either.

"Very well," she said.

"You were serving in the officer's mess yesterday?"

"Yes."

"The barbarian, the brute, he called Ottonius, has not returned, has he?"

"I do not think so."

"Why are we leaving?"

"They are seeking him in the wild, it seems as part of an
original mission. It is surmised he may have made contact with
certain barbarians, Otungs. Thus, those, with perhaps the help
of natives, Heruls or others, are to be sought, it being hoped to
thusly make contact through them with the barbarian."

The blonde lay back against the backrest.

"You may thank me for deigning to speak with you," said
the girl.

"Thank you, Mistress," said the blonde. She said this deferentially, as it was cold, and she knew that later she would be
terribly hungry, and would wish to be fed. Once she had used
the appropriate words, but had spoken with the least tincture of
some slight irony in her voice. She had then been seized and
beaten. She had not made that mistake again. Her lesson had
been well learned.

"You are welcome," said the girl, dismissing her.

The giant metal gate of the yard was swung open, and the first
treaded, armored vehicle, with Lysis now in its cab, rumbled out
the gate. The two hoverers now rose into the softly falling snow,
some twenty or thirty feet in the air, and then, some two hundred
yards apart, soared away to the south. The first of the horse-

drawn sleds then, harness bells jangling, followed the treaded vehicle. Other sleds followed, several flanked by horsemen, with rifles. Sledsmen, with their vehicles, were generally on foot, often beside the horses, with rope quirts, but some were on runners, and some on what were, in effect, wagon boxes, some of these at the front of the vehicle, and others at the rear. Sledsmen mounted on the runners, or the wagon boxes, utilized whips, of various lengths, some coil whips, and others little more than light, supple rods.

The blonde's sled was about a third of the way back in the line of vehicles.

There was a jerk and her sled moved. It slipped through the mud, which bubbled and squeaked beneath the runners; then, with a sudden scratching, startling her, it rode over some gravel; then, in a few moments, it was outside the gate, and running smoothly on snow.

In some fifteen minutes they were through the charged wires, which served as the walls of Venitzia.

Corelius was captain of one of the hoverers, and Ronisius of the other. Neither hoverer could now be seen. As visibility was decreasing they would doubtless soon rejoin the column, setting the hoverers down on the sleds designed to carry them. Qualius, the porcine stockman, was in the second armored vehicle, which would bring up the rear of the column.

Snow was falling more heavily now.

The blonde moved a little inside the fur sack. It was soft, and warm, and, within it, she was quite comfortable. Outside it, of course, she would be naked, and helpless, in the Tangaran winter.

Who is my confederate, wondered the blonde. Why has he not made himself known to me? Is he even on this world, and, if not, what might that mean for me?

What if some terrible mistake might be made?

I have no way to prove that I am a free woman, an aristocrat, even a patrician, of the senatorial class! I could be taken for a slave girl. I could be given away, as a gift, on a provincial world. I might have to remain here, forever, as a chattel of barbarians.

But the blonde knew that the ideal place for her work to be accomplished was the wilderness, that, surely, into which she was now being taken.

This must be part of a plan, but what if it was not?

Surely the deed should not take place in Venitzia, under the jurisdiction of the provincial governor, where she might be simply taken as a murderess, and executed, or returned to Inez IV, under secure guard, with affidavits, to be tried there, and then doubtless to suffer the same fate. No, the wilderness was the place, she thence, after the deed, to be whisked away to safety, perhaps in some hoverer, or armored vehicle, to some secret rendezvous with the shuttle, and thence to a second rendezvous, that with the *Narcona*, in orbit, and thence to return to civilization, and new-found wealth, position and power.

She heard a jangle of spurs to her right and a soldier, riding there for a moment, looked down upon her.

She looked up.

How men looked at women they thought to be slaves, she thought.

Her face, startled, exquisite, was almost hidden, framed in the furred hood.

He seemed a handsome fellow. In the last few weeks she had become acutely conscious of such things.

She squirmed a little, in the sack, under the two broad leather belts, one above her knees, the other about her waist.

He spurred away.

"You learn quickly, Cornhair, slave slut," said the girl next to her.

The blonde was startled. Then she said, deferentially, "Yes, Mistress."

"Beware, slave girl," said the other. "You are a slave, and men may call your tease, and have exactly what, and anything, they want of you."

"Yes, Mistress," whispered the blonde, deferentially.

The blonde then squirmed down in the warm sack. She turned her head, brushing away the snow on her eyelashes, against the edge of the hood. Within the sack she was conscious of her nudity, which she gathered could set men afire, and she reluctantly sensed, as though from afar, how she herself might be set similarly afire, how she might be swept up, like a sheet of begging flame, helplessly, in passions so fierce, so intense, so irresistible, that she had always denied, hitherto, that they could exist.

She thought she sensed then how it might be that a slave could crawl to a man, begging.

I will buy and sell all of them, she told herself.

Within the fur, she clutched the disk on its chain, on her

throat. She jerked at it. It was on her, like the chain. She could not remove it.

I wonder what it would be like, she thought, to be truly a slave girl.

The column continued on its way. The sky was darker now. Snow continued to fall.

· · · CHAPTER 29 · · ·

"The meat will soon be cooked," said Ulrich. "Then it will begin, the claiming."

The giant nodded.

There was a tiny stirring beneath the table, to the giant's left. There, beneath the table, head down, bent over, small, deliciously curved, her body oriented toward the center of the hall, her wrists bound together before her body, the right wrist bound over the left, the strand which had run from her bound wrists now taken back and used to fasten her crossed ankles together, knelt his slave, Yata.

He put one hand gently upon her.

She seemed afraid.

She whimpered.

"Be silent," he said.

"Yes, Master," she said.

He withdrew his hand.

He wondered why she was so afraid. She understands, perhaps better than I, he thought, the nature of this feast.

The fire in the fire pit, that long pit, was now sturdily ablaze.

The boar turned slowly, succulently, on the spit.

Its odor hung tantalizingly in the air.

But the men seemed dark, and tense.

Had it been another time and place, the giant thought, there might have been much fellowship in the hall, among such men.

But it was not so here, in this place, this Otung hall.

Perhaps he should dance the slave for them. Might that not please them?

She did not know the subtleties of slave dance, but she was

beautiful, and, being female, could doubtless move well, and provocatively, before them. Even in her ignorance she might impress upon them, these lost, confused, defeated, isolated, forlorn, spiritless warriors, what might, on far worlds, as a consequence of successful adventuring, could they but recall the songs of their blood, and the lure of the stars, fall to their lot in the way of diverse booties, in the way of various riches, including such as she, such tender, delicious, exquisite loot. Too, of course, she would obey instantaneously and unquestioningly. He had seen to that but recently.

But somehow he did not think the men in the hall were now in the mood to consider such matters, pleasant as they might be in prospect.

"Which is the hero's portion?" asked the giant.

"The right, back thigh," said Ulrich.

"He whom you call Urta names the king?" asked the giant.

"Yes," said Ulrich.

"How is it done?"

"He judges the dispute, the contest, the slaughter, if there is one," said Ulrich. "He adjudicates it. Usually there is little to be judged, for commonly only one of the nobles, or the noble's champions, remains on his feet."

"But someone must name the winner?"

"Yes," said Ulrich. "If it is a noble, then he is the year king. If it is a noble's champion, then it is his lord who is the year king."

"Who named Urta the King Namer?" asked the giant.

"Heruls," said Ulrich.

"Is Urta loyal to the Otungs?"

"He is Otung," said Ulrich. "He does what he must."

"Who is the current year king?" asked the giant.

"Fuldan, the Old," said Ulrich.

"He who was sent for?" asked Otto.

"Yes," said Ulrich.

"I do not understand," said Otto.

"The bloodshed and slaughter at the last king naming was so plenteous, the champions wounded, or slain, so numerous," said Ulrich, "that, in the end, few were willing, or fit, to claim the kingship. Fuldan, the Old, seeing at last the madness of it, hobbled to the boar and thrust his knife into the right, rear thigh. 'Who will kill me, who will kill one who rode with Genserix, who will kill one who has shed his blood a hundred times in the cause of Otungs, who will kill an old man?' he asked. By that time the stomach for killing one another had been muchly abated. 'Let him be king,' said men. 'You are king,' said Urta, the King Namer, and thus came Fuldan, the Old, to the kingship of the Otungs.''

"But Fuldan is not here," said Otto.

" 'I am king, but there is no king,' had said Fuldan," said Ulrich. "He avoids the hall. He avoids the folk."

"Then there is no king, truly," said Otto.

"There is one who was named king," said Ulrich.

"If you would have no king, then name Fuldan king again," said Otto.

"No," said Ulrich. "A year king can be a king but for one year only, and now, after the year, the nobles are ready, once more, none willing to yield place to another, to fly at one another's throats."

"This must please the Heruls," said Otto.

"They will have it no other way," said Ulrich.

"I would have it otherwise," said Otto.

"It is a long time since the pelt of a white vi-cat has been in the hall of the Otungs," said Ulrich.

"It is here now," said Otto.

"The meat will soon be done," said Ulrich.

"I am hungry," said Otto.

"One does not eat the meat, of course," said Ulrich.

"Why not?"

"Its cost tends to dampen hunger," said Ulrich. "Its price is high, and paid in blood. One tends to lose one's appetite."

"One should have a stronger appetite," said Otto.

"Perhaps," said Ulrich.

"There is no drink, no bread," said Otto.

"We do not eat nor drink at the feast of the king naming," said Ulrich.

"It is a poor feast," said Otto.

"It is not a feast," said Ulrich. "It is the Killing Time."

· · · CHAPTER 30 · · ·

Julian, codes exchanged, brought the hoverer down in the muddy yard outside the administration building.

There was, with the change in inertia, as the craft decelerated, a small, soft, startled cry from the object lying on its side in its net behind Julian and to his right.

"Inform the governor of the arrival of Julian, of the Aurelianii, kin to the emperor!" called Julian.

"Yes, your excellency!" said a guard.

Guards, shielding their faces from the spattering mud and water, whirled by the lifters, had hurried to the gunwales of the small craft, even as it had landed.

Julian cut the motors, and the craft eased into the mud.

The object in its net, lying behind Julian and to his right, whimpered. It could move but little, its legs drawn up, in the net.

The trip from the *festung* of Sim Giadini had been a bitterly cold one, and the small hoverer had been often buffeted with winds. Sometimes it had been impossible to see more than a few feet before the windscreen. They had been forced to land several times. More than once the tiny craft had been dug out of the snow by mittened hands, or, lifters roaring, had torn itself free, in its urgency, even at the cost of precious fuel.

"The yard is muchly empty," said Tuvo Ausonius. There were only two vehicles in the yard, both covered with canvas.

There were few lights in the barracks, at one side of the yard. The slave shed was dark, and no smoke emerged from its two chimneys.

Too, there were few supplies in view, though these might be housed in the dark warehouses to the north.

"The stables seem empty," said Tuvo Ausonius.

"Hold!" called Julian to the guard, who turned about.

"Summon, too," said Julian, "Phidias, captain of the *Narcona*, and Lysis, officer of supply, with the *Narcona*!"

"The shuttle has departed," called the guard. "Phidias is

· 260 ·

gone. Lysis, and other officers, and several men, with equipment and trade goods, have gone.''

"The trade expedition has departed?"

"Yes, your excellency," said the guard.

"It is being led by the blond-haired captain, Ottonius?"

"The barbarian?"

"He."

"No, it seeks him."

"He is not with the expedition?"

"No, your excellency."

"It is imperative," said Julian, "that I follow them and make contact with the expedition immediately. I will need their route, seven hoverers, fuel for a month, a hundred men, draft animals, two dozen sleds, perimeter defenses, weapons and supplies!"

"The garrison is muchly gone," said the guard. "There is little left, even fuel, until the next supply ship."

"Go!" said Julian.

The guard turned about, again, and hurried toward the administration building.

"Surely all is not lost?" said Tuvo Ausonius to Julian.

"We shall leave Venitzia within the hour," said Julian.

The two men looked down at the object at their feet. It was lying on its side, in its heavy furs, on the metal decking of the hoverer, its legs drawn up. The net was of closely linked chain, a slave security net, though it may be used also for the securing of cargo, that usually done, however, with a rope net. The chain net cannot be chewed through, nor cut with a knife. The slave is inserted into the net, usually sideways, and then the opening is closed and padlocked, with a single lock, a massive one, about one of the deck rings. This makes it impossible for the slave to rise to her feet, to interfere in any way with the operation of the craft, even to extrude a hand from the net. Too, perhaps most importantly, it assures her safety, or, perhaps more realistically, the safety of the master's cargo, that she, or it, will be kept within the craft should it, say, engage in unusual maneuvers, as in evading predators, giant insects, or insectoidals, on some worlds, winged lizards on others, magnetic air mines, other ships, or such, or encounter turbulence. A strong wind can occasionally invert such light, disklike craft. But even in fine weather such confinements, or others, are often resorted to, as their imposition pleases the masters, and is experienced as informative by the slaves. This is not unusual as that which pleases the masters is often found instructive by the slaves, even extremely so.

A wisp of Nika's red hair emerged from within the heavy fur hood.

She looked up, her eyes wide and frightened, over her shoulder, at Julian.

"We expect to soon encounter the Lady Publennia," said Julian, looking down at the confined, lovely slave. "When you see her you are to identify her for us, immediately and clearly."

"But she is my mistress, Master!" said the slave.

"She is an outlaw and traitress, and no longer possesses property," said Julian. "And you are a slave and we are free men. You will obey us instantly and unquestioningly."

"Yes, Master," moaned the girl.

"As soon as you see her, thusly, you will identify her for us, immediately and clearly."

"I will try, Master," whispered the girl.

Julian kicked her, with the side of his foot, through the chain net, with a sound of chain. "And you will succeed," he said.

"Yes, Master!" she said.

"Or die," said Julian.

"Yes, Master!" she said.

"Sir," said the guard, returning. "The governor inquires as to your rank."

"Ensign," said Julian, angrily.

"Your requests are to be conveyed through channels," said the guard, "your excellency."

"I am Julian, of the Aurelianii," said Julian, "kin to the emperor, on a mission of importance and delicacy."

"Such a mission is already in progress, and under the imperial seals of secrecy," said the guard.

"I would know its route, and consult its maps," said Julian.

"The seals are imperial," said the guard. "The governor suggests you avail yourself of the hospitality of the junior officers' quarters. He is prepared to see you tomorrow."

"I want the hoverer refueled, now," said Julian.

"There is no authorization for that," said the guard.

"What of sleds, and men?" asked Julian.

"Resources are limited," said the guard. "It is our hope that the fence holds, and the expedition soon returns."

"What of those vehicles?" asked Julian, indicating the two vehicles under canvas in the yard.

"They are in need of repair, and are not fueled," said the guard.

Julian smote down on the gunwales of the hoverer with his mittened fists.

"The governor," said Tuvo Ausonius, "seems unduly rigid, and severe."

"No," said Julian, straightening, angrily. "That is the fury of it! We must admire him! His behavior, under the circumstances, is impeccably correct. He cannot be faulted. His behavior is in strict accord not only with protocol and regulation, but, I fear, good judgment. He is not, upon the petition of any nobleman, short of the emperor or his representative, to break imperial seals. Too, he is acting in accordance with his primary charge, the security of Venitzia. If he would not rush to grant an audience to any junior officer, why should he grant me one, as that is, precisely, my rank. We must admire him for putting duty before an attempt to curry favoritism with a patrician. Would there were more like him!"

"At this point," said Tuvo Ausonius, "we could use a sycophant. The last thing we need now is an incorruptible official, an honest man and a good officer."

"Sir," said the guard, "the governor would be honored, unofficially, of course, if you, and your companion, were to have dinner with him this evening."

"Thank him," said Julian, "on behalf of my friend and myself, for the honor would be ours, but inquire if we may not, instead, have snowshoes, and a single sled, a small one, with supplies, such as may be drawn even by a slave."

"Yes, your excellency," said the guard, turning about.

"Surely you have no intention of leaving tonight?" said Tuvo Ausonius.

"That is my intention," said Julian.

"You do not know where to find the expedition, or where, even, to look," said Tuvo Ausonius.

"We must do what we can," said Julian. He looked down at Nika in the closely linked, stout meshes of her confinement. "I had thought, my dear," said he to the exquisite slave, "that we might be in time, and that, tonight, we might have spent pleasant hours in a pleasant, cozy tavern, well-appointed and well-stocked, and well-lit with roaring fires, with you and your former mistress."

"With us, Master?" asked the girl.

"Yes, to let you both, a free woman and a woman's slave, see what true women are like, women in an exquisite, enhanced, refined order of nature."

Nika regarded him, wide-eyed and trembling.

"It would do you both good," said Julian, "to let you see true women, slaves, in wisps of slave silk, in collars, aroused and begging."

"Yes, Master," she whispered.

"To let you, too, both of you, a free woman, and one once a mere woman's slave, feel silk, and metal, upon your own bodies, and firelight, and sense what it would be, what it will be, to be at the command of, and in the power of, men."

"Yes, Master," she whispered.

"But," said Julian, "it seems that it is not to be, and that rather it is the winter night of Tangara, and a dangerous, doubtless fruitless, journey, which lies before us."

"It is madness, milord, to so enter the night," said Tuvo Ausonius.

"The life of Ottonius is at stake," said Julian.

"It is madness nonetheless," said Tuvo Ausonius.

"Do not accompany me, friend Ausonius," said Julian.

"No, milord," said Tuvo Ausonius. "I would rather share a glorious madness, a noble madness, than linger indefinitely, wormlike, counting days, until the end, in a dusty, terminal sanity."

"We may not return," said Julian.

"That is true of any journey, milord."

Shortly thereafter, a sled and supplies provided, the sled drawn by a small, trudging figure, Julian and Tuvo Ausonius left Venitzia.

They trekked north by northeast, following speculations afforded earlier by Brother Benjamin, of the *festung* of Sim Giadini, which speculations, in broad outline, tended to be confirmed by various officers in the garrison.

On the sled, among other supplies, was, wrapped in silk, and then coarse cloth, a small object, weighing about a pound and a half. It had been given to them by Brother Benjamin, while they were in the *festung* of Sim Giadini.

When they were beyond the fence something like a hour's trek through the frozen, crackling, moonlit snow, Tuvo Ausonius, looking about, said, "We are being followed."

"I know," said Julian.

What they did not know, nor had Brother Benjamin, nor the garrison officers, was that the location of the territories of the Otungs, little more now than their pastures and fields, had changed several times over the years, due largely to the demands and pressures of Heruls. The trading expedition, under Lysis, supply officer of the *Narcona*, had had somewhat better information, information obtained by the governor of Venitzia through secret agents, posing as trappers, traders and such. The locations of Herul groupings and those of other barbarians, such as Otungs and Basungs, were, as on many worlds, seldom publicly disclosed, and tended to be known only in a very general way. Even the trade expedition, as we have noted, was counting on obtaining a refinement of information in the wilds themselves, presumably from natives.

"How are our friends doing?" asked Julian of Tuvo Ausonius, after another hour's march.

Tuvo Ausonius looked back. "They are much closer now," he said.

"Then they are not simply following us," said Julian.

"No," said Tuvo Ausonius.

"What do you think their intention is?" asked Julian.

"I do not know, milord," said Tuvo Ausonius.

"And they have made no attempt to contact us, either by light, or by shouting, or such."

"No, milord."

"They are closing in for the kill," said Julian.

"What shall we do?" asked Tuvo Ausonius.

"We shall accustom them to seeing only two pairs of snow-shoe tracks," said Julian. "I shall ride on the sled for a time. You draw it, if you would. Nika will walk where I have been walking. Later, in a wood, by clinging to branches, or over rocks, where there is no snow, I will leave the sled and circle about, coming up behind them."

"What will you do then?" asked Tuvo Ausonius.

"Kill them," said Julian.

· · · **CHAPTER 31** · · ·

"Draw again the sled, slave girl," said Tuvo Ausonius, after a time.

She swiftly crossed before the sled, and, in a moment, with the help of Tuvo Ausonius, was fitted into the harness.

"Master?" she asked, for the harness was not simply slipped into, as it had been with Tuvo Ausonius, when he had drawn the sled, but it was tightened and buckled on her, even to a ring and band about her throat, through which, by means of a rein running back to the sled, pressure might be exerted upon her. A bridle, too, was put upon her, with its bit, headstall and reins. Her small hands, too, were buckled behind her in the leather cuffs, between the fur sleeves and the fur mittens.

No more then could she speak for the bit was back, between her teeth, fastened there, she helpless.

She looked wildly, questioningly, at Tuvo Ausonius, but he paid her no attention.

The bit would keep her quiet.

She whimpered.

Tuvo Ausonius raised his hand angrily, menacingly, and she was instantly, totally silent.

Things had not been thus with her when she had been a lady's maid, with little to worry her but her mistress's hair, clothes and switch, but she was now in the power of men.

Nika secured, at least to that moment, to that extent, though not at that moment in ankle hobbles, Tuvo Ausonius freed his rifle from the sled. Fifteen minutes earlier, as Tuvo Ausonius had counted, as Julian had prescribed, Julian had stepped from the sled to rocks, between which the sled was conducted. Julian had then, snowshoes on his back, rifle in his mittened hand, left them.

They waited there for some five minutes when, suddenly, on the backtrail, perhaps a half mile or more behind them, there were three flashes, sudden and bright, one after the other, brilliant in the cold, pure air. He saw them reflected even from the lowering clouds, and flashed back, a lighter, sudden, momentarily flickering gray, on the snow.

After a minute or two there were more flashes.

"There were flankers!" said Tuvo Ausonius, angrily.

In a moment there was another flash, and then only the stillness of the winter night.

Tuvo Ausonius, stopping only for a moment, began to parallel the backtrail, hurrying beside it, a few yards from it, rifle in hand.

In a few minutes he came on a burned body in the snow. He could see flesh inside the blackened, opened fur.

He turned the body over with the rifle muzzle.

It was not Julian.

"Do not fire!" called a voice from the side.

"Milord!" cried Tuvo Ausonius.

"There were five," said Julian.

"And how many are accounted for, milord?"

"Five," said Julian. "One fled, wounded, returning to Venitzia. I followed the blood for a few yards. It was plenteous. I finished him by firing into the snow in which he had sought to hide himself.

"There," said Julian.

Tuvo Ausonius' glance followed the muzzle of Julian's rifle. A body lay there, its lower portions frozen in ice. In the flash of heat from the rifle, the snow had spumed upward, yards into the air, then rained down in droplets and crystals. About the body itself, it and its vicinity momentarily torrid with heat, the snow had melted, forming a small lake in a hollow, which fluid had then, in moments, frozen. The lower body lay then locked in ice, as in a congealing pond, its image distorted. The furs had been muchly burned away, and the skeleton, the upper right quadrant, was partly exposed. Julian had fired from short range with a wide setting on the muzzle. He had not been certain where in the mound of snow the target had been hidden. With that setting, effective only within a few feet, it did not much matter.

"We are safe now," said Tuvo Ausonius.

"No," said Julian. "These fellows may have inadvertently accomplished their purpose."

"How so, milord?"

"The light, the flashes, the concussions in the air, the burned flesh, the scent of blood," said Julian, "may attract animals, vi-cats, wolves, such things. In the winter they might sense such things, for miles about.''

"We have ammunition," said Tuvo Ausonius.

"It is limited," said Julian.

In a few minutes they had returned to the sled.

Nika, of course, was waiting for them, in the harness. She was a highly intelligent young woman, and would have remained where she was, of course, knowing herself a captive of the sled, and well fastened to it, even had Tuvo Ausonius not, in that brief moment before he had addressed himself to the backtrail, assured himself of it, locking her in slave hobbles.

"Let us be on our way," said Julian.

Tuvo Ausonius removed the slave hobbles from the girl, the flat, fixed ankle bands, joined by the short, stout, inflexible metal bar, four inches in length, and put them on the sled.

"Move," said Tuvo Ausonius.

"Yes, Master," she said, struggling, thrusting her small body against the straps of the harness.

There was a grating on the crusted snow and the sled moved. There was little sound then save that marked by the sliding passage of the two runners, and the pressing of the snowshoes into the snow, other than, after a time, in the far distance, the baying of wolves.

· · · CHAPTER 32 · · ·

"Who will stand for king?" called Urta, the King Namer.

The carcass of the roast boar, hot, basted, steaming, glistening, now lay, lengthwise, on the heavy, stained planks, laid over four trestles, before the dais on which stood, alone, the simple, wooden empty throne, the dais at the end of the hall, away from the entrance, down its flat, stone steps.

"Rolof, of the lineage of Ondax," said a man, rising from behind one of the long tables, to the side of the hall.

"The Gri!" said a man.

There were cries of anger, murmurs of discontent.

Rolof looked about himself, with contempt. Men near him,

retainers, rose, their hands on the hilts of blades. "Yes," said Rolof, "Rolof, of the lineage of Ondax, of clan Gri."

"Valdemar!" cried a stout fellow from the opposite side of the room, rising to his feet, he, too, flanked by armed men. "Valdemar, of the lineage of Alberich, of the clan Tiri!"

This entry, too, was met with a menacing roll of anger, like thunder, far off.

"Better Gundar!" cried a man.

"Yes!" cried another.

"Clan Oni!"

"No!" cried other voices.

Eyes turned toward a blond fellow, with braided hair. He rose to his feet.

"Gundar," said he, "of the lineage of Asa, of the Oni."

"No!" said another man, rising. "I, Hartnar, son of Tasach, son of Sala, scion of clan Reni!"

"Gelerich," said another man, rising, a lean man, "of the line of Pertinax, clan Orti."

"Astarax," said another, rising, "of the line of Fendash, clan Eni."

"Each of you," asked Urta, "have champions?"

Assent was nodded to this. At the right hand of each was a sullen, stalwart fellow, a helmet cradled in his arm. Some were of the clans in question, others mercenaries.

"Six clans are contestants, and claimants," said Urta. "What of the other clans?"

None others spoke, or rose from behind the tables.

"They are coward clans," said a man.

"No!" cried men.

"Be silent!" commanded Urta.

"Is there no champion on behalf of Lord Ulrich, son of Emmerich?"

"None," said Ulrich.

"Clan Elbi, Lord Ulrich, first of the clans of the Otungs, first tribe of the Vandal peoples, proposes no champion?" asked Urta.

"The Elbi propose no champion," said Ulrich.

There was a murmur of disappointment about the tables.

"What has become of the Elbi?" asked a man.

"What has become of the clan of Genserix?" asked another.

"Propose a champion," pressed a man.

"No," said Ulrich.

"They are cowards," said a man.

"Say no words which may be washed away only with blood," said Ulrich.

"Forgive me, milord," said the man who had spoken.

"I do not think I heard such words," said Ulrich.

"They were not spoken," said the man.

"It is only his concern for the Elbi, and the Otungs, that prompted his speech, milord," said a scarred man.

"What speech?" asked Ulrich.

"That which was not spoken," said the scarred man.

"The matter is done," said Ulrich.

"There are six claimant clans," said Urta. He then looked about. "Will no clan yield place to another?"

"No," said each of those who had spoken, in turn.

"I implore you to yield place, or to let the lots decide the matter, letting chance choose from amongst you," said Urta.

"No," said Rolof, looking about.

"None yields to any," snarled Gelerich.

"If there is to be gambling, let it be that of blades," said Valdemar.

"Yes!" said men.

"We shall laugh with steel," said a man.

"Yes," agreed the others.

A woman wept.

"Let it be understood that none but claimants or their champions may participate," said Urta.

Men looked angrily about.

"It is understood," said Valdemar.

The others, the claimants, murmured assent to this.

Grumbling came from retainers, and dark, suspicious looks were cast about.

"I shall prepare the lots, to determine the composition and order of the matches," said Urta.

"Proceed," said Rolof.

"Proceed," said Valdemar.

"There is yet time to withdraw," said Urta.

"Proceed!" said Gundar.

"Each of you claims the hero's portion?" said Urta. He looked from one to the other, in turn.

"Yes," said Rolof.

"Yes," said Valdemar.

"Yes," said Gundar.

"Yes," said Hartnar.

"Yes," said Gelerich.

"Yes," said Astarax.

"Behold," cried Ulrich, suddenly, elatedly, rising, pointing, "you are too late! It is already claimed!"

There were cries of rage, and of astonishment, throughout the hall.

On the table itself, towering there, legs spread, stood the blond giant. The great blade, five feet in length, was thrust into the body of the boar. He had held with two hands the hilt of the great blade, above his head, the point downward, and then plunged it downward. The point of the blade could be seen beneath the table where it had emerged, splintering the plank.

"Kill him!" cried men.

"Sacrilege!" cried others.

"Blasphemy!" cried others.

"How dare you do what you have done?" cried Urta, aghast.

"I am hungry," said the giant.

"Kill him!" screamed men.

The giant loosened the blade, and, lifting it, with three blows, hacked away the right, rear thigh of the massive boar.

He then, with the blade, sliced away a slab of hot meat, running with blood and juice.

He bit into this, deliberately, looking about himself, the blood and juice running at the side of his mouth.

"Kill him!" cried men.

"Surely others are hungry as well," he said.

He cut another piece of meat, and held it out to Urta, who drew back.

The giant then turned about.

"Untie the slave," he called.

One of the men at Ulrich's table crouched down behind the table and freed Yata's wrists and ankles. He wrapped the leather several times about her left ankle, and knotted it there, rather in the nature of a slave anklet. The slave may not undo such a knot without permission. It can be death to do so. Too, in this fashion, carrying the leather with her, she may be conveniently, instantly, bound, leashed or tethered, that at one's discretion.

The giant motioned that she should approach, and she did so, hesitantly, self-consciously, the eyes of all upon her.

She knelt below the table on which he stood, waiting, and he threw her the piece of meat which Urta had refused, and pointed back, toward Ulrich.

She rose and carried the meat to Ulrich, placed it before him, on the bare table, and then knelt near the table, facing the giant, her master.

"What is wrong?" asked the giant, calling to the tables. "Have you never seen a naked slave serve at a feast before?"

Ulrich did not touch the meat, but, eyes glistening, kept his eyes on the giant.

"Women of the empire," said the giant, "serve such feasts well."

He recalled perhaps a small feast at which, on Vellmer, three women of the empire had so served, and well, Flora, Renata and Sesella. Another had served, too, and well, Gerune, but she had not been of the empire. She had been once a Drisriak, and then an Ortung, and then but livestock, a slave.

"On behalf of whom do you claim this meat?" asked Urta.

"On my own behalf," said the giant.

"By what right?"

"By the right of my hunger," said the giant.

"That is not enough," said Urta.

"By the right of my pleasure then," said the giant.

"That is not enough," said Urta.

"By the right of my will then," said the giant.

"That is not enough," said Urta.

"Then by the right of my sword," said the giant.

"Whose champion are you?" asked Urta.

"I am my own champion," said the giant.

"You cannot claim this meat," protested Urta.

"Dispute it with me who will," said the giant, cutting another piece of meat.

He then, piece by piece, cut meat, throwing the meat to the slave, who carried it to one warrior or another, as indicated by the giant. He read the warriors, and in reading them, seeing who seemed young, and virile, and dangerous, and perhaps fit to be a companion, accordingly made his selections. None touched the meat put before them, but the eyes of many shone, and the hands of more than one inched toward the steaming, juicy provender.

"He gives meat!" cried a retainer of Rolof.

"He is a giver of meat," said a man, in awe.

"You are not a lord, to provide for companions, for a retinue!" said Urta.

"I have seen one who looked much like him, once before, long ago!" said a man.

"Where is Fuldan, the Old?" asked another.

"He has been sent for," said another.

"He is a stranger," said Hartnar, angrily.

"He has brought to the hall the pelt of a white vi-cat," said Ulrich. "It is the first time in a generation such a pelt has been in this place, not since Genserix."

"It means nothing!" cried a man.

"Such was the mantle of Genserix," said Ulrich.

The man was silent.

"Who are you, stranger?" demanded a man.

"A peasant, a fighter, one who was lifted upon the shields of Wolfungs, a Vandal people, as are the Otungs, a captain in the *auxilia* of Telnaria, come simply to recruit a company," said the giant.

"What is your people?" asked a man.

"I do not know," said the giant.

"I think you are Otung," said a man, in awe.

"Then," said the giant, "I am come home, and would be welcomed."

"Think, think!" cried Ulrich. "The Heruls put upon us year kings, insult kings, kings to divide us, kings to be replaced, kings who are to us as prisons and fetters, kings we despise and ignore, kings who are nothing, a kind of kings created by our enemies, kings who have but a compromised, meretricious, bestowed prestige, and one bought dearly with our own blood. The Heruls defeated us once, in battle, now they defeat us each year, by guile. Why do you think the Elbi propose no king, no champion? We will not play the game of the Heruls. I say, make no king, or make a true king!"

"The Heruls will not permit a true king," said Urta.

"Then make no king!" said Ulrich.

"The Heruls will be displeased," said Urta.

"Let them be displeased," said Ulrich.

"Yes," said men, softly.

"We cannot meet them, unmounted, on the plains," said Urta.

"And I do not think they will much care to seek us out in the darkness of the forest, in the shadows, in the growth and underbrush," said Ulrich. "Long ago, Telnaria lost armies in such endeavors."

"No more false kings," said a man.

"No king unless it be a true king!" said a man.

There were cries of approval from about the tables.

"It will mean war," said Urta.

"Lift me upon the shields," said Rolof. "I will be true king."

"No!" cried Valdemar.

"No!" cried other claimants.

"There would then be but one slaughter," said Rolof.

"We will not risk a king of clan Gri," said Astarax.

"Then year kings again it must be," said Valdemar.

"It is madness!" cried Ulrich. "Why must the clans and houses, the families, the lineages, war with one another? Are we not all Otung?"

"I yield to no one," said Gelerich.

"Nor I!" said Astarax.

"I would not hide all my days in the forest," said Ulrich. "I would one day come forth from the forest, bravely, with oxen and wagons, with songs, and arms, marching. We have hidden here long enough, imprisoned not by Heruls but by our own vanities and rivalries."

"We are not yet strong enough," said Urta.

"Let us take the first step, the first step on our march," said Ulrich. "If we must have a king, and cannot have a true king, then let us make a year king, but one who has no party, one who is not of the table of a given house, one who has taken rings from no man, one by means of whom to satisfy, and yet reprove and mystify, Heruls."

"Only a stranger could be such," said a man.

"Yes," said Ulrich.

Eyes turned toward the giant.

"No!" cried Rolof.

"He has brought to the hall the pelt of the white vi-cat," said Ulrich.

"Such was the mantle of Genserix," said a man.

"It is the medallion and chain which are important," said a man.

"The medallion and chain were lost," said a man.

"It fell to the lot of Heruls," said a man.

"There can be no true king without the medallion and chain," said a man.

"It was that, allegiance to it, sworn by the fathers of the clans, that united the people," said a man.

"Yes," said another.

"So there can be no true king," said a man.

"I do not come amongst you to be king," said the giant. "I come amongst you to recruit *comitates*, *comites*, fellows, companions, swordsmen, fighters."

"He is a spy for Telnaria!" said a man.

"He is a Herul spy. See the Herul knife!" said another.

The giant cut more meat, indeed, with the Herul knife, which, by means of Yata, he distributed, indicating likely recipients.

Then he rose up, from where he had crouched, cutting meat, and stood again on the table.

"Begone, stranger," said Rolof.

The giant freed the great blade of the meat, into which he had thrust it.

"Make the stranger year king," said Ulrich. "In that way no clan, and no house, takes precedence over another. Why should you, Rolof, or you, Valdemar, or Gundar, or Hartnar, or Gelerich or Astarax, or any other Otung of noble blood, stain his honor by accepting the post of year king? It is dishonor to accept it, not honor. To accept such a kingship is not glory, but shame. It is to serve not Otungs, but Heruls."

"In yielding to the stranger," said a man, "you lose nothing in honor, for no rival takes precedence over you."

"And you show contempt for Heruls," said another.

"No!" said Rolof. "I would be king, even if for a year!"

"I!" said Valdemar.

"No!" cried the others. "I! I!"

"Alas," said Ulrich. "All is lost."

"No," said the giant.

"How so?" asked Ulrich.

"For the hero's portion has been claimed," said the giant.

"That is true, milords," said Urta. "One stands between you and the kingship."

Retainers rose to their feet.

But more than a dozen young men before whom meat had been placed rose, too, to their feet.

"Hold!" cried Urta.

"My company," said the giant, "is open to all clans, to all Otungs, and to others, as well."

"And in such a company," said a man, "to whom is allegiance owed—to Telnaria, our hated foe, to whom we owe our exile on Tangara?"

"No," said the giant, "not to Telnaria."

"Then to whom?" asked the man.

"To me," said the giant.

There was silence in the hall.

"Kill him," said Rolof, gesturing toward the giant. Six men hurried toward the table.

"No!" cried others.

It was a mistake, of course, that the noble, Rolof, had given the order he had.

It was not in accord with the customs of the Otungs. Too, he did not understand the nature of the giant. But then, at that time, few did. His mistake was then twofold, on the one hand, a breach of civility, on the other, as it turned out, an error of judgment, not that one should blame Rolof severely for that, as, at that time, as we have suggested, the nature of the giant was not clearly understood.

The accounts differ troublesomely on what exactly occurred.

They concur, however, on the cry.

With a sudden, wild cry, a cry which astonished those in the hall, a glad, elated cry, as though of the release of long pent-up frustration, of patience too long restrained, a cry of savage joy, of feral gladness, a releasing, laughing, merciful, discharging cry, a cry like the flashing of fire, like the sudden, unexpected, exultant crack of thunder from violent, aching, swollen clouds, a cry bestial, grateful and exultant, a cry that might have been that of a starving man who sees food, that of a man dying of thirst who sees water, the giant leapt from the table, the huge blade in flight, hurtling, bearing with it all its edged, cruel weight, that mighty blade which the giant handled as if it might have been a straw, sped with all its momentum, that of his movement and of its own swift, smooth arc, like a steel wind, almost invisible.

Accounts of what matters then occurred, and the order in which these matters occurred, tend to vary amongst the chroniclers. Whereas this is regrettable, it is also quite understandable, as it is a commonplace that when a complex event occurs suddenly, precipitately, in a crowded area, and is hastily resolved, that even eyewitnesses tend to produce conflicting reports of what occurred. Doubtless they are startled, and perhaps confused; much happens quickly; it is soon done; perspectives differ; some vantages are superior to others; what one notes may depend in part on one's expectations; and memory, too, tends to be fallible, particularly in the case of such events, where so much happens so quickly; too, one must remember that the hall was doubtless poorly lit.

I have elected to follow here, in the main, the account of Orban, of the house of Orix, as reported in the second chronicle of Armenion, as revised by Teminius. I have selected it not because I regard it as that likely to be most accurate, but rather because, as I do not know which account is the most accurate, it is the most restrained.

I apologize for the account, but it must be remembered that the times were other than ours.

Six men, it may be recalled, hurried toward the table, these retainers of Rolof, his champion, and five others, these coming from the giant's right.

The mighty blade, which might have felled a small tree, or cut the head from a horse, with one blow, like a live, leaping thing, rising up, a flat, edged living wind, a flash under the torches, caught the men doubled on one another, they not anticipating the attack, they having foolishly thought it was they who were the aggressors, the first two stopping, suddenly, startled, others stumbling against one another, the men falling amongst themselves, none set, none in the guard position, caught the first two men to the right, cutting upward through the armpit of the first, slashing away the arm and upper torso and neck and head, and flighting thence, in the same arc, to cleave away the upper skull of the second man, the blade turning then, in its back stroke, to cut away the hand and split the ribs of a third man. The other three, half fallen, looked up, wildly, and one amongst them was cleaved at the side of the head, the stroke, downward, at the right eye, ceasing its dividing stroke only at the last of three sheared ribs. Two others turned to flee but another stroke cut both feet from under one, and he hobbled on stumps to the table of Rolof, beneath which he fell, and the last was caught against that very table itself, the table of Rolof, where he fell before his lord, the table itself splintered then in twain, the body, half cut in two, folded in upon itself, descending, sliding, in the collapsed planks. The giant scarcely noted the horrified eyes of Rolof behind the table, when his arena sense, alert to the tiniest of sounds, was that the movement of a foot in the dust, brought him full about to see men of lord Valdemar advancing toward him.

"Stop!" cried Urta.

The giant laughed, to see more meat for his sword, and men hesitated.

"Stop!" again cried Urta, the namer of kings.

"Kill him!" cried Valdemar, and his champion edged forward, but one blow of the long blade smote through a shield, flinging the arm, caught in the device's straps, across the hall.

The man to his right was blinded by the blood, and in a moment, unseeing, screaming, thrust his hand downward, into his own guts, where it was caught, tangled, and in his terror, with two hands, clutching, in madness and pain, disemboweled himself.

Other men of Valdemar drew back, four others.

The giant looked about himself, crouching down, like an animal, turning with feral, almost inhuman quickness.

"Kill him!" called Rolof, as though to the hall itself.

The giant's eyes were bright.

There was blood on his hands and furs.

"It is Genserix," said a man.

"It is more terrible than Genserix," said another.

"Kill him!" cried Valdemar to his reluctant liegemen.

The blood on the blade had run sidewise in narrow channels, these streamlets consequent upon the motion of the article.

It was this quickness apparently, this seeming capacity to move with unnatural speed, which was one of the first things to have struck, or caught, even enflamed, the imaginations of many men of the time, doubtless rude, simple men, sword-wielders, spearmen and such. There is much agreement on this quickness, it seems, as one of the giant's properties. And yet, as certain chronicles have it, the field diaries of Lucian, for example, the speeds with which he moved tended, even in battle, to shift and vary deceptively, distractively, startling foes, disturbing their anticipations, necessitating costly adjustments, a thousandth of a second sometimes the difference of an inch or more in the reach and thrust of a blade. Such things cannot be taught, not in their fullness of subtlety, not in their diverse pacings, their delicate temporal modalities, their seemingly instantaneous sensings, not in their odd admixture of violence and sensitivity, brutality and refinement. They are bred into warriors, generation by generation, over thousands of years, much as hunting and killing, generation by generation, over thousands of years, is bred into the lion, the vi-cat, the wolf. Sometimes, it is said, he seemed somnolent, slow to act, silent like rock, massive like stone, and then again, sometimes without warning, it seemed that great body could explode, bomblike, destructive to all within its compass. Sometimes he seemed slow, awkward, inarticulate. Certainly he was illiterate, like many of his time. But it seems, too, he was not unintelligent. There is much evidence that he could be patient, reflective and thoughtful. We know little in detail of such things, however, his plans and long thoughts, as he muchly kept his own counsel. Few people claimed to know him well. There is universal agreement, however, that his anger was not a light thing. It could arise suddenly, unpredictably, stormlike. It could seldom be assuaged without blood. Doubtless this was his greatest weakness. Certainly, politically, it was his most grievous flaw. To be sure, his concept of statecraft in any event was rudimentary, being founded on little more, as was common with his sorts of peoples in those times, than simple virtues, such as the keeping of pledged words. He was not equally at home in the saddle and on a throne. But this was not unusual, too, for many leaders of his time. We know little of the deeper currents within him, or if there were such. He is said, once in the darkness of the woods, thinking himself alone, to have howled, as though in great pain. Men never saw him cry. Little is known of his inner life, or if he, in effect, had one. It is speculated that men in his time were less self-aware, less self-conscious, than men in our time, that they were simpler, and more like animals, than we. One does not know, of course. Too, on such matters it is difficult to speculate.

The giant looked about himself.

The warriors of Valdemar had drawn back.

The giant went back to the table and, with the great blade, cut another piece of meat.

Yata ran to him and knelt before him, her head down, her hands lifted, and he put the meat in her small hands, her tiny fingers clutching it, warm juice running between her fingers.

She looked up at her master.

He looked about.

At the tables a young man had risen.

The giant pointed to the young man and Yata hurried to him, and placed the meat before him. His eyes shone. Yata then drew back from the table, knelt, put her head to the dirt, and then turned, on her knees, lifting her head a little, to face the giant.

How next would she be commanded?

The young man had scarcely glanced at the lovely young slave before him, though she would doubtless have brought a high price in many markets.

Mightier things were afoot.

She was only a female, and a slave.

"I have at this time no rings to give," said the giant.

"I would not serve for rings," said the young man.

"What is your name?" said the giant.

"Vandar," said the young man.

"It is a good name," said the giant.

"I am ready!" said the young man. "Summon me to your side!"

"At my side is danger," said the giant.

"I would rather die at the side of one such as you than live elsewhere," said the man.

"Do not move," said a man.

"The night is cold, and the stars are indifferent," said the young man. "I answer only to myself."

"Cease your obscure rantings," said a man.

"Milord!" cried the young man to the giant.

"Remain where you are!" said the giant.

The young man cried out in misery.

"Can you not see?" asked a man. "He stands alone."

"At this time one such as he must stand alone," said another.

"He who cannot stand alone deserves to have none stand with him," said another.

"He has brought to the hall the pelt of a white vi-cat," said Ulrich.

"No, no!" cried Valdemar, looking about himself. "Kill him! Kill him!"

One of his men turned to him. "We follow you, my liege," he said.

Valdemar did not move.

Then his men drew away from him.

"You are no longer first among the Tiri," said a man.

"No!" cried Valdemar.

Valdemar drew his blade, and cried out, and he, then followed instantly by several men, those of the Tiri in the hall, rushed toward the giant.

"No!" cried Urta. "Only the lord, or his champion, may challenge!"

But none gave ear to the plaint of the King Namer.

The giant struck about him with the great sword.

A shield was cut in twain.

Men were struck to the side, buffeted.

The mighty sword flashed again, and sparks, like flaming snow, bright from three blades, exploded in the hall.

Men pressed forward.

"Stop!" cried the King Namer.

"Stop!" cried others.

The giant, looking about himself, backed away.

The fire pit was behind him, long, some eighteen feet in length, some five feet in width, a foot deep with glowing coals. The two supports on which the spit had been mounted were still in place. The spit itself, one end pointed for insertion in the meat, the other end bent to a handle that the device might be turned, that spit on which the boar had been roasted, lay to one side, on a wooden rack.

The giant felt the heat behind him.

Valdemar lunged forward, his charge turned by the great blade, and the noble, screaming, losing his footing, fell into the pit. Otto forced the retainers back with a terrible blow, and spun about, turning to Valdemar, who, screaming, twisted in the coals, rose up wildly, slipped, fell, climbed again to his feet, and began to wade, frenziedly, stumbling, to the edge of the pit, but the giant turned about and plunged after him, wading into the coals, and seized Valdemar at the edge of the pit, by the collar of his furs, and threw him back, on his back, into the coals. Two men plunged after the giant, but he cut them down with one stroke, over the body of Valdemar, which he forced down, deeper, with one foot, into the coals. He then, to the horror of the liegemen, who hesitated, aware they could not reach him with their smaller blades, not having time to circle the pit, raised his blade above his head, holding it there with two hands, as he had, earlier, over the roast boar.

"No!" cried one of the liegemen, raising his hand.

"Strike!" cried Valdemar.

The sword was poised.

The liegemen cast their weapons to the floor of the hall.

"Strike!" screamed Valdemar.

But the giant stepped back from the body, through the coals, ascending the far side of the pit.

Valdemar's liegemen drew him swiftly from the coals, covering his own body with theirs, to smother flames.

Two other bodies were drawn, too, slashed, half dismembered, from the coals, one leg hanging by a muscle to a trunk, furs blackened, and, at the sides, burned away.

A grayish smoke, like haze, hung over the coals.

There was an ugly, sweet odor of burned flesh, of skin, of muscle and fat, in the hall.

The left side of Valdemar's face was gone, burned away.

The giant came about the pit, and stood over Valdemar, looking down at him.

Valdemar's men drew back.

Valdemar looked up, unblinking, staring, his right eyelid burned away.

"You are Otung," he whispered.

"I do not know," said the giant.

The giant wiped on his furred thigh the long blade.

"Aii!" cried a man.

Too, at the same time, the slave had screamed, but the giant had already slipped to the side.

The blow of Rolof's sword rang on the thick iron spit, it lying on its rack.

Sparks sprang upward.

"A felon's stroke!" cried a man.

"Pig!" cried another.

The giant rolled beneath the spit, the long blade lost, and another blow struck down, again ringing, showering sparks, from the spit.

"No longer are you first among the Gri!" cried an angered retainer.

Rolof snarled, and put his foot on the blade of the great sword, holding his own blade ready.

"Pig!" cried a man.

The noble of the Gri was flanked by two cohorts.

The giant now crouched behind the heavy iron spit, it on its rack, a foot above the ground, its metal now twice scarred from the blade of Rolof.

Before him was the noble, and his two fellows, and three blades.

He did not take his eyes from the steel. The giant's eyes were terrible. From his throat there came a rumbling, growling noise.

"Sheath your weapon!" called Urta to Rolof.

"I sheath my weapon for no man," said Rolof. "I am king!"

The huge hands of the giant felt for, and closed upon, the long, thick, weighty, still-warm spit on its rack.

Before him were Rolof, and two of the Gri, behind him, glowing, bright with heat, deep with coals, was the fire pit. Its heat was fierce upon his back and legs.

The hands of the giant were upon the spit.

The spit had held the weight, unbending, of the great boar, which, ungutted, had weighed better than four hundred pounds. Two men had turned the spit in its mounts.

Rolof raised his sword.

With a cry of rage the giant rose up. The spit, like a snake, striking, was not even lifted from the rack, but shattered free, bursting, scattering wood.

The man to the giant's right had no time even to scream, for the spit, a yard from its end, caught him beneath the left ear, breaking the neck, half tearing the head from the body. Rolof and his fellow were struck to the side by the same blow, and fell, rolling, to the floor. The giant kicked aside the remnants of the rack. Rolof scrambled back. The man to the giant's left was struck on the return of the spit, and his arm, the elbow smashed, running with blood, hung like rope to the side. He put up his left hand to fend the next blow, but the crook in the spit's handle, tearing back through the fingers, struck him in the throat, crushing it back, breaking cartilage, inches. Rolof reached for his lost blade. The giant lifted and plunged the portion of the spit handle, two feet long, parallel to its shaft, down twice, once through the jaw and mouth of the man, then on his back, breaking teeth and bone, and driving through tissue, and, then, more carefully, through the forehead, until it stopped, inches deep, in the dirt floor of the hall. Rolof now had his sword in hand but backed away from the giant, who was now regarding him eagerly, terribly, who now held the huge spit, drawn free, its length well beyond the reach of even the great blade, holding it as one might have held the peasant's weapon, one hand at the center, the other below, the long staff.

Suddenly Rolof cried out, flung down his weapon, and fled toward the entrance of the hall.

The giant pursued him, in fury, the spit, its pointed end forward, lifted over his head in both hands.

Rolof fled up the stairs, toward the wooden door of the hall.

But of course the two beams, barring the door, the hall having been entered, were now in place, secure in their brackets.

Rolof turned about, suddenly, wildly, at the door, knowing he had no time to lift the two beams from the braces.

He stood there, for a moment, on the level before the door, his back to the door.

"No!" he cried.

"Aii!" cried men.

Women screamed.

The giant worked the spit free of the door, through which the point had penetrated, emerging on the other side, and then he carried the spit, on which the body of Rolof was impaled down the stairs, and to the side of the fire pit.

The hall was silent.

He stood near the fire pit, the spit still in the body of Rolof, who, toward the lower end of the spit, had slipped toward its point, and lay on the floor, near the coals, one side of the body illuminated by their light.

One of the liegemen of the Tiri looked up, from his knees, where he knelt beside a seared body.

"Lord Valdemar is dead," said the man.

"He died as first among the Tiri," said another.

"Yes," said another.

The giant, with his foot, thrust the body of Rolof from the spit, and cast the spit aside.

He then, from near the fire pit, retrieved the great sword.

He then looked about the hall, from face to face, Ulrich, Gundar, Hartnar, Gelerich, Astarax, the others.

He then turned to face Urta, the King Namer.

"Who is king?" asked the giant.

"You are king," said Urta.

"Let us eat," said the giant. "I am hungry."

· · · CHAPTER 33 · · ·

There is little more to tell, at this time, though, in a sense, this was the beginning, not that it was then recognized as such.

On a winter night, after feasting, the giant, outside the hall, in the snow, for such things are done outside, in the light of a sun, or of stars, was lifted upon the shields of Otungs.

His nature, and his lineage, no more than his destiny, were at that time unknown.

He refused to sit upon the empty throne, that upon the dais in the hall, as he had not yet, at that time, in his view, earned such a right. Too, the medallion and chain, which was the token of an Otung king's office, his heritage and right, was not with the Otungs. It was that on which the heads of clans, long ago, had sworn the honoring of the kingship, even before the time of Genserix. Until that was found there was little assurance, and even less hope, that the nobles of the Otungen would long respect the kingship, such being the force of ambition amongst them.

Fuldan, the Old, who had been sought, that he might look upon the stranger, and speak upon his appearance, which had so intrigued some members of the hall, was not found in his hut, for he had, in desolation and grief, in sorrow for the debasement of the Otungen, even before the time of the king naming, left the forest, borne upon a litter, in furs, his bones ancient with pain, and misery, with ten retainers.

"They are no longer the folk, no longer the Otungen," he had said.

He did not know then, mercifully enough, one supposes, of the election of a stranger as king, which matter might have caused him even greater pain.

Urta, for he was the King Namer, slipped away later, that he might inform the Heruls of what had occurred.

The chieftains of the Heruls were not pleased to learn that the Otungen had lifted one upon the shields, even a stranger, for year kings are not lifted upon the shields, but only other sorts of leaders, such as lords of clans, chieftains, commanders of battle groups, and such, and kings.

Too, they were disturbed to learn that the stranger had brought to the hall the pelt of a white vi-cat.

Such things were not permitted to year kings.

To be sure, he who had been lifted upon the shields did not have the medallion and chain, which had seemingly been lost.

In a sense then, though he might be king, he was not to be feared as might have been a king who wore both the mantle of the white vi-cat and the ancient medallion and chain of the Otungen. The medallion and chain might unite not only the clans of the Otungen, but the other tribes, as well, of the Vandal nation.

Urta, bowing, withdrew from the council of the Heruls. They did not put him to death, but gave him golden *darins*, from Venitzia.

An old Herul warrior, whose name was Hunlaki, one of the far riders and hard fighters of that warlike nomadic people, might, if urged, or pressed, have been able to supply some informed speculation as to the possible whereabouts of the medallion and chain, but he was not of the high council of the Heruls, and he had not, in his own knowledge, an understanding of its significance, even though, once, years ago, after a campaign against Basungs, it seems quite possible that he may have held it in his hands. The high council knew its meaning, as Hunlaki did not. Hunlaki, on the other hand, might have had some sense of its fate, and whereabouts, as did neither the council nor the Otungen. To be sure, memory tends to be fallible, and the incident, if it had occurred, had occurred long ago.

It seemed quite clear to the Heruls that the Otungen had elected a king who was not a year king, but, against their wishes, and their clearly expressed ordinance and policy, in some sense, a true king, even if one lacking the medallion and chain. Accordingly they decided to move against the Otungen.

We do not know, exactly, why the stranger took the hero's portion at the feast of the king naming.

He may have taken the hero's portion that the strife amongst the Otungs might be thusly resolved, that their lack of unity and the plight of their rivalries might be abolished, or at least, for a time, assuaged. Too, he may have adopted this course of action simply as an instrumentality conducive to the recruitment of men, *comitates, comites*, companions, a retinue, for a mercenary company. Ostensibly, at least, such seems to have been his original purpose in approaching Otungs. Others see some sensing of an obscure reality in the matter, a sensing of fittingness, a response to a prompting of blood or instinct, thusly not so much that he saw an opportunity, in a time of confusion, uncertainty, and chaos, to seize a kingship, as that it seemed to him fitting that he should do so, that it, in some sense, was his, that it belonged to him. To be sure, this possibility is perhaps too uncertain and too disturbing to be accepted as a hypothesis. Others see the matter merely as a warrior's dark *jeu d'esprit*, brief, terrible, and celebratory, no more than a momentary, exultant gesture, or game, or festival, of blood and steel, and some, even, that it was merely that he was indeed hungry, and had decided to feed, in his uncouth, boorish manner, and that one event had led to another. We do not know the truth of the matter. Perhaps there are many truths, and they are woven somehow together, to form the tapestry of existence, the subtle, somber, some bright, some dark, threads, or cords, of reality. In historical studies it is often hard, trying to peer back into the mists of time, to ascertain even the deeds of men; how much harder it is then to look into their hearts. Too, it is a sobering thought, but it is well to remember that those hearts may be quite different from our own. Our beliefs, our values, our worlds, may not be the beliefs, values, or worlds of others. Doubtless we would find it difficult to enter the experience of the serpent, the wolf, the hawk, the vi-cat. Perhaps, too, then, we would find it difficult to enter into the experiences of men which may be quite different from ours, experiences perhaps more akin to those of the serpent, the hawk, the wolf, and the vi-cat, to those of predators, to those of beasts, than they are to ours. But, doubtless, even so, there is a kinship. It seems likely that nothing which is human can be utterly alien to us. Each of us, doubtless, carries in our heart many things. In historical studies it is not impossible to find the present, and ourselves.

No sooner had the giant leapt down into the snow, under the stars, from the shields, to the shouting and the clashing of weapons, than a warrior thrust aside others, and confronted him. "Let us laugh with steel!" he cried, tears in his eyes. The warrior was seized by those about, and, struggling, held fast. A blade was instantly at his heart, poised there by young Vandar, the first of the Otungs who had seized up the hot meat on the table before him, and fed upon it, his eyes on his lord, Otto, who had just been acknowledged by Urta as king of the Otungs.

Otto gestured that Vandar should lower his weapon.

Otto gestured that the warrior should be released.

"Let us laugh with steel," said again the warrior, to Otto, king of the Otungen.

Men cried out with rage for their lord had again been threatened. Had Otto not raised his hand, conveying to them that they must desist, furs would have surged about the bold fellow, the press of a hundred knives, in turn, responding to his insolence.

"Let him laugh with me!" cried Vandar.

"No, with me!" cried others.

Men looked angrily at one another.

Each would vie with each to defend to the death their liege lord.

"How is it that you so speak to your king?" asked Otto of the bold fellow.

"I want the slave girl," said Citherix.

There was a soft, startled cry from the side where, miserable, shivering, partly bent over, her arms clutched about her, stood blond Yata, the slave of Otto. She had crept forth from the hall, and, until then, had been muchly unnoticed. Aware of eyes upon her, she knelt in the snow, putting her head down to it.

"I will give you a thousand sheep, and a thousand pigs, for her," said Citherix.

Men cried out, amazed, at the bounty of such an offer.

"She is not for sale," said Otto.

"Let us laugh with steel," said Citherix.

"You must want her very much," said Otto.

"I must have her," said Citherix.

"But she is not yours," said the giant.

"I will have her or die," said Citherix.

"I do not understand," said the giant.

"I love her," said Citherix, angrily.

The slave, to the side, cried out, startled, softly.

There was rude laughter amongst the men and women outside the hall. "He loves a slave!" laughed a man.

"A slave!" laughed another.

"He is a fool!" said a man.

"Yes," said another.

There was more laughter.

"I will have her or die," said Citherix.

"As you wish," said Otto. "Bring me my sword," said he to Vandar.

In a moment the great sword was in his hands.

"Do you think you can best me?" asked the giant.

"No," said Citherix.

"But yet you would laugh with steel?"

"Yes," said Citherix.

Men cleared a space in the snow about them. It was some fifteen feet in diameter.

"Please, no, Master!" cried the slave.

"Cuff her," said Otto.

The nearest warrior struck the slave to her side in the snow.

She lay in the snow, weeping.

"See that he has a shield," said Otto. A shield was handed to Citherix.

The moonlight was bright, the shadows dark, the snow, where not trampled, away from the hall, away from the crowd, glistened.

The great blade struck, cutting away the upper part of the shield.

Citherix stumbled backward, slipping in the snow. Another blow cleaved away much of the left side of the shield. Citherix cast it aside and, two hands on the hilt of his sword, tried desperately to interpose it between himself and the great blade, which, with blow after blow, ringing, mighty, patient, merciless, with terrible weight, beat down upon it. Down Citherix was forced to his knees, each blow pounding his own blade down, forcing it down, driving it closer and closer to his head, his face and body. And then he was on his back, and the giant was over him, and again the great blade rang down. The arms of Citherix trembled, and shook, and ached. The hilt of his sword burned in his stung, tortured hands. Then the giant's blade, on the last stroke, turning, not lifting away for yet another onslaught, caught Citherix's blade under the guard, in that tiny moment just after the last pounding, ringing blow, when the grip loosened, to be instantly readjusted, retightened, for meeting the next stroke, and tore it up, away from his hands, and flung it high, and aside, over the heads of men, yards away, into the night, and the snow.

"Ah," said men, softly, and the business was for all intents and purposes finished.

The giant raised the blade over his head.

"No!" screamed a voice, and a small body flung itself, sobbing, across Citherix, who lay in the snow, shielding him, clinging to him. "No, no, please, Master!" it cried. "Kill me, instead!"

Otto, puzzled, lowered the sword.

The blow, of course, from such a blade, wielded with the might of the giant, which could fell small trees, and cut the heads from horses, might have cut through both bodies, arresting itself only, at last, in the frozen ground. But the giant lowered the sword.

"Kneel," said he to the slave girl, who, in terror, drew back from the body of Citherix and knelt to one side in the trampled snow. The giant, with one hand, bent her head down and threw her hair forward, exposing that small fine neck, the vertebrae of which he might have snapped in one hand.

"Very well," said he, "it is her life for yours."

The giant rested the edge of the blade on the back of the slave's neck, and then lifted it, for the blow.

"No!" said Citherix, his hand extended, half rising. "No!" He turned and crawled to the slave. He, on his knees, took her in his arms, shielding her, putting his body between hers and the blade. "Let her live," said he. "It is I who am guilty. It is I who raised steel against my king. That is treason, and the punishment for it is death."

"That is true, milord," said Ulrich.

"The king may kill," said Otto. "The king may pardon. The king may do as he pleases."

"That is true, milord," said Ulrich.

There was assent to this among the men.

"I pardon you," said Otto to Citherix. "Rise up. Be Otung."

Citherix rose, unsteadily, to his feet. "Why do you pardon me, milord?" he asked.

"I have need," said Otto, "of men bold enough to challenge kings."

Men looked at one another.

"Only of such men," said Otto, "would I be king."

"What of the slave, milord?" asked Ulrich.

Otto looked down at the slave who, kneeling in the snow, shivering, put her head down.

"Sometimes," said Otto, to the girl, "it takes a slave some time, in straps and chains, to learn who is her true master."

"Yes, Master," she whispered.

Otto turned to Citherix. "Do you think you can teach her?"

"Milord?" said Citherix.

"It seems she is more your slave than mine," said Otto.

"My slave?" said Citherix, astonished.

He looked down at the slave, who looked up at him, tears in her eyes. She smiled, through her tears, and nodded, a tiny, almost imperceptible movement of her head, so small a movement that it seemed she almost feared that it might be detected.

"I could give her to you," said Otto, "but I would rather sell her to you."

"Anything!" cried Citherix.

"One pig," said Otto. "I want her clearly to understand her value."

"Done, milord!" cried Citherix.

"To him, slut," said Otto.

Yata hurried on her knees to Citherix, and, laughing and crying, performed obeisance before him, and then, putting herself to her belly in the snow and holding to his ankles, one after the other, pressed kisses upon his snowy boots.

"I thought you hated me," said Citherix.

"I have always loved you, Master," she said. "I have always wanted to be owned by you, wholly, uncompromisingly, as a slave is truly owned. I have always wanted to be yours, completely, and to have no choice but to obey you perfectly, helplessly, will-lessly, in all things. That is how much I love you! So much so that I wanted to be your slave! So much so that I must be your slave! So much so that I can be only your slave! I have always wanted to be your slave! I have always dreamed of being of your slave, even from the time I was a little girl and you were a little boy! And I had hoped that you might accept me not only as your slave, but that you might one day come to realize that I was not only your helpless slave, yours to do with as you wished, in any way, but that I was, too, your love slave! No matter how you may despise or mistreat me, Master, I cannot help but be your helpless love slave!"

"You will be kept, of course, as a slave," said Citherix.

"Yes, Master!"

"As a total slave."

"Of my own will, were it permitted me, I would have it no other way, Master."

She shivered, in the snow. "Forgive me, Master!" she said, frightened.

"You are Hortense," he said, naming her.

"I am Hortense," she said. This name would serve to remind everyone that she was once Hortense, though she wore the name now only as a slave name, only as a pig or dog might be named, by the will of her master.

"Many times did I dream of owning the troublesome, insolent Hortense," he said.

"She is now yours," said the slave.

He bent down and folded her shivering body in his cloak, and lifted her up.

"I will carry you within the hall," he said, "and warm you by the fire pit, and then you will serve me, beneath the table, at my place."

"Yes, Master!" she said.

She wept with joy, kissing him.

"I have waited long to own you," he said.

"I have waited long to be owned by you," she said.

He gathered her more closely to him.

"How shall I treat you?" he asked.

"Remember that I cost only a pig, Master," she said.

"I shall," he said.

He turned about and carried her within the hall.

"Citherix would now die for you," said Ulrich.

The giant turned about. "I would have a woman," he said. "Where are the slaves of the Otungs?"

Men looked to one another, abashed.

"There is only one slave among the Otungs," said a man, "and that is the slave of Citherix."

"The Heruls do not permit us slaves," said another man.

"It is part of their policy," said another, "to so exercise their will over us, to mock and humiliate us, to keep us weak, to deny us the rights of dominance and possession, the rights of conquering manhood."

"That will change," said Otto. "Men need slaves."

"Slaves, too, need masters, milord," said a woman, almost inaudibly.

"There are many women in the empire," said Otto, "who need masters."

"And elsewhere, milord," said a woman, softly.

"Do not become aroused by the example of a despicable slave," said a man, angrily.

"No, no, of course not!" said the woman.

"They are different," said the man. "You are not such as they!"

"No, of course not!" exclaimed the woman.

"You are different!" he said.

"Yes, yes!" she said.

"You are proud, noble, and free!" he said.

"Yes," she said. "Yes!"

The giant looked at the woman. He sized her up, as men who are practiced with women do. He did not think she would look badly, in chains. She would lick and kiss eagerly, and within the hour, with scarcely a touch of the whip, he thought.

"I think some women can be found," said the giant. He, at

that time, of course, believed that the women embarked from Inez IV were in Venitzia. To be sure, that was days away.

"The king," said Hartnar, "will need a queen." He thrust a young woman forward. "My daughter, Gertrude," he said, "is a comely lass."

The giant pushed up the girl's chin and looked into her eyes, which she suddenly, frightened, turned away. Never had she been so looked upon. Surely she was not in a slaver's house, for sale! Surely she was not upon a slave block!

"I have this niece," said Gelerich. "She is of the lineage of Pertinax, of the Orti."

Another woman was pushed forward.

"Not of the Orti!" said Astarax. "Take a woman of the Eni, Una, of the house of Fendash, or Tuse, or Gretchen, of the house of Hertzaufen. Una, Tuse, Gretchen, come forward!"

"The daughters of Gundar, Esa and Estrid, are beauties," said a man, of the clan Oni.

"Where has he hidden them?" laughed a man.

"He does not want the Heruls to learn of them and take them for slaves," said a man.

"Perhaps they should be slaves," said a man.

The giant supposed that many women should be slaves, and of the Otungs, too, for their women, too, were women. Many, he supposed, might be better off, taken to far, rich, exotic worlds, in chains, there to serve strong masters.

But the Otungs, too, he thought, must have women.

"There are many comely women," said Ulrich, "and from the Elbi, too!"

Women crowded about. Some had been thrust forward, others guided forward, or urged forward, but others had come forward of their own will, some hurrying forward.

It is not unlike the wares in a slaver's house, thought the giant, on those rare occasions when a strong man, one deemed a desirable master, a possible buyer, is given the liberty of the premises. To be sure, the goods were not in brief silks, or stripped, and, either silked or stripped, in collars, kneeling.

The thought of Filene crossed the giant's mind. He remembered her, from the night he had tied her at the foot of his bed. He had heard, at times during the night, when she had thought him asleep, her restlessness, her tiny, half-restrained inadvertent whimpers, and moans.

There had seemed something different about her, though he had not been sure what it was. He supposed that it was only that she had not yet learned her slavery.

That could be remedied, easily.

And she was on Tangara, presumably in Venitzia.

The giant looked upon the free women.

One smiled. Another turned, that he might conjecture her figure.

They are free, they are dangerous, he thought. They have all the power of their freedom, of custom, of rude law protecting them, rendering them invulnerable, permitting them to strive in a thousand sly ways against men, capable of reducing and diminishing men, of denying them, of using their bodies to buy what they wanted, of withholding them for gain, of offering favors for bribes, and all with impunity.

How different the slave, who is owned, and must please!

Women are the enemy, thought the giant. Why should not men then, who are stronger, simply subdue them, and then let them find themselves the spoils of war, owned and mastered. It is pleasant to tame women, to make them obedient, dutiful, passionate slaves, and to drive them to sexual ecstasies a thousand times beyond those attainable by the free woman, to have them at the foot of your bed, on the floor, perhaps bound hand and foot there, begging for your touch. Yes, thought the giant, women should be slaves; they belong in collars, and shackles. And women, interestingly, thought the giant, dream of masters. They long for the chains in which they know themselves rightfully to belong. At the master's feet is the place of women, and this, deny it, and fear it and fight it as they will, in their hearts, they know.

The man who does not put them to their knees they despise. They respond, in the fullness of their sexuality, only to the man before whom they must kneel.

How luscious, thought the giant, was Filene. And she is somewhere in Venitzia! I must arrange for the trading mission he thought. I must go, with men, to Venitzia.

It was the next day that the giant learned, to his elation, after a night of terrible and restless torment, that the trade expedition, with vehicles, and goods, and tents and equipment, under the command of Lysis, attempting to follow him, had arrived near the edge of the forest, only hours away.

Heruls, apparently curious to see what would ensue, had

brought the expedition that far. They would not venture into the forest.

The next day, toward evening, at the head of some ten picked men, including Vandar, the giant emerged from the forest, and saw, in the distance, the camp compound and its defensive perimeter, illuminated by floodlights.

The men with him had never seen such a camp. It was quite different from the wagons of the Heruls.

In a short time the giant had approached the camp, and, from a distance of several yards outside the fence, made himself known.

Lysis himself, and the young blond officer, having ascertained through sentries that the guest from the night was indeed Otto, came themselves through the fence.

They seized him, and embraced him warmly.

"We had hoped we could make contact with you here," said Lysis, supply officer of the *Narcona*. "Why did you leave Venitzia without us?"

"It was important to come alone, to prepare the way," said Otto.

"Telnarians are not welcome in the forest?" asked Corelius, the young blond officer.

"There are many places Telnarians are not welcome," said Otto.

"Did your mission go well?" asked Lysis.

"I think we have cause to be pleased," said Otto.

"Who are those with you?" asked Lysis.

"Otungs," said Otto. "I would not approach them too closely, as two have bows."

"How many are there?" asked Lysis.

"Ten," said Otto.

"That does not seem too many," said Corelius.

"They are welcome," said Lysis.

"Telnarians and Otungs are enemies," said Otto. "I think it is better that we do not bring soldiers and Otungs together, until we have prepared both."

"He is right," said Corelius. "A gesture, a shove, a heated word, a drawn knife or pistol, and the work of Ottonius could go for naught."

"The mercenary company I have been charged to form," said Otto, "as it is currently conceived, will be much its own unit, functioning substantially independently, muchly under its own command. Ideally, it will have as little close interaction with regular Telnarian forces as possible, in particular, with those of the fixed sort.''

Here the giant was referring to the border, or garrison troops, as distinguished from the mobile forces.

''Fraternization would be dangerous?'' said Lysis.

''Better,'' said Otto, ''to house *arn* bears and vi-cats in the same cage.''

Both animals, it might be noted, aside from being natural enemies, tend to be restless, short-tempered, aggressive, and territorial.

''Perhaps you should return to them, and have them wait, until we have discussed matters fully.''

''My thoughts, as well,'' said Otto.

''You will enjoy our hospitality, in the compound, I trust,'' said Lysis.

''Yes,'' said Otto.

''We will have a splendid supper,'' said Lysis.

''I shall return in a moment,'' said Otto. He went back and conversed with his men. He told them to return to the hall, and he would join them later.

They faded away, back into the darkness of the forest.

In a few moments Otto had rejoined Lysis and Corelius.

''Tonight,'' said Otto, ''after we talk, and after supper, I will need a woman.''

''We will have one prepared for you,'' said Lysis.

''Who?'' asked Otto.

''Filene,'' said Corelius.

''Excellent,'' said Otto.